The Fate of the Arrow

The Fate of the Arrow

Shel Pais

The Fate of the Arrow

© 2019 by Shel Pais. All rights reserved.

This book is a work of fiction. Names, characters, places, and incidents either are products of the author's imagination or are used fictitiously. Any resemblance to actual persons, living or dead, events, or locales is entirely coincidental.

All rights reserved. No part of this publication may be reproduced or transmitted in any form or by any means, electronic or mechanical, including photocopy, recording, or any information storage and retrieval system, without permission in writing from the publisher.

Please contact publisher for permission to make copies of any part of this work.

Windy City Publishers
2118 Plum Grove Road, #349
Rolling Meadows, IL 60008
www.windycitypublishers.com

Published in the United States of America

ISBN:
978-1-941478-70-7

Library of Congress Control Number:
2018951078

Cover Design by Nicole Hutton of Cover Shot Creations

WINDY CITY PUBLISHERS
CHICAGO

Acknowledgments & Dedications

My sincere thanks to my wonderful family for their incredible love and support throughout this journey from inception to publication. In particular, special thanks to my son Matthew, a professional journalist, for his invaluable assistance. I also want to thank my many friends for their enthusiastic encouragement as well.

A special thanks to Lise and Dawn of Windy City Publishers. Working with them has been a joy, and I am looking forward to a long and mutually successful relationship together.

This book is dedicated to the memory of my beloved mother and father. My father was a Holocaust survivor, and my mother's family fled Russia at the end of the nineteenth century due to persecution.

I also dedicate this book to my late mother-in-law, a Holocaust survivor, who miraculously survived the horrors of Auschwitz, and my late father-in-law, a decorated U.S. medic in WWII.

Finally, a very special dedication in memory of my best friend for almost fifty years, Les Pock, who never got to read the story he was so excited about.

Prologue

Northampton, England – June 1264

It always started with men yelling in the street. The crash of broken-down doors and smashed furniture. The screams of frightened women and children. The smell of smoke, and the all-too-familiar smell of death.

Sarah quickly got out of bed and ran to her children in the next room. "Get up, get up. Everyone to Jerusalem!"

David raised his head, understanding the urgency of his mother's cries. He leapt out of bed and pulled back a corner of the curtain covering the second-story window of the bedroom he shared with his brother Benjamin to glimpse the commotion outside. His friend Samuel's house was on fire, so close David could feel the heat. Groups of men moved wildly from house to house. Right now, the mob was three homes away.

"Benjamin, get downstairs NOW!" he yelled. Benjamin obeyed, running past his brother to get to the first floor. David hurried to the next room where his sister Rachel slept. She was already awake, a frightened look on her face.

"David, are they coming for us, too?"

David picked her up and carried her down the stairs without saying a word. There was one possible place of safety. Mordecai, David's father, had built a small shelter underneath the floor in the rear of their house. He secretly had dug it out himself, careful not to let anyone know what he was doing. He had discreetly dispersed the dirt and ensured the family understood the magnitude of this secret. He called the underground haven Jerusalem.

The tumult outside was growing louder. There was no time to lose. David put Rachel down. "Help me, David," his mother said. She was trying to keep calm for Benjamin and Rachel, but David knew inside she was panicking.

The opening to Jerusalem was covered by a carpet underneath their dining table. The table was heavy, but David and Sarah somehow found the strength to pick it up and move it just enough to access the opening. David pulled back the carpet and found the indentation his father had cut to be able to lift it up. It sat on pegs that kept it level and secure.

"Hurry," his mother said. "Down the ladder."

The shelter was small, about six feet deep and eight feet across. It was only designed to hide Sarah and the children. Mordecai always figured he would be home if something happened, and he would get them to safety. This time, however, he had gone to London, believing the quiet in Northampton—it had been a year without incident since Jacob had been beaten and robbed—would continue.

Suddenly, a bang on the door. "Sarah, it's Meir. Let me in."

Meir was Mordecai's best friend and the only one outside the family who knew about Jerusalem—the only one Mordecai trusted to know. Sarah could not put back the table by herself, so Meir had come to help her.

Sarah removed the wooden bar from the door, let him in, and replaced the bar. Blood from Meir's nose and cheek dripped onto the floor.

"What happened to you?"

"It's nothing. I'm all right. Two of them jumped me, but I managed to get away when they left me and ran after a girl."

"Did you see who it was?"

"Yes. It was Miriam, Joshua's daughter. I couldn't help her. Let's get the children hidden."

Benjamin went down the narrow ladder first and waited as David lowered Rachel into his arms. Then David started down.

"Mother, you can't stay up there."

"I have to. They won't hurt me. Now let me cover the shelter, and Meir and I will put the table back. I can't do it by myself."

"I love you, Mother. May God protect you."

"I love all of you. I will see you soon after everything calms down."

Sarah hoped her children could not hear the fear in her voice. To her it was deafening. The mob was enraged, and she expected the worst.

Mordecai had a blacksmith make four hollow tubes that extended outside the rear of the house. One had to look very hard to find them.

They not only brought fresh air into the shelter, but permitted a candle to remain lit. Otherwise, Jerusalem would be in total darkness.

David lit the candle as Rachel hugged Benjamin. The eldest sibling heard the top of the shelter being replaced, and the table moved back into position.

"David, I'm so scared. I want Mother," Rachel sobbed.

"Don't worry. We'll be safe down here, and she will be fine. We must remain quiet."

The shouts of the mob were getting louder. It sounded like they were inside Asher's house next door. His family had no shelter. David heard shrieking, and then suddenly it stopped. The mob had moved on. They were next.

Chapter One

Northampton – May 1266

People began to stir as the town, its noises and smells, sprang to life. Fresh milk from the cowherd, fresh bread from the baker, and fresh eggs from the egg seller were all typical. A few women came out to make some purchases, but otherwise activity was limited. The sun beamed, and only a few clouds interrupted the sky's endless deep blue. A light breeze rustled the leaves in an isolated tree. It was a Friday spring morning like any other.

It was not much of a town. While there were several stone houses, most resembled huts, with thatched roofs and not much else. Some were inhabited by some of Baron Geoffrey's servants, who paid only slightly less for their housing than they earned from him since he owned the town and, in many ways, the people who worked for him. At least their families never went hungry. The baron always ate quite well, insisting on freshly made dishes at every meal. More often than not, there were table scraps for the servants to bring home.

West End was named for its location at the western side of Northampton, not far from the baron's castle. The town was unique from many other towns in one way—it contained a Jewish population of thirty families, as well as a small synagogue. More than one hundred years before, a Jewish physician who happened to be passing through saved the life of the baron, who insisted the physician stay. He sent for his family, and gradually more families settled there as well, even when succeeding barons were not as friendly to the Jews.

David did not want to get up. It was time to prepare for the morning prayer service, Shacharit, before cheder. Unlike most of the other boys in the Jewish community of West End, David hated going to services. He did not know why, but somehow none of the prayers or what the rabbis said they were supposed to mean made any sense to him. Why must the Christians, or at least most of them, hate us? If God is so kind and loving, why is there so much misery? He could not answer these questions and did not know anyone who could.

Certainly, his father could not. David often would get into heated debates with him. Mordecai was like all the other men David knew. Devotion to God and daily prayers, morning, afternoon, and night, was his life, while loving his family and working very hard for very little money to keep them fed.

David was much taller and stronger than the other boys. At fourteen, he already was five foot eight, and still growing. He could run faster and throw a stone much farther than even the eighteen-year-olds. He also looked a little different from the others in the area known by the Christians as Jewtown. His sister Rachel was three years younger, and they looked nothing alike. Rachel somewhat resembled their brother Benjamin, who was twelve. Why didn't he? While that always puzzled him, he felt he was the best looking in the family, so he did not think too much about it.

Unlike the other boys, David was not afraid to defend himself when provoked or when he saw one of his friends or neighbors made fun of or worse by the Christian boys. Even the Christian men learned David probably could beat them in a fight and so he was usually left alone.

The baron had never come to West End, and David had never been inside the castle. His father had been there several times. As an apothecary, he helped ill or wounded men-at-arms and had cured the baron's brother when no one else could. As a reward, the baron gave Mordecai a few gold pieces and a barrel of wine, which had made an impression on David. Perhaps the baron was not like most of those in authority.

David did see the baron joust once, and he never forgot it. He was about ten at the time and had gone with his father to watch a tournament. He loved the pageantry, the colorful banners, the heraldry, the glamour of it all. He wanted to be part of it. But that was impossible. Jews could not own weapons or armor or become warriors. Jews were not allowed to fight. It was forbidden. That was something else David could not understand, and questions frequently ran through his head. What are the Christians afraid of? That we would revolt and take over? There are so few of us and we are scattered. Why can't our people have the right to defend ourselves?

Baron Geoffrey's attitude was not the norm. Persecution of Jews in England was commonplace, but had been rare in West End because

Baron Geoffrey had followed the king's edict that all Jews belonged to the king, and therefore an attack on one of them was the same as attacking the king. That was another thing that David could not understand. How could he belong to the king? He was not a slave. He did not feel he belonged to anyone.

"David," his father said. "Time to get up. It's almost time to go to Shul."

"Father, you know I don't want to go."

"David, my son. Please do not argue. We must go. It is our duty. It is our life."

"Why, Father? What will happen if we do not? Will the earth tremble? Will the sea drown us? Will the soldiers come and kill us? It seems they'll do that anyway. Since God does not listen, why should we continue to worship him?"

"David, no one knows better than I the difficulty in continuing one's faith after tragedy. I cannot explain or even truly understand why God would allow these things to happen. But our people have continued to pray and follow our customs for thousands of years under tremendous adversity. So many have tried to destroy us, but we are still here, and they are not. Does that not affect you at all? Can you not see that we must remain true to our faith or we are no better than those who want to destroy us, and ultimately that will help them win?"

"I understand that, Father. I will go for you, but my heart is not in it. I will not disgrace you. I love and respect you too much. I also will go for mother, as I remember how important our Jewish life was to her. That's something that makes my blood boil. I want to avenge her death, and I want those Christian maggots who killed her to know that a Jew is the one who is doing it. Someday I will find them."

"Stop!" Mordecai said. "No more talk of revenge or killing. It is not our way, and we have no means. God, in his time, will avenge your mother."

"You don't really believe that, Father, do you? The baron and the sheriff did nothing. What will God do? Our prayers fall on deaf ears."

David could tell that his father was getting upset. He also thought his father was beginning to look older than his forty-year-old body, his hair and beard graying, and even his medium build appeared shorter.

"I'm sorry, Father. I don't want to upset you. I won't speak of this again. Let's go to Shul together."

"I understand your frustration. I really do. This is just how it is. We must live as best we can, keeping our traditions and faith as our forefathers did. We must not antagonize the Christians. Things have been relatively calm for the past two years. God willing, it will stay that way."

David just nodded his head. He knew he could not change his father's mind. If only there was a way...

The rest of Mordecai's household stirred as he and David dressed and prepared to leave. Benjamin and Rachel awoke, dressed, and prepared a breakfast of bread, cheese, and smoked fish for all of them.

As they walked to Shul, neither David nor his father spoke. David was immersed in thought. One truth repeated in his head—this is not the kind of life I want.

York – May 1266

Baron Henry de Percy was quite ill. A burly man over six feet tall, approaching forty-two years old, with brown eyes, medium-length black hair, a short beard, a deep voice, and a temper to match, he had come down with a fever that would not break. The monk who had tried to bleed and cure him for almost a week with several foul-smelling and tasting medications, as he called them, was trembling.

"You're an incompetent fool!" the baron screamed at him, in as loud a voice as he could muster in his condition. "I should have you whipped. Get out of here!" The monk quickly bowed and left the baron's chamber.

"Bryce, come here, boy."

"I'm here, my lord," replied the baron's page.

"Go fetch Lady Eleanor. I believe she's in the kitchen."

"At once, my lord." Bryce hurried out to find the baron's wife. He ran down the stone stairs to the main castle floor, through the great hall and out towards the back to the castle's kitchen. Lady Eleanor was there, instructing the cook.

"My lady," he said, bowing, unable to mask his shortness of breath, "my lord baron requests your presence immediately."

"Has there been any change in his condition?"

"I don't think so, my lady. He demanded the monk leave immediately and ordered me to get you right away."

"Very well. Lucinda, I will return shortly. You may begin the meal as instructed." The cook bowed and returned to her work. Lady Eleanor and Bryce made their way through the castle to the baron's and her chamber.

"Honestly, Henry," she said, "it smells vile in here. We must do something about it. You will never recover if we don't. Bryce, get one of the servants to clean and freshen this room."

"Yes, my lady."

"Eleanor, please come here." She slowly walked up to her husband. His nightclothes were quite dirty, and he was still sweating.

"Lucinda is making you a stronger broth. I hope that will help you feel better."

"I doubt it," Henry said weakly. "I need someone who can cure me. The monks are useless. They do more harm than good."

"My poor husband. Do you want me to get someone else?"

"There's only one man who can help me."

"You mean Nehemiah, the Jew?"

"Yes. Please hurry."

"Very well. I will send Bryce to get him."

Eleanor found Bryce and told him to get Nehemiah and describe the baron's symptoms to him. After the entire York Jewish community was wiped out in the massacre of 1190, it took a few years, but slowly Jews returned and the community was rebuilt. The baron protected them, and no one would dare go against Baron Henry de Percy. Bryce was familiar with Nehemiah, as he had healed some of the men-at-arms' wounds after bandits attacked them. He found his home and knocked on the door. Nehemiah soon answered. "Hello, Bryce, are there more wounded men to heal?"

"No, the baron is quite ill, and no one has been able to cure him. He wants you to come to the castle right away."

"Do you know what is wrong?"

"He's had a high fever for several days. He's very weak and has no appetite."

"I will get my bag and be right along."

Nehemiah was the only physician in York. While the monks tried to practice what they called medicine, their methods were quite rudimentary and rarely produced results. Bryce and Nehemiah hurried to the castle. As they approached the gate, one of the guards recognized Nehemiah.

"Nehemiah. You've come to cure the baron?"

"Hello, Alain. How is your wound? Do you have any pain?"

"No pain at all. You completely healed me," the guard said smiling.

"I am very glad. Now to see if I can help the baron."

Bryce led him through the main gate, into the courtyard to the castle. They climbed a huge staircase and reached the baron's chamber. The door was open.

"My lord, Nehemiah is here as you ordered."

"Bring him in." They both entered the chamber. Eleanor was sitting on a chair next to her husband.

"Thank you, Bryce. You may go." Bryce bowed and left.

"Nehemiah, please come here and cure me," Henry said in a low, struggling voice.

Nehemiah approached the bed and bowed. "My lord, Lady Eleanor. I am sorry to see you in such a condition, my lord. Tell me what is wrong."

The baron coughed. "I've had this fever for over a week. One of the monks tried to cure me, but I think he made it worse. I have no appetite and am very weak."

Nehemiah felt the baron's forehead. It was extremely warm. "My lady, we need to get him into a cold bath right away. His fever is very high. I will prepare something to help bring down the fever, but the cold bath is necessary."

Eleanor left the room to do as Nehemiah asked. He prepared a coriander paste, adding some water to make it easier to swallow. "Here, my lord, please take this." The baron opened his mouth as the Jew placed the spoon in. It was not unpleasant, and he swallowed the entire amount. After a while, Bryce appeared. "My lord, your bath is ready."

Bryce and Nehemiah helped Henry get out of bed and supported him as they walked down the stairs to the wooden bath. Henry felt the water. "I can't go in this. It's too cold."

"Please, my lord, this will help break the fever. You will get used to it shortly." Reluctantly, the baron took off his nightshirt and slowly climbed into the tub. He shivered as the cold water engulfed his body.

"Nehemiah, this had better work or I'll be very angry with you."

Nehemiah nodded, and smiled at the baron. "Please be patient. I believe you will feel better soon."

The water gradually warmed, and the baron grew more comfortable. Nehemiah continually monitored Henry's fever by feeling his forehead. After several hours and twice refilling the tub with cold water, he could feel the fever was lower.

"Well, my lord, do you feel better?" he asked.

"Nehemiah, you are a wonder. I feel much better. May I get out now?"

"Not quite yet. I want to be sure the fever will not return."

As the baron sat in the tub, his demeanor continued to warm with the water, while his temperature slowly returned to almost normal.

"Tell me, Nehemiah, why are the monks so ignorant of what you know?"

Nehemiah thought carefully how he would answer, knowing the baron was a religious man. "I do not know for certain, my lord. I believe the Church feels that illnesses are punishments from God. We believe our cures come from God, so why would the illness come from Him as well? Has He nothing better to do than create problems so He can solve them?"

Henry thought about that for a moment. "The Church's teachings are not always correct, I suppose. I also once believed illnesses were punishments from God. But when my first-born became ill with fever soon after birth and died, I stopped believing that. The child committed no sin. God would not punish him for something I did. That's when I stopped believing such nonsense. There are diseases that anyone can get. I hope you will be around to cure whatever my family or I ever come down with."

"I will try my best, my lord, but not all conditions can be cured. One cannot blame the physician for something beyond his capability."

"Some call what you do witchcraft or sorcery."

"It is not. It is knowledge. Only the ignorant believe that."

"And there are so many who are ignorant."

After a few more minutes, Henry stood up and stepped out of the tub. Bryce gave him a fresh nightshirt and covered him with a wool robe. "I do feel much better."

"I am glad," Nehemiah said, "but you still must rest. The fever may return if you do not."

The baron returned to his chamber, which he noticed had been freshened. A clean sheet was on his bed, and as he laid back down he felt like a new man.

"Nehemiah, you will be rewarded for what you have done today. I will send my seneschal to you with a generous payment."

Nehemiah bowed. "You are very generous, my lord. I am happy to serve you, and I hope our two peoples can get along."

"I hope that as well. But if not, I will protect you. You have my word." Nehemiah thanked the baron again, bowed, and left.

As Nehemiah was leaving, Lady Eleanor stopped him. "Nehemiah, will he be all right?" she asked.

"Yes, my lady. I believe he will. Luckily, I was summoned before it was too late. His fever was dangerously high. He does not know how close to dying he came."

"I was not aware it was that serious. The monk said nothing of the sort."

"I am afraid it is true. Please watch him for a few days. If his condition does change back, please summon me. However, I do not believe that will be necessary. Good day, my lady," he said, bowing.

"Good day, Nehemiah, and thank you again."

As Nehemiah left the castle, he thought about the massacre seventy-six years earlier. Such a shame, he said to himself, sobbing. He prayed to God that would never happen again. He also prayed that if the conditions that caused it did reoccur, the Jews would have their own champion to protect them.

Chapter Two

Northampton Castle – May 1266

It was past mid-morning, but Baron Geoffrey Guernon remained in bed. His head was pounding from the vast amounts of ale and wine he consumed the previous night. While not normally an angry man, after drinking he was better off left alone. His page, Cyrus, waited patiently outside his door until called. Knowing what had happened last night, Cyrus worried the baron's temper would be fierce, and his nervousness showed.

The baron's chamber was at the east end of the castle. If the baron ordered Cyrus to fetch something, he would have to hurry or perhaps suffer his wrath.

As Cyrus waited, he heard footsteps approaching. He turned to see Lady Catherine, the baron's wife.

"My lady," he said, bowing.

"Is he still sleeping, Cyrus?"

"I think so, my lady. I sometimes hear his snoring, but then he's quiet. He hasn't called for me yet."

"I will check. Wait here."

The door to the baron's chamber creaked as Catherine opened it, and quietly walked over to him. He looked up and smiled. She was exceptionally beautiful, with radiant blue eyes, long, blonde hair, and a shapely figure that complemented her medium height. Even if he was in a bad mood, her appearance always softened him. He was madly in love with her.

"I see you are awake," she said.

"Barely. I don't feel like getting up yet. Are our guests still here?"

The previous night he had to provide lodging to Abbot Hubert and his cousin Alwyn, a priest. The baron hated them both. He thought they were mindless opportunists, using their titles and families for personal gain, and were perfect examples of what the Church did not stand for. Hubert had had Geoffrey's brother, Peter, excommunicated two years before, who killed himself due to his shame. Hubert said he had witnesses to Peter's heresy, but Geoffrey did not believe it. He was certain Hubert did it for his own personal reasons, although Geoffrey did not know what they were. One day he would discover them, and then he would avenge his brother's death. Geoffrey would have reported his suspicions to Bishop Basil, but he did not have any proof, and Basil was Hubert's cousin as well.

"No, they left at dawn. Said they had to get to London."

"Good. I hope they're waylaid on the road. I told them I couldn't spare anyone for an escort. I don't think they believed me."

"Well, you do make your feelings obvious. Maybe you should be a little more discreet?"

"Never. Not with them. If I thought I could get away with it, I'd slit both their throats myself."

The baron sat up and belched. He walked over to the chamber pot and urinated. Then he filled the basin with water and washed his face.

"Cyrus," he yelled. "Are you there?"

"Yes, my lord."

"Come here!"

Cyrus opened the huge oak door and entered the baron's chamber.

"Help me dress, then tell Theresa I want my favorite breakfast."

"I will leave you now," said Catherine. "I have some household matters to attend to."

Baron Geoffrey Guernon of Northampton was forty-five years old, stood about six foot tall, with long, black hair and a full beard. He was slightly overweight, and his right arm was exceptionally muscular from wielding his long broadsword. He did not like short blades. Better to give one some room to overcome your opponent, he would say. He had fought for the king in the Baron's War, earning him the everlasting gratitude of Henry III. That also earned him the enmity of the barons who did not agree with him. Geoffrey did not care. He had risen to knighthood, taking advantage of every opportunity to serve the king. Ironically, it was he who was described as the ultimate opportunist, but it had served him well so far. Despite being wounded, he saved the life of the king's favorite cousin while rousing his men to victory. As a reward, Henry awarded him the title of Baron Geoffrey of Northampton, where he oversees a manor of over two thousand acres and several villages. His wife, Baroness Catherine, is the daughter of Sir Mortimer of Wigmore, another staunch supporter of the king.

Cyrus helped the baron dress and hurried down to the kitchen.

"Theresa," he called out. "Where are you? The baron wants his favorite breakfast."

The baron's cook emerged from the pantry. She was approaching forty years old and could hardly walk. She was extremely overweight from sampling too many of the baron's favorite dishes and eating too much of the leftovers. She had pain in her legs whenever she moved and standing for long periods put her in agony. The baron considered replacing her, but she was such a fabulous cook, and her mother used to be the previous baron's cook, so he felt obligated to keep her on as long as she still could perform.

"Again?" she muttered to herself. That meant she had to bake his favorite oat bread, and she feared she was out of some of the ingredients. Lords of the baron's stature usually ate manchet, a fine white bread made of the best wheat. The baron was different. He came from the lower classes and still preferred the coarser oat bread his mother used to make.

While the baron insisted on it baked only occasionally, lately he was now asking for it every other day, and Theresa tried to make sure she kept everything she needed in stock. Luckily, she had enough this morning. The baron also liked boiled eggs and dried fish, both of which she had.

"How's his mood today, Cyrus?" she asked.

"So-so. He was ranting about the abbot and his cousin again."

"I agree with him. Hubert is a leech and a lecher," Theresa said quietly, crossing herself. "I've heard he tries to worm his way with every nobleman and king's officer he can, and lusts after many a maid. Because he's a bishop's cousin, he thinks he can get away with anything. And he's only a distant cousin at that. Alwyn, I'm sure, is no better. Would you like some breakfast, Cyrus?"

"Yes, I would. I didn't get to eat with the other servants. The baron wanted me to stay by his door until he needed me."

Theresa gave him some bread, cheese, and a cup of ale.

"Thank you, Theresa. You're very kind." Cyrus wolfed down the food but drank the ale slowly.

"Please hurry with his breakfast. He'll be angry if it takes too long."

"I'm going as fast as I can. The oven's hot, so the bread will bake quickly. But I must be sure not to burn it."

Cyrus brought the platter with the oat bread, three boiled eggs, some dried fish, and a mug of ale to the baron's chamber. The door was open, and Cyrus could see he was alone. Lady Catherine had not returned.

"Ah, Cyrus. Finally. Was Theresa angry with me? I know she doesn't like making my oat bread. She told me it's beneath me, but I still love it. Have you eaten? I know I kept you by me this morning, as I thought I might be ill from last night." The baron's foul mood had dissipated.

"Yes, my lord. Theresa gave me something to eat."

"Good. I want you to run an errand for me today."

"Yes, my lord."

"I want you to take a letter to the Jewish part of town."

Fear immediately came across Cyrus' face. He had never met a Jew, although he had seen them. What he knew about them came from what he had heard from the priests, the men-at-arms, his parents, and some of the townspeople—stories of strange rituals, how they spoke a language that sounded like nothing they had ever heard and wrote with strange symbols that came from the devil. Some even said they killed little Christian children for their blood, though that he found hard to believe.

"My lord," he stammered. "Couldn't you send someone else?"

"Are you afraid, Cyrus? Afraid they might cast a spell on you?" Geoffrey said, enjoying his page's discomfort.

"I have heard of such things, my lord."

"Nonsense. I assure you they are people just like we are. They just have different beliefs and customs. They are no better or worse than we or any other Christians."

"But I've never been to that part of town."

"Then it's time you did." He handed Cyrus a sealed parchment. "Take this to Mordecai, the apothecary. You can ask around where his house is. Wait until he reads it and bring his response back to me. And don't tell anyone about this, do you understand?"

"Yes, my lord. I will obey."

"Good. Now off you go, and hurry back."

"What shall I do if he's not there?"

"Wait for him unless he's traveling. If that's the case, come right back with the letter. Do not give it to anyone else or leave it at his home."

Cyrus' heart raced as his fear increased. He still felt uneasy about his mission. The baron certainly is more knowledgeable then I am, he thought. But after years of hearing so many scary things about Jews, he still was apprehensive. He worked his way down several stairways to a side door of the castle and began his journey to the Jewish quarter—West End.

The streets were busy as the Sabbath was approaching, and women were buying vegetables and other foods for the Sabbath meal. A butcher was harking his kosher chickens. Cyrus had no idea what that meant and did not want to know. He saw men with strings hanging out of their shirts, and some had curls dangling near each ear. Many spoke a strange language he had never heard before. It sounded so foreign, nothing like the Latin in church. He asked a man where Mordecai the apothecary lived and was directed to a stone house in the middle of Green Street. He slowly approached it. His fear had subsided somewhat, but he still felt apprehensive as he knocked on the door. He noticed an unusual object attached to the doorpost with the strange symbols on it. He backed away from it, afraid of what might happen if he touched it. Then the door slowly opened, and a boy about his age stood in front of him.

"Yes. Can I help you?"

"I have a message for Mordecai, the apothecary, from Baron Geoffrey."

"He's my father," the boy said. "But he's not here. I can take it for him."

"No. Baron Geoffrey said I must give it to him personally, or if he won't be back soon to bring it back to the castle. When will he return?"

"He should be back soon. Would you like to wait for him inside?"

A chill descended Cyrus' spine. What should he do? The baron will be angry with him if he did not deliver the message when Mordecai was going to be available. He looked up at the sky, which grew dark and gray as a storm approached. He could not wait outside in the rain. "All right," he said. "But just for a short while. I have important things to do for the baron."

Cyrus slowly walked into the Jewish home. He looked around, noticing a candelabra and some small trinkets. There was nothing scary inside. He was not sure what he was expecting to see, but everything seemed normal.

As he looked around a young girl came out of a back room. Cyrus thought she was very attractive and stared at her while the boy addressed him. "I'm Benjamin, and this is my sister, Rachel. What's your name?"

"Cyrus. I'm Baron Geoffrey's personal page. He relies on me to do many things for him," he boasted.

Rachel smiled at him. Cyrus had long blonde hair and a muscular body for a boy his age. "It sounds like you have a very important position," she said.

"I do. The baron said soon I will begin training to be a squire, and then I will be a knight."

"My brother wants to be a knight but cannot because we are Jews."

"I never met a Jew before. This is my first time in West End." As the three of them talked, Cyrus became more at ease. The boy and girl seemed no different from Christian boys and girls. He then remembered what a priest had said about the Jews—that they killed our Savior and did not believe he was the son of God.

"Do you live in the castle?" Benjamin asked.

"I do. I don't have my own chamber, but I must stay near the baron so I can do his bidding whenever he needs me."

"Where are you from?" Rachel asked.

"A small village near York. One day Baron Geoffrey stopped there, and I watered and fed his horse. His page had just died of the flux, and he asked me if I would like to replace him. I was living with my uncle after my parents died. My uncle welcomed the baron's offer, so I left." Cyrus looked at the candelabra again. "What's that used for?"

"It's for Hanukkah," Rachel answered. "It's one of our holidays. We add a candle each night for eight nights to remember a miracle from long ago. We often celebrate it while you are celebrating Christmas."

Cyrus looked confused. "You don't celebrate Christmas?" he asked. Before either Benjamin or Rachel could answer, some of the priest's words began to come back to him.

"Why did you kill Christ?" he asked angrily.

Benjamin and Rachel looked at each other and started to feel uncomfortable. "We didn't kill anybody," Benjamin said.

"Yes, you did. The priest said the Jews killed Christ, and you're Jews."

Benjamin started to raise his voice. "That was a long time ago, and we weren't living then. I don't know about such things." He saw Rachel was beginning to cry. "Perhaps you should leave now."

The door to the house opened, and the children were relieved to see their father had returned. Mordecai saw the blonde boy and noticed Rachel's tears.

"What is happening here? Who are you?" he gruffly asked Cyrus.

"I am Cyrus, page to Baron Geoffrey. Are you Mordecai, the apothecary?"

"Yes."

Cyrus handed him the message. "This is for you."

Mordecai opened the parchment and read it. "Tell the baron I will be there tomorrow after Sabbath prayers."

Cyrus nodded and left.

"What was that about, Father?" Benjamin asked.

"First tell me what happened. Rachel was crying when I walked in, and your voice was raised."

"Cyrus asked us why we killed Christ. I told him we didn't kill anybody and we weren't even alive then."

"Oh, I see," Mordecai said. "That again. I am sorry I was not here. Sit down, children." Mordecai then realized David was not there. "Where is David? Shabbos is approaching. He should be home."

"I don't know, Father. Cheder ended on time before Shabbos, and I came straight home."

Mordecai sighed. "Benjamin and Rachel. Our people have suffered for many years because of what happened a long time ago. The truth has been twisted by some to make the Christians hate us. Some say the Church is afraid Christians will become Jews if they see who we really are. We have our beliefs, and they have theirs. The Romans were responsible for killing Jesus. You two have nothing to feel guilty about. You have never harmed anyone. Do you understand?"

Benjamin and Rachel nodded. Mordecai kissed them both. "We had better prepare the Shabbos meal. It's getting closer to sundown."

The next afternoon Mordecai walked to the castle. He had no idea what the baron could want of him. Two guards stood at the gate.

"What do you want, Jew?" one of them growled, lowering his pike to block Mordecai's path.

"I am Mordecai, the apothecary. Baron Geoffrey summoned me."

The guard looked at his comrade. "Do you know about this?" he asked.

"Aye. Sir Walter told me to expect him. He can pass."

Mordecai bowed slightly as the guard raised his weapon, giving Mordecai a little push on his backside as he passed. Mordecai continued into the courtyard and saw Cyrus sitting on a stump, munching on what was left of a piece of bread. "Oh, it's you," Cyrus said. "Come with me. I'll take you to the baron."

"Thank you," Mordecai said. He followed Cyrus into the castle where he entered a large room. Baron Geoffrey sat at a huge table, drinking wine, and cutting pieces from a slab of mutton. He saw Cyrus and Mordecai approaching.

"My lord," Cyrus said, bowing deeply. "The Jew Mordecai as you commanded."

"Thank you, Cyrus. You may go."

"Mordecai," the baron said, "it's good to see you. Come sit with me and have some wine."

"My lord," Mordecai said bowing. "I have come as you asked."

The baron poured a glass of wine for Mordecai and handed it to him. Mordecai reluctantly took it.

"To your health," Geoffrey said as he gulped down the red liquid.

Mordecai put the glass near his lips but did not drink. "And to yours, my lord," Mordecai said.

"A fine wine, is it not? I have it brought in from Italy. I much prefer it to the French wines. To me they taste like vinegar."

Mordecai nodded.

"Mordecai, I need your help."

"In what way?"

"What I'm going to ask of you is in the strictest confidence. I want no one to know of this, understand?"

"Yes, my lord, I understand."

"You are an expert in medicines and potions to help cure illnesses and conditions. You also know about poisons and how to prepare them, do you not?"

"Yes, my lord. An apothecary must know what is helpful along with what is dangerous. There are many natural poisons, as well as those that can be prepared."

"I want to have a poison prepared that will make it seem the victim died of natural causes. There can be no trace of it. Can you do that?"

Mordecai was stunned at the baron's request. While he had prepared poisons to kill rodents, he had not prepared one that would intentionally kill another human being.

"I have never done that before, my lord. I also am not comfortable performing such a task."

"Mordecai, I understand this will be difficult for you, but I absolve you of all responsibility. I want you to do this, and I will give you some time to complete it. I don't need it immediately but want to have it on hand. Therefore, it must be potent for a while."

"Cannot another apothecary do this for you?"

The baron looked sternly at Mordecai. "No. I don't trust anyone else with this. I know you won't break my confidence. And you know what will happen if you do."

Mordecai nodded. "I will see what I can do."

"Good. I'll give you until August, when I'll send for you."

"I will obey, my lord."

Mordecai bowed. As he walked past the guards at the gate, he did not hear them making fun of him, his mind thinking only about this task he did not want to perform. What choice did he have? The baron ordered him to prepare a poison. It could be used only for one purpose. Perhaps he should discuss it with the rabbi. No, he cannot, as that would no doubt lead to his betraying the confidence the baron demanded. He had no choice. He must prepare it.

When he returned home, all three children were waiting for him.

"What did the baron want?" David asked.

Mordecai had not thought how to answer that question. He paused for a moment. "I have to prepare something for him. I cannot discuss it with anyone as he told me not to."

David assumed the baron or someone in his household must be ill and did not want anyone to know about it. His father must have been asked to prepare some special medicine to cure it. "I understand, Father. We won't ask you about it again."

Benjamin and Rachel looked at each other. "We don't understand," Benjamin said. "Please tell us."

Mordecai looked at them and pointed. "Enough. I cannot speak about it. And this is very important—do not say anything about it to anyone or I will be in trouble. Do not disobey me."

Rachel and Benjamin nodded and said at the same time, "We won't say anything to anyone, Father. We promise."

"Good. Now let us forget we even discussed this."

Chapter Three

The Road to London – May 1266

Abbott Hubert turned to look at his cousin, Father Alwyn. "What do you mean?" Hubert asked.

The two of them had left Baron Geoffrey's castle and were on their way to London on horseback. It could be a dangerous journey, even in daylight. Thieves and cutthroats seemed to be everywhere. Sheriffs Alan de Insh, Warin de Basingburn, and the latest, John de Oxenden, had tried to capture some of them, but largely had been unsuccessful. There were just too many outlaws, and there never were enough soldiers. Requests for help were always answered the same way—no excuses, take care of the problem with the men you have. It had been considered to press some men from the town, but they were untrained and would not be of much good. Hubert did not like traveling without an escort, but he was unable to hire one on short notice, and Geoffrey said he could not spare even one man.

"I mean Geoffrey is dangerous and will stop at nothing to harm you, and perhaps me as well."

"I do not trust him either," Hubert responded, "but I don't think he would dare to harm me. You, I do not know."

"Thank you, cousin. That makes me feel better."

"What do you think he's up to?"

"I overheard some of the servants talking. If one quietly walks around a castle and listens carefully, one can learn quite a lot."

"Well, what did you hear?"

"Geoffrey still blames you for his brother's suicide. He's planning revenge."

"That's old news. You were there when I told him his brother committed heresy and I had to excommunicate him. There were witnesses."

Alwyn pulled on the reins to stop his already slow-moving horse, and Hubert did the same. "Yes, but Geoffrey does not believe them."

"The matter is closed. I am not concerned."

"Well, I believe you should be. Servants hear everything and know what is going on. And they usually have loose tongues."

"He gave us his best hospitality, did he not?" Hubert said.

"Only because he had to. I told you we were foolish to stop there."

"I appreciate your concern, but he wouldn't dare. The king would know immediately Geoffrey was the culprit and arrest him, confiscate his lands, and have him executed. Now no more talk of him. Let's continue our journey being mindful of the scum that inhabit these woods."

"All right, cousin. I won't bring it up again."

They continued their journey without incident or any further discussion. Hubert was to meet with his cousin, Bishop Basil, in three days. Basil had sent a priest for him, although the priest said he did not know what this was about. The priest did not wait to accompany him, but said he had to return immediately.

They stopped at an inn for the night, feasting on shepherd's pie and ale. They continued on the next morning, reaching London in the late afternoon. They went directly to the bishop's residence and knocked.

A priest peered through a small opening, looking suspiciously at the two men on the other side.

"Open up. I am Abbot Hubert, the bishop's cousin." He neglected to mention Alwyn.

"I am sorry, Your Grace, but the bishop is not here and left no instructions to admit anyone."

Indignant at the apparent insult, Hubert further raised his voice. "Let us in right now or I will have you flogged when my cousin returns. I am sure he would not deny me entry."

The priest, a timid man of about fifty, reluctantly admitted them. "That's better," Hubert said. "Now, get us food and drink. We've had a long journey and we are tired and hungry." The priest escorted them to the parlor and shuffled out.

"Hubert, I think you scared him half to death," Alwyn grinned.

"He is nothing. Basil surrounds himself with weaklings to make him feel stronger. How Basil became a bishop is beyond me. He probably knows something about someone he should not," Hubert said, winking at Alwyn.

Alwyn kept his thoughts to himself. Inside he hated Hubert, but knew he needed him to advance in the Church. Hubert was forty-seven, about five foot seven with a medium build, brown eyes, and black thinning hair that was starting to turn gray. Most considered him a boisterous, self-centered loudmouth who felt he could order everyone to do his bidding. Alwyn was ten years younger, a few inches taller, with brown hair and green eyes. Alwyn had never met Bishop Basil, and all he knew about him was from Hubert. Basil and Hubert, while only distant cousins, had grown up near each other. Basil was ten years older, and they did not appear to have much, if any, of a relationship. What Basil could want of Hubert, Alwyn could not even guess.

Hubert and Alwyn waited three more days in the bishop's residence until Basil finally returned. Hubert expressed his outrage at the extra-long wait to the priest, who apologized, explaining he did not know why the bishop was delayed. They were sitting in the parlor as evening approached when they heard Basil.

"I am back, Father Eustace. Was anything amiss while I was away?"

"Not amiss, Your Grace," Eustace stammered. "Abbot Hubert and a priest arrived four days ago and insisted on staying here. I told them you had not left any instructions, but he said he would have me flogged if I did not let him in."

"And you did?" Basil saw Eustace shaking with nervousness. "It's all right. Where are they now?"

"I am here, cousin," Hubert said. He walked quickly to Basil and embraced him. Basil pushed him back with a scowl. The bishop was quite tall, standing over six foot, with deep, blue eyes. Hubert thought he looked older than his fifty-seven years.

"I am a bishop. Kiss my ring and treat me with the proper respect!" Basil commanded, raising his voice.

Hubert knelt down on one knee and kissed Basil's ring. "My humble apologies, Your Grace. Since we're related, I was hoping we could be less formal."

Basil frowned. "We are distant cousins. I'm not even certain how we are related. Do not speak of any family relationship again." He then looked at Alwyn, who stood behind Hubert. "And who might you be?" he asked.

Hubert started to answer. "He is my cousin as well."

"He can answer for himself. Be silent, Hubert."

Humbled again, Hubert bowed his head and mumbled something no one else in the room could hear.

"Well?" Basil asked Alwyn.

"I am Father Alwyn, Your Grace, of York. I am Hubert's second cousin on his mother's side. I was visiting him when he asked me to accompany him upon receiving your summons."

"I see. You may stay. I may find you useful." Basil's demeanor then softened. "Eustace, bring wine and food for our guests."

"So, Hubert. By what route did you come?"

"Through Northampton. Unfortunately, that meant I had to ask for Baron Geoffrey's hospitality."

"Does he still blame you for his brother's suicide?"

"Yes, he does."

"Why did you stay there if there is still tension between you two? Were you not fearful he would cut your throat?"

Alwyn looked at Hubert, wondering how he would answer. Hubert had told Alwyn he was unable to stay at the priory or an inn. The baron's castle had the best available accommodations, and there would not be any cost.

"There were no other places available that night. The priory looked filthy and the only inn fit for an abbot was full. I did not want to send some poor soul into the cold, wet night when the baron could not refuse me shelter. I do not fear Geoffrey. He would not dare harm me."

Alwyn smiled at his cousin's predictable dishonesty. Basil grunted as he listened. He expected as much from Hubert. But Basil planned to put Hubert's pompousness to good use for his own aims. "So, Hubert, what news in Northampton?"

"Nothing lately. Geoffrey said it has been quiet."

"No trouble with the Jews?"

Hubert looked surprised. "The Jews? Not that I know of. Why do you ask?"

Eustace arrived with bread, cheese, and wine. "Thank you, Eustace. You may go. Refresh yourselves first, and then we will talk," Basil said, his voice more caring.

Basil watched the two of them devour the food and guzzle the wine. One would think they had not eaten for days, he thought. Alwyn at least had some manners, but not Hubert. Basil sighed, wondering if Hubert was truly able to carry out his wishes. Time would tell.

"So," Hubert said. "What can I do for you?"

"Are you happy where you are now? Have you considered relocating?"

"Yes, Your Grace. I am happy where I am, and no, I have not considered relocating, although I am always ready to move up in the Church. Why do you ask?"

"There is a problem with Hedgestone Priory, and I want to replace the current prior with a much stronger man. Prior Bartholomew is old and cannot handle his duties anymore."

Hubert was puzzled. He knew Basil did not care for him. Why, he thought, would he want to make me prior of Hedgestone at Northampton? It was a smaller monastery than his current posting, but it could be a unique opportunity. Northampton was closer to London, and perhaps could lead to an even better position. Also, the bishop would be in his debt, and that always could be useful.

"I am flattered, Your Grace. However, usually the senior monks elect the next prior."

"I know. You have been at your current station for some time, and while I do not care for some of your methods, I need someone like you for this. Even though it may seem like a step down, it is only temporary. Are you interested?"

Hubert nodded. "Yes, Your Grace, I am very interested. However, is not Hedgestone out of your jurisdiction?"

"Yes, but I have been given the authority to replace Bartholomew. You need not concern yourself with that."

"Very well. Please tell me more."

"What I am going to say is very confidential. Hubert and Alwyn, do you swear by Our Lady you will not divulge this to anyone?" Alwyn had been listening intently to the bishop, trying to figure out what he was getting at.

"Yes, Your Grace, we swear," the two men said simultaneously.

"The priory at Hedgestone is being poorly run. You yourself mentioned how filthy it was when you stopped there. Its finances are in terrible shape, the buildings are deteriorating, and the monks are lazy. Also, the prior has become too friendly with the Jews."

Hedgestone stood outside Northampton, not far from the Jewish quarter at West End. Hubert thought he was beginning to understand what Basil wanted. Clueless, Alwyn kept silent.

"Prior Bartholomew? Why would he get too friendly with the Jews? I've never met him, but my friend, Prior Xavier, knows him well, and never said anything like that about him."

"I do not know why. However, it was reported to me he has been attending some of their services, and often discusses scripture with the rabbi. This is dangerous, and I want it stopped."

"I have heard of a monk in Germany who committed the ultimate heresy of converting to Judaism. You don't want that to happen here, I suppose."

"Absolutely not. Prior Bartholomew will be retired, and you will take his place."

"What about my current abbey? Who will replace me?"

"I will take care of that. I want you to go back to your abbey, get your belongings, and meet me at Hedgestone in mid-July. If you arrive before me, say nothing to Bartholomew or anyone else. Just say I told you to meet me there, understand?"

"Yes, Your Grace. I understand. And thank you for this opportunity."

Basil grunted. "Just do as I ask and you will please me."

"What about me?" Alwyn asked.

Basil thought for a moment. "Hubert, please leave the room. I want to talk to Alwyn alone." Hubert looked annoyed and insulted. Why did he have to leave when a mere priest did not? He reluctantly bowed and left, closing the door behind him.

Basil took a long look at Alwyn. "How long have you been at York?"

"About seven years. I've been assisting the bishops. There have been three in the last few years."

"Yes, I know. While I do not know you, if it is agreeable, I would like you to go to Hedgestone with Hubert. I want you to report back to me if he does anything against my orders. Will you do that?"

Alwyn answered without hesitation. "Yes, Your Grace. Hubert is my cousin, but I have no love for him. I will be happy to honor your wishes."

"Good. I am counting on you. You will find it very beneficial to have me on your side."

"May I ask why you want me to do this?"

"I do not trust him. I want him to do exactly what I say and nothing more. His reputation as an opportunist scares me, but with your eyes on him I would feel better. Are you comfortable with that?"

"Yes, Your Grace. I want nothing more than to serve you."

"Then remember that. Now go prepare for your journey."

The bishop sat and became immersed in his thoughts. Ever since he was a young priest, he wanted to enrich himself by appropriating money from the Jews. However, since they were protected by the king, he had to be very careful. Hubert will do the dirty work for me, Basil thought, smiling as he worked out his plan. He will not be able to resist his own greedy nature. Alwyn will keep me informed of his progress. When the time comes, Hubert will suffer the consequences, and I will reap the reward.

"Eustace," he called.

"Yes, Your Grace?" Eustace was always close. Perhaps too close, Basil thought. He may know too much. I will have to keep my eye on him as well. "Bring me more wine. I have much to ponder."

"Right away, Your Grace. Right away."

Alwyn returned to his chamber in the bishop's palace and found Hubert waiting for him.

"It's about time you returned. What did he want with you?"

Alwyn's face was blank. "Nothing in particular. He asked me to accompany you to Hedgestone, and inquired about the conditions in York, particularly about the Jews there." Alwyn hoped he was convincing, adding the lie about the Jews. He never considered himself a very good liar, and when the bishop asked him to spy on Hubert, he feared he could not do it without giving himself away.

"He asked you to go with me and about the Jews? Why would I have to leave his presence for that?"

"I don't know," Alwyn said in a low, soft voice.

"He's up to something, I know it. Alwyn, I'm glad you'll be accompanying me. I was going to ask Basil myself for you to come with me anyway. Listen. I want you to keep your eyes and ears open and tell me anything that involves him. Do you understand?"

Alwyn began to show a little fear. By nature, he was not a brave man. "He's a bishop. I cannot spy on him for you."

Hubert looked sternly at his cousin. "Do you want me to tell him about your frequent escapades with Brother Thomas?"

Alwyn shuddered. That swine, he whispered to himself under his breath. He is always holding that over me. "No, cousin. Of course not. I will do as you ask. But please do not tell anyone about that."

Hubert smiled. "Don't worry, I won't. As long as you do as I tell you and are loyal to me, your secret is safe. However, if you betray me…"

"I will not betray you," Alwyn said sheepishly.

"Good," Hubert replied. "Now, let us pack our things and prepare to leave."

Chapter Four

West End – June 1266

It was a short walk from Mordecai's house to the synagogue. As he slowly approached the old structure, Mordecai thought of all the time he has spent there, including attending the minyan that morning.

More than one hundred years old, the synagogue building used to be a tavern. When the owner died, he owed a considerable amount of money to Isaac, the wealthiest moneylender in West End at the time. In an unusual display of generosity, Isaac donated it to the community to be converted into a synagogue since the previous one, a ramshackle wooden building, had burned down. Arson was suspected, but it could not be proven, and the sheriff showed no interest in trying to identify the perpetrator. Fortunately, the rabbi had managed to save the Torah.

Isaac was not known to be a very kind or considerate individual. He often clashed with the synagogue elders in both religious and secular matters. He always wanted everything his way, which alienated him from almost everyone. While the community thanked him for his gift, it was generally believed he only did it to try to make amends for his sins against God and man, since he was more than seventy years old. Mordecai had gotten along with him, even though they did not have much in common. Isaac was killed the same night as Mordecai's wife.

Mordecai opened the heavy wooden door and saw the rabbi sitting in a small room near the back of the chapel. There were only two chairs and a small table with a lit candle on it.

"Shalom, Mordecai. Thank you for coming," Rabbi Ezra greeted him. "I hope you are well. Please sit down. You are probably wondering why I asked to see you."

"Shalom, Rabbi. Yes, I am well enough. And yes, I am wondering why. What is this about?" Mordecai sat in a chair that for years had threatened to outlive its usefulness.

"We are worried, Mordecai. The council and I are worried about your son David."

"Worried? About what? Has he done something wrong?"

"Mordecai, we know how hard it has been for you since that awful day, losing your wife and your best friend. And we understand how much more difficult it has been for your children."

"Yes, of course. Please get to the point."

"As you wish. David is showing more and more a lack of interest in his studies and in his prayers. When you are away, he often does not even show up. He also has been talking to some of the other boys about tournaments, jousting and fighting with weapons. He actually told one he wishes he could become a knight! Imagine that, a Jewish knight. How absurd."

"Rabbi, you know this is nothing new. David has never been afraid to defend himself. He was very upset he could not help save his mother. I've spoken to him several times about this. He understands we are forbidden to have weapons. He understands we cannot learn about such things. But he does not agree with these restrictions, and I do not as well."

"Are you saying you would let him fight if he could?"

"Yes, I am. Our history has many examples of how we fought tyranny and won. Today is different. We are scattered and prevented by laws and edicts that keep us from defending ourselves. The Church says it protects us, but often incites the people against us. We rely on a lord or sheriff for protection when they usually have no love for us as well. The king considers us his property. Bar Kochba and Judah Maccabee would not have lived like this. They would fight back if they lived today under these conditions, and I think David just feels the same way."

"Mordecai, we must never speak like that. Do you not think such talk is dangerous, for everyone else as well as David? If the people start hearing these things there will be trouble."

"Rabbi, there's always the chance of trouble occurring. The Gentiles do not need any excuses—they make up their own. Perhaps if there were more like David, willing to fight back, there would be less trouble for us."

The rabbi stood and pointed at Mordecai. "We want him to stop all this talk and bad behavior. We want him to be like all the other boys. Talk to him again. Make him understand. He must attend all classes and prayers. We will hold you responsible if he does not."

"Rabbi, I will talk to him, but not because of what you said. I will talk to him because he cannot get his wish. He will never be able to fight with a weapon for himself or our people. He will never be able to be a knight. I do not know where his destiny lies. Not everyone is a good student or has the same desires as everyone else. Somehow, he must learn to live his life as best he can under the conditions our people are required to live. But I will say again, Rabbi, if he could pursue his dream, I would let him."

Mordecai left without saying goodbye. As he walked slowly home, he thought about what the rabbi had said. Mordecai always had been a man of peace and tried to avoid confrontation. As a boy, he often had been harassed by the Christian children when walking to cheder or simply playing in the street. He had been beaten up a few times, but it was mostly his pride that was injured. He admired David's feelings and his willingness to fight. He especially admired his lack of fear or when he defended other Jews who were being harassed. His size and strength enabled him to do this. However, what he wants cannot be. Not now. Not ever.

David sat with his best friend Avram by the side of the river Nene. The stench from the offal and human waste thrown into it usually made it impossible to be this close. Today, however, it was not so bad. They both were tossing small stones, watching the ripples slowly fade away. Avram was David's age, but several inches shorter and about thirty pounds lighter. He was a thin boy, with brown hair and brown eyes. David liked to tease him about being so skinny. He would tell him how easy it would be to break him in half. Avram would laugh and compare himself to the biblical David and David to Goliath. It was all in fun.

"Avram, the rabbi spoke to my father about me."

"I'm not surprised. You haven't exactly been a model student lately."

"I know."

"Was your father angry with you?"

"Actually, no, and that surprised me."

"I'm surprised as well. My father would have been very angry with me. He constantly tells me study not only brings me closer to God, but also is important to separate us from the Gentiles. I'm not sure what it means, but he's adamant about it."

"I think my father changed after what happened to my mother. He still has not forgiven himself for not being here or God, for that matter, for taking her away from us. Perhaps that's why he isn't angry with me."

"He hasn't forgiven God? That's serious. Do the elders know about his feelings?"

"They do, but under the circumstances they don't hold him responsible for them, the same way they did when Joshua's daughter Miriam was raped and killed that same night."

"Poor Joshua. He was never the same. They say he died shortly afterwards of a broken heart. She was his pride and joy after his wife died on their passage here."

"Well, I tell you, Avram, I'm sick of all of this. I want to fight back."

"But you know you can't. How could that ever happen? Jews cannot have weapons, cannot be a man-at-arms or anything like that. Only Christians can. It's the law. Even if you could somehow get a weapon, how could you learn to use it? Where could you hide it? I'm afraid it's impossible."

David looked down at the water. "I know. I know. There must be a way. I just have to find it."

Avram put his right hand on his best friend's shoulder. "If you ever do, I'll be there for you. I'll keep your secret and help you in any way I can."

"Thank you, Avram. I know it's mad, but I just can't get those thoughts out of my mind."

The two friends headed back to West End. It was getting late, and it soon would be dark. It was Friday night, and the Sabbath shortly would begin.

Sabbath at Mordecai's house generally resembled Sabbath at all the Jewish houses in West End. The female of the house would light the Sabbath candles, covering her eyes as she said the blessing. Rachel performed this, even though she was still a little too young. At the Sabbath meal, blessings were said over the wine and bread. The meal usually consisted of chicken, although sometimes fish would be served. Side dishes may be a vegetable or soup, depending upon what was fresh at the market. Rachel would take it upon herself to prepare the meals. Mordecai could not afford a housekeeper like his brother.

After the meal, grace would be chanted, and the family would gather together. Mordecai would tell the children stories from the Torah and about his youth and their grandparents.

On Saturday mornings, after a brief breakfast, the entire family would walk to the synagogue for services. Since the men and women sit separately, Rachel would go to the women's side, usually sitting with her best friend, Malka. The service always seemed too long, and the sounds of men chanting in an unfamiliar language could be heard outside the building. After services, the family would return home for their dinner, usually resting afterwards. Sometimes they would have a visitor, and he and Mordecai would discuss scripture or the events of the week. David preferred to take walks when the weather permitted, as he was too bored not doing anything for so long. As darkness approached, Rachel would light the Havdalah candle signaling the end of the Sabbath. Then the family would have their supper. Another Sabbath, another week. It seemed like nothing would ever change.

Chapter Five

West End – June 1266

Mordecai looked at David asleep and smiled. He thought how he wished he could help him. Mordecai knew he is who he is and would probably never change. David is very smart, but not in classroom ways. He knows his environment, and he knows how to talk to people, especially Christians. He is never afraid to stand up to them. Why could I not be more like him? Why are not more of our people like him? Being submissive was never appealing to Mordecai, but it constantly had been repeated to him by his father.

Mordecai's father Tuvia was born and raised in Paris. Mordecai decided to leave France after a series of anti-Jewish incidents that resulted in the murder of his parents. While there seemed to be a relative calm between Christians and Jews for quite a while, it did not take much for something to ignite. Usually it was the same thing—a debtor did not want to pay his moneylender (the occupation forced upon most Jews), and made up some story to incite a few hateful people that resulted in terrible consequences.

Mordecai chose to go to England because his brother Baruch had resettled there, he knew some of the language, and could speak French, which was widely spoken by the Normans. Baruch was ten years older than Mordecai and had decided to leave France eight years earlier. Baruch had a temper that could convert a small, seemingly insignificant incident into a major situation. One evening, Baruch was leaving the small Paris synagogue his family attended. He had hurried out after services because he was invited to dinner at his friend Gabriel's. Baruch was excited, because Gabriel had a very pretty sister, Chava. While the custom was for marriages to be arranged, Baruch was never one to hope to chance when there was something he wanted. Chava was fourteen, and Gabriel, like Baruch, was sixteen. He was determined to someday make her his wife.

As Baruch ran down the street on the way to Gabriel's house, he accidentally collided with a knight walking with two other knights to an inn. The knight stumbled, twisted his ankle, and cried out in pain.

"Watch where you're going, Jew," the knight curtly said. "Bow down and apologize." His two companions, Sir Nicholas of Rouen and Sir Guibert of Caan, moved around him, so Baruch basically was surrounded.

Baruch tried to escape. One of the knights tripped him, and he stumbled onto the filthy street, his anger growing as they laughed. A small crowd of onlookers began to gather.

"Nice work, Nicholas," the apparently aggrieved knight said. "You made him bow down." The knight, Sir Jacque of Navarre, put his right boot on Baruch's back, pinning him down. "Now we'll make him apologize."

Baruch quickly assessed the situation, looking for some way out. He knew he could not simply apologize and do the knight's bidding. They would not let him off without a beating or something worse.

"Sir Knight," he said. "You must let me go. I'm on an important errand." He figured it was a futile attempt to escape unscathed, but this was the only thing he could think of.

"What errand, you lying pig?" the knight replied.

Baruch's temper got the better of him, and without thinking, he said, "The only pig I see is you."

Jacque pressed down harder with his boot and started to pull out his dagger. "I'll cut out your tongue for that."

"No, Jacque," Nicholas said. "I have a better idea." He spotted a well down the street. "Let's toss him down that well."

"And poison the water? No. I want to cut his tongue out. Turn him over and hold him down."

Nicholas and Guibert did as Jacque asked. However, as they turned him over, Baruch saw they were squatting and took a chance. He gathered all his strength and pushed. Both knights fell onto their backs. Baruch quickly got to his feet and ran, but a townsman grabbed his arm and held him. Nicholas and Guibert jumped to their feet and pulled the struggling Baruch away from his captor. The three knights were all quite angry now that this Jewish boy had embarrassed them in front of everyone.

"Now you'll pay," Jacque said as he drew his sword.

"Stop this!" A familiar voice was heard over the growing crowd. "Let the boy go." The crowd turned around to see who had spoken, and then separated to let two men through. They were Father Pierre, the local priest, along with Samuel, the local rabbi. A murmur rose from the crowd as they tried to understand why those two were together. Father Pierre walked right up to Jacque and stood directly in front of him. Pierre was not a small man, standing almost six foot tall and husky. He had been a man-at-arms before suffering a wound that prevented him from holding a sword, becoming a priest after his wife died.

Jacque was the same height as Pierre, and he met the priest's stare. "Why should we?" he growled.

"This boy is under my protection."

"Your protection? He said he was running an important errand when he barreled into me. I said he was a lying pig."

"He was telling the truth. Rabbi Samuel here asked him to do something for me."

Jacque looked at the priest with the greatest suspicion. "Do what?"

"That's none of your business. Did he apologize?"

"No, he didn't."

The priest walked up to Baruch and freed him from his two captors. "Apologize to the knight," he ordered. Baruch saw the priest was trying to get him out of this predicament, and he reluctantly nodded.

"I apologize, Sir Knight." His voice was muted, and few could hear him.

"That's not good enough. He called me a pig. I demand his punishment."

Pierre winked at Rabbi Samuel. "We will punish him for his insolence. Now be on your way."

Jacque's two friends had grown weary and wanted to get to the inn. "Come, Jacque," Nicholas said, taking his friend by the arm. "We're hungry and thirsty. Let this priest take care of him."

Jacque nodded and looked at Baruch. "I won't forget this. The next time we meet you won't have a savior." The three walked away, and the crowd dispersed, unhappy they did not see the knight punish the Jew.

"I guess I should thank you," Baruch said.

Pierre grabbed him by the shoulders. "That was a very stupid thing you did. Samuel and I are trying to help our two peoples get along better, and you stir up a hornet's nest with your mouth. I know of this Jacque. He is a very vindictive man. He will track you down and kill you for what you said."

"Baruch, Father Pierre is a good friend. He's right. We must go talk to your father, as I think you must leave France."

"Leave France?" Baruch was astonished.

"I'm afraid so," Pierre said. "He will find you if you do not leave the country entirely." After discussing what happened with his father, Baruch decided to leave. He sailed for England, and after exploring London, eventually settled in Northampton.

Mordecai decided to visit his brother to discuss David. He slowly walked to Gold Street where the wealthier Jews lived. Like most Jews, Baruch was a moneylender, and had done well for himself. When it came to business, he curbed his temper, although he knew when to exercise it to collect his due. Most of his customers considered him honest and fair and did not want to anger him.

Mordecai approached the stone house and knocked on the fine oak door.

"Shalom, Mordecai. Nice to see you. What brings you to me at this time of night?"

"I could not sleep and have a problem I thought that perhaps you could help me with."

"Of course, my brother. Whatever I can do."

"It's David, Baruch. He's worrying the elders again with his talk of fighting and his desire to be a knight."

"Mordecai, I've told you before I agree with him. In my youth, I felt the same way. To this day, I wish I had taken care of Sir Jacque. If I ever find him, I still might do so."

"That was many years ago. He's probably dead by now. Baruch, you are not helping me. What David wants can never be. I was hoping you would talk to him and make him forget those crazy ideas."

"Mordecai, I would do anything for you, but that I cannot. Perhaps David will get his chance to do something to help our people. Perhaps not. However, I will not try to dissuade him from something I believe in. I wouldn't worry, though. As you say, what he wants is not possible, right?"

Mordecai sighed. "I suppose you're right. It is impossible. He will have to forget about it and live his life as we all do."

"Would you like some wine?"

"I guess a little may also help me sleep."

Baruch poured two glasses and handed one to his brother.

"L'chaim," they said simultaneously as they clinked them together and each took a drink.

"These are beautiful glasses," Mordecai said.

"They're from Morocco. I got them from a trader who could not repay his debt. Notice the gold and jewels around them? I have ten more. Mordecai, I've asked you many times to go into business with me. Why do you always refuse?"

Mordecai put down his glass.

"I've told you I just am not comfortable doing that. Our father, may he rest in peace, was an apothecary who taught me the trade, and I like carrying on his profession."

Baruch nodded and smiled. "How I miss our father and mother. I believe father was right in making me leave France, but it hurt both of us." Baruch had heard the story of what had happened to their parents many times, and both men were silent as they each thought about it.

Paris, France – April 1242

Tuvia ben Shimon, their father, and Devorah, their mother, lived quietly in a section of Paris near other Jewish families. An apothecary, Tuvia was known for his success in helping to cure Jews and Gentiles alike. Devorah was an attractive woman, and although she tried to hide her face behind a thin veil when she went to the market, she was often the target of Christian men who taunted her with not very subtle sexual suggestions. She always ignored them, and until that fateful day, there had not been any real trouble.

One early afternoon before Passover, as she walked by the market stalls shopping for vegetables in preparation for the holiday, a mercenary by the name of Roul of Laval spied her and could not take his eyes away. Half-drunk from too much wine, he walked up to her, blocking her path. He was accompanied by two other mercenaries, who also had been drinking.

"Where are you going?" he said. She stopped, ignored him, and started to turn around, but the other two men blocked her path. "Come. Take off your veil so I can see your true beauty."

"Roul, she's a Jewess," one of his companions said. "An infidel."

"I've never had a Jewess," he said. "At least not one as pretty."

Devorah quivered with fear, wondering what to do as all three of them laughed at his remark.

"If you won't take it off, I'll do it for you." Roul reached up to pull off her veil. Devorah wore a ring on her right hand, and with the back of it, hit him hard on his right cheek. The ring caused a deep cut, and blood began to flow. The slap stunned all three men, and Devorah tried to run. Roul grabbed his cheek and cried out in pain. "Get that Jewess!" he yelled. His friends tried to run after her, but they were too drunk. None of the people in the street tried to stop her. Devorah was able to make it home, locking the door and sobbing as she told Tuvia what had happened.

Roul, embarrassed and enraged at being attacked and wounded by a Jewess in public, offered a denier as a reward, and kept asking everyone who she was until he found someone who could help him. A Christian man, whose wife had been so ill that Tuvia unfortunately could not save her, had recognized her. The man blamed Tuvia for his wife's death, even though Tuvia had explained the medicine probably would not help. This was his opportunity for revenge. He told Roul where she lived, as well as lies about Tuvia, how he was a wizard and Roul should be careful that Tuvia does not turn him into a beast. Roul told the man he would kill them both.

Later that night, Roul and the same two mercenary friends broke into Tuvia's house while he and Devorah were sleeping. Mordecai had stayed with a friend that night, and therefore was not at home.

The next day, the entire Jewish community was enraged at what had taken place. Not only did Roul kill Tuvia and Devorah, but Devorah had been raped by all three mercenaries. They killed Tuvia first, since Roul did not want to take a chance that the wizard would put spells on them. Devorah's body was found naked and stabbed through her heart. When Mordecai returned home that morning, he stumbled upon the gruesome scene. After their burials, he decided he could not live there anymore and left for England to join his brother, wishing he could punish the perpetrators. The authorities made only superficial efforts to try to identify the culprits, and Mordecai knew he could do nothing.

Baruch and Mordecai both had tears in their eyes as thoughts of their parents subsided.

"I had better return home," Mordecai said. "I think I'll be able to sleep now."

"Be careful, my brother. The streets can be dangerous at night."

"I'll be all right. Good night, Baruch." The brothers embraced, and Mordecai left and arrived home without incident.

The next day, Mordecai sat for a while thinking about his conversation with his brother. So many of his people had suffered at different times. He knew about the massacres Crusaders had perpetrated, believing Jews were just as much infidels as Muslims. How ironic, he thought, that in ancient times the Israelites were respected for their bravery and heroism. The armies of Solomon and David could not be defeated. Then there were the conquerors—Babylonians, Persians,

Macedonians, and others until finally the Romans. The Maccabees established the Hasmonean State in Israel while still under the Romans. However, since the Roman expulsion after the failed Bar Kochba revolt, not only was Judea renamed Palestine, but almost all Jews were dispersed throughout the Empire. In his heart, he believed David and Baruch were right. But again, it was impossible.

Chapter Six

West End – June 1266

"David, it's Sunday, and I want you to run an errand for me."

"Yes, Father. What do you want me to do?"

"I have a preparation for Arthur of Coby Hollow I would like you to bring to him. He has already paid me. Do you know where that is?"

"It's at the far edge of Salcey Forest. I'll take Avram with me."

"Good. Here it is. It's for his wife. Tell Arthur she needs to take all of it at once and then rest. It will make her sleepy anyway. You should be back before dark if you leave now. It's about a half-day's journey, and the morning is still young. Be careful and watch out for bandits."

David took the preparation, kissed his father goodbye, and left. He went straight to Avram's house and knocked on the door. After a short while, it opened.

"David," said a still-sleepy Avram as he stood in the doorway, "it's Sunday, and I was going to sleep in."

"Not today, Avram. Get dressed. You're going with me to Coby Hollow."

"Coby Hollow? There's nothing there but a few huts. Why are you going there?"

"*We* are going there. I have to deliver a preparation to someone named Arthur. His wife is ill and my father said this will cure her."

"Very well. Come in. I'll dress and then we can go. I'll eat my breakfast on the way."

Avram dressed quickly, grabbed some bread and cheese, and began walking with his friend.

"Honestly, David, I wanted to stay in today. I was even going to miss services."

"Avram, it's a beautiful day and you need the exercise."

The two friends reached the end of the open road and stopped at the edge of the forest. Avram looked down the overhanging trees and shuddered.

"This is a perfect place for an ambush." He looked at David. "Well, Sir Knight, where are your weapons to protect me?" Avram said, raising the pitch of his voice so he sounded like a girl.

"That's not funny, Avram. Don't jest."

"I'm sorry, David. It's just that I'm frightened. Who knows what lurks in the forest? Wild beasts? Thieves? Elves and goblins? Witches?"

"Elves, goblins, and witches? Do you really believe in any of that nonsense?"

"I don't know. I've never seen them, but then I never venture into the forest. I'm only doing this for you."

After walking along the forest road for a while, they saw a man approaching. He was a forester, officially appointed to hunt and maintain the forests. He had a sword at his side, a bow around his shoulder and a quiver of arrows at his back. David greeted him as they came face to face.

"Good day, sir," he said.

"Good day. What are you two doing here?" the man said, looking them over.

"We're on our way to Coby Hollow. Is the way safe?" Avram said.

The man looked straight at Avram. "Should be. Of course, I know a wild boar down the road that loves to attack Jews. Maybe I should call him."

Avram could see his friend was getting angry and might even try to hit the forester. Avram grabbed David by the arm and started to walk away. "Thank you, sir," he said. "We'll watch out for that boar."

The forester laughed and went on his way. Avram looked at David. "Are you mad? You were really thinking about hitting him, weren't you?"

"Why not?"

"They were only words. I'm not like you, David. I can't fight and don't want to."

"You could learn. I wanted to take his weapons from him."

"You're mad if that's what you were thinking," Avram said, shaking his head.

Eventually they reached Coby Hollow, a tiny village of about fifteen families. The villagers worked the fields of Baron Geoffrey, as his lands were quite extensive. They found Arthur, who was very grateful and thanked them. He offered them food and drink, but they declined in keeping with their dietary laws. They turned around and began the journey back.

Both boys were eager to return to West End. Avram kept complaining he was tired, and David just wanted to eat. He was angry at himself for not taking any food with him. As they were getting closer to home, not far from the spot where they had seen the forester that morning, they saw a man sitting on the side of the road, leaning against a tree. It looked like he was sleeping.

"Avram, look. It's the forester, fast asleep. Now's my chance."

"Don't you dare! He'll wake up, draw his sword and cut us both in two."

They slowly and silently approached the man. Avram stayed back a bit while David got close to him.

"Something's wrong, Avram. It looks like he's not breathing."

David gently nudged the man, and he fell over on his side.

"Oh my God, David. He's dead!" Avram cried.

David put his hand over the man's chest. "There's no heartbeat. He is dead."

"But there's no blood, no wound. What could have happened? Perhaps he was ill, although he looked healthy when we saw him this morning. And he isn't very old," Avram said, panic in his voice.

"I don't know. My father told me sometimes people just die without being ill. No one knows why."

"We'd better get out of here. If someone sees us with him or even near him they'll think we cast a spell on him and killed him."

Avram could see David was engrossed in thought. Then a huge smile appeared on David's face. He began to remove the forester's weapons and looked in one of the man's pockets for extra bowstrings. He found three and took them as well.

"Are you crazy?" Avram exclaimed. "You can't keep those. It's forbidden."

"Why not? He has no use for them."

"But where will you hide them? And what if someone recognizes them and blames you and maybe me as well for murdering him?" Avram's voice was shaking.

"I know a place where I can hide them. I won't even tell you in order to protect you. These aren't custom weapons. They're just common ones many foresters and men-at-arms have."

"How do you know?"

"Avram, I know about these things. I've asked soldiers to show me their weapons. While some told me no since I'm Jewish, others were happy to show them off. I've seen weapons just like these before. Held them. Admired them. They can't be traced to any one person if I can get them to a hiding place before anyone sees us."

David moved the body away from the road and hid it under some brush as a precaution. No need to make it easy to find him, he thought. David found a fallen branch and wiped away their footprints. He then picked up the sword, bow and quiver, and they hurried away from the dead forester. They did not see anyone else on the road in either direction. After a while David stopped. "Avram, I want you to go on ahead without me. I have to hide these."

"Be careful, David. What you're doing is dangerous. I'm worried about what may happen to you."

"Go home, Avram. Forget about what happened today. Never tell anyone. Remember your promise to me."

"I remember. I've forgotten already." Avram looked at his friend and shook his head. "I just don't understand what you're going to do with them. You can't use them and you can't get anyone to teach you how to use them."

"Let me worry about that. Now, go home."

Avram briskly walked away, anxious to get out of the forest.

David walked a short while down the road as Avram's image faded. He then turned off it, carefully lowering himself down an embankment when he saw it—a small cave hidden by some evergreens. He had stumbled on this spot a year ago while wandering in the forest. He thought at that time if ever he would find any type of weapon, he would hide it in there. It was off the road enough, and the evergreens in front of it would keep it hidden all year, so probably no one would find it, unless by accident. He carefully slid around the evergreens and looked into the cave to be sure there was no animal inside. There were no tracks, so he got down on his hands and knees and crawled inside.

The cave was very small, with a low ceiling. He released the bowstring and placed the weapons inside. He put all four bowstrings in his pocket to keep them dry. I'll have to come back and wrap everything in something to protect them, he thought.

David crawled out of the cave and climbed back up to the road, again using a fallen branch to cover his footprints. His mind raced the rest of the way, as he could not believe his luck. He had weapons. The bow was made of yew and looked to be new. The quiver contained one dozen arrows, more than enough to train with as long as he could reuse them. He knew he could not easily replace any if they were lost or broken. The sword had seen some use. David guessed it had been used by more than one forester since it had been forged. Now he would have to find time to sneak away and try to teach himself how to use the bow. He did not think he could teach himself how to use the sword.

As he walked, he tried to figure out how he could get away for a while to practice without anyone getting suspicious. His father usually did not have deliveries for him to make, and he often stayed out of the forest. Then, it came to him: David would tell his father he wanted to get closer to God by spending time alone in the forest, praying. The solitude, he would explain, would let him gather his thoughts so he could try to honor his father's wishes. Since he did not want to lie, he planned to pray in the forest a short while each time before practicing. He also decided he needed to prepare a target. Using trees would be too risky if he wanted to use the arrows over and over. As he left the forest, he noticed pieces of straw lying in a field. At archery tournaments, he had seen the targets they used were made of cloth filled with straw. He would find some old cloth, gather some straw, and make a target the best he could.

Soon he was past the fields and close to home. His father was waiting for him as he entered.

"Shalom, Father."

"Shalom. Welcome home. Did everything go all right?"

"Yes, Father. I found Arthur easily enough, and he said to tell you he's very grateful."

"How was the journey? Anything happen? Did you see anyone on the road?"

He decided to tell some of the truth. "Only a forester on the way to Arthur's. He didn't bother us, but he made a crude comment about knowing a wild boar who loves to attack Jews."

Mordecai sighed. "It never ends," he said. "I hope you didn't reply and make him angry."

"No, Father. I wanted to, but Avram helped to hold me back. Father, as I was walking in the woods I got to thinking."

"About what?"

"The forest can be a fine place to gather one's thoughts and pray alone to God."

"I guess it could be if a safe place could be found. As long as one stays near the edge, it should be fine. What are you saying?"

"I would like to spend some time praying alone in the forest. I think it will help me to get more interested in my studies and our way of life." David smiled as he watched his father absorb his words.

"It's fine with me if it will help you do that. I would rather not have to go before the rabbi again about you. Just please tell me when you are going there, so I will know where you are."

"I will, Father, I will."

Northampton – June 1266

The sheriff picked up his mug of ale, took a sip, and looked at his friend Jack. The two of them had stopped at the Rams Head Inn for a meal and a few mugs. Jack was a forester and had just returned from York.

"I heard Ronald is missing," Jack said, ale dripping from his bearded chin onto his dirty linen shirt.

"Aye. I heard that too. He never returned home a few days ago. His wife has been searching for him with his brother. I fear he was ambushed while on duty."

"Are you going to do anything about it?"

"I've asked the baron for some men to help me look for him. I expect they'll arrive shortly."

Jack and the sheriff finished their meal of mutton and left the inn. They saw a group of men-at-arms approaching on horseback and walked up to greet them.

"Are you Baron Geoffrey's men?" he asked.

"Aye," said one, a mean-looking sergeant with a scraggly beard, worn boots, and a helmet with multiple dents on it. He looked to be about forty years old, and apparently had seen many years of service. There were five other men-at-arms with him. "You must be the sheriff."

Jack laughed as the sheriff nodded. "I am John de Oxenden, recently appointed by the king. Who are you, and did the baron tell you why you are here?"

"I am Sir Walter of Glenhaven. I've been in Geoffrey's service for ten years. He said Ronald the forester is missing and we're to help you find him."

"Good. He's been missing for several days. I'll get my weapons and we'll start the search."

"You're going with us?" Walter said, scowling. "Baron Geoffrey said there will be a reward for the man who finds him. We were planning to find him on our own. We don't want to share it with anyone."

"I don't care about the reward. What's so important about this forester anyway? Do you know?"

"Ronald is the baron's cousin. He fought with him when the king granted Geoffrey his title, and Geoffrey got him his appointment. I fought with him as well, and he's my friend."

"I see. Well, we'd better get started. Follow me."

The sheriff stopped at home to get his sword, helmet, and horse. Jack had gone on his way saying he had other things to do, and he never liked Ronald anyway. As the seven of them rode to the edge of town, they could see the forest about two miles ahead. Walter whistled softly, while his men were quiet. The sheriff looked at Walter. "You should be quiet. We don't want to announce our venture."

"Why?" asked Walter. "Are you afraid of bandits?"

The sheriff put his hand on the hilt of his sword. "How dare you speak to me like that," he said. "I'm in charge here. If I tell you to do something, just obey me without saying anything."

Walter was not used to being spoken to in that manner. His service to Geoffrey had placed him in a position of authority. However, he knew the baron was very concerned about his cousin, and that was the first priority. Walter calmed himself down and hoped he would get a chance later to put the sheriff in his place.

"Very well, my lord," Walter said. "What are your orders?"

"When we reach the forest, I want groups of two to search. We'll meet where the road meets the river. I'll stay with you, Walter, and one of your men. That will give us three groups searching."

"Yes, my lord," Walter said. He pointed at his men. "Aldrich, you and Preston search together, and Sedgwick, you go with Ulmer. Wolfe, you stay with the sheriff and me. We will meet where the road meets the river."

The three groups separated and began searching. Walter tried not to take the lead with the sheriff in his party but felt hampered by his presence. After searching for about two hours, they arrived at the meeting place. About thirty minutes later, Aldrich and Preston appeared, but there was no sign of Ulmer and Sedgwick.

"Any luck?" the sheriff asked before Walter could.

"No, my lord. We searched everywhere but saw nothing."

They waited somewhat impatiently for about another hour. Then they saw Ulmer, alone.

"My lord," he said. "We found him. Sedgwick is there with him while I came to find you."

"Well," John said. "Is he alive?"

"No, my lord. He's dead. We found his body covered with brush. His weapons were gone, but…" Ulmer stammered.

"But what, man? Speak up!" John ordered.

"There isn't a wound on him. No blood, no evidence of a blow. Nothing. It's like a spell was cast on him."

John laughed under his breath. "A spell? Are you mad? You both must not have looked close enough. Show me. Lead me to him."

The three men followed Ulmer, who started to shake as he approached the site. Sedgwick was standing over the body. "My lord," he said. "Here he is."

John knelt down and examined Ronald's corpse. He did appear to have been dead for several days. The animals had not found him yet, or there would not have been much left, he surmised.

"You're right. There is no evidence of any violence. And no footprints, no weapons, just a dead body. The baron will not be pleased when we report this. Men, look around. See if you can find anything."

They all searched the area a while more but found nothing. John overheard some of the men muttering about spells and witchcraft again. The sheriff had Walter's men make a litter out of some sturdy branches. Then they carefully put Ronald's body on the litter and started back to Northampton.

"I'll go to the baron with you, Walter. As sheriff, I must report this myself. Don't worry. I'll tell him Ulmer and Sedgwick found the body. You can divide the reward as you like."

Since that was Walter and his men's main concern, they nodded in agreement their acceptance. Slowly they made their way out of the forest to the castle.

"Sir Walter," a guard said, "I see you found Ronald. The baron instructed me to personally tell him when you returned. All of you follow me."

They followed him through the gate. "Wait here," he said. "I'll fetch the baron."

They lowered the litter and waited for the baron. After several minutes, Baron Geoffrey appeared with Cyrus following. Geoffrey looked at Ronald's corpse, examining it for wounds.

"John and Walter. You found him like this? No wounds, nothing?"

Before John could answer Walter spoke quickly and loudly.

"That's correct, my lord. Not a mark on him, and his weapons were gone."

"Perhaps he was poisoned. Did you see anything that might indicate that's what happened?"

"No, my lord. There was no cup or food of any kind by him."

Geoffrey examined Ronald's head, checking carefully for evidence of a blow, but found nothing. "Very strange. He wasn't very old. And his weapons couldn't be found. We may never know what happened to him. Let's give him a proper burial. Cyrus, go tell Father Leon. We'll bury him in the churchyard."

Geoffrey turned to John and Walter. "I want you both to go back where you found him and look again for any signs of what may have happened or his weapons. Are they identifiable if we can find them?"

Walter thought for a moment. "Probably not. His sword was old, and I don't think it had anything unique on it. The bow, arrows and quiver were common. I doubt we could identify them."

"Very well. Do the best you can."

"My lord," John began. "Why do I have to return to look for anything? I have duties of the sheriff to perform."

"I'm sure your duties can wait. I want someone to go with Walter, and you were already at the site. It will be dark in a few hours anyway. However, you do not have to return here when your search is done."

The sheriff's face indicated he was not pleased. "Yes, my lord. As you wish."

Geoffrey told one of the guards to stay with the body until Father Leon arrived to take charge of it. The baron slowly walked into the castle and sat down to ponder what had happened.

John and Walter, along with two more men-at-arms Walter ordered to accompany them, mounted their horses, and proceeded back into the forest. It was not difficult to find the spot where Ronald was found since they had marked it well. Walter again gave the orders. "Search everywhere around here. See if you can find anything that might be a clue as to what happened to Ronald or his weapons."

The men began to search, spreading out to cover more ground. After about an hour of searching, one of the men-at-arms called out.

"Sir Walter, I think I found something." Walter hurried over to see what it could be. Garrett, the man-at-arms, pointed to two sets of footprints. They were somewhat faded, but still visible. Walter knelt to examine them. Both appeared to be smaller than a full-grown man's.

"Sir Walter," Garrett asked, "do you think these are footprints of two who may have had something to do with Ronald's death?"

"I don't know, Garrett. Perhaps. They appear to belong to two boys, with one bigger than the other. If they were involved, maybe they found Ronald and took his weapons. Or maybe someone else did. It looks like they were going back to town. There are many boys in this shire, so it's not much of a clue. Come, let's return to the castle."

When Walter met up with the sheriff, he told him about the two sets of footprints. "John, I think you should ask around if any boys know anything about what happened, or about the weapons. If anybody does, it may help."

"I will, although I doubt it will do any good."

Chapter Seven

West End – July 1266

David was lying on his bed, his hands behind his head and his mind racing. I finally have some weapons, he thought. Now, what can I do with them? I have to learn how to use them, and I can't ask anyone to teach me. Whom would there be to ask? No one in the West End Jewish community certainly. I don't know any men-at-arms. Even if I did, I doubt anyone would help me. How could I explain where I got them? And it is against the law.

He began to regret taking them. All were well hidden, though, so he believed they were safe. Even if someone were to accidentally find the weapons, there was nothing to tie him to them.

No, he continued to think to himself, I will have to teach myself. If I can, I'll watch very carefully at tournaments the techniques archers use, and how knights fight with swords. On second thought, he still doubted he could teach himself the proper way to fight with a sword. Archery, though, he could do. He just had to get into the forest by himself to practice. He trusted Avram not to say anything to anyone about what had happened, since it was very dangerous for both of them.

Later that day, David was walking back from the marketplace with some vegetables for dinner when he heard someone calling, "David, David."

"Shalom, Avram. What's wrong?"

Avram looked around to be sure no one could hear them. "They found the dead forester, and the sheriff has been asking boys about our age if they know anything about him and the missing weapons."

"Why would he do that?" David asked.

"Apparently, they found two sets of footprints, our footprints, around where the forester died, and they believe they belong to two boys heading back to town. They think if they can find them it will help solve their mystery. I overheard some of the Christian boys talking about it."

David said nothing as he thought for a moment. He had told his father about seeing the forester, but nothing about finding him dead.

Still, just the fact they had seen him might arouse enough suspicion that the sheriff would want to question them. If he used any of the methods David had heard about, he was certain Avram would tell what had happened.

"Avram, let's stay calm. If we're asked, we'll say we saw a forester on our way to Coby Hollow, but we didn't see him again, or anyone else for that matter, the rest of our journey. It's almost the truth. Since I told my father about seeing the forester, I'll ask him not to say anything. He'll understand if he did, we might be under suspicion. Did you tell anyone about seeing him?"

"No, I didn't. I was going to tell my father as well, but he wasn't home when I returned, and then I forgot about it."

"Good. Then let's hope we're not asked. Perhaps he'll only ask the Christian boys anyway. There's nothing to tie us to the body. Go on your way and forget about it again."

"I will, David. I will." Avram ran off towards his house.

David returned home as well, his mind focused on this new fear. *I will have to be extra careful*, he thought. *I cannot risk beginning to practice archery for a while. If I'm seen with the weapons...* He shuddered to think about what might happen.

I've waited this long, David told himself. *I can wait a while longer.*

Northampton – July 1266

Walter went right in to the sheriff's office. The sheriff was finishing a leg of mutton.

"Don't you knock before entering?" John asked.

"Sometimes. The baron sent me to find out if you learned anything."

"I'm afraid not. I questioned a number of boys, but no one knew anything, or said they had not even been in the forest."

"Humph," Walter grunted. "Liars, no doubt. Very well. I guess we've done all we can for now. Keep listening for anything that might slip by.

I've learned most people have a hard time keeping something a secret. The baron wants you to stay on this, understand?"

"Yes, Walter, tell the baron I will do all I can for him."

Walter left without acknowledging the sheriff's request. He had no intention of telling the baron anything except that John had not found out a thing.

Walter decided to take a walk amongst the shops, stopping only if one of the food stalls interested him. When he approached the bakery, the smells enticed him.

"Good day, sir," a plump man in an apron said.

"Are you the baker?" Walter asked.

"I am indeed. Every day I bake delicious breads and cakes. I even bake for the baron at festival time."

Walter looked at the baker's assortment and selected a scone.

"What garbage are you trying to sell me? I almost broke a tooth on this. It's as hard as a rock. I should report you to the baron."

The baker began to tremble. "Please, kind sir, it was left over and I had forgotten it was there. It wasn't meant for someone as you, but only for some poor villager." The baker picked up another one and handed it to Walter. "This was just baked this morning. Please take it at no charge with my apologies."

Walter took the scone. It was fresh and very tasty.

"All right, I won't say anything this time. But I want you to do something for me."

"Anything, sir. What do you want of me?"

"A forester was recently found dead without any wounds, and his weapons were gone. We're trying to find out what happened to him and his weapons. I want you to keep your ears open. I would think most of the townspeople come by your bakery."

"That they do, sir. Except for the Jews, of course."

Walter stopped and thought for a moment. The Jews; I wonder if any of them were queried about what happened.

"Of course. They stay to themselves and don't eat what we eat. Never mind them. If you hear anything, I want you to tell me immediately and not the sheriff, do you understand? I am Sir Walter, the baron's sergeant."

"Yes, Sir Walter, I know who you are. I will only tell you. Anyway, the sheriff already questioned my son."

"He did? How old is your boy?"

"He's ten. But he never goes into the forest. It's too dangerous, I always tell him."

"Tell him to keep his ears open as well. If you help me, I'll see you are rewarded. But if you tell the sheriff before you tell me, or if what you tell me isn't true, I'll cut off your ears."

"Don't worry, Sir Walter. Anything I learn, you will hear it first."

"Good."

Walter was not certain the baker could help him, but it would not hurt to have someone like him as a spy in the town. He thought again about the Jews. Could one of them have been involved with Ronald's death and taken the weapons? The more he thought about it, the more he decided it could not have happened. Jews know they cannot have weapons, and they would not know the first thing what to do with them. He laughed to himself. They cannot fight. Their boys just study and pray. I have seen them. But then he thought about the one he had heard about who could fight with his fists and did not seem to be afraid like the other Jewish boys. He laughed again. A Jew with weapons? Absurd. He continued laughing as he returned to the castle.

The Road to Hedgestone Priory – July 1266

Upon returning to their previous postings, Abbot Hubert and Father Alwyn gathered their belongings, and made the uneventful journey to Hedgestone Priory. It was close to mid-July and quite hot. A priest drove a wagon with several chests, mostly containing Hubert's personal items. Alwyn had many fewer belongings.

As Hedgestone came into view, they both noticed how run down it appeared. The buildings showed evidence of disrepair and neglect, and the grounds were unkempt. It would take considerable work and funds to fix everything. Hubert began wondering what he had gotten himself into. Did Basil give him this assignment to punish him? How was he to finance everything? It seemed like this was going to be a very difficult job, but he was determined to successfully complete it as quickly as he could. He did not want to be stuck there for a long time. His ambitions were to become a bishop, but they did not stop there. He would do anything necessary to eventually become a cardinal.

"It doesn't look like much, does it?" Alwyn said.

"No, it doesn't. It's going to take a lot of work to turn this place around. I will need your full cooperation, Alwyn, and to follow my orders to the letter. However, I will welcome your input and expect you to assist me as much as you are able."

Alwyn nodded while his thoughts returned to what a pompous ass Hubert is. I am just as capable as he is, he thought. He reminded himself that Bishop Basil was relying on him to keep an eye on Hubert. Alwyn had no problem with Hubert failing or at least suffering the bishop's wrath. Alwyn had his own ambitions, and maybe he could accomplish them without Hubert.

They rode up to the door of the priory and dismounted. Hubert pulled the bell cord. No one came, so this time he rang the bell harder and pounded on the door. "Open up. It's Abbot Hubert."

They heard the shuffling of feet and the murmur of voices. There was a small hole cut out in the door, and it slowly opened. "Who are you?" a voice called out.

"I already told you. I'm Abbot Hubert. Now let me in!"

"We were not expecting any visitors. Wait here. I'll get Prior Bartholomew."

Hubert became furious. "Open this door immediately. I am here on the bishop's business."

This stunned Alwyn. Bishop Basil had explicitly told Hubert not to tell Bartholomew why he was there.

Hubert did not faze the man behind the door. "I will get the prior," he repeated. He closed the little door, and they heard him walking away.

"Hedgestone definitely needs my special talents," Hubert said to Alwyn. "I will show them how to pay respect to me."

Alwyn smiled and said nothing. After several minutes, they again heard footsteps and the priory door slowly creaked open. They saw a very old man and a somewhat younger man standing in front of them. The older man used a walking stick to help support himself.

"Greetings, Abbot Hubert, is it? I am Prior Bartholomew. This is Father Ambrose. We are sorry to keep you waiting. We were not expecting any visitors, and do not understand why anyone would come on the bishop's business."

Hubert studied both men. The little hair Bartholomew had left was completely white. He wore a very dirty robe that had several small tears in it. Covered with food stains, it looked like it had never been washed. Ambrose had gray hair, and his robe was not quite as dirty as Bartholomew's was. Both men smelled terribly.

"Yes, I am Abbot Hubert. This is Father Alwyn. We are here on the bishop's business but cannot tell you anything more at this time. I am appalled at how both of you look. Do you not care about cleanliness?"

"I am sorry, Your Grace. There has been sickness here—ague and the flux. Many of us are just getting over it. We chose to stay this way until all had passed."

Hubert looked worried. "I see. Is it safe to enter?"

"I do not know, Your Grace. I believe so, but one can never be sure," Bartholomew said. "We do have clean quarters available where there was no sickness, if that meets with your approval."

"Very well. Lead us."

Hubert had been to a few priories, and this one looked smaller than most. There was a chapel building, a main building, and a structure that resembled a barn that no doubt doubled as a stable. Hubert noticed it looked even worse on the inside than what one could see on the outside. A well stood in the middle of an unkempt courtyard. The walls surrounding the priory also showed signs of neglect. The more he saw, the more Hubert realized this was going to be harder than he thought if the bishop really did want to restore Hedgestone. When Basil arrived, he would have to discuss this with him. Hubert wanted to be sure both of them agreed completely on what exactly is expected of him. He did not want any margin of error.

The quarters Bartholomew and Ambrose showed them were actually better than Hubert expected. They were guest rooms, no doubt intended for higher-ranking churchmen, and larger than the usual, cell-like accommodations he was used to. Hubert was surprised to see how clean they were, considering the rest of the priory. Each room had a table with a vase of fresh flowers. However, Hubert wondered if anyone had come to visit there in the last several years. He had many questions to ask about Hedgestone, but he would have to be patient until Bishop Basil arrived and announced Hubert would now be in charge.

"These will do just fine, Bartholomew," Hubert said.

"Good. Then we will leave you two to rest after your journey."

Alwyn went into his own room, and Hubert sat on the bed. The mattress seemed to be fresh, and there were no bugs.

After a few minutes, Alwyn appeared at the doorway of Hubert's room. "Are you as surprised as I am with the state of these rooms?"

"I am. From what we have seen so far of this priory, I expected much worse. I want to tour the grounds and start thinking about what needs to be done."

"I suggest you be careful, Hubert."

"What for? Bartholomew is old, and he has to assume he would be replaced soon."

"Yes, but you are an outsider. Priors are usually elected by the senior monks, are they not?"

"Usually. But the bishop can override that and appoint whomever he wants. Anyway, I am only doing this to help the bishop. After all, an abbot is higher than a prior is. I plan to turn this place around, ensure there are no issues with the Jews, and move on to my next assignment, no doubt on the bishop's staff. Then he or the monks can have whomever they want as the next prior unless it's you."

Alwyn hid his anger. "We will see, Hubert. There is much to be done here, and it will be expensive."

About an hour later, one of the monks appeared. "Prior Bartholomew would like both of you to join him in the refectory for some refreshment. Please come with me."

Hubert and Alwyn followed the monk into the refectory. It was extremely barren, with only a long table and benches. Prior

Bartholomew sat at one end. Father Ambrose was next to him on his left. They both had bathed and now wore clean robes.

"Please sit down. Brother Mark, bring food and wine for our guests." The monk nodded and left the room.

"Your Grace, may I call you Hubert? At my age I don't have much need for standing on ceremony."

"Certainly, Bartholomew. I know you have served the Church well for many years. How long have you been prior here?"

Bartholomew thought for a moment. "I believe it is just over thirty years. Much has changed since I first came here as a young man and eventually was elected prior."

Hubert nodded and smiled. "I am certain that is true." He paused and looked directly at Bartholomew. "Tell me, the priory does not appear to be in a good condition. Have you not been able to keep it up?"

Father Ambrose began to answer, but Bartholomew raised his hand to indicate he should not.

"We have done our best, but conditions have been harsh. Our parishioners are poor, and we have not been able to generate much income. It's hard enough to keep us fed."

"I do not understand. The peasants are supposed to work your land for free and to pay for church services, such as baptisms. You have not been collecting these, have you?"

Hubert could see Ambrose was getting angry. He stood and addressed Hubert. "You have no right to criticize Prior Bartholomew. You have just arrived and know nothing about our life here." Ambrose was almost yelling.

"Ambrose, please contain yourself," Bartholomew ordered. "I am sure Abbot Hubert meant no disrespect."

"My apologies to both of you," Hubert said, bowing his head slightly. "Father Ambrose is right. I do not know anything about life here, although I am most eager to learn. Perhaps I can be of some assistance."

Bartholomew looked intently at Hubert. "I am sure I will be replaced soon, as I had recently received word from Bishop Basil he will be arriving in a few days. I can only assume you will be replacing me."

Hubert did his best not to respond, but Bartholomew noticed a slight smile on the abbot's face.

"This is the only life I have ever known, and I was hoping to perform my duties until I died. Now that may not be possible." He paused and took a deep breath.

"There are very good people here, Hubert. And not only the monks. We have established strong relationships with the townspeople, and even the Jews. I have made it a priority to take care of the parishioners first. That is why our priory may seem a bit run down. Our mission is not to acquire wealth, but to foster the wealth of the human heart and spirit. We believe that is what God prefers, and what our Savior preached. There is too much greed in this world, and it only causes sin and sinners."

Bartholomew's words took Hubert by surprise. He especially wanted to question him about his statement regarding the Jews. However, he would wait until he took over. Yes, he thought, there is much to change here. Now I understand why Basil chose me to undertake this task.

Brother Mark then arrived, carrying a tray with wine and bowls of stew, which Hubert noticed smelled quite good. Mark poured wine for all four of them, and after saying grace, they ate in silence.

"Thank you for this delicious meal, Bartholomew. I must say I am surprised you have provided such a tasty and abundant supper. With the conditions I have seen so far, there is much work to be done here," Hubert said. With a smirk on his face he added, "Whoever is charged with this responsibility will have much to do."

Bartholomew smiled. "I trust you will wait until Bishop Basil arrives and officially makes the change before you do anything?"

This time Hubert stared blankly and ignored Bartholomew's words. "We are tired. Come, Alwyn, let us rest before Vespers." They both arose and returned to their quarters.

Ambrose waited until they had left. "I don't have a good feeling about him, Bartholomew. He will cause problems, I'm sure of it."

"Perhaps," Bartholomew said. "Even if I am not prior, I still will be here and will be able to keep an eye on him. I am not in such a poor condition that I am helpless. If I get the chance, I will discuss my concerns with Bishop Basil. I do not want to see Hubert unravel in a short time what we have accomplished after years of effort. I still believe in what we have done, especially our relationship with the Jews."

Ambrose nodded. "I agree. Why would any Jew consider accepting Christ if we treat them so poorly? By setting an example of kindness and caring, we have nurtured an understanding I believe will begin to bear fruit. Hubert will not continue that, I am sure, and all our work will have been for nothing."

Bartholomew sighed. "I am afraid you may be correct. If we are criticized for being too close with the Jews, it will not be the first time."

"And no doubt not the last time either," Ambrose added.

Chapter Eight

Salcey Forest – Northamptonshire – July 1266

David walked carefully as he approached the hiding place where he left the forester's weapons. Avram tagged along behind him, frantically scanning all directions for outlaws, wild animals, foresters, or the king's men.

"Stop being so afraid, Avram. Nothing's going to happen to us."

"I'm not as sure as you are, David. The forest is full of danger. You've heard the stories as well as I have."

David laughed. "Yes, they're stories, just that. If you aren't afraid, you have nothing to fear. Do you still think there are evil spirits here?"

"Don't make fun of me. I came to help you, not to be your bodyguard. I will watch out for any signs of danger or anyone approaching while you practice your archery, but that's all. I cannot and will not fight anyone or anything."

"I know, Avram. I know. Don't worry. I'll protect you."

Avram stayed back while David found the hiding place. Everything was as he had left it. He had brought materials to make a target and cloth to wrap around the weapons to help protect them. He removed the bow and arrows, examining them for any defects. There were none. David returned, showing Avram the bow.

"This is so beautiful," he said. "Look how the wood is crafted, how it's carved so perfectly. I have never seen a more wonderful bow."

"Well, how many have you seen anyway? Especially up close?"

"A few. Maybe not so close. But I have been to an archery tournament."

"You are really enamored with it."

"Avram, you know I am. I still cannot believe I have this."

"You'd better keep it between us or you won't have it anymore. You'll be arrested, and God only knows what could happen to you."

"Can you imagine what everyone would say? A Jewish archer? Not since biblical times has there been one, I guess. Or at least not since the expulsion by the Romans."

David carefully strung the bow, held it in his left hand, and tried to pull back the string with his right arm. He hardly could move it.

"This is going to be harder than I thought. I will have to get stronger."

David knew archers practiced for years before they could use a longbow. This was not a longbow, but a shorter one used by the foresters for hunting. The draw was still difficult for him. It would take some time, but he knew he eventually could do it, and would keep working at it. Avram was disappointed.

"So, I came all the way here, risking my life, and you can't even shoot one arrow?"

"I'm sorry. I didn't know this would be so hard. I promise that soon you'll be able to watch me shoot."

David decided not to build the target yet, since he would not need it for a while. He practiced pulling the string until his arm ached and his fingers hurt. "I think I'm done for today, Avram. Let's go home." David unstrung the bow and returned it and the arrows to the hiding place, being careful to conceal it well, again using a branch to wipe away any footprints.

The boys saw no one else on the road as they returned to West End. Mordecai was waiting for David when he arrived.

"Where have you been?"

"Avram and I were walking in the forest. I enjoy the peace and solitude, except for Avram's fear of witches and spirits."

Mordecai laughed. "It's not witches and spirits I fear but outlaws and Jew-haters who would just as soon kill you as look at you."

"Now, Father, I can take care of myself."

"Perhaps you could fight off an outlaw, but Avram could not."

"True, Father. I've offered to teach him, but he doesn't want to learn and has no confidence in himself."

"He doesn't have the strength you do, that is certain," Mordecai said. "Please, David, you must not take chances. I don't know what I would do if I lost you."

"I'll be careful, Father. I promise."

"Good. Now let's prepare for supper."

Hedgestone Priory – mid-July 1266

Bishop Basil arrived at Hedgestone with a small entourage. Basil and Father Eustace rode horses, while two other priests rode in a wagon that carried the bishop's baggage. Eustace pulled on the bell rope, ringing it several times. After a few minutes, a monk appeared at the small opening cut into the door. Eustace spoke without greeting him.

"Bishop Basil is here to see Prior Bartholomew. Let us in."

The monk looked at the four men. While he did not know the bishop, Prior Bartholomew had advised everyone he was coming.

"Welcome, Your Grace. I am Brother Andrew. Please follow me, and I will get Prior Bartholomew."

Andrew took Basil's and Eustace's horses, and they all followed him into the priory. While several monks were doing chores, the priory courtyard was otherwise deserted.

"Where is everyone?" Basil asked.

"Many are getting over the flux, Your Grace. Almost all have been ill."

Basil grunted. "Perhaps it's because Bartholomew has let this place run down or has not properly kept his vows."

Andrew restrained himself from defending Bartholomew. As they walked towards the main priory building, Basil saw Hubert running out to greet him.

"Your Grace," he said as he bowed, kissing Basil's ring. "I've been waiting for you. I trust your journey was not difficult."

"Hello, Hubert. It was uneventful. How long have you been here?"

"Alwyn and I arrived a week ago. It allowed me time to inspect the priory without disclosing the reason for my presence. However, Bartholomew is no fool. He assumed I would be replacing him."

"I'm not surprised. Have you formulated any plans yet?"

"Nothing specific. There is a question of funds we must discuss for me to fully improve this place."

Basil glared at Hubert. "We'll discuss that later. I'll meet with you in private to give you my recommendations. There are certain changes I want you to make, and we will discuss how to pay for them as well."

"Of course, Your Grace. As you wish."

Bartholomew and Ambrose then appeared.

"Welcome to Hedgestone, Your Grace," Bartholomew said, bowing and kissing Basil's ring. Ambrose bowed his head but said nothing.

"Thank you, Bartholomew. It has been a long time since we've seen each other."

"Yes, Your Grace. It was when I was in London several years ago. You have not called me there since, nor have you come to visit."

"I have been very busy with Church affairs." He looked at Ambrose. "And who might you be?"

"I am Father Ambrose, Prior Bartholomew's assistant."

Basil ignored him and studied Bartholomew. "You have aged quite a bit since then. Have you not been well?"

Bartholomew did not like the bishop's tone. "There has been much sickness here. Most, including me, have had a very bad case of the flux. Some are still ill. Otherwise, I believe I am faring quite well for a man of my age."

"We will speak later of this. Also, we will not eat with the monks tonight. Please show us to our quarters, as I wish to rest. Hubert, I will see you at supper."

Bartholomew and Ambrose led them to their rooms. Hubert went to see Alwyn, who was lying down in his chamber. He shook the priest awake.

"Alwyn," he said, "he's here."

Alwyn was still a bit sleepy as he spoke. "Did he say anything significant to you?"

"Only that he has some recommendations for me. When I asked him about funding, he said we would discuss it later."

"I'm curious to hear what he has in mind."

In the early evening following Vespers, they all sat down to eat in the refectory after the monks had eaten. Basil led grace, and they ate a meal of bland chicken with asparagus. Afterwards, Basil, Hubert, and Bartholomew met. Basil said there was to be no wine during the meeting.

"Prior Bartholomew, I have decided it is time for you to be replaced. You have spent a great many years serving Hedgestone, but I am afraid the job has gotten too difficult for you. You have let it get too run-down. This priory is an embarrassment to Mother Church. Your monks are lazy due to your lack of leadership. You have not brought in any revenue. In addition, I am very unhappy with your relationship with the Jews."

Bartholomew looked at the bishop, shaking his head. While he knew this day was coming, he did not feel he should be spoken to in that manner.

"Your Grace. I am not a young man. I have done the best I could under the circumstances. The little money we have been able to raise we used to sustain ourselves in a meager fashion, and to help the poor. We decided not to use any funds for our own comfort. That is why the priory may appear to be run-down. But every one of our monks has dedicated himself to serve God by helping our fellow man."

Basil frowned. "I do not agree with you. Why would anyone want to come here in this condition? Why would any of the poor you speak about want to pray in your church in its condition? We serve God best by showing beauty and strength."

Hubert just listened. He knew his turn would come soon enough.

Basil continued. "Abbot Hubert is to take your place, effective immediately. I expect everyone to give him their full cooperation."

"But Your Grace, monks are supposed to elect their own prior," Bartholomew said.

"Not this time. When Hubert has finished his work here, perhaps they may elect his successor. However, I make no promises at this time."

"Replacing me is within your power, Your Grace. But it is not right. The monks would elect Father Ambrose, if you would let them. He is well qualified."

"That may be, but it is not my desire. I want an outsider in charge here. Ambrose just would continue your ways."

Bartholomew realized Basil's mind was made up.

"Very well, Your Grace. We will honor your wishes and give Hubert our full cooperation. Just one question, however. Why are you unhappy with my relationship, as you describe it, with the Jews?"

"I will be blunt. I have heard you often invite the chief rabbi here as well as other Jews, and you have actually attended some Jewish services! Blasphemy! You're lucky I don't have you whipped, but I believe you are too old and would not survive."

Bartholomew rose and pointed at Basil. Hubert could see the old prior was angry. "I have done nothing wrong. How can we expect Jews to follow Our Lord if we treat them cruelly? We do have some things in common. All we have done is try to learn about them and to teach them about us and our faith. What is wrong with that? I have heard the Holy Father does the same thing."

Now Basil was becoming angry. "You know nothing about the Holy Father. And you are not the Holy Father. There is nothing more to discuss. Hubert takes over, and other than providing counsel to him as he wishes, your duties are completed."

"Very well. I am too old to argue with you. However, I am afraid Hubert very quickly will undo all the work we have done here, especially with respect to the Jews."

"Enough, Bartholomew. Do not speak about the Jews again."

"What about Father Ambrose? He's been my very capable assistant and counsel. He can help Hubert in many ways."

"He may stay, but Father Alwyn will be Hubert's assistant. Ambrose agrees with you on all matters, I suppose?"

"Not all, but most."

"He still may stay, but if he poses a problem for Hubert or Alwyn, I will transfer him, understand? You may relay that to him yourself."

Bartholomew bowed and left the room. Basil looked at Hubert.

"I think that went about as well as it could have," Basil said.

"I'm not so sure. I don't trust him. And I especially don't trust Ambrose. He's younger than Bartholomew and could incite dissension amongst the monks. I will have to watch him."

Basil nodded. "That's why I didn't include him during our meeting. I want you and especially Alwyn to watch him closely. I'm sure he will resent you as the new prior since he did not have the opportunity to be elected. The other monks as well will be resentful. I want you to be firm with them. They need discipline. Things here have been lax way too long. No doubt Ambrose will also resent your new methods, shall we say?"

"I'm sure he will, Your Grace. I can handle Ambrose, as well as all the monks."

"Tell Alwyn to gather all the monks in the refectory. I want to address them now. But not Bartholomew. He is not to attend."

Hubert left to do the bishop's bidding. He felt excited as well as a bit apprehensive about this assignment. Again, he told himself, this was an opportunity to please the bishop and rise in the future. However, he must be sure he completes his mission such that the bishop is entirely pleased with the results. Otherwise all may be for naught. Basil was a hard man to understand. Hubert was still suspicious of why Basil spoke to Alwyn in private. Hubert reminded himself he would have to keep an extra eye on Alwyn. Perhaps he even could use Ambrose to spy on Alwyn. The more he thought about it, the more he liked it. He would speak to Ambrose after Basil had left.

Hubert found Alwyn in his chamber and repeated the bishop's orders. Alwyn ordered all the monks into the refectory. There were twenty brothers, plus Father Ambrose. Basil kept them waiting for about fifteen minutes. He finally walked in with Hubert, and the monks immediately became quiet. They all noticed Bartholomew's absence.

"Gentlemen," he began. "Most of you do not know me. I am Bishop Basil from London. I have come to thank Prior Bartholomew for his long and loyal service to the priory and to introduce you to your new prior, Abbot Hubert. Abbot Hubert is to assume the prior's duties effective immediately. Father Alwyn will be his assistant. I expect all of you to obey Hubert. This priory has become an eyesore, and I want it turned around. You will all work to make this effort a success. Hubert has my complete confidence, and he is not to be questioned in anything he does by anyone except by me. He will be assigning each one of you your duties." Basil paused to observe the monk's reactions. Most just nodded without saying anything. He then continued.

"One more thing. Jews are not allowed at Hedgestone anymore without Abbot Hubert's permission. In addition, none of you are to have any outside contact with them."

This brought a reaction from one.

"Your Grace. I am Brother Xavier. May I ask some questions?"

"Certainly, Brother Xavier. What do you wish to know?"

"I think I can speak for all the brothers when I say we believe Prior Bartholomew has done a very good job maintaining Hedgestone as we all believe God would wish it. While, yes, there needs to be some repairs done, most are cosmetic and the priory is functioning effectively."

Basil interrupted him. "I do not agree. There is much work to be done here. Hedgestone is a disgrace." Some of the monks began murmuring, but what they were saying could not be heard. "What questions do you have?"

"For one, Your Grace, why can we not elect our own prior, as is custom?"

Basil stared at Xavier, unfazed. "I've decided it is best to have Hubert make Hedgestone as I want it to be. Once his work is completed, I may permit you to elect the next prior. That decision will be based on how cooperative all of you are with Hubert. If there are no problems, we will all get along just fine. However, I will be receiving reports from him regularly, and if there are problems, they will not be tolerated. Hubert has my mandate to do whatever he feels is necessary to complete his mission."

Xavier was not pleased with the answer, but felt he had no recourse to argue. "My last question is about the Jews. As you may know, we have established a very good relationship with them, and both sides have benefited from it. Why can it not continue?"

At this, Basil became angry. "Brother Xavier and all of you. Listen to me. Prior Bartholomew, Father Ambrose and most, if not all of you, may have believed becoming friendly with the Jews will bring them to Our Lord and Mother Church. I strongly disagree. Under Abbot Hubert, and as long as I am bishop, this will stop. If there is to be any contact with the Jews, Hubert or Alwyn are the only ones who will make it. There is to be no more socializing or religious discussions with them. Anyone who disobeys this will be subject to expulsion and excommunication."

At this tirade, the monks merely nodded in silence. Brother Xavier also was speechless. It was futile, he thought, to argue with the bishop.

"Any more questions?" Basil asked. No one spoke. "Very well. Return to your work. Hubert and Alwyn will meet with each one of you soon to explain any new assignments." Remaining silent, they all filed out. Father Ambrose glared at Basil and left as well.

"Hubert. Watch that Xavier. I feel he also may be a problem."

"Yes, Your Grace. I will. Don't worry. I can handle all of them."

Basil's eyes narrowed. "We shall see. I want regular reports sent to me without fail. Have Alwyn deliver them."

Hubert was surprised at this. "Alwyn, Your Grace? But he's my assistant. What shall I do when he's gone?"

"Use Father Ambrose. He is experienced, and you need to get him to change his way of thinking." Basil could see Hubert was not happy.

"Your Grace. I do not understand. Why Alwyn?"

"Because he is the only one I trust. Not only will he deliver your reports, but I can query him, and I know he will be truthful. I do not trust any of these Hedgestone monks. I am sure they all hope you will fail and may do everything they can to make that happen. Now do you understand?"

Hubert nodded. While he still believed Alwyn might be spying on him for Basil, the bishop's answer made sense. "All right. I will send Alwyn."

"Good. Now let us have something to drink. I am quite thirsty."

The next day, Basil, Hubert, and Alwyn met in the scriptorium.

"Hubert, I'll be leaving soon, but before I go I want to discuss a few items with you."

"Yes, Your Grace."

"First, I want you to make a list of all the improvements you believe should be made, in order of importance. Then I want you to find out how much each one will cost. I also want you to make a list of ways Hedgestone can obtain revenue. I suspect that in order for you to make at least some of the necessary improvements, you will have to borrow money from the Jews. Bartholomew will know who the best moneylender is. Borrow as much as you can for the longest term you can, and, of course, at the lowest rate."

"I will. But will we be able to repay the loan on time?"

"Leave that to me. Make sure the payments are not to be made more than quarterly. And I must have a full accounting of every penny. Do you understand? If there are any discrepancies you will answer to me, is that clear?" Basil said.

"Of course, Your Grace. Every penny. You can trust me."

"One more thing. Do not spend even a penny of the loan without my permission."

At this Hubert and Alwyn were a bit puzzled. Why would Basil say that if he wants the priory restored? "I will not, Your Grace. I will obey," Hubert responded, somewhat sheepishly.

"I expect nothing less. Are there any questions?"

Both men shook their heads. "Very good. Then I will return to London tomorrow." He looked at Alwyn. "I will expect your first report in the next few weeks. Do not wait too long as I don't want any surprises." He then looked at Hubert. "Remember, I want to approve everything before you do it."

Hubert frowned. "But, Your Grace. You said I have your complete confidence to do what is necessary here. I do not understand."

"You do not have to. I said that for your benefit in front of the monks. I have plans I want to complete, and it is very important to me that you do as I ask."

"Very well," Hubert said, obvious reluctance in his voice. "I understand."

Basil retired to his chamber to rest. Hubert and Alwyn stayed in the scriptorium.

"Well," Hubert said to Alwyn, "what do you think he's up to?"

Alwyn did not answer.

"Well? Speak up!"

"I'm not sure. I'm as surprised as you he wants to approve everything. It sounds to me he does not want to spend much. Perhaps he wants the money from the loan for something else?"

"You may be right. I always thought he was using me for another purpose, but I had no idea what it could be. I will have to be vigilant, and I want you to be as well. If you learn anything, you must tell me at once. Remember what I know."

"You never let me forget it."

"Then I will not have to worry about you."

Chapter Nine

Salcey Forest – Late August 1266

David was getting stronger. He had found some heavy rocks near the river and used them to strengthen the muscles in his right arm. He would have to greatly improve his strength to be able to fully pull the bowstring. Until he had tried it, he had no idea how difficult it was. He knew the king's archers used longbows, and they were even harder to pull.

It was easy to go down to the river after being dismissed from cheder. It was not far, and there was enough vegetation so he could do this without being observed. Sometimes Avram would go with him. He said he was acting as a lookout, although David had told him it was not necessary.

After strengthening himself with the rocks for a few weeks, David decided it was time to try the bow again. On a hot Saturday afternoon after services, he told his father he was going for a walk. As usual, he saw no one else on the road. It took him more than an hour to reach his hiding place. He looked around one more time, and there was no one. David carefully unconcealed the opening of the cave. There they were, undisturbed. While he thought this was a very safe hiding place, he did worry a little someone would stumble upon it or, even worse, follow him. Not today, though. All was fine.

David removed the bow from the cloth he had wrapped it in, took a bowstring, and carefully set it. It was taut and ready. He gripped the center of the bow with his left hand, and with two fingers and the thumb of his right began to pull back the string. He smiled. He was doing it. His strength had improved. He pulled back the string to almost its full draw. He did not release it since he knew doing so could break a bow if there was no arrow. He pulled back the bowstring several more times, and each time it was easier.

David returned the bow to the cave and decided to make his target. He took out the large piece of cloth he had brought previously. He had taken some dye and painted a circle in the center. Then he took the straw he had collected and, with a needle and some thread, sewed the cloth closed around the back, just enough to keep the straw from falling out. It was not a great target, but it would do for now. He placed it against a tree and retrieved the bow and three arrows. It was time to shoot his first arrow.

David stepped back about twenty paces and looked around before notching the arrow on the bowstring. He pulled back on it, aimed, and released. The arrow fell harmlessly about ten paces away. Undaunted, he retrieved it, returned to his original spot, notched the arrow again, pulled back and released. This time the arrow reached near the bottom of the target but did not hit it.

David continued to practice for about an hour. With each try, the arrows grew closer to the target. Meanwhile, his fingers were becoming quite sore and beginning to feel raw. One more shot, he said to himself. He carefully set, pulled back, aimed, and released. The arrow shot straight into the target's center circle.

"Yes!" he said. "I did it."

For a few moments, he admired that arrow. It was not perfectly in the center, but it was in the paint.

"One day I will be an archer," he told himself. He gathered the bow, arrows, and the target, unstrung the bow, and hid everything in the cave. He again was careful to conceal the entrance and erase his tracks. He was encouraged by his first real attempt at shooting. He knew it would take a while, but eventually he would become very proficient. When he arrived at home, Mordecai was waiting for him.

"How was your walk?" he asked.

"Very nice, Father. I enjoy the solitude of the forest. It helps me to clear my mind and prepare for this week's studies."

Mordecai smiled. "I'm very glad to hear that. It looks like you listened to me after all. Perhaps I will accompany you next week."

David shuddered at the idea. While he did not want to hurt his father's feelings, he obviously could not practice with him there.

"That would be nice, Father. However, I don't know if you could walk as far as I do. My walks are quite long, and I don't sit and rest."

"You're right, my son. I cannot walk as far as you, especially when the pain in my foot returns. Perhaps we can just stroll around town."

"Any time, Father. I would enjoy that."

West End – Late August 1266

Mordecai sat thinking about the baron's order. The apothecary still did not want to comply, but felt he had no choice. Soon the baron would send for him and expect the poison. He decided to keep it simple. Either an arsenic-based formula or belladonna will probably work best and be easy to prepare. He also had all of the ingredients. He thought about which one to use. In the end, he decided to prepare one of each. Then the baron could do with them whatever he wanted. Mordecai did not want to know the baron's purpose, or, more specifically, who his intended victim or victims would be. It was hard enough for him to have to prepare them. However, he must obey Geoffrey.

The first one Mordecai prepared was in a small clay jar that contained concentrated belladonna roots, the most toxic part of the belladonna plant, along with a few leaves and a number of berries he made into a paste. He added some crushed blueberries that made the concoction look and smell like preserves. The second was a small vial of arsenic powder that could be added to either food or drink. Then he carefully secured and hid them to be sure his children would not find them. He would wait until Baron Geoffrey summoned him.

York – Late August 1266

The servants to Baron Henry de Percy had packed his clothes and other items he considered necessary for his trip to Northampton. Baron Geoffrey had invited him to come for a visit and hunt. Henry loved to hunt, especially with his prized falcon, Saladin. The baron was quite proud of that name, one he had heard about from an earlier Crusade. He had grown a bit bored hunting around Yorkshire and was eager for a change of scenery.

"Bryce," he called. "Come here."

Bryce hurried into Henry's chamber.

"Yes, my lord, I'm here."

Henry looked at the boy. Bryce was fourteen, the son of Henry's blacksmith. Henry liked him. He would grow into a fine man, Henry thought. I think he will make a good man-at-arms.

"How would you like to accompany me to Northampton?"

The baron's question surprised him. He had never been far from York before, and only lately had gone with the baron on a hunt to help recover the game his falcon had killed.

"I would be honored, my lord."

"Good. Go pack some of your things. We will leave at first light tomorrow with six men-at-arms. Tell your father you'll be gone about a fortnight. I can't imagine staying with Geoffrey much longer than that."

"Thank you, my lord. I'll be ready at first light." Bryce bowed and dashed from the baron's chamber. He could not believe what he had heard. He would be traveling with the baron to Northampton. He ran down the castle's stairs and out the side door to his father's forge. Quinn, Bryce's father, was responsible for making weapons and armor.

"Father," Bryce said, panting from running so fast. "I have great news."

"Well, what is it?"

"The baron is traveling to Northampton and is taking me along."

Quinn put down his hammer and hugged his son.

"That's wonderful. How long will you be gone?"

"He said about a fortnight."

"You'd better tell your mother. I don't think she'll be as happy as I am with this news."

"Why not, Father? I'm not a little boy anymore."

"You know she worries about everything. I'm sure she'll worry about you until you return."

Bryce nodded. "I know. I'll tell her now." He scampered off to their small house just outside the castle walls. He found his mother preparing supper.

"Mother! I have exciting news!"

Grace, his mother, looked up from cutting some vegetables.

"What is so exciting?"

Bryce hugged her and then burst out, "Baron Henry is going to Northampton and is taking me with him!"

His mother took a moment to absorb the news. She knew someday this might happen, with the baron's fondness for her only son. "Is it safe to travel there?"

"Of course, Mother. The baron is a great warrior and is taking six men-at-arms with him. I can fight too, if needs be."

Grace hugged her son. "You will be careful, right? Stay with the baron. Never wander off on your own, especially in the forest."

"I'll be careful. The baron needs me. I can't leave his side."

"Very well. Let me pack some clothes for you. I'm sure Baron Henry will take good care of you."

While she was speaking, Quinn entered. "Well, I see the news is out. Grace, are you all right with it?"

He saw a few tears in his wife's eyes. While Bryce was their only son, their daughter, Elsabeth, died almost five years ago when she was only three. They had tried to have more children but could not. Grace always feared something would happen to Bryce. "I guess so. He is growing up and can't stay here forever. I'm sure he'll be safe with the baron. He's a good man."

Bryce could hardly sleep that night and awoke just as dawn was breaking. He gathered up a small sack with his clothes, kissed his mother and father goodbye, and ran to the stables. The baron's steward, Garth, was there with a small wagon pulled by only one horse.

"Well, I see you're ready to go."

"Are you going too?" Bryce asked.

"Of course," Garth replied. "You'll stay close to me and help me with the baron's needs. We'll ride with his personal items."

Bryce looked in the wagon, but a blanket covered whatever was in there. Soon the six men-at-arms accompanying them arrived. Bryce was friends with one of them, Brom of Leicester. Brom was a large, brutish man, and he had taken a liking to the wiry, blonde boy.

"Well, look who's here. Now I'm not afraid of any outlaws ambushing us. Bryce will protect us," Brom said to the other five men-at-arms as he laughed.

Bryce was not amused. "Give me a sword, and I'll protect you."

Brom and the others laughed harder.

Brom patted Bryce on the back. "Don't get upset, my friend. I was only joking. I'm sure when you're old enough you'll make a fine man-at-arms. But we'll have to fatten you up a bit first. You're too skinny. I don't think you could hardly hold my sword now."

Bryce was tempted to respond belligerently, but understood he meant well. Perhaps, he thought, soon Brom will show me how to use a sword.

Baron Henry de Percy then appeared, wearing a black surcoat over his chainmail. He was not wearing a helmet and carried his long sword at his side. Bryce guessed the baron's other weapons were hidden in the wagon.

The baron smiled when he saw Bryce. "So, is my little traveler ready?" Bryce did not like the reference to being little, but to the baron he could not express his displeasure.

"Yes, my lord. I believe we are all ready."

"Let's proceed then."

The small entourage started to move. The guards on the battlements watched as they crossed the drawbridge and disappeared down the road.

The pace was slow and bumpy, but at least he did not have to walk. The baron, the only one riding a horse, often would gallop ahead until he was out of sight and then stop to rest. By the time they caught up to him, he liked to gallop off again.

By nightfall, they had reached an inn outside of Sheffield. The baron took the largest room for himself. Garth, Bryce, and the men-at-arms shared one room. After a meal of mutton, bread, and ale, they all retired. Brom took the bed, small as it was, and the rest of them slept on the straw-covered floor.

As tired as Bryce was, the loud snoring of Brom and three of the other men-at-arms kept him awake but did not bother Garth. Bryce finally was so sleepy the snoring did not matter, and he drifted off.

Their journey continued for three more days until they reached Northampton castle. When the guards announced strangers were approaching, Baron Geoffrey assumed it was Baron Henry and his party, so he sent Sir Walter to greet them. Walter recognized the baron's coat of arms.

"Welcome, Baron," Walter said as he bowed.

"Thank you, Walter. It's been quite a while since I've seen you. How have you been?"

"Well enough, my lord. My wound from the outlaw ambush last year has healed. I'll never let that happen again."

Walter referred to an incident when he was returning to the castle through Salcey Forest and five outlaws jumped him and threw him off his horse. After fighting off two of them, he managed to draw his sword. He slashed one in the face, and with a thrust killed another right through his heart. Of the other three, one fled with fright while the other two continued to fight with him. Neither carried a sword, but one tried to stab Walter with a large dagger. The one without the dagger jumped on Walter's back, allowing the other man to try to stab him. His chainmail absorbed most of the impact, but the outlaw had found an opening. The dagger pierced Walter's skin on his left side. Enraged, Walter tossed the outlaw on his back over his head, and immediately disemboweled him. The outlaw with the dagger attempted to run, but Walter hurled his sword at him like a spear and killed him as the weapon went through to its hilt.

"I am sure you will not."

"Come, my lord. Baron Geoffrey is eager to see you."

Henry followed Walter into the castle, while his entourage was greeted by Baron Geoffrey's steward, who showed them their quarters. The men-at-arms would stay with Geoffrey's men-at arms, and Garth with the steward. Bryce would be with Cyrus, Geoffrey's page.

Walter led Baron Henry to a small room off the castle's main hall. Geoffrey was there waiting, and they embraced.

"Welcome, my friend. I'm glad to see you. How was your journey?"

"Thank you, Geoffrey. It is good to see you again. The journey was fine. No outlaws this time. I think perhaps I scared them away." Both barons laughed.

"I doubt it. I've sent men into Salcey without much luck. They managed to catch two I hanged, but I don't even know how many outlaws are living there now."

"I saw their bodies hanging at the edge of the forest."

"Good. I hope that scared the rest of them off. Let someone else take care of them. Come, sit and have some wine."

Henry and Geoffrey sat at a small table. Henry looked around the room, which was barren except for a tapestry covering a portion of the wall. Although a bit musty, the room was comfortable.

"This is my thinking room," Geoffrey said. "I prefer this to the great hall. It also gives me some privacy."

"I see. No windows and only one door. It makes me nervous. No way to escape."

Geoffrey laughed. "Escape from what, Henry? A servant? I don't fear in my own castle. Tell me, how are things at York?"

"Quiet at the moment. The taxes have been collected and sent to the king, and the harvest should be very good this year. We are already beginning to prepare for winter." Henry sipped his wine. "How about here?"

Geoffrey belched. "Quiet here as well. Nothing since de Montfort's attacks two years ago. The castle could use some repairs, but I don't want to borrow any more money from the Jews."

"I know what you mean. I am too indebted to Aaron of York."

"And I of Baruch here in Northampton."

"Do you plan to do anything about it?" Henry asked.

"I'm not planning to kill him, if that is what you mean. It's not my way, and the king forbids it."

"After the massacre we had in 1190, York cannot have another such incident. It was difficult to lure Jews back to York after that."

"I've maintained a good relationship with them. I find it beneficial when I need something. Our Prior Bartholomew has also established good relations with them. It helps to keep things quiet. The townspeople have left them alone, so there has not been much trouble lately. Of course, there are isolated incidents, and if they are serious, we punish the perpetrators. We did have an unfortunate incident, however, but not involving any Jews."

Henry finished his goblet and Geoffrey refilled it. "What was that?"

"One of my foresters, my cousin Ronald actually, was found dead in the forest and his weapons were taken. There were no wounds on him, and only footprints, apparently of two older boys, were found. He was a fairly young man and had not been ill. We're still trying to find out what happened to him."

"Hmmm," Henry said. "Most unusual. The devil's work, perhaps?"

The men laughed. "I don't believe in that any more than you do. I know people can die without any clue as to what happened. I just don't understand about Ronald. At least I want to punish whoever took his weapons. It probably was an outlaw."

"I hope you find the culprit." Henry changed the subject. "So, Geoffrey, I was glad to get your invitation. Did you miss my pretty face?"

Geoffrey laughed. "No, that's not why. Do you know Abbot Hubert and his cousin from York, Father Alwyn?"

"I don't know Hubert, although I have heard of him. I do know Alwyn. He hears my confessions. Why do you ask?"

"Hubert had my brother Peter excommunicated under false pretenses. He accused him of heresy. Peter was very religious and was so upset he killed himself."

"Do you know why Hubert did that if the charge was unwarranted?"

"I didn't know for certain until recently when a pilgrim I gave shelter to told me. After the king made me baron, he gave Peter fifty acres and a small manor house as a reward for his services. We didn't know they happened to be next to Hubert's brother, Abbot Oswald's property, near Kent. After Peter's suicide, Oswald confiscated the property in the name of the Church. I petitioned the king to reverse it, but he didn't want to antagonize him or the Church. He did make Oswald pay for the land, but it was a pittance of what it was worth. Hubert recently stopped here with Alwyn, asking for shelter on their way to London just to aggravate me. I reluctantly let them stay, using his visit as an opportunity to figure out a way to get revenge. They left the next morning but wouldn't tell me the purpose of their journey. I haven't heard of them since."

"I have," Henry said. "Alwyn returned to York to gather his belongings. He is near here, at Hedgestone Priory with Hubert. Bishop Basil ordered Hubert to clean up Hedgestone and change the previous prior's attitudes towards the Jews, and Alwyn is to assist him."

"What? He's at Hedgestone? How long will he be here?"

"I don't know. Alwyn told me Basil ordered Hubert to do what he had to do. He did say Hubert wants to accomplish this as soon as he can. He doesn't want to stay here too long. He has huge ambitions to rise in the Church and remaining at Hedgestone more than is necessary would certainly hinder him."

Geoffrey considered this as he stroked his beard. "I see. That is indeed interesting news. While I'm sure I eventually would have heard of it, it's better to know of it now."

"Are you planning to do something to Hubert to thwart him?"

"Henry, I will get my revenge. How, I do not know, and I certainly wouldn't want you to be implicated. I'll have to think about how to proceed."

"Be careful, Geoffrey. I understand that while Hubert is disliked in Church circles, he does get results. That's why Basil chose him to take over Hedgestone. You could jeopardize everything you've gained if you make a mistake."

"Thank you for your advice, my friend. I would never do anything that could hurt me. Or be traced to me," he said, laughing.

Chapter Ten

Salcey Forest – October 1266

David wore a heavier cloak as he headed to the cave where his weapons were hidden. Already the weather was turning colder. Many of the leaves had fallen, with some trees and shrubs completely bare. This bothered David, as it might make it easier for him to be discovered. He figured with the first snow he would not be able to continue practicing anyway. It would be too risky. He would leave tracks in the snow, and as much as he wanted to work on his skills, he would have to wait for spring.

David followed his usual routine. He removed the bow, three arrows and the target he had made. He set up the target on the same tree he had been using and attached a bowstring. He notched an arrow, took aim, and shot. The arrow ran true and landed near the painted center. David smiled. He was getting stronger and better. He shot the next two arrows, and they hit the target as well. He practiced for about two hours until his arm felt quite sore. He put everything away, being especially careful to cover his tracks. The sheriff was still asking questions, even though it was several months since the forester was found.

When David returned home, his father was waiting for him as was Avram.

"How was your walk?"

"Fine, Father, fine. Hello, Avram."

Mordecai noticed three of the fingers on David's right hand looked red and somewhat raw. "Are you all right? What's wrong with your fingers?"

"I found a fallen branch on the ground and used it as a staff to walk with. I must have gripped it too tightly," he said, thinking quickly of an excuse.

Mordecai did not think that was plausible but did not question him further. David and Avram went into David's room and closed the door.

"Well," Avram began, "I can guess where you've been."

"Avram, I'm getting good. I hit the middle of the target several times today, and from a greater distance. I think I have a knack for archery."

"I'm still worried, David. The sheriff continues to ask questions, and if anyone sees you…"

"I know. Winter's coming soon, and I won't be able to practice. It will be too risky to leave tracks in the snow. That should help, though, as with time passing, the sheriff will lose interest and finally give up."

"I don't agree, David. He seems pretty dedicated to solving this mystery. You've been lucky so far."

David shook his head. "The sheriff doesn't suspect a Jew could be involved. He has never done his questioning in West End. It's been several months already, and as I said, with winter coming, the first snows will make it even harder if he tries to search again. My treasure is well hidden." David hesitated for a moment. "As long as you don't say anything."

Avram looked disappointed. "How could you say that? You know I would never say anything."

"Really, Avram? What if the sheriff stopped you and started questioning you? What if he asked you directly if you knew anything about the forester's death or the missing weapons? What if you were not convincing in your answer and he took you in for further questioning? You know they have terrible ways to get anyone to say anything."

"You're right, David. Let's hope the sheriff doesn't extend his investigation to West End. He has no reason to, after all. Even so, please don't worry. I may not be very brave, but I can lie quite well when I want to. Your secret is safe with me."

"You're right, my friend. You can lie convincingly when you want to. Let's not speak of this again."

Hedgestone Priory – October 1266

Hubert and Alwyn sat in Hubert's chamber. There was a parchment on the small table, along with a pitcher of wine and two cups.

"This wine is awful," Hubert said, spitting some onto the floor.

"I like it. I don't like strong wine."

Hubert grunted. "It tastes like horse piss. Alwyn, you have no class whatsoever. You would like anything liquid, I presume."

"Hubert, you insult me. I just have different standards depending upon the situation. This is the best we can afford right now. Hopefully soon we will be able to afford better. Perhaps some good French wine?"

Hubert looked at the parchment and turned it around so Alwyn could see it better. "What do you think about this list? Have we covered everything?"

Alwyn began reading out loud. "Roof repairs to the refectory, rebuild the south outer wall, replace the stables, build a new chapel, granary, and expand the kitchen and scriptorium." Alwyn stopped reading and looked at Hubert. "The list goes on. This will cost a fortune. Basil will never approve all of these."

Hubert smiled. "I disagree. I believe Basil wants me to obtain the largest loan I can from the Jews, and while these may seem somewhat extravagant for a relatively small priory as Hedgestone, I think he will approve them all."

"I don't understand, Hubert. Why would Basil want to commit so much money for such a place as this?"

"Because, cousin, he wants the moneylender, whoever he is, to believe the loan is to make these improvements. These can only increase the priory's visibility, and, as such, it will attract more revenue. Then Basil can take the money, or at least as much as he wants, without giving away his scheme, leaving me responsible for the debt and not being able to do the work or repay the loan."

Alwyn thought he was beginning to understand. "But why couldn't Basil simply negotiate his own loan?" he asked.

"Alwyn, I can see you don't know how Basil thinks. I believe he doesn't want to associate himself with borrowing from the Jews. And if the loan is in default, his name would not be a part of it. Mine would be. Do you see now?"

"I think so. If what you say is true, he's playing you for a pawn."

Hubert started to take another sip of wine, remembered how he thought it tasted, and threw the pottery cup against the cold, stone wall, startling Alwyn, as it broke into dozens of pieces. Hubert then thought, two can play this game, cousin. I cannot share my plan with you because I believe you are spying on me for Basil. I must keep quiet.

"Are you all right, Hubert?" Alwyn asked.

"I have no choice, Alwyn. I must do the bishop's bidding. I believe he will want you to report to him now. Please take this list and see what he wants me to do."

"Yes, Hubert. I think it is time for me to go to London. I'll return as soon as I can."

"What will you tell him?" Hubert asked, a bit sarcastically.

"I'll tell him you had the monks clean up the priory. The floors and grounds look much better, and you've given everyone assignments. You punished a few for being lazy, a few for being late for prayers, and two for socializing with the Jews when in town. You also carefully prepared this list of major improvements."

"Very good," Hubert said. "You should leave at first light."

Alwyn left the room. As soon as he leaves, I will talk to Father Ambrose, Hubert thought. Enough time has elapsed here that I now can get him to spy for me. Basil cannot use me as he wishes, but I must be careful.

Alwyn left the next morning with two monks. Hubert wished him well on his journey, and then walked the grounds as he did each dawn. He was happy with the small improvements he had made. He occasionally had requested Bartholomew's advice, primarily just to try to have the old prior warm up to him. He also wanted Ambrose to get to know him better. Hubert tried to watch every move the priest made, looking for anything he could use against him in case Ambrose was resistant to the idea of spying on Alwyn.

As Hubert continued his walk, he saw Ambrose coming out of the lavatorium.

"Good morning, Father Ambrose," Hubert said, making sure his voice sounded kind and friendly.

"Good morning to you, Abbot."

"Will you join me as I finish my daily walk?"

This surprised Ambrose since Hubert never had asked him before. "Certainly. I would be most happy to." The two men walked slowly around the perimeter of the priory.

"Tell, me Ambrose, what do you think about the improvements we've made so far?"

Ambrose was surprised Hubert said "we" instead of "I."

"May I speak honestly?"

"Of course. I would most welcome your opinions," Hubert lied.

"Most of what you have done Bartholomew would have ordered himself. The timing of all this was most unfortunate; as you recall, there had been much illness here when you arrived. I will admit some of the brothers had become lazy, and Bartholomew did not address that. He was not strict enough, in my opinion. When he did ask one about something, there was always an excuse, and he just nodded his head and said meekly they should try to be better. I had spoken to him about it, but he just replied God makes many different types of people, and we must not try to change someone."

"He actually said that?" Hubert said. He felt Ambrose was starting to tell him things about Bartholomew he never would have just a few days before.

"Yes, he did. I think you have instilled fear into most of the brothers, but your punishments have been too harsh. Especially with Brothers Tybalt and Cassius."

Hubert stopped and looked at Ambrose. "They were flogged for socializing with Jews. I was in Northampton and saw them. They knew the rules."

Ambrose's face reddened. "The rules are too harsh. They were not socializing. Tybalt and Cassius had been trying to convert Jews before you came. You heard Bartholomew. Your danger is misplaced and wrong. There is nothing evil about talking to Jews. With your logic, you wouldn't have spoken to Our Lord."

Ignoring Ambrose's comment, Hubert began to get angry. "The danger is not misplaced nor wrong. If we are not strict, it will be too easy for someone to stray. I will not take that chance, and neither will the bishop. He is very concerned about this here."

"Nonsense. There is no one here who would denounce his religion and convert to Judaism. That's absurd!"

Hubert continued. "And another thing: I do not believe Jews can be converted without forcing them. They are a strange people, and the fact they did not embrace Christ over a thousand years ago and still have not only convinces me even more."

Ambrose laughed. "I'm sorry, but that is so misguided. One must first understand the other side before being able to change their thinking. No one wants to be forced to do anything. I am not very knowledgeable when it comes to history, but I do know conquerors have almost always made the mistake of alienating the people they have conquered. What has that brought? Enslavement and even more animosity against them. Remember, the Jewish religion is a lot older than Christianity. Do you know that even when the Hebrews had a strong army, they rarely forced anyone to convert? It's not their way. Our Church decided a long time ago to go in the other direction, and many have died because of it. We believe there must be a better way."

"I can see Bartholomew has truly poisoned the minds of everyone here with that heresy. The problem is much worse than I or Bishop Basil believed."

Ambrose shook his head. "You're wrong again, Abbot. No one here has a poisoned mind. We are free thinkers. While we know Christ is the true way for us, others think differently. We call them infidels just as they call us infidels. I will say it again—we will have a much better chance of converting some if we show them our kindness and consideration. That going our way is the correct way towards righteousness. If we are hypocrites, then why should they trust us?"

"I've heard enough. No one here will follow that course. You and everyone else will do exactly as I say. This discussion is over." He stomped off, convinced he cannot trust Ambrose.

Ambrose watched the abbot walk away. Such a little man, he thought as he slowly walked back to the dormitory. It is thinking such as that that will only cause more pain and death and will not bring anyone closer to Christ. I am sure of it.

West End – October 1266

Mordecai was about to leave the synagogue when Rabbi Ezra stopped him. "Good Shabbos, Mordecai. How have you been?"

"As best as can be expected, Rabbi."

"Is anything wrong?" he asked.

Mordecai looked down at the floor, holding back tears. "I still am having a problem dealing with Sarah's death. Or murder, I should say. I feel so guilty I wasn't there to save her, and the culprits have not been caught or even pursued."

Ezra patted Mordecai on the shoulder. "I know it has been very difficult for you. It has been difficult for many others as well. That was a terrible night. So many suffered losses. We must trust in God, and he will help to heal all wounds."

"I want to believe that, but it's so hard. She was such a beautiful person. She never harmed anyone her whole life. Her only crime was being Jewish. Why was she taken from me?" Tears flowed down Mordecai's cheeks as he sobbed.

"I do not have an answer for that. Some say everything is God's will, but I personally do not believe that. I believe God gave man the ability to think and understand what is right and what is wrong. What is good and what is evil. Just as there is beauty in this world, there is ugliness as well. There are calm, gorgeous days and terrible storms, too. Each man must decide in his heart if he is to be good or evil. Unfortunately, some pretend to be good and mask their evil in the name of God, for their own ambitions. We can only hope they will get their day of reckoning."

Mordecai dried his eyes. "I'm sorry to have lost my composure, Rabbi."

"Have you considered remarrying?"

"I've thought about it. At least to have someone to help take care of my children."

"May I make a suggestion?" Ezra asked. Mordecai nodded.

"My youngest sister, Hannah, lost her husband last year, as he was very ill. They had no children. I wrote to her about you, and she responded she would be interested in meeting you."

"Where does she live?"

"In Bristol. She would be happy to come visit me, and then you two could meet."

"I don't know, Rabbi. Does she know about my children?"

"Of course. While she could never replace Sarah, I am sure she would make a fine stepmother for them. She always wanted to have children."

"Very well. I guess it's time we had a woman in the house. I will meet her if she comes."

"Very good. I will send for her. Now, something else. Bartholomew, the former prior, will be here shortly to meet with me and some of the elders. We would like you to stay and join us."

"I am honored you would ask me. Certainly, I will stay."

He followed Rabbi Ezra into another room, where Rabbi Tanchum ben Jacob, Moshe ben Joseph, and Joshua ben Isaac were waiting. "Come join us for some bread, wine and cheese."

About thirty minutes later, Bartholomew arrived. "Good Shabbos, gentlemen," he said.

"Good Shabbos, Prior," they all replied.

Ezra then introduced Mordecai. "You know everyone except Mordecai." Bartholomew extended his hand as Mordecai arose and took it. "We met when I cured him a few years ago," Mordecai said. "It's good to see you again. I understand you are no longer prior."

"That's why I've come." Mordecai sat, and Bartholomew took the last empty chair.

"Would you like some wine and something to eat?" Ezra asked Bartholomew.

"Just some wine, thank you. I've already eaten." Moshe poured him a glass.

"As you know, I am no longer prior, and the new prior was not chosen from among our brothers." They all nodded.

"Bishop Basil has made Abbot Hubert prior, even though it is a bit of a demotion. Basil said he was not happy with the way I was running the priory. We disagreed with him to no avail. Of course, internal priory matters should not concern you. However, there is one matter that does, as well as all the Jews of West End, and that's what I wanted to talk to you about. I have always believed, and I have made it no secret, that God does not want us to be enemies over worshiping Him.

I have also not made it a secret that while we can have our differences, we have much in common. We've shared bread together and have had many discussions about the Bible and the differences and similarities in our religious beliefs. Only by understanding one another can we create a better world, as were we not all created in God's image?" The men again nodded in agreement.

"Unfortunately, Basil and Hubert do not agree with our philosophy. They have forbidden any of the brothers to even speak to Jews. Two were flogged for doing so."

"Aren't you afraid of being caught talking to us and getting flogged yourself?" Ezra asked.

"I'm an old man. No one would dare to do that to me. However, with this new edict, I cannot come again. I will miss our debates, as they truly stimulated my mind and Father Ambrose's as well."

"Do the other brothers agree with you or the bishop?" Rabbi Tanchum asked.

"Most, if not all, agree with me. When the edict was announced there was much dissension. But it didn't matter. The bishop wouldn't budge, and Hubert is merely doing his bidding, although he believes the same way."

Ezra stood up and walked about the room, engrossed in thought. "I had been hopeful we were making progress by getting to know each other better and understanding our similarities as well as our differences. Now I am quite concerned it has been for naught, and our peoples will never be able to truly coexist. The king says we belong to him, and he dictates what we can and cannot do. We are resented for our successes when we fulfill those dictates. This resentment breeds hate, as well as those in the Church that preach against us. We are outcasts based on long ago events we had nothing to do with. Bartholomew, I am truly grateful and appreciative for your efforts to reach out to us. No doubt you were hoping to convert some of us, but that is no matter. Any man or woman who has true faith cannot be swayed, I believe. God lets each person make his or her own decisions. When other men make laws or by a king's ruling deny anyone the right to make their own decisions, there is no freedom. We have our own laws and customs that we live by to honor God in our own way, and for many they may seem difficult. But they have helped to sustain us as best as we can."

Bartholomew stood and embraced Ezra. "I am hopeful someday there will be no more hate, and every man can simply live by his own beliefs and let others do the same. Unfortunately, we will not see that in our lifetimes, or in your children's, I'm afraid. Instead, I see more trouble ahead. But I will pray and ask God to help bring us all together."

"That's all we can ask for," Ezra said.

"I must go now. May God be with you all."

"And with you too," they all replied.

After Bartholomew left, they sat in silence for a few minutes.

"What do you think this means, what the new prior has ordered?" Mordecai asked.

"It's another indication of the deep separation we have with the Gentiles, or perhaps I should say they have with us. They do not respect us, and they believe that their way is the only way. Until that changes, we will always live with the fear that at any time they will turn against us. And, as history as shown, they will." Ezra paused. "It's time to pray. Let us prepare."

Chapter Eleven

London – November 1266

Alwyn sat waiting for the bishop to meet with him. Eustace greeted him coldly as usual but did offer him some refreshment. For the journey from Hedgestone, Alwyn left the two brothers at a dilapidated inn. He had told them they must be frugal. He, however, would stay at a much nicer inn, unless the bishop offered to let him stay in his palace. After what seemed a very long time, Bishop Basil appeared.

"Alwyn, nice to see you. I'm sorry to have kept you waiting. Church business."

Alwyn stood, bowed, and kissed the bishop's ring. "Thank you, Your Grace. It's nice to see you as well."

"How was your journey?"

"Other than the cold winds that kept blowing in our faces, we had no problems. Once the snows start, traveling certainly will be much more difficult."

"I will not keep you long. Let us sit, so you can give me your report."

They both sat at a small table on high quality, cushioned chairs.

"Hubert ordered the brothers to clean up Hedgestone, and it looks much better. He punished a few of them for their slothfulness, making them work extra duty. He also flogged two for socializing with the Jews."

Basil's eyes opened wide. "Flogged them?"

"Five lashes each. They said they were simply trying to convert them, but Hubert was following your ultimatum that no one but him was allowed to even speak to a Jew."

Basil nodded. "I assume they all learned their lesson, then?"

"There have not been any other instances."

"Good. Tell Hubert I approve. That's one reason I wanted Hubert to reform, shall we say, Hedgestone. What about the improvements I asked for?"

Alwyn produced the parchment and handed it to the bishop. Basil took a few minutes to read it.

"Very good. This is exactly what I wanted. Now, when you return, I want Hubert to negotiate the largest loan he can. Do you know who the most successful moneylender in Northampton is?"

Alwyn thought for a moment. "I believe his name is Baruch."

"Can he loan a large amount? Hubert's list is quite extensive, and it will be expensive to complete everything."

"Hubert had me make some subtle inquiries, and we believe this Baruch can without engaging any other resources."

"Excellent. I will prepare a document giving Hubert my approval of his plans and to secure the loan. When he has received the money, I want him to hide it securely. He may take out a small amount to start work on a project so as not to arouse any suspicion. Then I want you to report to me this has been completed. I will then send for the balance."

Basil stood up. "Do not tell anyone about this except Hubert, do you understand?"

"I will not, Your Grace. You can trust me completely."

"I want you to return to Hedgestone tomorrow. I would like the transaction to be completed before the summer solstice. I am counting on you, Alwyn. Do this, and you will find me very grateful."

Alwyn stood, bowed, and again kissed the bishop's ring.

"Come back in the morning before you depart, and I will give you the approval document. Go then with God." Basil turned and left the room.

Why does he need Hubert to obtain the loan for him? Alwyn thought. What are his plans? Why does he want it several months from now? Will he require Hubert to repay the loan? If he reneges on repayment, will Hubert be responsible? I do not know what he needs the money for, nor why he cannot obtain it himself. It sounds like Hubert's assumptions may be correct. However, I must obey.

Alwyn went to the inn where the two brothers were staying and told them they would be leaving in the morning. He then returned to the much nicer inn where he was staying, ordered a supper of mutton and ale, and retired for the night. The next day he received the written approval from Basil and began the return journey to Hedgestone.

Northampton – November 1266

Even while at home, John de Oxenden, Sheriff of Northampton, remained obsessed with discovering the truth about Ronald the forester's death and the missing weapons. He was not sure why. The forester was Baron Geoffrey's cousin, and his death was mysterious, but the weapons were only a bow, some arrows, and a sword. However, John did not like unsolved crimes. If innocence could not be proven, then the party was guilty; it was as simple as that to him. At least the crime was solved, and his conscience was clear. His job was to uphold the law. As he pondered the situation, his wife Mary came into the room.

"What are you thinking about, John? The dead forester again?" she asked.

"You think I should give up, don't you?"

"John, I understand you feel if you can solve this the baron will be extremely grateful to you, and perhaps reward you. Frankly, I don't believe he still cares that much about it, so why should you?"

"I think you're right. Perhaps one day the truth will be known. For now, I'll concentrate on other matters. Did I tell you Abbot Hubert wants to meet with me?"

"Abbot Hubert? I thought he was Prior Hubert."

"He's an abbot who was asked by Bishop Basil to take over Hedgestone Priory from Prior Bartholomew."

"I see. You haven't met him yet?"

"No, my dear, I haven't."

"Do you know why he wants to meet with you? Do you know what he's like?"

"Not exactly. I've heard he has already started to reform the monks, correcting Bartholomew's mistakes."

"Mistakes? Such as what?"

"I heard Bartholomew wasn't a good administrator, and he also had become too friendly with the Jews, at least to Bishop Basil."

"Too friendly? I wonder what that means."

"I don't know. I'm sure Hubert will tell me what he wants me to know."

"What do you know about him?"

"Not very much. I believe he's pretty much kept to the priory. I've never seen him in Northampton."

"When is your meeting?"

"Tomorrow morning. I'll tell you about it when I return."

John kissed his wife. "Keep your ears open, just in case you do hear anything about Ronald's death."

"Of course I will," she said, kissing him back.

The next morning, right after breakfast, John arrived at Hedgestone. He pulled the bell cord, and a young monk appeared. "Yes, can I help you?"

"I am Sheriff John de Oxenden of Northampton, and Abbot Hubert wants me to meet with him."

The monk quickly opened the door. "Good morning, Sheriff. Abbot Hubert instructed me to wait for you here. Please come in. I will lead you to him."

John followed the young monk, who he guessed to be only about twenty. John noticed the priory was quite clean. It looked like fallen leaves recently had been removed, and the grounds actually looked quite nice, he thought. He followed the monk into a room off the scriptorium. "Please sit," the monk said. "Abbot Hubert will be with you shortly."

The room was quite barren, except for the table and four chairs around it. There was a small window, but a candle on the table was the source of most of the light in the room. John grew impatient, as it seemed like he had been kept waiting too long when Hubert arrived.

"Hello, Sheriff. Thank you for coming. I'm sorry to have kept you waiting, but I was unavoidably detained."

John rose and slightly bowed not believing him. "I'm honored, Abbot, for your invitation. It's good to finally meet you."

Hubert saw the table was empty. "Were you not offered any refreshment?" John shook his head.

"Brother Dominic! Come here at once!" Hubert shouted. The young monk appeared almost immediately. "You neglected to offer our guest wine or ale."

Dominic became nervous, seeing the abbot was angry with him.

"My apologies. What is your pleasure, sir?"

"Ale, if you please." Dominic hurried out.

"Please sit down, Sheriff. May I call you John?"

"Of course."

"Please call me Hubert."

"So," John began, "I understand you were sent here by Bishop Basil on, shall we say, a special assignment."

"You understand correctly. The bishop was very unhappy with the conditions here, and I have been given the task of turning Hedgestone around."

Dominic arrived with a large tankard of ale and carefully handed it to the sheriff. "Thank you, Dominic. You may go, and please close the door behind you." Without a word, the monk left, ensuring the door was shut.

John took a sip of the ale. It was strong and quite tasty. "Very good ale, Hubert. Where's it from?"

"I have it brought in from Normandy. Surprising, no? The French can make good ale if they want to. It is from a priory in Bayeux. Most think the French only can make wine."

"You were saying you are charged with turning Hedgestone around."

"Yes. Besides the physical changes, I must, shall we say, reeducate most of the monks here. They have strayed from the Church and must be properly returned."

John took another sip of ale. "Strayed? How so?"

"Well, for one, they have become much too friendly with the Jews. Bartholomew actually attended some of their prayer services. Some of the other monks have as well. I have stopped this fraternizing."

"Why should the prior or any of the monks attend a Jewish service?"

Hubert slightly raised his voice. "Their excuse was that in order to convert them we must show them how kind we are and convince them what the true way is. Going to one of their synagogues is heresy, do you not agree?"

"I suppose so. I don't know many of the Jews here. They live in the West End section of Northampton. I only know one of their rabbis, Ezra, and Baruch, the moneylender." At this, Hubert's eyes widened.

"You know Baruch? Well?"

"Not well, but I've done business with him. He loaned the baron the money for expanding the cells in the castle, and I was the baron's agent. The dungeon was too small for the number of criminals we find here."

"I want to meet him. Would you be so kind as to arrange a meeting between us?"

"Of course, Hubert. Shall I say what the meeting is for?"

"No. Just tell him I may need his services in the future."

"Very well. I will try to arrange a meeting for tomorrow. Where do you want the meeting to take place?"

"Tell him to come here tomorrow in the early afternoon. I will meet with him then."

The sheriff left, reflecting on the meeting. Hubert is a cunning fellow, he thought. I do not get the feeling he can be trusted. He uses people for his own gain, I am afraid, and I will not let him use me.

John rode back to Northampton and stopped at Baruch's house. He dismounted, tied his horse, and knocked on Baruch's door. His housekeeper answered. "May I help you?" she asked. She looked to be an older woman of about fifty.

"I am John de Oxenden, Sheriff of Northampton. I must see your master, Baruch."

"Please come in, my lord. I'll get him for you."

John entered, looking around at how the stone house was furnished. A fine oak table stood in the center of the large main room, with eight nicely cushioned chairs around it. There were some Jewish artifacts, mostly made of silver and quite exquisite. He noticed several candelabras, also made of silver, some with extensively detailed scenes. He guessed they may be from the Bible, but he was not sure. As he examined one, Baruch entered.

"Sheriff, welcome. I hope you have been well."

"Hello, Baruch. Yes, I have. How have you been?"

"I am fine as well, thank you. Please sit down. Emma, please bring wine for our guest," he ordered in a loud voice.

"So," Baruch asked, "what brings you to me? Do you or the baron need another loan?"

The sheriff laughed. "No, neither the baron nor I need one. I am delivering an invitation to you."

"An invitation?"

"Yes. You've heard Hedgestone Priory has a new prior?"

"Yes, I have. He's an abbot, is he not?"

John nodded. "I met with him a short while ago, and he asked me to arrange a meeting so he could meet you."

"No doubt he wants to negotiate a loan. Why else would he want to meet me?"

"I don't know, Baruch. I'm only doing him a favor."

"Can you tell me what kind of a man he is?"

"I just met him, so I can't tell you much. I've heard, as you probably have as well, that he is very thorough." Emma entered carrying a tray with wine and two silver cups. She placed the tray on the table and filled both cups.

Baruch handed one to the sheriff and lifted his own. "L'chaim, John," he said as he drank. He saw John was uncomfortable with what he said. "It means, 'to life.'"

"Oh, I see. Abbot Hubert told me he was charged by Bishop Basil of London to reform the priory and the monks, as they had strayed from their mission and the way of the Church."

"Humph," Baruch grunted. "I know what some of the reform means. I know he has forbidden Prior Bartholomew and the monks from associating with any Jew. I know he had two monks flogged for merely speaking to Jews. I cannot speak to what he is doing inside the priory, but I do know he is not interested in any relationship with my people."

"Again, Baruch, I don't know about such things. Will you meet with him?"

"Of course, John. How else can I conduct any business? If I refused to meet with any Gentile who did not like Jews, I would have almost no one to do business with."

"Good. Then be at the priory tomorrow after the noon meal."

"Very well. I shall be there. Tell me, have you learned anything more about the dead forester?"

"I'm afraid not. I don't think I ever will. His missing weapons have not turned up, and there still is no evidence or information about what happened to him. I suppose you don't know anything about it?"

"Now, Sheriff, what could I know?"

"Don't you have a nephew who has a reputation for fighting?"

The question surprised Baruch. "Do you mean David, son of my brother Mordecai?"

"Yes, I believe that's who I'm referring to."

"Yes, he is my nephew, and he used to fight some. But he's changed his ways and is a dedicated student now. What are you thinking? That he had something to do with the forester's death?"

"Not really. It was just a thought. The Assize of Arms forbids Jews to have weapons. I don't believe Jews can fight, and what on earth could a Jew do with a sword and a bow and arrows?"

Baruch ignored this. "Why such a long-running interest in a dead forester anyway?"

"He was Ronald, cousin to Baron Geoffrey. The baron would like to know exactly what happened to him."

"I see. Well, I'm sure David had nothing to do with it. Seems preposterous to me. However, I hope you do find out what you want if it pleases the baron."

"Thank you. If you do hear of anything, you'll tell me?"

"Of course. I'm a law-abiding person, even if the law says I cannot be a citizen."

"Thank you for the wine. I hope your meeting with the abbot is successful."

"Thank you for coming, Sheriff."

So, Baruch thought, refilling his cup, Abbot Hubert wants to see me. Any arrangement we make will have to be very well constructed, since I will not suffer any loss from him.

The next afternoon Baruch arrived at the priory and pulled the bell cord. Brother Dominic answered. As he heard Baruch identify himself, he opened the door and gestured him to come in. Baruch never had been inside a priory before, and he looked around to get a sense of the place. It was quite clean, he noticed, with several monks performing various duties around the grounds. "I am Brother Dominic. I will bring you to the abbot."

Dominic led him to the small room off the scriptorium. "Please sit. The abbot will be with you shortly."

Baruch noted how cold and lifeless the room was. He sat for a few minutes until the door opened. He rose and slightly bowed his head in respect.

"Baruch, is it not? I am Abbot Hubert, Prior of Hedgestone."

"Yes, Abbot, I am Baruch. The sheriff said you wanted to meet me."

"Please sit. Would you like anything?"

"No, thank you."

Hubert studied the Jew seated in front of him. Baruch was well-dressed with a shirt, breeches, and a robe of a very high quality. He also wore nicely made shoes that looked like they were of the finest leather. Hubert was about to say something when Baruch started the conversation.

"So, Your Grace, how much do you want to borrow?"

Hubert laughed. "Is that why you think I invited you here?"

"Of course. Why else would an abbot want to speak to a Jewish moneylender, especially the most successful one in Northampton? I didn't think it was to debate scripture or to establish a social relationship. In fact, I have heard you've forbidden the monks here to have any contact with a Jew."

Hubert smiled. "No, you are correct. I did not invite you here to debate scripture. And, yes, I did give that order. It had nothing to do with you, Baruch. The monks have much to do here to restore Hedgestone, and no time for socializing with anyone. At this time, I don't have any need for a loan. I merely wanted to make your acquaintance, so if I do have any need of your services, I'll know who I'm dealing with."

"I see. I must admit, Your Grace, no one has ever done this to me before. Previously, it was always just business."

Hubert tried to hide his true emotions. "Baruch, let me ask you something. As the most successful moneylender here, I would suspect both Jews and Gentiles alike are jealous of you."

"Of course. Success always breeds jealousy. I do not hide my success. As long as I am not permitted most other professions, I will be a moneylender. Why do you ask?"

"I was just curious. I have never borrowed money from anyone before. My previous abbey was well-funded, we maintained a steady revenue, and I watched expenses very carefully."

"I see. I assume Hedgestone is not like your previous abbey. Therefore, you will be borrowing from me in the near future."

"Perhaps. You aren't the only moneylender here, are you?"

"Of course not. But as the most successful, I can lend larger amounts at better rates."

Hubert decided to change the subject. "Tell me, are you married?"

Baruch at first thought he would tell Hubert it was none of his business. Then he determined he might as well be cordial since it hopefully would pay off in the future. "No, I'm not. Many years ago, I was to be married, but she was killed two months before the wedding."

"I'm sorry. I know there have been many Jews killed in towns and cities throughout Europe." Hubert did not sound apologetic and did not ask why he did not seek another wife. "Do you have any family here?"

"Yes. My brother Mordecai lives in West End with his three children. His wife was killed more than two years ago by another murderous Christian mob."

Hubert realized that while he should not have started this conversation, he must show compassion. "Again, I'm sorry. When mobs get started there's no stopping them."

"This one was started by Simon de Montfort and his mercenaries. There was no reason for it. There never is. A legitimate one, at least."

"Is your brother a moneylender as well?"

"No. He's an apothecary. Our father was an apothecary, and Mordecai decided to carry on his profession." Baruch paused. "If you don't have any business to conduct, Your Grace, I must beg your leave. I have business this afternoon I must attend to."

"Certainly, Baruch. Thank you for coming. If and when I am in need of your services, I will contact you."

"Until then."

Hubert called for a monk to walk Baruch out of the priory. This Baruch is shrewd, he thought. I must be careful with him, as he is no fool. I must use him to obtain the sum I want, since it will be too complicated and suspicious if I use several small moneylenders.

Baruch returned home, feeling it was a strange meeting. Hubert only wanted to meet him? It made no sense. Hubert's order forbidding the monks to have any contact with a Jew also bothered him. He remained quite suspicious of this abbot made temporary prior. When he did request a loan, Baruch decided he would require extra collateral to protect himself.

Instead of returning home, Baruch stopped at Mordecai's house. He found only David at home.

"Shalom, Uncle," David greeted him with a hug.

"Shalom, David. Where is everyone?"

"Father took Benjamin and Rachel to the market. I didn't want to go. Please come in."

Baruch entered and sat down in an old, worn chair. Every time he visited, he could not help noticing how poor his brother was, especially compared to him. While he had offered assistance to Mordecai, his brother had always refused, saying he appreciated it, but he could not take anything and they did not need it. No matter what Baruch offered, Mordecai always declined.

David took a chair next to his uncle. "So, David, how have you been?"

"Very well, Uncle. What about you?"

"I am fine. I've just come from Hedgestone Priory."

"Are you thinking of becoming a monk?"

They both laughed. "No, the new prior, Abbot Hubert, wanted to meet me. He didn't want a loan now but said if he did in the future he prefers to know with whom he is doing business. So, David, what's new with you? How are your studies going?"

David appeared solemn. "You know I'm only going to cheder because of father and my mother's memory, may she rest in peace."

"I know. You are growing into quite a man. Have you thought about joining me as a moneylender?"

David had figured one day Baruch would ask him that. Since Baruch had no children, David always felt he was his uncle's favorite nephew, and was almost like a son to him.

"Frankly, I have thought about it. There are so few options available to Jews. But you know what I would do if I could."

"And a fine soldier you would make. But we must be realistic, David. I hope you aren't thinking of being baptized to become a Christian so you can be a soldier."

"No, I'm not. It would hurt my father deeply and be an insult to my mother. Even though I don't feel religious, I always will be Jewish. That's what torments me—that I can't be who I am and become what I want to be."

"The world is a hateful place, I am afraid," Baruch said. "It always was, and I am afraid it always will be. I lend money at lower rates than the Christian moneylenders, who do it against Church laws, and yet I am the one who is accused and accursed."

David always had a good relationship with his uncle. For some reason, it often was easier to talk to him about certain matters than his father.

"Tell me, Uncle Baruch, I don't understand all the persecution we Jews must withstand. After my mother was killed I begged my father to leave England. He said there was no place to go. He wouldn't go back to Paris. We didn't speak any of the other languages of Europe. Who would take us in? he said. I am tired of this hatred. I wish there was something I could do to end it all."

Baruch saw David had tears in his eyes and put his hand on David's shoulder. "David. David. Your sadness is something our people have felt for many, many years. I find it ironic that decisions made more than twelve hundred years ago by men who were not even our direct ancestors can so direct our lives. So many of our kinsmen have been murdered. And for what? For believing something different and refusing to be intimidated by those who tried to force conversion on us. I'm not a very religious man either, as you know. But I do believe in maintaining our heritage. Unfortunately, it is easy to hate, easy to believe lies, and easy to incite the uneducated. Since we're dispersed, we don't have the strength in numbers to defend ourselves. Perhaps one day things will be different, but I do not see it happening in my lifetime. Can you understand that?"

David wiped a tear from his eye. "Yes, Uncle, I guess so. Thank you."

"David, I believe you will find your destiny. You are not afraid to stand up and fight. I only hope you'll be safe. There's danger everywhere, and you must be careful."

David nodded.

Baruch embraced his nephew. "I must go now. Tell your father I'll see him soon."

"I will," David said. "My destiny," he said to himself. "What can it be?"

Hedgestone Priory – November 1266

Alwyn returned from London, and reported to Hubert. One of the monks told him the abbot was in his chamber, ill. Alwyn hurried there and found the door open. Hubert laid in his bed as a monk wiped his forehead with a wet cloth.

"Hubert, what's the matter? Alwyn asked.

Hubert slowly sat up. "Alwyn, I'm glad you've returned. Brother Gabriel, you may go now, and close the door." The monk left, shutting the door behind him as ordered.

"Tell me what Basil said."

"First, tell me what's wrong with you."

"I came down with a fever and some other conditions I would rather not disclose. The brothers here have no idea how to take care of any illness. I am surprised any survived the diseases they had when we arrived here."

Alwyn laughed. "I don't believe you think they can do anything correctly."

Hubert let out a loud cough. "Tell me about Basil."

"It sounds like you have the lung congestion. That can be dangerous."

"I'll be fine. Now, tell me about Basil."

"Very well. He approved all of your plans and wants you to secure the largest loan you can from the Jews by the summer solstice. He gave me this written approval for you." Alwyn held out the parchment.

"Put it on the table. That long? Why not now?"

"I don't know. Those were his orders. I will say he also approved of your punishments for disobeying your orders regarding talking to the Jews."

Hubert coughed again, this time spitting mucus onto the floor. "I am impressed. I didn't think he had the stomach for that. What else did he say?"

"Hubert, I'm worried about you. You need to see a physician."

"Are there any in Northampton? Any Christian ones?"

"I don't know, but I'll find out. And, no, he didn't say much else. I told him you already had made significant progress here, and he was pleased. Now, let me go and get help for you."

Hubert fell back on his bed. "Very well. If you insist."

Brother Gabriel was standing outside Hubert's door.

"Gabriel, I want you to watch him. I'm going to bring a physician."

Gabriel looked surprised. "Physician? There is none around here. There used to be one, but he was a Jew killed in the riots two years ago. There is an apothecary, though."

"Apothecary? Can he cure diseases?"

"I believe he has knowledge of what herbs can help cure certain conditions. He cured Prior Bartholomew once."

"Then go fetch him immediately, and take a horse. Tell him Abbot Hubert is very ill, has a high fever and his lungs are congested."

"He's a Jew, Father Alwyn. I'm not allowed to even speak to him."

"I permit you to do this. Now go."

Gabriel appeared nervous. "But Father Alwyn, Abbot Hubert will be angry if I do this."

"He'll be angry if you don't. I told you to go."

Gabriel left without responding. Alwyn returned to Hubert's room. Hubert frowned when he saw him.

"What are you doing here? I told you to go get the physician," Hubert said, his voice slightly raised.

"Brother Gabriel told me there are no physicians near here. There is an apothecary, though, and I sent him to bring him here. He cured Prior Bartholomew once." Alwyn intentionally neglected to mention the apothecary was a Jew.

Hubert started to get angry, assuming this apothecary also must be a Jew. But then he remembered Baruch telling him his brother was an apothecary. He probably was the only apothecary in Northampton anyway.

"Very well. I pray he arrives soon." Hubert closed his eyes and soon fell asleep.

Gabriel arrived at Mordecai's house and knocked on the door. He had been there before when he had summoned Mordecai the time Bartholomew had developed a very high fever.

"Brother Gabriel. What brings you to my door?" Mordecai asked. "It must be important, since Abbot Hubert doesn't allow monks to converse with Jews."

"I'm sorry to disturb you, Mordecai. Father Alwyn sent me. Abbot Hubert is very ill, and since there is no physician, Alwyn wants you to help cure him."

Mordecai laughed under his breath. "I see. We aren't good enough to interact with the priory unless there are no Christians to help. What are his symptoms?"

"He has a high fever and his lungs are very congested. He coughs and coughs."

"Is he coughing up blood?"

"I don't know. Please hurry. Father Alwyn will be angry with me if we don't return soon."

"I believe I have what can help him. I'll need a few minutes to prepare it. Would you like to come in?"

Gabriel thought he should not but then realized it probably would be better not to be seen standing outside a Jew's house. "Yes, thank you."

"Please be seated. I won't be long."

This was the first time he had ever been inside a Jewish house. When Prior Bartholomew was ill several years before, Mordecai had not been at home, so he had left a message with his wife to come to the priory as soon as he could. While Gabriel thought about that, a young man entered the room.

"I'm David, Mordecai's son."

"I'm Brother Gabriel from Hedgestone Priory."

"I know. My father just told me. Can I get you some wine?"

"No, thank you. You must know we are not allowed to even speak to Jews."

"Yes, I know. We aren't wanted except when we can be useful. What do you think about that, Brother Gabriel?"

Gabriel appeared very uneasy. "It's not for me to say. The abbot gave the order, and we must obey him."

"Do you like being a monk? Do you enjoy not being able to think for yourself?"

Gabriel did not answer as Mordecai entered the room.

"David. Do not disrespect Brother Gabriel. He's come to me for help, and I will help, regardless of religion or circumstances. Come, Gabriel, I have what I believe will help the abbot."

"Father, Brother Gabriel, I meant no disrespect. At least no more than the Christians give us."

"Gabriel, I apologize for my son. He does not understand the world we must live in."

David laughed. "I understand very well, Father. Very well."

"Shalom, David. I'm leaving."

Gabriel gave Mordecai the horse and instructed him to ride to the priory while he would walk. Father Alwyn was waiting for him.

"You must be the apothecary," Alwyn said.

"I am Mordecai. Gabriel said it was urgent."

Alwyn led Mordecai to Hubert, who still was sleeping. Alwyn lightly shook him.

"Wake up, Your Grace. The apothecary is here."

Hubert slowly opened his eyes to see Mordecai standing over him. He started to raise himself up.

"Let me help you, Your Grace," Mordecai said.

"Who are you?" Hubert asked.

"I am Mordecai, the apothecary."

"Do you have a brother Baruch?"

Mordecai showed his surprise. "Yes, I do. How do you know that?"

Hubert coughed again. "I recently sent for Baruch, as I may have need of his services someday. He told me his brother was an apothecary. I assume you are the only apothecary in Northampton?"

"Yes, I am. I often assist Baron Geoffrey."

At this, Hubert scowled. "Perhaps I can get you to poison him." Hubert tried to laugh, but the congestion made him cough even more.

"I do not poison anyone, Your Grace. I only help heal. Now, let me look at you."

Mordecai bent down to look at Hubert's condition, examining his eyes and feeling his forehead.

"You kill rats and other vermin with your potions, do you not?"

"I believe they bring disease and are unhealthy. Let me see if I can help you."

Mordecai opened the small bag he had brought with him and took out three small, clay jars.

"What are those?" Hubert asked.

"Mugwort, vervain, and angelica. I believe these will cure you."

Mordecai mixed them together into a paste. He then took a wooden spoon and placed about half of the paste onto it. "Please open your mouth, Your Grace."

Hubert reluctantly obeyed. The mixture tasted bitter and terrible. He almost spit it out but did swallow it. "Water! Give me water!"

Alwyn gave him a cup of water, and Hubert drank it quickly.

"Now he must rest. If he is not better tomorrow, give him the rest of this."

Hubert laid back in his bed. "Mordecai, I want to ask you something."

"Yes?"

"You know about my orders that the monks are not to even talk to Jews?"

"Of course."

"Then why do you help me?"

"God has given us ways to help our fellow man. Even though you may hate us, we must use God's tools to help heal when we can. Did not Jesus teach peace and love? We are not evil people. We are not against the Church or your beliefs. We only want to worship God as we want to. Our way. The Church says since we do not believe what you believe we are infidels and will burn in Hell. The truth is I respect the fact you can believe whatever you want to. You twist our religion and our customs to your own advantage. The Old Testament, as you call it, is our Torah, our Bible. God gave it to us, and we have shared it with the world. It is up to each man to decide which course to follow. I am not an expert in Christian teachings. I believe if the Messiah had already come, the world would be a better place, and it is not. And not because we have not embraced Jesus. No, we cannot be blamed for that. We are so few, and yet we have managed to survive all the evil perpetrated against us. So many of us have died. Your Crusades only have brought more hatred and death, and for what?"

Mordecai suddenly stopped. "I'm sorry, Your Grace. You are ill, and I didn't mean to go off on a tirade. I only can hope to have taught you something today, to at least have helped you to understand we are all made in God's image, and to not treat any man equally is actually sacrilege."

Hubert was stunned. While he had never had any debate or religious discussion with a Jew before, he also never had been spoken to like that.

"Mordecai, out of respect for you helping me today, I will not respond to your heretical statements. However, I warn you. Keep your sentiments to yourself. I will not allow this in my priory."

Hubert coughed again, this brief exertion tired him out, and he quickly was asleep. Mordecai began to hurry out, but Alwyn stopped him.

"Mordecai, I'm sorry for what just happened."

"I am as well, Father Alwyn. The differences between us are deep, I know, and it frustrates me and most of my people. The discussions we used to have with Prior Bartholomew were helping us to better understand one another. Only through mutual respect and communication will we be able to live with our differences. Force is not the way, and not God's way. If that were true, why would not God have made us all the same? Every man must decide for himself."

"Your points are well taken. I'm afraid, however, that Church doctrine and the beliefs of many will never embrace those concepts. Both of us cannot be right."

"I must go. If the abbot is not better in a few days, please let me know. If you please, my fee is one pound."

Alwyn paid him and watched as he hurried out, walking as fast as he could away from Hedgestone. Mordecai's frustrations showed on his face. He started thinking about David and his desire to fight back. The more he thought about it, the more he started to wish somehow David could. And not just David, but other Jews as well.

Chapter Twelve

West End – May 1267

After a rough winter, spring had finally arrived. David was eager to get back to the forest and continue practicing to be an archer. He had to wait until the heavy snows had all melted, since he could not risk leaving footprints anywhere near his hiding place. There was also the problem of the melting snow causing the dirt road to become a virtual sea of mud. Not only was it difficult to traverse, but again David worried about leaving any sign someone had been near the cave that held his treasures. As April ended and May began, the mud dried up, and travel returned to normal.

David knew he could not practice only once a week. I will never get good enough, he thought. Somehow, I must be able to shoot several times a week. The dilemma was how, if the weather cooperated, and if he could even get away. As he looked around his house, he noticed his father's clay containers of the herbs, roots, and other ingredients he used in his profession. He realized his father often would have to go into the woods to find the proper ingredients. What if he could learn what these are, and help his father? It would be a perfect excuse to travel to the forest. While he did not know if the area near his hiding place had any of the herbs his father could use, if he would teach him, it could be the solution. Also, he thought, maybe Avram could help. If I could learn about them, I could teach him.

That evening, after supper David approached his father.

"May I speak to you, Father?" he asked.

"Of course, my son. What's on your mind?"

"Well," David began, "I've been thinking about my future. I don't know much about what you do. Perhaps you could teach me, and I can become an apothecary."

"You want to become an apothecary? You never expressed any interest before."

"I know, Father, but I am getting older. You know Uncle Baruch keeps asking me if he could teach me moneylending. I don't think I want to do that. There aren't many professions a Jew is allowed. I'm not a scholar, nor religious. Perhaps being an apothecary would be right for me."

Mordecai was shocked. He never thought David would ever be interested in continuing with the same profession as he and his own father.

"David, are you truly interested in learning this trade? Moneylending can be considerably more lucrative."

"I know. However, it's dangerous as well. At any time the loans can be cancelled and significant losses can occur. Jealous mobs can and do kill, as we well know. Being an apothecary is not only safer, but I like the idea of helping our people. Since I can't do it with weapons, maybe I can by other means."

Mordecai smiled at his eldest child. "Very well. If you want to learn, I will teach you."

"Thank you, Father. I thought we could start with me going to the forest and finding the herbs and other materials you use. This way I would be helping you as well as learning."

"That's a good idea. I could use the help. Not only is it getting harder for me to bend down and gather them, it takes me more time as well. I'll teach you about each of what I use. However, I must caution you. While most of the herbs and plants I use are harmless by themselves, when mixed in certain combinations they can be deadly. I wouldn't want you to make a mistake that hurts you or someone you were treating."

"I'll try not to, Father. I'll be careful."

"We'll start tomorrow, then."

David retired to his bed to think about what he had just committed to. He did not want to be an apothecary. He was planning to learn just enough to be able to quickly find what his father told him to, and then spend the rest of his time practicing archery. He also planned to enlist his friend Avram to help whenever he could. This way Avram could gather the herbs and plants while David shot. David thought the plan was ingenious.

The next morning after breakfast and the morning minyan, David had his first lesson. He sat at the table while Mordecai selected four small clay jars and placed them in front of him.

"David, what do you know about herbs and their use?"

"Father, even though I have watched you work for many years, I'm sorry I didn't show any interest until now. I'm afraid I don't know anything."

"I'm glad. It's better to start at the beginning than to have any false information that may cause harm. Look at the four jars. What do you see?"

"I see they're labeled the numbers three, four, eight and nine."

"That's correct. I don't label herbs, plants or medicines, but use a number code."

David seemed puzzled. "Why, Father, and how do you know which one is which?"

Mordecai took a book off the shelf, and removed a parchment hidden inside.

"This lists all the codes and what the jars contain. I learned this from your grandfather. When he was first an apothecary, a woman whose husband died after taking a mixture he had prepared accused him of witchcraft. She brought her complaint to the local lord, who went to your grandfather's house to investigate. While the lord was not superstitious and did not believe in witches, when he saw the jars labeled with Hebrew letters, he became quite uncomfortable. However, after examining the body and questioning the woman further, he determined her husband had been ill for quite some time, and your grandfather was not responsible. Ever since then, he decided to use numbers to identify each herb and preparation in case there was another difficult situation. This is what I've always used."

"Aren't you worried something will happen to the parchment?"

"I have a second copy hidden somewhere else. After using them for a while, I know what most of them are. You will too. Now, open the first jar, pour a little out and examine it."

David slowly removed the lid, tried to pour out a small amount, and almost emptied the jar by mistake. "Sorry, Father."

"That's all right. Do you know what this is?"

David looked at the green leaves. They looked like any other green leaf to him. "No, Father, I don't."

"This is called comfrey. It usually is found by the side of roads. It's used to speed the healing of cuts and bruises. Study the leaves so you can identify them. I use this more than most, since so many people suffer cuts and bruises. From the leaves I make an ointment that is usually quite effective if infection has not yet set in."

David started to wonder if he could learn just enough for his plan to succeed. "I understand, Father."

"Good. Now open the second jar, being careful not to mix up the two." David did as he was told. The jar contained green leaves with some white flowers.

"This is called deadnettle. It also grows by the roadside and may have white or red flowers. I only use the plants that have white ones."

"What does this cure, Father?"

"I use it for bleeding of the mouth, gout, and aches and pains of joints."

"Father, there is so much to learn here. And it seems like both of these look the same, except for the flower."

"Don't worry, my son. I believed as you when I first started learning the trade. As you get more experience, you will feel more at ease. We'll work slowly. You don't have to learn everything all at once."

David felt relieved. If he could learn about a few herbs and plants, it would make it much easier to satisfy his father and be able to spend as much time as he could practicing his archery. "Can we just start with these two? I think if you give me any more I'll be too confused."

"Very well. I was hoping to get you started with a few more, but I understand this could be somewhat difficult to learn. I would rather you take it slowly so you don't make any mistakes."

"Thank you, Father. What do you want me to do next?"

"Study these for a while. Then I'll send you out to find both of them."

David sat for a while staring at the two piles of plants. However, he was soon bored, and began to wish he had never started this. He began returning them to their jars.

"David, make sure you never mix them up. While I can tell what they are, you cannot. Using the wrong one can cause serious problems."

"Yes, Father." David carefully kept the two separate, put everything back correctly, and returned the jars to the shelf. "When do you want me to attempt my first search?"

"Whenever you want. I can always use both of them."

This is what David wanted to hear. While he was not certain he properly could identify either the comfrey or the deadnettle, at least he now had a legitimate reason to be in the forest. "I will go tomorrow."

The next morning he was up early and went right to Avram's house. He snuck up to Avram's bedroom window.

"Avram," he whispered. "Are you awake?"

After two more attempts, the curtain covering the window moved, and Avram's head peeked out. "David, is that you?"

"Yes. Get dressed and come outside."

"What's going on? Why are you here so early?"

"I'll tell you when you come out."

"Very well. I'll be out shortly."

David paced for what seemed a long time but was only a few minutes. Soon Avram appeared. "David, what's so important it couldn't wait?"

"I need your help today. I need you to go to Salcey with me."

Avram gave David one of his not again looks. "Salcey? Do you have another delivery to make?"

David laughed. "No, I need to practice, and you're going to help me."

"Help you? How? I won't retrieve your arrows, if that's all you want me for."

"No, it isn't. I figured out a way to get to practice more than once each week."

David told Avram about his plan and his offer to become an apothecary.

"Are you mad? You would never become an apothecary. You don't have the patience for learning everything you'll need to know. I can't believe your father thought you were serious."

"He started to teach me about herbs and plants. I need to bring some back with me."

"So why do you need me?"

"I'll show you the two plants he taught me about yesterday. Then, while I practice, I need you to gather some of them. I don't want to spend the time looking."

"I don't know, David. You know I don't like walking around in the forest, especially by myself. Where do we find these plants?"

"My father said they usually grow by the roadside. You shouldn't have any problem finding some."

"Very well. I'll do it today. But not every day, mind you. I must go to cheder, and I have my own responsibilities. I will help you when I can, but that's all."

"I understand. Thank you for helping me today."

As they entered Salcey Forest and walked down the road, David kept his eyes open for comfrey and deadnettle. As he looked, all the vegetation looked the same to him. He tried to remember what his father showed him, but he admitted he was quite confused.

"Avram, I don't remember what my father showed me yesterday."

"Describe them to me again."

David tried his best to detail the characteristics of the two plants. As the boys continued to look at the side of the road, David realized they were getting closer to his hiding place. Then he saw the white flower of a deadnettle.

"Avram, there's one!" David almost shouted, then realized he should be quiet.

"David, keep your voice down. There may be bandits or God knows what roaming around here."

"Sorry. I guess I just got a bit excited."

David carefully removed the deadnettle, and placed it into one of the two cloth bags he brought, one for each type of plant. There were several more, and he removed them as well.

"Avram, I must leave you now to go to my hiding place. Try to find some more deadnettle."

"What about the comfrey? I don't know what they look like."

"Just do the best you can. If you see some plants that look the same, just take them. It will have to do. My father can't expect me to learn everything in one day."

"How long will you be? I don't want to spend all day here."

"I promise I won't be too long. I'm still building my strength, and my fingers get sore as well. Meet me here at high noon. Now, turn away so you don't see in what direction I'm going."

Avram walked slowly to try to help his friend. David carefully maneuvered his way through the brush and down an embankment to the cave. The brush covering it was exactly as he had last left it. He uncovered the weapons, examining them as he always did, not just to see if anything had happened to them, but because he thought they were so beautiful. He strung the bow, gathered the quiver of arrows and target he had made, and proceeded to his practice tree. He mounted the target and walked back about twenty paces. David carefully notched the arrow, pulled back on the string, aimed and fired. The arrow hit the target just to the left of the center. Not bad, he thought.

As David practiced, he saw the sun was arcing higher and higher. Soon it would be high noon. He looked at his fingers that were beginning to look raw. While he had not hit the exact center of the target, he had moved back several paces from when he started. It was getting easier to pull back the bowstring farther and farther. The arrows seemed to be traveling faster and with greater force. He was getting stronger and better. "I am made for this," he said to himself out loud. He was startled when there was a reply.

"I guess you are," the voice from behind said.

"Avram, what are you doing here? I told you I didn't want you anywhere near me when I was shooting."

"I know. But I got tired of waiting for you and started exploring. I heard what I thought was you and followed the sounds. Please don't be angry with me."

"I'm not. I only want to protect you. How did your searching go?"

"I found a bunch of deadnettle. I picked up a bunch of something else that may be comfrey, but since I've never seen it, I can't be sure. Here, look."

Avram opened one of the bags. "Avram, these are just common weeds, not comfrey."

"Sorry. I didn't know. What will you tell your father?"

"Just that I couldn't find any comfrey. It's the truth, after all. Now I need you to go back to the road. I must return these to my hiding place."

Avram headed for the road. David gathered everything up, returned them to the cave, and secured them as usual. He then checked the cave entrance, satisfied the brush prevented anyone from seeing the entrance. He then met Avram. As they walked back, David kept looking for comfrey. As they got within sight of the edge of the forest, he thought he saw some.

"Avram, I believe this is comfrey. I'll take it and show it to my father."

David gathered several of the plants and placed them in the second bag.

Mordecai greeted David as he walked into the house. "So, my, son, how did you do? You were gone quite a while."

"I think I found the deadnettle, but the comfrey I'm not so sure. Please take a look." Mordecai opened the first bag and examined the contents. "Yes, this is good deadnettle. Let me see the other." Mordecai opened the second and took out a handful of its contents. "This is comfrey, but these are just weeds."

"I'm sorry, Father."

"Don't be. You did well. It takes time to learn how to identify each plant and herb. There are so many, and they tend to look alike. I'm sure next time will be easier."

David went to his room and laid on his bed. Not too bad, he thought. I think I had a very good practice session, even though I am sore and my fingers hurt. I wonder how long it will take before I am an accomplished archer. As he thought more about it, he closed his eyes and fell asleep.

Hedgestone Priory – May 1267

Abbot Hubert was taking his daily inspection walk around the priory. He noticed his changes were making progress at Hedgestone. The monks were almost always working. Some were cleaning, while others were assigned to the kitchen. He not only improved the appearance of the priory but wanted the monks to eat better. He believed that while he worked them harder and longer, keeping them better fed would help to make them happy. As he concluded his walk, Alwyn approached.

"Hello, Hubert. A beautiful day, is it not?"

The sun's warmth took away the morning chill, and the blue sky contrasted with the green leaves that were slowly filling up the trees.

"Yes, Alwyn. It is. Walk with me."

"Hubert, since it's spring, I believe you should negotiate Basil's loan. I'll have to report back to him soon, and that's the first thing he'll want to know."

"Yes, I realize that. In fact, I've sent Brother Dominic to Baruch's house to set up a meeting for tomorrow."

"Very good. How much are you going to ask for?"

"From what we have calculated based on the plans Basil approved, I'm going to request fifteen hundred pounds."

Alwyn stopped and stared at Hubert. "Fifteen hundred pounds? That's an enormous sum. Baruch will never loan you that much. How could you ever assure him you will be able to make the payments? Hedgestone never could generate enough revenue to cover that much."

"Alwyn, you have no faith in me. I know Baruch never will lend us that much. One never asks for what one wants, always more. I figure we only need about one hundred fifty pounds at the most to make just a few improvements. But I want at least one thousand."

"Do you plan on keeping some of it for yourself?"

Hubert raised his eyebrows. "Alwyn, you forget yourself. We know Basil wants me to secure as much money as I can under my name, and then he will take possession of it. I figure he has no intention of making any of the payments. He'll insist I do that. While I plan on bringing in some revenue to Hedgestone, I doubt it would be enough. I must keep some in reserve, shall we say. After all, one never knows when another riot will occur and debts will be forgiven."

"That may be so, but the king may require all outstanding debts to be paid to the treasury."

"That's a risk I'll have to take. I can't worry about that now."

"I hope you know what you're doing. If you're wrong, you may be in big trouble."

Hubert then saw Brother Dominic had returned. "Brother Dominic, what did Baruch say?"

"He will be here tomorrow morning, as you requested."

"Very good. Thank you."

Alwyn's jaw dropped. "Hubert, I don't think I've ever heard you thank anyone for doing anything."

"I'm in a good mood. Let's see if tomorrow I still am." Alwyn watched Hubert walk away. There will be trouble, he thought.

The next morning, Baruch arrived as requested. Brother Dominic escorted him to the same small room where he had met Hubert before. This time, however, Hubert was waiting for him. The abbot stood and greeted him. Alwyn was also present but did not stand up.

"Baruch, nice to see you again. Thank you for coming. You remember Father Alwyn."

"Good morning, Abbot. Father. I'm here as requested. I understand you now want to discuss a loan."

"That is correct. May we get you some wine?"

"No, thank you. I never have wine when discussing business. One never knows what may be in it, or what it could do to one's judgment," he said, smiling.

"Very wise."

"Well, how much do you want, and what do you want it for?"

"You certainly get right to the point. You are aware Bishop Basil has ordered me to make substantial improvements here at Hedgestone?"

"I know. We discussed it briefly last time."

"Yes, we did. I've prepared a list of the improvements, and the bishop approved them." He handed Baruch the parchment. Baruch quickly examined the list and handed it back.

"I don't see any costs included."

"No, those have been calculated separately."

"I see. How much do you need?"

Hubert slowly paced and looked right at Baruch. "We would need fifteen hundred pounds."

Baruch laughed. "You must be joking. Fifteen hundred pounds for your little priory? You never could generate enough revenue to make the payments."

Baruch began to walk out. "I am not a fool, and do not do business with fools."

Hubert felt a degree of panic and quickly moved to stop him. "Please don't leave. I meant no disrespect. I never have done this before."

"Very well. However, you must be serious with your request. Abbot, in order for me to grant you a loan, I will need you to show me exactly how much you want based on the details you provide, and how you will generate the revenue to make your payments. The more details you provide, the easier it will be for us to negotiate. It's called negotiating in good faith. I will, and I expect you to do so."

Hubert realized he had underestimated Baruch. His own lack of experience showed, and he was embarrassed by his ignorance. I should have learned the process, he thought.

"Baruch, please accept my apology. I must admit I am ignorant of these matters. I was under the impression one merely had to request the sum, arrange the payment terms, and conclude the arrangement."

Baruch shook his head. "I meant no disrespect to you. I did not know you were not informed of how I do business. Perhaps other moneylenders are quick to make loans without properly understanding the purpose of the funds and how they would be repaid, but not me. Besides, no moneylender I have ever heard of would loan such an amount without the proper security. I hope you understand."

"I believe I do understand. In my business, we put our trust in faith. However, I can see in yours, much more than faith is required. I'll prepare the details you requested. When they're ready, I shall send for you, and hopefully we can obtain our loan. There's much we'd like to improve here."

"Very well. I will await your summons." He bowed slightly and left, Brother Dominic waiting outside to escort him out of the priory.

"Honestly, Hubert, did you really believe he would give you fifteen hundred pounds just like that?" Alwyn asked.

"That is none of your concern. I need to obtain the largest loan I can for our bishop friend. And, no, I did not expect him to just hand over the money. But I needed to know how he thinks, how he operates. And now I do. Alwyn, I want you to prepare a detailed list of all the projects Basil approved, along with as many cost details as you can. Get some of the brothers to help. I will develop a plan to show this Jew how we'll pay for his loan."

Alwyn looked surprised. "It will not total fifteen hundred pounds. Give me a more realistic figure to work with."

Hubert shook his head vigorously. "No, I will not. You just prepare the cost estimates."

"I'll do my best for you, cousin."

How can I project revenue I probably will not be able to generate? Hubert thought. I must be creative.

Chapter Thirteen

Hedgestone Priory – June 1267

Alwyn worked on the details for Hubert, but it was taking much longer than he expected. Hubert wanted to be sure the data was accurate and covered everything, since he assumed Baruch would only give him the largest loan if there were proper support for the figures. While determining costs was not too difficult, revenue was another matter altogether. Clever ways to do this first had to be identified and then well-documented. Hubert solicited the monks to generate ideas. Besides the usual christenings, weddings, and funerals, also considered were to raise sheep for wool, sell some of the vegetables they grow, and possibly learn blacksmithing, pottery-making or glassblowing to make items to sell. When Alwyn met with Hubert to discuss them, Hubert replied it did not matter, as these were only to secure the loan. Hubert would only do the bare minimum so his plan would be successful. All he wanted were well-detailed plans he could show Baruch. Alwyn did not believe Baruch would agree to any of this, and was frank in expressing his opinion to Hubert, who always disagreed and insisted upon doing it his way. Finally, everything was ready, and Hubert sent for Baruch. He arrived the following day.

"Baruch, thank you for returning. We've been hard at work preparing what you asked for."

"I hope so. I don't like wasting time, and unless you have everything in order that will be the result of this meeting."

"Please sit. Alwyn, would you be so kind to give Baruch what we have prepared?"

Alwyn handed Baruch several parchments. Three were labeled revenue and five expenses. Baruch briefly glanced at them. "Well, you certainly have been busy. There is considerable detail here. I'd like to take them home with me to study everything."

"I'm sorry, Baruch, but these cannot leave the priory. I fear if it did, some of our ideas may be stolen."

Baruch grunted. "I see nothing secret here, nothing so unique no one must know. Have you lowered the amount of the loan you are asking for?"

"Yes and no. I propose the loan be made in three phases. For the first phase, we will need two hundred pounds. Then, as we show you the revenue being produced, we will need another eight hundred pounds. Finally, as the third phase is implemented, the last five hundred pounds will be required."

Baruch stared at Hubert, incredulous. "Three phases? Three separate loans? With what security?"

Hubert smiled. "I don't suppose my word would be enough?"

"No, it is not enough," Baruch replied sternly.

"I did not think so, and anyway, I was joking."

"I do not joke when negotiating a loan. This is serious business and must be treated as such. I am an honorable man, and I expect the same from you."

Hubert began to realize he had made another mistake with the Jew. His gamble Baruch would be impressed with the information provided, and the three phases to gradually obtain the funds would be agreeable to him, had failed.

"Baruch, again I must apologize to you. I thought the details we prepared would satisfy you."

"Abbot Hubert, I'm not saying I won't be satisfied, but I'm not satisfied at this moment. I need to study your figures and plans. If, and I mean if, they look good to me, then we can discuss terms and security."

"But Baruch, the only security we have is the priory and the little land surrounding it, and it is owned by the Church. I would need Bishop Basil's permission to use it as security. However, a Jew could never own a priory, so how could I satisfy your demand?"

"You are correct, Hubert. In the event of a default, I could not take over the priory. You will need a guarantor."

"A guarantor? You mean someone else to ensure I will pay, and, if not, they will suffer the loss?"

"That's correct. I often loan money based on a guarantor. It may not be easy to find someone, but it is the only way I will loan you what you are asking for."

Hubert's heart sank. Who could I get to do this for me? he thought. The bishop certainly will not. Baron Geoffrey? Not after what he believes I did to his brother.

Hubert showed his disappointment. "I'll have to think about this and get back to you. However, isn't there any other way we can do business?"

"Perhaps if you lower your request considerably."

An idea entered Hubert's mind. "Baruch, may I propose this? Let us start with a loan of one hundred pounds. I will demonstrate my good faith by making the proper timely payments that we agree upon. After some amount of time of me honoring my commitment, we will agree to negotiate a second loan."

Baruch said nothing for what seemed to be several minutes. "One hundred to start? With no security?"

Hubert nodded. Alwyn smiled slightly, somewhat pleased with Hubert's suggestion. However, Alwyn did not think the bishop would be pleased with that arrangement.

"And what will you use the funds for?"

"You will note our plans have been prepared in the three phases I mentioned. We would start with some of the phase one items. While the hundred pounds would not be enough to complete the phase, it would give us a good start."

"And how will you generate the revenue to make your payments?"

"We'll start implementing our ideas. Surely if they all don't work, at least one or two will."

Baruch studied this man, who literally was begging for a loan. "Tell me, Abbot, why this insistence on meeting my terms? There may be other moneylenders willing to do business with you who are not as, shall we say, difficult as I am."

"That may be true, but you are the most successful moneylender in Northampton. You have, I believe, the resources to help us meet our goals, to satisfy the wishes of the bishop. I understand you do not renege on agreements, like others I have heard of."

"Hubert, I have not heard that, but it is of no matter. I will think about your proposal and give you an answer next week. I hope that will be acceptable."

"Very well. It will have to do. I'll await your decision, which I hope will be positive."

"Good bye Hubert. Alwyn."

"Well, Alwyn, what do you think?" Hubert asked.

"I think you made a huge mistake. I think he doesn't trust you and may not loan you anything."

"Do you think I will be outdone by a Jew? I don't care who he is. Bishop Basil instructed me to obtain the largest loan I could. He never said how much it should be. I've been establishing a position eventually to dictate my own terms, can you not understand that? Baruch never will turn down an opportunity to increase his wealth. You do not understand how Jews think. I believe I do."

Alwyn smirked.

"Do you mock me, Alwyn? Do you think I'm a fool?"

"No Hubert, I am not mocking you, and I don't think you're a fool. But I don't think Baruch is either. He doesn't seem the type to take huge risks, and that is what you asked him to do."

"Well, we'll see when he gives us his answer. I hope you won't report to Basil until this matter is settled."

"No, of course not. I don't have anything to report except what has not happened yet. I'm sure he'll be expecting me soon, but I must wait, at least until next week."

"Yes," Hubert repeated. "Next week."

Salcey Forest – June 1267

David had stumbled on a patch of ground not far from his hiding place full of comfrey and deadnettle. He was able to bring back a few of each plant each time he went out. This satisfied his father and allowed him ample time to practice. Not only was his aim improving, but he had increased his distance to the target threefold. Unfortunately, this was as far as he could go if he stayed near the cave. While he wanted to find another spot where he could increase the distance to the target, he felt it was too risky. There was too great a chance of discovery. He did not know where his archery skill would lead him, but he knew if he were discovered, not only would it all have been for nothing, he would be severely punished, and perhaps even executed. He would have to be satisfied with the current situation.

However, as David repeated the same routine over and over, he began to get bored. He had been careful with the arrows, losing only three of the dozen that the forester had on him. Two broke when they became stuck in a tree next to the target. One went wild into the forest, and after spending a good while looking for it he finally gave up. The broken ones he carefully split into small pieces, burying them as deep as he could to be sure no one would find them. As he took a short rest, he thought maybe he could try to hunt at least a small animal, such as a squirrel or rabbit. He would never eat one, of course, but he was tempted to try his archery skill as a hunter. The more he thought about it, the more he realized it was not a good idea. For one, he might lose one or more arrows, and that he could not afford to do. After all, how could he replace even one? He could never buy any from an arrow maker. If he even tried, he probably would be reported to the sheriff, who still was asking questions one year later about the forester's death and the missing weapons. He also did not like the thought of killing an animal just for killing's sake. The other aspect that bothered him was what would he do with it? He would have to bury it, and again that brought risk. No, he would have to be content with shooting at the target.

He usually did not bring Avram with him on his almost-daily treks to Salcey. Mordecai tried to teach David about other herbs and medicinal plants, but he acted as if he was losing interest and was content just finding the comfrey and deadnettle. Mordecai did not challenge him. If David truly wants to become an apothecary, which he now doubted, he wanted David to learn of his own free will.

West End – June 1267

Baruch sat in his comfortable, well-upholstered chair, sipping a glass of wine. His gut feeling was he should not get involved with Abbot Hubert and his phased loan request. While business lately had been slow, Baruch was in a position where he did not have to take huge risks or any risks at all. However, there was something intriguing to him about Abbot Hubert and Hedgestone Priory. He was not sure what it was, but the Church often borrowed money from Jews. They did this primarily because even though usury by Christians was forbidden, some did do moneylending, and at much higher rates than Jewish moneylenders charged. He continued to mull it over until he made a decision. He would go to Hedgestone tomorrow, three days sooner than Hubert would be expecting him.

The next morning after breakfast, Baruch walked to the priory. It was a beautiful June day, and he wanted to enjoy the sunshine and fresh air. He arrived and pulled the bell cord. Brother Dominic soon appeared. "Hello, Dominic," Baruch greeted him. "I need to speak to Abbot Hubert."

Dominic brought him to the same room where they had met twice before. Baruch sat to wait for Hubert. After a few minutes, Hubert and Alwyn entered.

"Good morning, Baruch. I hope you have good news for me."

"Hello, Abbot, Father Alwyn. Before I give you my answer, may I please see your figures again?"

"Certainly. Alwyn, please get them right away." Alwyn left to fetch the parchments.

"Well, Baruch, I did not expect you for three more days. I'm surprised to see you so soon."

"I've spent a great deal of time thinking about your proposal, and the entire request. After I review the figures again, I'll give you my answer."

Alwyn returned with the parchments. Baruch spent some time reviewing the documents. Hubert was growing antsy.

"Abbot Hubert," Baruch finally said. "You have set forth some very ambitious plans. Your cost figures are quite detailed, and they look accurate to me. However, I don't think you can accomplish everything in the timeframe you estimate. I also don't think you can generate the revenue you project as well. With that in mind, I will consider the phased approach you proposed. But not three distinct phases. I will loan you fifty pounds at fifteen percent interest with no security, provided you make quarterly payments of at least ten percent of the balance plus interest. After one year of successful payments, I will lend you three hundred additional pounds at terms to be agreed to at that time. We will continue to do this, perhaps increasing the amount each year, until the entire amount you need is loaned. This will get you started on your improvements and allow time to get your revenue flowing."

The disappointment on Hubert's face was obvious. This is nowhere near what he wanted to do and would not please Bishop Basil. But what options did he have?

"Baruch, I thank you for your offer, but it saddens me. I was hoping to start with one hundred pounds. Will you consider one hundred?"

"I'm sorry, Abbot, but the risk is too great. Fifty is all I'm willing to lend at this time."

"What if you make the second loan after six months instead of one year?"

"I can make no promises. That is my offer today. If you are agreeable, I will have the documents prepared."

"Please give me a few minutes. I want to discuss this with Alwyn."

"Certainly."

Hubert and Alwyn stepped out of the room. "Well, Alwyn, what do you think?"

"I think you don't have a choice. Take his offer, make your payments, maybe even more than two in six months, and perhaps then you will be in a better position to increase the loan. I will report to Basil you did your best, and there was no choice but to accept these terms at this time."

Hubert sighed. He hated losing, and that is what he felt was happening. He was especially bitter a Jew was doing this to him.

They returned to Baruch. "I accept the terms as you described them. I hope that in six months you will be pleased with our progress and when I have kept my part, you will be open to a new negotiation."

"I will have the documents prepared, and we must meet at the archa to have them formally recorded. I will let you know when all is ready."

"I will await your summons."

Baruch bowed slightly as usual and left. Hubert looked scornfully at Alwyn. "Hubert, what are you thinking about?"

"Nothing. I was hoping to obtain considerably more and this entire business would not be so difficult. Perhaps I have erred in insisting on doing business with this Baruch."

"That may be so, but what is done is done, and since your requests were so large, there was not much choice."

"I guess you're right. However, I am not happy about this, and someday will rectify the situation."

Three days later Hubert, accompanied by Alwyn, met Baruch at the office of Northampton's archa. Two parchments had been prepared detailing the loan agreement. After Hubert and Baruch signed them, one copy was placed in the archa, and Baruch kept the other. The archa was required by the king to keep a record of all moneylending by the Jews. Jews could only live in towns with an archa. Upon completion, Baruch gave Hubert fifty pounds worth of silver coin. Hubert counted the money, examining each one to be sure none was clipped. Coin clipping was practiced by some, Jews and Gentiles alike, to shave off some of the silver, and was illegal. Those caught doing it were severely punished, and some even executed.

"Hubert, you can see all the coins are perfect. I am an honest man and would never coin clip," Baruch stated, insulted Hubert would even consider that possibility.

"I meant no disrespect, Baruch. I was merely ensuring the transaction is totally to my satisfaction."

"Very well. I will expect your first payment in three months as agreed."

"As agreed."

Northampton Castle – October 1267

"My lord, Baron Henry de Percy approaches!" Cyrus excitedly exclaimed to Baron Geoffrey.

Geoffrey's face exploded into a smile. "That's excellent news. I always enjoy his company. Cyrus, inform Lady Catherine, and tell Theresa to prepare a special feast tonight."

"Yes, my lord."

Geoffrey hurried down to the castle's main gate. Henry and his party were just crossing the drawbridge. Sir Walter greeted him with a bow.

"Welcome, Baron. What a nice surprise. What brings you to us?"

"Walter, my friend. So good to see you. I hope my unannounced visit will be permissible. Is Geoffrey here?"

As soon as the words left his mouth, Henry saw Geoffrey running to greet him.

"Henry! Why didn't you send word you were coming? I didn't expect you."

The two friends embraced. "I'm returning from a visit to London, and thought I would surprise you, and I did."

They both laughed. "Come, I'll secure quarters for your men."

"First, I need tankards of ale. My throat is parched."

"Cyrus, prepare ale for Henry and his men."

"Bryce, I'm glad you're here. Come help me fetch the ale."

Bryce looked at Henry, who nodded his approval, and the two boys ran off. Sir Walter took care of Henry's six men-at-arms while Geoffrey led Henry into the great hall. "Sit, my friend. Try my new chair."

Henry sat in a very plush chair. "I think this is too comfortable. I may never get up."

The pages soon arrived with two very large tankards filled to the top with ale. They were very careful not to spill even a drop. They put them on the table, bowed, and left the hall.

"So, Henry, what brought you to London without stopping here on the way? You must have been in a hurry."

"I was. The king summoned me."

"Why? And why only you?"

"Since de Montfort is dead and the Second Baron's War over, he wanted me to reaffirm my loyalty to him. I don't know why, as I was always loyal and sent men to fight de Montfort."

"Was Edward present?"

"Yes, he was."

"That's why. Henry is weak, but Edward is dangerous, and I believe it was he who made you reaffirm your oath."

"I think you're right. When Henry dies and Edward becomes king, he'll make it more difficult for all the barons."

"Did you meet with anyone else in London?"

"Other than wenches?" They both laughed.

"I saw Bishop Basil. He asked me questions about my former priest, Father Alwyn."

"What kind of questions?"

"He wanted to know if he could trust him."

"Trust him? Why would he ask that? I hope you told him since they are all related and he's Hubert's cousin, he must be a swine as well."

"He wouldn't tell me, other than Alwyn is here with Abbot Hubert, as you know. I could not answer him definitively, as I don't know him that well."

Geoffrey took a long drink, finishing the entire tankard. "Cyrus, bring more ale," he yelled. "I've avoided them since they got here last year."

"So, you haven't done anything revengeful?"

"My dear Henry, why would I do that?" Geoffrey said, laughing.

Cyrus and Bryce both returned with pitchers of ale, refilled their baron's tankards, bowed and left.

"What else did Basil ask of you?"

"He wanted to know about the Jews."

"The Jews? What about them?"

"Most specifically, he wanted to know about the moneylenders, how they worked, who the wealthiest in York are, and about any loans I made with them."

"Aren't there enough moneylenders in London? You know, I don't trust him either, especially since he's related somehow to that cur Hubert."

"I have nothing to do with him. He isn't my bishop."

"Did the king say anything interesting to you?"

"Only that he was not happy with the Dictum of Kenilworth, even though peace has been restored and the rebels paid their fines to restore their forfeited lands. He did thank me for my loyalty."

"I'm against rebellions. I'm glad Henry reaffirmed the Magna Carta, even if reluctantly, but I believe there are other ways to accomplish one's objectives. I'm tired of war and seeing too many men die."

"And yet it earned you your knighthood and title as baron."

"True enough, Henry. I wasn't high-born like you. I sometimes wonder why you're my friend because of my commoner blood."

They both laughed. "Come, Geoffrey, you know that doesn't matter to me."

The two friends chatted for a while and then retired for an afternoon nap. That evening Theresa prepared an exquisite feast for Henry and his men. After eating and drinking too much, they all retired for the night.

Henry stayed for three more days. Most of the time he and Geoffrey stayed drunk with a never-ending supply of ale. Finally, as the evening of the fourth day approached, Henry announced he must leave the following morning.

"I understand. It's hard to be away for so long."

"Tell me," Henry said, "whatever happened with the dead forester, your cousin I believe? Did you ever find out what happened to him or what happened to the weapons?"

"I'm afraid not. The coroner couldn't determine the cause of death, since there were absolutely no wounds, and the sheriff never discovered who took the weapons. Some thief in Salcey Forest, I suspect."

"No doubt."

"Be careful, Henry. The thieves have become bolder lately."

"I can handle them, especially with my men-at-arms. They would make short work of any thief or group of them."

Hedgestone Priory – October 1267

Father Alwyn returned from London after his latest visit to Bishop Basil. He was not looking forward to relaying the bishop's message to Hubert. Alwyn was just following orders. He saw Hubert talking to Brother Dominic.

"Alwyn. You have returned."

"Yes, Hubert. Just now."

"Come. Tell me what Basil said."

They went into Hubert's room, and Hubert closed the door. "Well, was Basil pleased?"

Alwyn took a slow breath. "Hubert, I am sorry, but Basil was very unhappy with most of my report."

"Unhappy? Why?"

"He said you never should have asked Baruch for fifteen hundred pounds. He is worried you frightened him, and now he will be too wary of loaning you a substantial sum. He also was displeased since now it will take you much longer to finalize the amounts. He did comment he was happy with how you are managing the brothers so far."

Hubert was visibly upset. "Oh, he's worried and displeased, is he? Let him negotiate his own loans. I did the best I could. He wanted a large loan, and that's what I tried to get for him." Hubert was almost fuming. "What else did our dear bishop tell you?"

"He's willing to give you until next Easter to get him the money. If not, you'll be replaced and he'll see to it that you will be sent to an abbey in Wales."

"Alwyn, he's just using me. Very well. I'll satisfy him. But mark my word, I will not forget this. He will owe me, and I will collect. When do you have to report back to him again?"

"Not until after Easter."

"Humph. Very well. I'll make sure that he gets what he wants. And I will as well."

Chapter Fourteen

Salcey Forest – October 1267

Avram accompanied David into the forest, the first time he had done so in a while. David continually reassured him there was nothing to worry about. After all, he had been going to Salcey for more than a year, usually by himself, without even one incident. Avram remained unconvinced it was safe.

The two friends reached the area near the cave where David kept his weapons.

"Avram, this is as far as you should go."

"David, you know I've watched you practice."

"Yes, but you don't know where my hiding place is, and I don't want you to know."

David had gone out only to practice his archery. He was not going to collect any herbs or plants for his father. Lately he had admitted he was losing interest in being an apothecary, although he was willing to collect plants for him. His father had told him he was not surprised, was grateful for David trying to learn the trade, and for any assistance.

Avram waited while David went to the cave to retrieve the bow and arrows. From the original dozen, he was now down to five. He knew he needed to replace some, but still did not know how.

As usual, David found the brush covering the cave exactly as he had left it. He carefully made his preparations, recovered the entrance, and returned to Avram.

"Your target looks like it's seen better days," Avram said.

The cloth David had used to make it showed evidence of numerous hits, with multiple holes almost everywhere, including the painted center.

"I know, but I just haven't taken the time to replace it."

"I have an old piece of cloth that will work. I'll give it to you later."

"Many thanks. It has to be better than this one."

David set up the target and began shooting from a distance of about forty paces. His first shot just missed the center of the target.

"You've improved, David. You've become an archer."

David smiled. "I hope so. I find it hard to compare me to the archers I've seen at the tournament, since I haven't witnessed one for several years."

"Perhaps you will soon. I wish you could compete against them."

David sighed. "I do too. But how? Sometimes I wonder why I've spent all this time to become this skilled. I'm resolved I'll just have to keep this secret and only practice in the forest until I run out of arrows."

"What will you do when that happens?"

"I have no idea. I could try to buy some from an arrow maker, but how without him getting suspicious and possibly reporting me to the sheriff? It would no doubt take a considerable amount of money to keep him from doing that."

"There must be a way. We'll think of something when the time comes."

He watched David continue practicing. Almost every arrow hit the target, and quite a few in the painted center. After a while, David sat down to rest with his friend. They both were leaning against a tree and had started to close their eyes when they heard some commotion. It sounded like it was coming from the road.

Northampton Castle – October 1267

Baron Henry de Percy planned on rising early to begin his journey home to York soon after dawn. Baron Geoffrey had thrown a huge feast the night before to send his friend on his way. Unfortunately, both Henry and his six men-at-arms had all eaten and drunk way too much. Henry had slept later than he had planned but felt fine when he awoke. However, when he checked on his men, he had to throw buckets of cold water on them to get them up. They were not in the best condition, he noted, but he did not want to delay his departure.

Geoffrey found his friend preparing to leave. "Henry, your men are not very fit for travel. I'm worried they may not be able to keep up with you. Only you are on horseback, while they must walk. Make sure you stay close to them."

"Don't worry, my friend. Are you afraid I'll be set upon by thieves and my men won't be able to rescue me?"

"I just don't want you traveling alone in Salcey. The thieves have become bolder, and I'm sure they'd be very happy to either rob you or hold you for ransom if they don't kill you. Let me send some of my men with you, at least until you're through the forest."

"I appreciate your concern, but we'll be fine. Even after being drunk, my men can fight."

"I think you're too optimistic, but very well. I'll respect your wishes."

The baron mounted his horse, and Bryce rode in the cart with one of the men-at-arms. Garth had taken ill and would stay behind. The other five would walk, taking turns driving the cart, even though Bryce insisted on driving it himself. Henry said goodbye to Geoffrey and Catherine, and Bryce bid farewell to Cyrus.

As the group left the castle and proceeded through Northampton, Henry kept getting ahead, but would slow or stop to allow the rest to catch up. When they reached Salcey Forest, Henry addressed his men. "Keep your eyes open and your weapons handy. Geoffrey said there are many outlaws in the forest. I'm sure we can fight off any that may dare to attack us, but let's not be ambushed. We must be through the forest before dark. I don't want to camp here."

The men-at-arms were slowly returning to normal, Henry concluded, but they still were traveling slower than he liked. He kept looking around as his horse walked slowly on the narrow road that wound through Salcey. Everything was quiet, except for the birds, squirrels, chipmunks, and the occasional duck, goose, and deer. Henry listened for any sounds of trouble but did not hear any. He started to daydream, thinking about returning to Eleanor and home. After a while, he did not notice he was far ahead of his men. When he did hear the sound of trouble, it was too late.

The three of them came from behind and his right and left without any warning. They pulled him off his horse and threw him onto the forest floor at the side of the road, a stone pushing into his back. He saw the three outlaws. One had a sword pointed against his throat.

"Well, look what we found," the man with the sword said. He was filthy, dressed in old, torn breeches, a raggedy shirt, and a well-worn cap. "A rich baron, no doubt. And who might you be?"

Henry started to push the sword away from his throat. The other two outlaws, dressed in clothes even more filthy and torn than the first man, held out daggers and made gestures indicating they were not afraid to use them.

"I am Baron Henry de Percy of York. Let me up. I'm traveling with men-at-arms right behind me."

"Is that so?" said the first outlaw. "We've been watching them. They, along with the boy, stopped to rest way back a spell. The boy did not want to, but your men insisted. They said their brave baron could take care of himself."

Good boy, Bryce, Henry thought. He has more brains than my idiot men do. I will deal with them later.

"I have almost no money on me. I'm traveling home after a long journey. Here, take my purse." Henry threw it at the outlaw, who picked it up while still holding the sword near the baron's throat. "Bullocks. He's right," he said to his companions. "There's only a few pennies here."

"What shall we do, Tom?" one of the other outlaws asked. "Hold him for ransom?"

"No, we can't. His family will send soldiers to find us and rescue him. It's too dangerous. We will just have to kill him and wait for the next traveler."

"But he's a baron, Tom. He's rich."

"Search him to see if he has anything else on him."

The second outlaw searched Henry but found nothing of value.

"So, my lord," the outlaw called Tom said, "it appears you can't help us. Guy and Flynn. Kill him. Then we'll throw him in the river."

"Are you sure, Tom?" the one named Flynn asked.

Tom was becoming angry. "Don't keep questioning me. Just do it."

All of a sudden there was a *swoosh* of air, and an arrow landed right in Tom's heart. Guy and Flynn turned to see where the arrow came from, and two more found their marks and both men dropped. Flynn was dead, an arrow through his left eye; Guy was severely wounded, an arrow in his stomach. Henry quickly got up, grabbed Tom's sword, and ran Guy through. Then he looked around to see who had saved him and saw no one.

"Come out, my friends, come out. You saved me, and I want to thank you," he called. Still no one came. Then he saw a young man carrying a bow work his way through the brush.

Salcey Forest – October 1267

"Avram, do you hear that?" David whispered.

"Yes. It's coming over there by the road."

"Follow me and stay down. Let's see what it is," David said, taking his bow and the five arrows with him.

The two boys crept along the forest by the road, as the sounds of voices were becoming louder. Then they saw it. A man who looked like a nobleman was lying on the ground, and three outlaws stood over him. One had a sword pointed at the man's throat, and the other two held daggers. David tried to hear what they were saying, but it was difficult, since they were keeping their voices down.

"Avram, they're going to kill him. I heard one of them say so."

"But what can we do about it? There are three of them, and if they see us, they'll kill us too."

David made a decision. "Avram, stay here until I call for you." He began to crawl a little closer to get a better view of what was happening. Then David heard the outlaw holding the sword say, "Don't keep questioning me. Just do it."

David perched himself on one knee, notched an arrow, aimed, and released it. The arrow hit the outlaw right in his chest. He quickly notched a second arrow and shot at another outlaw, hitting him in his left eye as he looked over to see where the shooter was. He fell over immediately. The third arrow hit the last outlaw in his stomach. David watched as the man fell, and the nobleman quickly got up, took the other outlaw's sword, and killed him with a thrust through his heart.

David froze. He began to realize what he had done. I just killed three men. I did it almost without thinking. He started shaking, but then calmed down. The nobleman was calling for him. Should he go? He said he wanted to thank me. David slowly walked out of the brush.

"My lord, are you all right?" he asked, bowing his head as he stood in front of Henry.

Henry gazed at the boy standing in front of him, carrying a bow and two arrows.

"Was it you who saved me?"

"It was, my lord."

"But you're only a boy. Your shots were perfect. I would have been killed if you hadn't been there. What's your name?"

David did not answer immediately. He could not tell him his real name, or that he was Jewish. He might be in enough trouble anyway, so he decided he would use a different name. "I am called Donald, my lord."

"Do you know who I am?"

"No, my lord, I'm sorry but I don't."

"I am Baron Henry de Percy of York. Donald, I am deeply in your debt. Where did you learn to shoot so well? Come. Tell me all about it while we wait for my lazy escort."

"I taught myself, my lord, for the last year or so."

"I'm impressed. You apparently were born with the skill. I wish my archers could shoot as well, even after years of practice."

Henry then remembered the incident with the dead forester. "Tell me, Donald, where did you get your bow and arrows?"

David did not know how to answer. He had not thought of any story to cover himself if he was discovered.

"Don't worry, Donald. I assume you found them on the dead forester, am I correct, and were afraid to report it?"

David felt he could not lie. "Yes, my lord. I always wanted to be an archer, and when I stumbled upon the forester, I decided to take advantage of the opportunity. I beg you not to report me."

"I won't. And I suggest we keep that our secret. It's better you don't tell anyone else, either. After all, you saved my life. If you hadn't found them and not been out here at this time, I probably would be dead. I want to reward you. What is your pleasure?"

Almost without thinking, David answered. "I want to be a knight."

Henry laughed. "How old are you?"

"Fifteen."

"Do you know what it takes to become a knight?"

"I guess I don't, my lord."

"You first must be a squire. Can you come with me to York and train to be one?"

David could not believe what he had just heard. "Yes, my lord, I can."

"What about your family. Where do you live?"

Now David had to think fast. While he did not want to lie, he had no choice. "I have no family, my lord. They died when I was very young. I've been living near here with a poor family who took me in."

"So, there would be no problem for you coming with me now?"

"No, my lord. I have a friend near here who can tell the family. Give me a few minutes, and I will return shortly."

"Very well but be quick. I hear my men approaching, and I want to leave."

David ran back through the brush. "Avram," he whispered. "Come here."

Avram stepped out from behind a tree. "David, I heard what the baron said. You can't be serious. You can't just leave your father, brother and sister like that."

"I have no choice. This is my chance. I can't travel to York by myself. If I don't go now, I'll never go."

"And what do I tell your father? That you killed three thieves, saved a baron's life, and now you're going to York to train as a knight?"

"Not a knight. A squire. And, no, you can't tell him anything of what happened."

"What happens when they find out you're a Jew?"

"They won't. I'll keep it a secret."

"How can you possibly do that? What do you know about living as a Christian? Even if you can fool them for a while, eventually they'll find out, or become suspicious. You know you can never let anyone see you naked."

"I know. Somehow, I'll just have to learn how to be a Christian. And you must never tell my father that. Please, Avram, just tell my father I had to leave for a while, but I will be back. I promise."

"David, you're my best friend, and I'll do what you ask, but I don't know how. Your father will ask me many questions."

"Just do your best. I'll try to get word to him as soon as I can. Goodbye, Avram. I hope to see you again soon."

The boys embraced, and Avram left. David ran to the cave to retrieve the sword. Then he hurried back to where the baron was yelling at his men, berating them for resting and not staying with him.

"Ah, Donald. I see you have a sword as well. Do you know how to use it?"

"No, my lord. I don't."

"We'll teach you. Men, this is Donald. While you were loafing, he saved my life."

Henry's men-at-arms greeted Donald with mutterings, obviously embarrassed a boy had saved their master from certain death. Bryce jumped down from the cart. "I'm Bryce, the baron's page. Thank you for saving him." Bryce glared at the men-at-arms while he spoke.

"Donald, you can ride with Bryce. Everyone else can walk the entire way back to York."

David and Bryce climbed into the cart, and Bryce took the reins. "You'll like living at York castle. Baron Henry sets a fine table, and we eat well."

David felt regretful as he thought about what Bryce had said. I have never eaten non-kosher food. I may have to eat pork and who knows what else. I may have to go to church. I cannot celebrate the High Holidays. I will be going against all I have learned and what my family has endured. Then his thoughts changed. If I can learn how to be a warrior, maybe even become a knight, perhaps I can be a champion for my people. Perhaps one day I can avenge my mother's death. Maybe I can show them Jews can fight given the opportunity. He began to feel a bit better about what at first felt like the worst thing he could do to betray his religion, his people, and his family. God gave me this opportunity, and now it is up to me to make the best of it. And I will.

"Do you live there?" David asked.

"Usually. My father is the baron's blacksmith and chief armorer. I stay at the castle when the baron needs me, but I go home whenever he lets me."

Bryce looked at David. "You're lucky. You don't have to start your training as a page, like me. Where did you get your bow and arrows?'

He was comfortable telling Baron Henry the truth, but not Bryce or anyone else. He decided to ignore Bryce's question.

"That's all right, Donald. I was just curious. I don't have to know. Be careful of Baron Henry's men, though. Since it was their fault for leaving him unprotected, they'll resent you for what you did and will most likely try to find some way to get back at you."

"Thank you. I'll be careful."

West End – October 1267

Avram quickly walked out of the forest, always fearful of the many dangers he always believed were present there. However, he was more nervous about how he was going to tell David's father his son was not coming home for a while. *Knowing what I know, how can I keep David's secret? Mordecai will most assuredly not let me go with a simple explanation. David, what have you gotten me into?*

As Avram reached the town and got closer to David's house, he decided he just had to tell him the bare minimum. He would not lie to Mordecai. He just would not tell him the details.

He finally arrived at David's house, took a deep breath and knocked on the door. Benjamin answered.

"Avram. Where's David? We thought the two of you had gone looking for more plants and herbs."

"Is your father home? I must speak to him."

Benjamin sensed something was wrong. "Is David all right?"

"He's fine. Now, where is your father?"

Mordecai then appeared. "Avram, is David not with you?"

Avram took another deep breath. "No, Mordecai, he isn't. Don't worry, he's fine. He wanted me to tell you he had to go away for a while, and he will get word to you as soon as he can."

Mordecai was stunned. "Went away? Where? Why?"

Now Avram had to do his best to honor David's wishes. If he told Mordecai the truth, Mordecai would most certainly travel to York to get David. That would immediately reveal David's secret and ruin his opportunity.

"Mordecai, I'm sorry, but I cannot tell you anything more. Just know he is safe."

Mordecai relaxed a bit. While he did not know why David wanted to spend as much time in Salcey as he did, his father always suspected that perhaps it was his son who found the weapons. If so, that may have something to do with this.

"Avram, you've been David's best friend for a long time. If you're keeping something from me because David asked you to, I will respect that. I know David always maintained thoughts of leaving West End and our life here. Something must have happened to cause him to do this without any warning. Since he apparently could not tell me himself, it must be something I would not approve of. I'm sure I'll find out what it is, but I won't make you betray his confidence."

Great relief washed over Avram. He had honored David's wishes and still maintained a good relationship with Mordecai. "Thank you, Mordecai. That means a lot to me."

Mordecai looked at Benjamin and Rachel, who had just entered. "Come here, my children. I must talk to you. Your brother David had to go away for a while. I don't know where or why he has gone, but he is safe, and will get word to us as soon as he can."

Rachel began to cry, and Mordecai embraced her. "It will be all right. We all know David wanted a different kind of life. I can only assume he left us for a good reason. When he's ready, he'll tell us what that is."

"What will we tell people when they ask about him?" Benjamin asked.

"I don't know just yet. I'll think of something."

Both children looked at each other, sad and confused about the entire situation. All of a sudden, their brother was gone with no explanation?

And he was safe? Something must have happened to him. It made no sense. "I'll try to find out what happened, Rachel," Benjamin said as he consoled his still weeping sister. "I must know."

Chapter Fifteen

York – October 1267

David gazed in awe upon York Castle. It had experienced considerable turmoil since it was built after the Norman Conquest. King Henry III recently had rebuilt it out of stone from the original wood. The keep had a design called a quatrefoil, with an outer bailey wall and gatehouse. David knew about the massacre of Jews that occurred there in 1190, and he tried to hide his sadness about being on the exact spot. It made him angry inside. *If my people could have fought back or at least had our own protection, perhaps that horrible event would not have happened,* he thought.

"Well, Donald, isn't it magnificent?" Baron Henry said. "I've petitioned the king to make some additional improvements. You can see we are well-protected."

"Yes, my lord. I've only seen Northampton Castle from the outside, and it's nothing like this."

"Bryce, come here," the baron commanded. Bryce was unloading the cart with the baron's personal items.

"Yes, my lord?"

"I want you to take good care of Donald. He can stay in your quarters with you. Tell Carleton to have an extra bed brought in. I think there's room for two."

"Yes, my lord. Come with me, Donald. I'll show you around."

"Who's Carleton?" David asked.

"He's the baron's seneschal. He runs the castle, making sure there is enough food for Baron Henry, his family, and eventually us," Bryce answered with a grin.

David followed Bryce through a side door that led into the kitchen. David saw people preparing what he guessed was the baron's supper. When he saw a huge pig roasting on a spit, he knew his first test of keeping his identity secret would come quickly. He saw other dishes being prepared that may not have been kosher but were not as blatantly against his religion as the pork. Also, the chickens, ducks, and geese he saw being prepared may not have been ritually slaughtered, but at least they were permissible.

Bryce showed him the great hall where the baron held his feasts, his court and council. The two boys stepped on the dais where the baron and Lady Eleanor sat. Bryce sat in the baron's chair.

"Look, Donald. I'm Baron Bryce."

They both laughed, as Donald sat down next to him.

"Donald, that's Lady Eleanor's chair. Maybe I should call you Lady Donald!"

David immediately stood, and they both laughed again.

"I'm glad you're here, Donald. I think we'll have a good time. Baron Henry said we can train to be squires together."

"I hope that doesn't mean we will have to fight each other. I wouldn't want to hurt you."

Bryce appeared offended at David's remark, then grinned. "I don't want to hurt you," he responded back.

Bryce took David to his room. While small, it was not too far from the baron's chamber, so his page could be available when the baron needed him.

"Bryce," David asked, "when you're training to be a squire, will you still be a page?"

"Baron Henry said when I train a new page I can concentrate on my squire training. I wouldn't want you to get too far ahead of me."

Carleton had a bed brought in, and although it was a bit tight, it fit. It was not as nice as the one he had at West End, but it was clean and seemed comfortable.

"Donald, tonight we'll attend the baron's feast to celebrate his return. You may meet some important people there. Be sure to bow and be polite. The baron requires we be courteous at all times. But be wary of Father Zacharias. He always will scold you for not paying attention during Mass or not following any Church law or custom. He watches everyone, especially the boys."

David knew this was another area where he had to be careful.

"Bryce, the poor people who took me in did not go to church very often, and when they did, they usually did not take me."

"You were baptized, weren't you?"

"I think so. I'm not really sure."

"Then you will have to discuss this with Father Zacharias. You may have to be baptized again."

David realized he had made a mistake. "No, I'm sure I was baptized, I remember hearing my parents talk of it when I was small."

"I hope you can meet my parents soon. They live just outside the castle walls." Bryce paused. "Donald, how did your parents die?"

David answered without hesitation. "They became quite ill. I don't know much more, as I was too young to understand."

"I'm sorry."

"I never knew them very well, so let's not talk about it again, if you please."

"Of course. Come, let's prepare for the feast."

Bryce looked David over. "You'll need some new clothes. The forest and the journey here made yours quite dirty."

In all the excitement of his new life, David had forgotten all he had was what was on his back. He could not have gone home to get anything. Baron Henry never mentioned anything about clothes. "I have no money. How can I buy some?"

"Don't worry, Donald. We'll visit the baron's seamstress. She can make you a new tunic and breeches. The baron takes care of his own."

"Everything happened so quickly. I didn't have much of anything else anyway."

Bryce looked at what David was wearing. His tunic and stockings looked to be of a better quality than someone who said he lived with a poor family. It started to arouse his curiosity, and then he shrugged. "Let's wash up a bit. You'll have to try to get as much dirt off your clothes as you can. I don't think any of my clothes will fit you."

While Bryce and David were the same age, David was several inches taller and huskier than Bryce. Using a washbasin, David did his best to remove as much dirt as he could. Luckily, most of it was on the surface, so when they dried, he looked almost clean.

"Very well done. I think the baron will be pleased. Come. Let's go down to the great hall."

David followed right behind Bryce, feeling more nervous the closer he got to the hall. This could be a very difficult night. He had to be very careful how he answered any question. One slip, just one suspicious person who even thought he was not who he said he was, could mean disaster. As they approached the great hall, he heard loud voices and music. The baron had sent one of his men on ahead with a borrowed horse to announce his return and ensure his welcome back feast would be as well attended as possible on such short notice. David counted eight tables with eight people at each. There were knights and ladies, and several others who looked to be very important, although he had no idea who they were.

David followed Bryce as they approached the baron's table. Henry sat there in a stunning blue tunic laced with gold, and a red cape. Lady Eleanor sat beside him, dressed in the most beautiful gown David had ever seen. It was pure white, decorated with embroidered flowers. When Henry saw David, he stood and immediately called to him.

"Donald! Come here, my boy!"

"Go ahead," Bryce said. "Our master calls."

David stood in front of the baron and bowed. "My lord."

Henry banged his cup on the table and called for silence. "My friends. This is Donald. He saved my life a few days ago. Tonight, we feast in his honor. Make places for him and Bryce in front of me."

David and Bryce took the places made for them when two guests, both knights who were not happy with the baron's order, had to find other seats. David looked to his left and saw he was sitting next to a large man. "Donald. I am Sir Michael of Northampton," the knight said in a heavy French accent as he patted David on the back.

"Hello, Sir Michael," David replied, somewhat sheepishly. When David heard Northampton, he began to worry. Would this knight recognize him? There was nothing he could do about it now, but it made him even warier.

"So, you saved Henry's life, did you? Well done, lad. Here, let's have a drink together." The knight handed David a mug of ale. David had never tasted ale before. His father had given him wine since he was twelve at each Sabbath meal and at Passover, but this was his first time for ale. He slowly brought the cup to his lips and tasted the warm brew. It was somewhat bitter but not distasteful. "To your health, Sir Knight," he toasted.

"To yours, my brave friend," the knight replied. "So, Donald, where are you from?"

David replied with the name of the only small village he knew. "Coby Hollow. I lived with some poor people after my parents died."

"I'm sorry. Where is Coby Hollow?"

"It's at the edge of Salcey Forest, several miles from Northampton."

"I was born in Northampton, but I haven't been there in years. My father took me to France when I was a child, and I just recently returned to England. I never heard of Coby Hollow."

"There's not much to hear of, Sir Michael."

The knight laughed, and there was no more conversation about what David had done, which greatly relieved him. Servants brought out platters and platters of food. David feasted on duck, mutton, and various vegetables, avoiding the pork. With so much food served, no one cared what he had taken. He had gotten through his first non-kosher meal. He was careful not to drink too much ale, as he knew that could loosen his tongue and he might say something that would expose him. He did feel somewhat guilty about what he had eaten, but he was beginning to feel comfortable around the Gentiles. He continued to worry, however, about when he had to attend Mass.

David spent a considerable amount of time observing during the meal. There were two knights and their ladies seated near Baron Henry. Baroness Eleanor looked radiant, he thought. She wore several pieces of jewelry, all looking to be quite expensive. The knights were also well-dressed, with colorful tunics. He never had seen anything like it.

There was one sight he could not take his eyes off of, however. She looked to be about his age, with radiant blonde hair that fell halfway down her back. She wore a magnificent red dress with silver threads and a lace collar and sat next to Lady Eleanor. Her daughter, David guessed. Sir Michael noticed David staring at her.

"So, my brave friend, I see you have an eye for a pretty face."

David lowered his eyes, embarrassed.

"Don't feel ashamed, Donald. She is Alycia, the baron's youngest daughter. And the prettiest, I may add."

"I was only looking around, Sir Michael."

The knight laughed. Bryce overheard Sir Michael and turned to David.

"Donald, don't even think about it. Not only could you never have a chance with her, you being a commoner, she's betrothed to Sir Edgar, the son of Earl Tristan."

David nodded. "I understand. But such beauty, I've never seen anyone like her before."

Sir Michael leaned over to David and whispered in his ear. "We must get you a wench to warm you at night. I'm sure there are many a maiden here who would accommodate you."

David tried to stifle a look of near-terror. This could never happen since he would be discovered in an instant. He had not thought about how to handle such a situation. He merely smiled at Sir Michael and changed the subject.

"Sir Michael, please tell me about some of your exploits."

The knight always was willing to talk about himself. David spent the rest of the evening listening to him brag about the battles he had fought in, the men he had killed, and the tournaments he had won. As the evening wore on, guests began to retire, including Baron Henry, the Baroness, and Alycia. Sir Michael, who had continued to empty mug after mug of ale, eventually became so drunk two servants had to help him to his chamber, almost carrying him. David and Bryce left as well.

"So, Donald, what do you think about everything?" Bryce asked.

"It's overwhelming. I come from a poor village, and to now stay in the castle and to feast like this ... I think I ate too much."

Bryce smiled at his new friend. "We don't eat like this every night. But when we do, I also think I eat too much. Let's get some sleep. Tomorrow, you'll start your new life here."

Bryce slid under his woolen blanket and was soon fast asleep. David did the same, but did not fall asleep immediately, even as tired as he was. He thought about what he had done, where he was now living, and what the future possibly could hold for him. What would everyone in West End think? That he betrayed his people and religion to try to become a knight? No, he would not do that. Somehow, he must maintain his heritage by pretending to be Donald for a while. When the right time comes, no matter what the danger, I will be David again. I only hope my father is not angry with me, and my brother and sister will be fine, since I will not be around to protect them. Eventually his thoughts faded as he finally drifted off.

The next morning after a light breakfast, Baron Henry told Bryce to bring David to him.

"Good morning, Baron," David said, bowing.

"Donald, did you sleep well after such a feast last night?"

"I did, my lord. Thank you." David noticed there was another man standing in the room.

"Donald, I want you to meet James. He's my champion archer."

David turned as James stepped forward. He was a short, squat man, with muscular arms.

"Hello, Donald. I hear you are quite skilled with a bow for being such a young lad, and you used your skill to save my master's life."

"Thank you. I was lucky to be in the vicinity when Baron Henry was attacked."

"Lucky, indeed. It took skill to drop three outlaws as quickly as you did."

"Donald," Baron Henry said, "I want you to work with James to start your training. He will make you an even better archer. When you are strong enough, he will teach you to use a longbow."

David was delighted with the news but then realized that no doubt meant he would not be training to be a knight.

"Baron Henry, James, please don't think me ungrateful or disrespectful, but I wish to train to be a knight, not an archer."

"I understand, Donald, and as I already explained to you, training for knighthood begins by becoming a squire. I want you to first improve your archery skills, for I may need you to use them someday. Besides, all my knights have squires at this time. When a position opens up, perhaps then. Now, please be satisfied with archery. However, I suppose we can include teaching you how to use a sword as well, don't you think so, James?"

"My lord, I believe that can be arranged."

A huge smile appeared on David. "Thank you, my lord. I am grateful for any opportunity you give me."

"Very well, then. James, you may start today. Bryce, you may join them. I promised your father I would give you a chance to become a squire or man-at-arms, so you might as well start now."

The two boys grinned at each other. They would train together.

Northampton – November 1267

Mordecai paid little attention to the Torah reading. Many at the synagogue had asked him where David was. His absence in the small Jewish community was quickly noticed. All Mordecai would say is that he had to go away for a while.

Rachel missed her brother but accepted the explanation her father had given. Benjamin, however, did not. "It makes no sense," he told his father. "Where could he have gone and why? I'm afraid for him. I need to know he's all right." Mordecai repeated Avram said he was fine and David would contact them soon. Benjamin decided he would do some investigating on his own and would question Avram directly.

News of the ambush eventually reached Northampton when a traveler found the three dead outlaws' bodies a few days later and reported it. Baron Geoffrey sent the sheriff and several men into Salcey to investigate. They returned with the bodies, all with arrow wounds and one with a sword wound as well.

"Well, John," Baron Geoffrey began, "what do you think happened there?"

"My lord, it's difficult to say. From the tracks that were still present, it looks like someone was ambushed by those outlaws and was saved by an archer."

"I wonder if it was Baron Henry who was ambushed. I know he often will ride ahead of his men, and if he did, that may explain his being attacked."

"Yes, but who killed the outlaws?"

"That I don't know. A forester, perhaps? Doubtful, though, as we probably would have had a report by now. Henry's men were only carrying swords and crossbows."

"My lord, it may have been the one who took Ronald's weapons."

"Yes, I guess that's possible, but not likely. While we never found out who did take them, I doubt he would have remained around here. Too risky."

"You're probably correct, my lord."

"Well, no matter. If it was Henry, he's safe. You may go, John."

John de Oxenden returned home. *I believe whoever killed those men was the one who took Ronald's weapons,* he thought. *It must be him. It must be.*

Hedgestone Priory – November 1267

With winter approaching, Hubert made sure his priory would be well-stocked with firewood and provisions. He had the monks working hard to ensure his preparation orders were completed. The fifty pounds he received from Baruch he used against Bishop Basil's orders. Alwyn reminded Hubert Basil had said he could only use a small amount. Hubert said that made no sense, and he would have to make substantial improvements to show the Jew the additional loan he required would bring in more revenue. He used most of the funds to enhance the small church with just enough items to improve the altar. A new altar cloth, crucifix, chalice, candleholders, patens, cruets, and purificator were purchased. Hubert wanted the metal items to be of the finest silver and had commissioned the best silversmith in Northampton to perform the work. He also made improvements to the inside of the church to brighten it. He had some wooden benches made so parishioners could sit instead of standing during services. Alwyn thought while it was a good idea, he had never heard of it done before. Hubert believed by not having to stand, people would be less tired and more inclined to attend. He also started to venture into Northampton to talk to townspeople on the street and ask them to attend his services, and use his church for baptisms, weddings, and funerals. Gradually attendance began to increase. People seemed to like to be able to sit, and even though their weekly contributions were relatively small, revenue began to increase. Hubert was pleased, and even Alwyn had to admit Hubert's ideas appeared to be working.

"So, Alwyn, what do you think of my improvements so far?"

"Hubert, I must admit I'm impressed. I didn't think you could do so much with fifty pounds, but you have, even though the bishop did not want you to use that much."

"I had no choice. Baruch must see progress from the use of his money, or he will never loan the rest."

"I suppose so, if he will even give you another loan."

"He will. I know he will."

"What makes you so sure?"

"He will because I know how to deal with Jews," he replied angrily. "They're all alike. He will not turn down an opportunity to increase his wealth, especially after I've shown him how trustworthy I am."

"Hubert, I'm sorry, but you're a fool. Not all Jews are alike, just as every people have their good and evil. Baruch is smart. He does not need to, nor will he, take on such a risk as you are planning to present to him. I believe you will fail in your attempt, and your plans, as well as Bishop Basil's, will falter."

"Oh, so you believe that I will fail? Perhaps you've spoken to Baruch and planted that seed in his head? Perhaps Basil has told you he wants me to fail?"

"No, I have not, nor had that thought entered my mind. I don't know why you would even think that, and frankly, I don't even care. You are under the impression that the bishop is giving you directions in order to use you for his own gain. Well, that may be. However, since he has not expressed that to me, I can't agree with your opinion. Watch yourself, Hubert. You continue to make enemies. While they have remained quiet, I don't believe they will remain so forever."

Northampton Castle – November 1267

Alone in his chamber, Baron Geoffrey stared at the two jars of poison Mordecai had provided. Lady Catherine had gone to London to visit her sister before the weather turned too cold. What shall I do with these, he asked himself. I have the means, but do I have the wherewithal? How can I do it without a finger being pointed at me? He rejected every idea after thinking about it. There always seemed to be a catch even an untrained person might see through. Abbot Hubert must have more enemies than me. No doubt, he has angered most of the monks at Hedgestone Priory. I can only speculate, however, if anyone else would consider harming him besides me. Who might the most ambitious one be? Alwyn comes to mind, but I do not believe he even would consider it. A knock on the door took him out of his thoughts.

"My lord, it is I, Sir Walter, as you requested."

"Please sit. There's something I want to discuss with you."

"Yes, my lord."

"Walter, you have been faithful to me for a long time, have you not?"

"Yes, my lord. And I hope to continue to serve you."

"I need to talk to you about a very secret matter. Can I trust you to never divulge it to anyone?"

"On my life, my lord."

"You know what happened to my brother?"

"Yes, my lord."

"I want revenge on Abbot Hubert. I want you to help me get it."

"Certainly, my lord. How can I help?"

"I want you to gather some information for me. I can't do it since Hubert and I are not on the best of terms. Do you know any of the monks at Hedgestone?"

"Not the monks, but I do know Prior Bartholomew, my lord."

"Can you get word to him? I need to know what's going on there. It may help me to decide how to proceed. Tell him I want to see him."

"I will, my lord."

"Thank you, Walter. I won't forget this."

"Baron, I only want to serve you. I will do the best I can." Walter bowed and left.

Geoffrey poured himself a mug of wine. If I can just learn one good piece of information. One good piece.

West End – November 1267

Benjamin knocked on Avram's door. He heard voices inside, and soon Avram's mother opened it.

"Benjamin. Come in. Did your father send you to borrow something?"

"No. I want to talk to Avram."

Avram appeared from behind a curtain. "Shalom, Benjamin. You want to talk to me?"

"Yes, can we go outside?"

Avram led Benjamin to the rear of the house and out the door.

"What's this about?"

"Tell me where my brother is."

Avram was not surprised at the request. He had expected it.

"I can't tell you any more than I have. He is safe and will be back."

"Avram, we heard three thieves were killed in the forest. It happened about the time you came to us and said that David had to go away for a while. Did he kill them? Was he arrested? Was he hurt?"

"No, David wasn't arrested and wasn't hurt. Don't you think if he were, your father would know about it? He just told me he had to go away for a while and that's all. Please believe me."

"Did he kill the thieves? You avoided the question."

"How could he? With what weapons? We can't have weapons, you know that."

"The dead forester. The missing weapons. There has been much talk about it. Did you and my brother find them?"

"No. I don't know anything about it. And I suggest you don't bring it up any more. Nothing good can come of it. It happened over a year ago, and the sheriff could find nothing. Now go home and leave me alone."

"Very well. I'll go. But I don't believe you. You're hiding something. One day we'll learn the truth. I only pray that David will be fine, and the secret you're keeping for him won't cause him or my family harm."

Avram felt nervous as he watched Benjamin run toward his home. The secret is still safe with me, he thought. I hope Benjamin does not pursue it further. If I'm questioned by the sheriff, I don't think I can remain silent. I know they have terrible ways to make people talk. I'm sure they would not hesitate to use them on a Jew, and David would not be there to help me this time. David, why did you do this to me? David, I wonder how you are doing.

Chapter Sixteen

York – December 1267

More snow was falling as Christmas was getting closer. David had been working on his archery with James. Bryce was starting to learn, but his skills lagged far behind David's. When James was not around, the boys would practice together. David was becoming a very good teacher himself, correcting Bryce's mistakes and helping him improve.

In David's first few weeks at York, he had avoided Father Zacharias, but only because the priest had gone on a pilgrimage and was not expected to return before Christmas. David attended an occasional Mass, observing what took place during the service. The Mass was in Latin, and while he could not understand any of the words, neither could anyone else. He would mouth the words when a hymn was sung, pretending to learn them.

Each Sabbath he prayed silently from memory as best he could, as long as he could find some privacy. He did not want to lose his Jewish identity, but he had to be extremely careful. Pretending to be someone else, especially from a different religion and culture, was much more difficult than he thought it would be. While he could not have prepared himself for what happened, he knew he had no choice but to accept Baron Henry's offer. He did not know where this would lead him, be it a knight, an archer, or a man-at-arms. He missed his family and his friends terribly, and he did not know when he would have a chance to see them. Still, life at the castle was pleasant enough so far. There was plenty of food, and since all the servants knew Donald had saved the baron's life, they showered him with extra attention.

As David was lying on his bed during a chilly afternoon in mid-December, he was startled by an older man who suddenly stood at his bedside. Dressed as a priest, he looked David over very carefully.

"Donald? I am Father Zacharias. We have not met."

David sat up and felt his nerves tingle. This day finally had come.

"Hello, Father. I understand you were on a pilgrimage."

"That's correct. I went to St. Olave's Priory in Norfolk. A long journey, but I'm descended from St. Olave, a Viking who converted to Christianity and established the Church in Norway."

David did not know whether to believe Zacharias or not. Bryce said the baron had told him quite often such tales, or the supposed relics of ancient saints, probably were not true, even though many believed them.

"I'm glad you had a safe journey."

"Tell me about yourself. I know you saved the baron's life, and he invited you to train here. Are you a good Christian? I do not see you wearing a crucifix."

"My parents died when I was very young, and I lived with a poor family until now. They could not afford one."

"Were you baptized?"

"Yes, I was. But the family I lived with did not attend church very often."

"I see. Well, we will correct that. I will talk to Baron Henry about getting you a crucifix to help keep you safe. I want to see you at Mass every Sunday. Perhaps we should baptize you again, just to be sure? When was the last time you went to confession?"

"Uh, I've never been to confession."

"Well, Donald, it seems we have a lot to teach you. After all, we do not want you to turn into a Jew," Zacharias said, chuckling.

David held his temper. "No," he replied. "I will never turn into a Jew, you can be sure of that," he said with a smile.

"I'll see you in church."

David laid back down. I am not a Christian, he thought. I don't know how to be a real Christian. I can pretend to be one around the castle, but in church I feel lost. I cannot avoid this priest. I will just have to be the best Christian a Jewish boy can be.

The next Sunday, David went to church with Bryce. He stood in the back but made sure Father Zacharias saw him. He decided he had better take the Eucharist. When the time came, he lined up with the other parishioners. But when it was his turn, Zacharias shook his head no. "Donald, you first must go to confession to cleanse your sins. Then you may take Holy Communion."

David nodded and returned to the rear of the church. After the service, he asked Bryce about confession.

"You never went to confession before?" Bryce started laughing loudly. "You must have quite a number of sins to confess. You'll be in the booth all day."

"Seriously, Bryce. What do I do?"

Bryce explained the confession process. David did not know if he could handle it. The problem was learning what the typical sins were to confess. Though he assumed there were quite a few everyday transgressions he could list when the time came, he was certain Father Zacharias would not let him go too long before his first confession.

Northampton Castle – December 1267

"Merry Christmas, Prior Bartholomew."

"Merry Christmas to you, Baron Geoffrey. You wanted to see me?"

"Please be seated. I'll pour you a cup of hot spiced wine."

"Thank you." Geoffrey handed the cup to Bartholomew, who took a long sip.

"I understand Abbot Hubert has replaced you."

"Yes. Bishop Basil insisted Hubert replace me."

"I don't understand. Northampton is not under Basil's authority."

"He asked for and received permission from Bishop Amos. Apparently, Amos owed Basil a favor. I do not know any more than that."

"It sounds to me Basil had his own reason for doing that. Why would he care who's prior at Hedgestone? And why choose Hubert?"

"Basil told me Hedgestone was being poorly run, and that I and the other brothers were becoming too friendly with the Jews."

Geoffrey looked surprised. "Too friendly with the Jews? I don't understand that either."

Bartholomew was pleased to tell the baron everything that had happened. He told him how Hubert tried to obtain a fifteen hundred pound loan from Baruch but had to settle for only fifty pounds. He described the changes Hubert was making as well. Geoffrey nodded as he listened carefully to every word.

"Does Hubert have Father Alwyn as his assistant?"

"Yes, Father Alwyn, his distant cousin, is his assistant. However, I know Basil has enlisted him to keep watch on Hubert and report back to him."

"So, Basil doesn't trust Hubert, apparently. Tell me, Bartholomew, how do you know all this?"

"Hubert does not confide in me, even though Basil told him to request my counsel. Father Ambrose was my assistant, and even though I still live at Hedgestone, I am not privy to much that happens that one cannot see. Ambrose, however, learns all, and he tells me."

"What do the brothers think of Hubert?"

"At first they all hated him. He made them work extra hard and actually had two flogged for what he said was socializing with the Jews. As time has passed, most are used to him. But there still is animosity."

"Do you think anyone would harm him?"

Bartholomew became suspicious of Geoffrey's motive for asking him over. "Why do you ask?"

"Prior, I'll be honest with you. Hubert wrongfully accused my brother of heresy, and because of it, my brother killed himself. I've never forgiven Hubert. I'm wondering if perhaps he has a few more enemies."

"I see. I'm sure he has many. He seems to make more enemies than friends, I would say."

"No surprise. Tell me, what do you think of Father Alwyn?"

"While Alwyn must obey Hubert, I can see he resents it. Hubert does not treat him well. He rarely lets Alwyn make any decision of consequence. He doesn't let Alwyn forget who the abbot is and who is not. Hubert seems to be easily threatened."

"Doesn't Alwyn wish to be prior?"

"Most certainly. He's hopeful Hubert will be successful, and after he leaves Hedgestone, he'll become prior. Frankly, I doubt that will happen."

"Why?"

"Because I believe Hubert will not support Alwyn if it does not benefit him personally. In addition, I believe Basil has some other motive for all this that will become evident eventually."

Geoffrey nodded in agreement as he listened to the old prior. "I wouldn't be surprised if everything you say is true. Hubert is only for Hubert. Alwyn knew my brother was innocent, and yet he didn't oppose Hubert. I hate them both."

"Baron Geoffrey," Bartholomew said, crossing himself. "I have no doubt you want to get revenge on Hubert. I could never assist you in that effort. However, Basil expects Hubert to obtain the large loan from the Jews. If Hubert fails, the bishop will be very angry and I believe have him exiled to some Godforsaken place."

After Bartholomew was gone, Geoffrey thought again about wanting to kill Hubert for what he did. But maybe he does not have to. If he can somehow stop Hubert from carrying out the bishop's orders, perhaps his failure will be worse than death. The thought made Geoffrey smile.

York – December 1267

It was Christmas Day. Baron Henry had ordered a spectacular feast in celebration of the birth of Christ. His kitchen staff was busy preparing a variety of foods, from fish to meat to vegetables and fruits. Henry also ordered a large supply of various cheeses be served since he was very partial to cheese.

After Christmas Mass, David decided to take a walk around the castle grounds. It was chilly, but not as cold as it had been. His woolen cloak kept him quite warm. A fresh layer of snow made everything quite pretty. As he approached the main gate, he saw Alycia, who had slipped on a patch of ice.

"Let me help you, my lady."

"Thank you. I feel so clumsy."

She took David's hand and stood. David had never touched the hand of a girl other than his sister before. Her skin was smooth and soft.

"You are Donald, correct? The one who saved my father's life?"

David found himself staring at her beauty, and at first did not answer.

"Yes," he finally replied.

"I never had the opportunity to thank you. That was a very brave thing you did. You could have been killed yourself by those bandits."

David felt a burst of extreme pride. "It was nothing. I saw only three and took care of them quickly."

"You saw only three, but there might have been many more you didn't see." Her dazzling blue eyes gazed at him while the slight breeze caught her golden hair.

"Merry Christmas, Donald. Will be you at the feast today?"

"Merry Christmas to you. I wouldn't miss it. Especially since you will be there."

David realized he should not have said that. She was the baron's daughter, and he was known as a poor boy who had performed a great deed. Alycia appeared surprised by the comment but did not admonish him.

"Then I'll see you later," she said with a huge smile as she hurried off. David watched her go into the castle.

One of the guards at the main gate witnessed the entire encounter. He was one of the men-at-arms who had accompanied the baron to and from Northampton, so he knew David.

"She is a beauty, isn't she?"

David turned to the guard. "Yes, she is."

"Do you know what the baron would do to you if you touched her?"

"I can imagine."

"No, lad, you can't. Last year, during one of the baron's feasts, the son of one of his guests got drunk and, before we could stop him, kissed her against her wishes. The boy, who was about your age, was given five lashes."

"Didn't his father try to stop the punishment?"

"He couldn't. He was indebted to the baron and had to admit his son's behavior was wrong, so he agreed to the flogging. Alycia is the baron's pride and joy. Protect her, and you will always earn his thanks. Anything else and you'll suffer his wrath."

"Thank you for the advice. I'll remember it."

"Be sure you do. There are plenty of wenches here who will give themselves to you. We've heard them talking. Stay away from Alycia. No good can come of it."

Later that day, David attended the feast with Bryce. Baron Henry always invited his entire household to celebrate the Christmas feast. While the cooks and servants had to work, they were allowed to eat with everyone else. All men-at-arms not on duty were in attendance with their families. Those on duty were allowed to rotate so they could eat as well. However, they were not allowed more than one mug of ale each.

When David arrived, Alycia was seated next to her father. She saw him and waved. David, afraid to acknowledge her, merely nodded. He was glad Henry had not noticed Alycia greeting him.

The Christmas feast was the grandest David had ever seen or could imagine. Besides the usual roasted pig, ducks, geese, mutton and fish, there were pheasants, quail, eel, whole sides of roasted beef, and several large wheels of cheese. David and Bryce sat near the rear of the hall. Sir Michael surprised David by sitting next to him.

"Donald, Merry Christmas!" he said, already quite drunk.

"Merry Christmas, Sir Michael."

Michael looked down at David's empty plate.

"Here, my boy. Let me serve you."

Before David could stop him, Michael dropped a chunk of pork and a large slice of cheese on David's plate.

"Enjoy, my boy. Stuff yourself."

David stared at the two items that were against his religion. Pork was the most forbidden food, of course, but Jews also did not eat dairy products with meat. He knew this day may come, and after silently asking forgiveness to God, his father and mother, he tasted the pork first. To his surprise, he liked it. It was a bit salty and greasy, but it was also juicy and flavorful. He then cut a small piece of cheese, making sure not to eat it until after swallowing the pork. *Will anything happen to me now that I have broken two of the most important dietary laws?*

he wondered to himself. What is the purpose of those laws anyway? He was told it was healthier to maintain them. For several weeks, he had seen Christians eat pork with dairy items and no one became ill. His guilt faded as he finished both the pork and cheese. He completed his meal primarily with beef and several different kinds of fowl.

Sir Michael ensured that both David and Bryce's mugs were always filled with ale. Bryce was drinking heavily, so much so that eventually he ran out quite ill. David sipped his slowly, reminding himself becoming drunk could cause him to say things that could expose his real identity.

After the main meal, trays of sweets were brought out. Cakes and pies of all different varieties were set on every table. David was already quite full, but again Sir Michael made sure David had more than enough.

Baron Henry, after consuming a huge amount of food, ale, and wine himself, went from table to table wishing his guests a Merry Christmas, gloating from the accolades showered on him. When he got to David's table, he stopped and, in his loudest voice, asked for quiet in the room. Everyone soon complied.

"My lords and ladies," he began, more than a little drunk, and pointed at David. "This is Donald, who saved my life when three outlaws attacked me in Salcey Forest. This brave boy protected me when my escort did not. Let us all give him a hearty Huzzah!" The room erupted with the sounds of the cheer.

David turned red, more than a little embarrassed at the attention the baron bestowed upon him. David saw Alycia smiling at him, and he turned away. He also noticed Father Zacharias looking at him with apparent suspicion.

"Merry Christmas, Donald," he said.

"Merry Christmas to you, Father."

"I have a present for you."

Zacharias handed David a silver cross on a cord. David tried to stifle what would have been a very negative reaction to the priest's gift. He must continue with his charade. It's only a piece of metal, he said to himself.

"Thank you, Father. That's very kind of you." David put the cord around his neck.

"Tell me, how did you save our Baron Henry?"

David swallowed hard, unsure if and how he should answer. If word got around with the details, perhaps Baron Geoffrey or the sheriff would find out, and they would know it was he who found Ronald and took the weapons. This time however, Baron Henry was standing by David and answered Zacharias's question.

"Father, he raised his mighty arm and, with the help of Our Lord, smote the varmints."

Everyone around David who had heard the baron's statement laughed and gave David another round of cheers. Zacharias was not satisfied but decided he would discover the answer at a later time.

Even as drunk as he was, Baron Henry winked at David, acknowledging that so far, his secret was safe. But for how long, David thought? What if it is discovered I took the forester's weapons? Even worse, what if it is discovered I am a Jew? Again, David realized he had not prepared himself very well to be in his current situation. So far, he had been successful. He had blended in with the Christians. He knew this was partly because of his looks, and he knew how to interact with them, unlike most of the Jews he knew from Northampton. While he was curious to explore York's Jewish community, he knew that would be extremely dangerous. If anyone from Northampton was visiting and recognized him, or if a Jew from York believed him to be one of them, he could be in serious trouble. Somehow, he must continue to maintain his facade, keep learning, and reach his goal of becoming a trained warrior. He also must stop thinking about Alycia. Unfortunately, that was becoming more difficult. Not only was he enthralled with her beauty, he believed she was expressing her own interest in him, and that made it even harder. He again told himself he must stay as far away from her as possible, as no good could come of any association with her, even if he was not Jewish.

As Christmas passed, it became the new year of 1268. The winter turned out to be mild, which permitted more time for training. David continued to improve his archery skills, and James began his training with a sword. Bryce was becoming a more proficient archer, but still was far behind David. He also did not seem to have as much natural talent or interest in archery. He was quite good with a sword, however, and soon caught up to David. The two of them would practice for hours with wooden swords and shields, lunging, parrying, and defending. Baron Henry would sometimes watch, occasionally giving pointers. He also enjoyed sparring with them, showing no mercy. He was becoming quite fond of David, and as Easter approached, invited him to have Easter dinner with him, Lady Eleanor, and Alycia. As much as he did not want to go, David knew he had no choice, and must accept. He was unhappy about the invitation not only because of Alycia, but because it also would be Passover. He felt guilty he could not celebrate the holiday. Passover always had been his favorite holiday when his mother had been alive. She always served a variety of delicious foods all strictly kosher for Passover. He missed the wonderful aromas as she prepared them, as well as the family retelling the story of Moses, the redemption from slavery and the exodus from Egypt. He had never attended an Easter dinner, although he assumed it was similar to the Christmas feast. He could not refuse to eat bread, as that would arouse suspicion. He wondered if Father Zacharias would be in attendance. Luckily, since the Christmas feast, he had not bothered with David. David made certain Zacharias saw him at each Sunday Mass, wearing his cross, but was able to avoid him the rest of the week.

When it became time for the Easter dinner, David dressed in a new shirt and breeches and cleaned his shoes. He had bathed, always making sure it was by himself, as he obviously could not let anyone see he was circumcised. This turned out to be easy, as the bathing tub for use by him and the men-at-arms was never in demand.

He knew it was an honor to be invited to eat with the baron and his family, an honor rarely given to someone like him. As he approached the hall, he became nervous, afraid his interest in Alycia would become obvious, and would put him in a difficult position.

"Ah, Donald," Baron Henry said. "Welcome. Come, my boy." David walked into the hall where Henry, Lady Eleanor, Alycia, Father Zacharias, and another man were already seated. David bowed to all of them. "My lord, Lady Eleanor, Alycia, Father Zacharias."

"Donald, allow me to introduce you to Sir Edgar of Ashby, Alycia's betrothed."

David suppressed his dismay at hearing Alycia was to marry this man, although there also was a bit of a relief. "Sir Edgar, congratulations," David said, bowing.

Edgar nodded. It was evident he had no use for this common boy, no matter what he had done to ingratiate himself to the baron.

Donald sat next to Father Zacharias and across from Alycia and Edgar. It was apparent this arranged betrothal was not to Alycia's liking. Edgar hardly spoke a word, and when he did, he only spoke of the dowry he was expecting and he hoped this marriage would increase his holdings. Actually, they were those of his father, Earl Tristan, and not his alone.

Edgar was a large man, and at twenty-eight almost twice Alycia's age, with long, black hair and a full beard. David could not understand how Baron Henry could even consider this man for his much-younger daughter. As they began the meal after Father Zacharias said grace, David saw Edgar had poor manners. He would be more at home with a group of men-at-arms than the baron and his family. Alycia remained quiet the entire time, obviously quite unhappy with the arrangement.

The Easter meal consisted of roasted beef, several varieties of fish, cheese, and the baron's favorite meat pasties. As always, there were large quantities of ale and wine. David watched as Edgar downed cup after cup, soon becoming quite drunk.

David kept quiet as the conversation primarily involved tentative plans for the wedding, as well as the usual political gossip. Baron Henry and Father Zacharias monopolized most of the discussion, and at times no one could hope to get a word in. David noticed Alycia looked extremely uncomfortable when the wedding was discussed and relaxed a bit when the subject changed. Father Zacharias hardly had spoken to David. It was Alycia who started talking to him.

"Donald, that's a nice crucifix you're wearing."

"Yes. Father Zacharias was kind enough to get it for me."

"Thank Baron Henry, Donald," Zacharias said. "It was he who gave it to you upon my request."

"And he has thanked me many times already, Father," Henry said. "Remember, Donald saved my life, and I will never forget it. He deserves every reward I can give him."

"Then, Father, why not let me marry Donald?" Alycia said, surprising everyone at the table.

Edgar looked up from his plate and turned to Alycia. He did not say a word, but his expression betrayed his anger.

"My dear, you know that's impossible. You must marry someone noble. Sir Edgar will make a fine husband for you. Do not tease Donald, as I am sure he is a normal young man, and to even think of such a thing with a girl as yourself will torture him."

David felt extremely embarrassed at Alycia's question. She obviously said it to incite a controversy and upset her fiancé. David worried Edgar may take out his anger on him.

"Baron, Sir Edgar," David said, "I am flattered by Alycia's suggestion, but I apologize for her using my name. I am a poor guest at Easter dinner and do not want to be the cause of any conflict from her statement." David raised his cup. "To you, Sir Edgar; may your marriage to Alycia be filled with joy and happiness."

To David's surprise, Edgar raised his cup, drank, and replied. "Thank you, Donald. It appears my future bride likes to stir up trouble. Baron, I assure you I will do my best to make your daughter as happy as I can."

Tears began to flow down Alycia's cheeks. She stood up and ran out of the room, the baron calling her to stop and return, but she ignored him. David noticed that Lady Eleanor gave the baron a scornful look.

"Sir Edgar," Henry said, "I apologize for my daughter's behavior. She has much to learn about respect and authority."

"She's a child, and I'll make her into a woman," Edgar said, his mouth stuffed with food.

After the meal ended, David thanked the baron and Lady Eleanor and asked to be excused. As he got up to leave, Father Zacharias stopped him. "Donald, come with me." David followed the priest into the courtyard, where they sat on a stone bench.

"Donald, I noticed you have regularly attended Sunday Mass, and I saw you today at the Easter service. I am happy you are setting a good example."

"Thank you, Father."

"However, you have not yet been to confession."

David swallowed hard. He did not want to go to confession. "I'm sorry, Father, I meant to, but just haven't."

"Then why don't we do it now?"

"Father, I don't know enough about the different kinds of sins to confess."

"I can see since you have never done it, you seem apprehensive. There is nothing to be worried about. Confessing cleanses the soul, and if after confessing you are required to do something in response to your sins, you'll be the stronger person and a better Christian for it."

"Very well."

The two went into the church, where Zacharias led David to a small alcove. "Now kneel down and hold your hands in prayer." David did as he directed.

"Now, say Father forgive me for I have sinned. This is my first confession."

David again complied. He was not sure what to say until he remembered the sins Jews confess together at Yom Kippur and decided to use some of those. "I have thought ill of my neighbor, I have had lustful feelings, I have been lazy at times, and I have acted selfishly." David continued with several more until he figured that should be enough.

"Well done, Donald. I'm impressed. You learn very quickly. I don't think you have to perform anything this time. You may go."

"Thank you, Father." David walked quickly as he did not want to see Zacharias for a while. He wondered if what he had said would make the priest suspicious. After all, first he said he did not know what to confess, and then he spit out a number of so-called sins. Did the priest know how Jews confess on Yom Kippur? How could he? David retired to his room where Bryce was waiting for him.

"So, how was your first confession?"

"All right, I guess. I wasn't sure what to say, but I guess Father Zacharias was pleased. Tell me, Bryce, how could the baron allow Alycia to marry that pig Edgar?"

"Careful, Donald. We must not talk like that. Marriages are arranged for the nobility, usually for the large dowries and lands that go with it."

"What about love? Can't one marry for love?"

Bryce laughed. "Donald, the longer you stay here the more you'll learn. Perhaps you and I can marry for love, but a nobleman's daughter must obey her father, and that means they marry only who he wants her to. Forget about Alycia. She will marry Sir Edgar and most probably spend the rest of her life miserable in his castle, bearing him many children, and hating every minute of her marriage."

While David knew that Jews often had arranged marriages as well, both parties had to agree. He did not know of anyone forced against their will.

"Very well. Of course, I'll forget her. I know she could never be mine."

"Good. Now let's get some sleep. Tomorrow we must go back to our training."

Chapter Seventeen

Hedgestone Priory – April 1268

Abbot Hubert finished his Easter meal, one of two feasts he permitted, the other being at Christmas. The monks took full advantage of it, all of them eating more than their fill. Hubert's austerity orders to save funds meant the priory grew most of its own food, only purchasing what Hubert deemed necessities. Hubert, however, kept his wine and ale stores well stocked, with cost no consideration.

Hubert had made good progress with the fifty pounds Baruch loaned him. Payments were made exactly on time, and revenue had increased as Hubert implemented a few of his proposals. Most significant was the wool venture. He had a few sheep purchased, and was hopeful a small herd would be built, eventually providing meat as well as wool for sale. Hubert knew another priory had established a profitable wool business, and wanted to do the same at Hedgestone. As ready as he was to try to negotiate the next, much-larger loan, he worried Baruch still would not give it to him. Bishop Basil no doubt was getting impatient, and if he did not produce results, perhaps the bishop would have him reassigned to some horrible abbey. Hubert would not let that happen at any cost.

After evening prayers, Hubert ordered Alwyn to meet with him in his chamber.

"Alwyn, do you think the monks enjoyed my feast?"

Alwyn grunted. "Of course, Hubert. You only allow them to stuff themselves twice a year. Obviously, they enjoyed it."

"Gluttony is a sin, remember. That's not why I wanted to talk to you. I want to meet with Baruch to negotiate the next loan. However, I am worried he will not agree to my request. What do you think?"

"Baruch is no fool, as we know. Even though you regularly have made your payments, sometimes with amounts greater than expected, I'm sure he will not give you want you want."

"Then we must come up with a way to make him give it to me."

"How are you going to do that? You can't force a Jew to make a loan."

"Alwyn, you underestimate me. I believe I can, and I think I have thought of a way."

"How?"

"Do you know what coin clipping is?"

"Of course. Many people, Jews and Gentiles have been accused of it, and quite a few hanged over it. The king has made it clear it will not be tolerated."

"That's correct. Tell me, how do we know Baruch has not clipped any coins?"

Alwyn began to understand what Hubert was saying. "You mean to accuse him of clipping?"

"Of course not. I can't accuse him without proof."

"What proof?"

Hubert again smiled at his assistant. "How hard do you think it would be to clip some coins?"

"I see," Alwyn said. "You think you can force him into giving you the loan?"

"Now, Alwyn, that would not be very Christian, would it? Anyway, it would be against a Jew."

"I don't know, cousin. Baruch has a stellar reputation. Why should he risk all he has to clip a few coins? What if the sheriff or the baron don't believe your accusation?"

"Trust me, they won't know because Baruch will agree to my terms, and I'll keep his secret, shall we call it."

"I still don't like it. I want no part of it."

Hubert frowned at Alwyn. "You'll do as I say. If Baruch does not agree and I must accuse him, you must back me up."

"Back you up? How?"

"If necessary, you will testify Baruch gave me clipped coins. That we both examined them, and we found them that way."

Alwyn started pacing. "I am no saint, Hubert, but I don't care to be included in lies and conspiracies."

Hubert then flashed the sly smile Alwyn hated, but knew was coming. "Very well. I then might be tempted to disclose what I know about you and, what was his name? Oh, yes, Brother Thomas."

Alwyn glared at Hubert and grabbed him by the front of his robe. "Why do you always hold that over my head? I am sick of you doing that. If I had no morals, I would kill you here and now."

Hubert's face went pale with fear. "Cousin, I'm sorry. I would never reveal your secret. I only say those things to convince you to do what I know is right."

Alwyn did not let go of Hubert. "I don't believe you. You would do whatever you thought is necessary to get what you want, no matter who's harmed when they're in your way. Baruch may be next, but I will not be. Do you understand? If you ever say anything about me to anyone, I'll make sure it's the last thing you ever say!"

Hubert pushed Alwyn away. "Very well. I won't accuse Baruch of coin clipping. I'll find another way that doesn't involve you. However, I warn you cousin. Don't ever grab me or threaten me again. Don't forget who I am."

"And you don't threaten me, understand?"

Hubert knew he had mentioned the one thing that upsets Alwyn, but he did not think the priest would react so violently. *I must be careful*, Hubert realized. *Alwyn might try to kill me in such a way he would not be suspect.*

Hubert called for Brother Dominic. "Bring me a parchment, quill and ink immediately," he ordered. Hubert then began to write. When he had finished, he rolled the parchment and sealed it with wax and his ring. Then he wrote on the outside "To be opened upon the event of my death" and hid it among other parchments. Eventually, he would entrust it to someone, but exactly who, he did not know at this time. *There*, he thought, *now everyone will know about Alwyn if he does something to me. You cannot outthink me, cousin. I will always be smarter than you.*

West End – April 1268

Mordecai, Benjamin, and Rachel were at Baruch's home for Passover. It was the night of the first Seder, the retelling of the exodus from Egypt. Baruch had invited his brother, nephew, and niece, as well as Rabbi Ezra, his family, and his sister Hannah, who was there to meet Mordecai. As the rabbi and his family entered, Mordecai stood to greet them.

"Mordecai, this is my sister, Hannah."

Mordecai had not been told Hannah was coming. It had been about a year and a half since Ezra approached Mordecai with the idea. While at first Hannah had been open to meeting Mordecai, she had had second thoughts, and it was only until now she had agreed to come to Northampton from her home in Bristol.

As they were introduced, it was apparent how awkward the situation was for both of them. Hannah was about ten years younger than Mordecai. She had brown eyes and brown hair, was slightly overweight and average-looking. She also had a very sweet smile and a voice that sounded musical.

"Shalom, Mordecai. I'm pleased to meet you."

"Shalom, Hannah. I am as well to meet you. This is my son, Benjamin, and my daughter, Rachel."

"They are beautiful children. You also have another son, do you not?"

The question surprised him. "Thank you. Yes, David is older and is away."

"I see. I'm sorry it's taken me quite a while to come to West End."

"It has been a while since Rabbi Ezra told me about you. Had you changed your mind about meeting me?"

"I am afraid I did. Certainly, not due to you. I was married to my husband for ten years before he died. Even though I lost him about three years ago, I found it difficult to consider meeting someone else. I hope you won't hold that against me."

"Of course not. I lost my wife about four years ago, and I didn't think about meeting someone else until your brother mentioned you. I didn't know he was not only a rabbi but a matchmaker."

They both laughed, and their awkwardness began to decrease. It was time to come to the table for the Passover Seder. Hannah sat next to Mordecai, with Rachel sitting on his other side. Baruch started the Seder with the Kiddush, the blessing over the wine. They recited the Haggadah, the book written to celebrate the holiday by retelling the story of the Hebrews' freedom from slavery. As the youngest, Rachel asked the four questions. Baruch took a piece of matzo, the unleavened bread eaten at Passover, and hid it for the afikomen. The child who found it would receive a coin from Baruch.

As they performed the various activities one does at a Seder, taking turns reading from the Haggadah, it eventually was time for the festive meal. Baruch's cook had prepared a variety of dishes, including chicken broth with matzo balls, roast chicken, a variety of vegetables, other side dishes, and desserts.

After the meal, the Seder continued until they read the entire Haggadah. Rachel found the afikomen with Benjamin's help, since he had seen where Baruch hid it. After the Seder, Mordecai and Hannah sat together to learn more about each other. Rabbi Ezra approached Rachel and Benjamin, who were not sure how they felt about their father considering marrying someone else.

"Did you enjoy the Seder?" he asked them.

"Yes, Rabbi," Benjamin said. "It was too long," Rachel replied.

"It may seem long, but remember our people were slaves in Egypt for hundreds of years, and then wandered in the desert for forty years. I think we can stand a few hours retelling the story without complaining, don't you agree?"

They both nodded. "Yes, Rabbi, when you put it that way," Rachel said.

It was getting late and Mordecai said goodbye to Hannah. They agreed to see each other again, since she was planning to stay with her brother for a while.

While they walked home, Mordecai spotted a group of men at the end of the street. He considered doubling back to avoid them, but they had seen him and began to approach. Being too far from Baruch's to return, they continued walking until the men, numbering five, stood right in from of them.

"What do we have here?" said one, a large man with a straggly beard, dirty tunic and breeches, holding what appeared to be a half-empty mug of ale.

"Jews," said another. "It's their Passover time. They must be coming from one of their celebrations."

The first man's face changed from aloof to angry. "Jews at Passover? I heard they kill Christian boys for their blood to make some of their Passover food."

Mordecai stood in front of the man. "That's a lie. Now get out of our way so we can return home in peace."

Rachel looked afraid, and Benjamin put his arm around her to comfort her.

"A lie, is it? Not according to the priests."

"They are wrong. All those stories are lies, pure lies. Now let me pass, or the baron shall hear of it. We Jews are protected by the king and Baron Geoffrey."

One of the men took a closer look at Mordecai. "Ulric, I know this man. He's the apothecary who saved my life after I was wounded. Let him go."

Mordecai did not recognize him. Apparently, he was an off-duty man-at-arms. Mordecai had helped a number of the baron's men over the years, so it was not unusual he did not know who he was.

"Go home, Jew," Ulric said. "Gavin saved you this time, but next time you may not be so lucky. And stay away from Christian boys."

Mordecai thanked the man called Gavin, and the three of them walked briskly back to their house. When they were safely inside, Rachel began to cry. "Why do they continue to hate us, Father?" she sobbed. "I don't understand it."

"David would have fought back," Benjamin said. "He would have taught them a lesson."

Mordecai shook his head. "I told you, we cannot fight back. We are too few and have no means but the king, Baron Geoffrey, and the laws to protect us."

"We need a champion," Benjamin said. "David would have been our champion. Oh, David, why don't you come home?"

Mordecai was thinking the same thing. Why have I not heard from David? And why has he not returned home? I pray God he is safe.

York – May 1268

As the weather improved, David's training regimen increased. He had learned how to throw an axe with startling accuracy. His strength also was increasing, and he was taller since he arrived at York. After improving his archery with James, David learned how to use a sword with the baron's sword master, Oliver, who had taken over for James. While not a knight, he was extremely skilled, not only in how to attack and defend, but in teaching as well. David took to the sword almost as quickly as he did to the bow and arrow. He learned how to thrust, parry, and block with sword and shield. They practiced with wooden swords until David was skilled enough to switch to steel. Oliver reported daily to Baron Henry, who often would watch David practice to monitor his progress. As David finished for the day, Henry approached him.

"Donald, come here."

"Yes, my lord?"

"I'm very proud of you. You seem to have a natural talent for the axe, bow, sword, and shield."

"Thank you, my lord. I also have great teachers. James and Oliver have both taught me quite a bit."

"Yes, but they have taught many other men who are not nearly as skilled as you. I want to ask you something. I'm leaving in two days to see my friend Baron Geoffrey again. Would you like to accompany me?"

David hoped this day might come, and he was prepared for it. "Thank you, my lord. I would be honored to be one of your guards."

"I'll give you time to see the family you lived with while we are there."

"Thank you. It would be nice to see them."

"Good. We leave at dawn the day after tomorrow."

"My lord, is Bryce going as well?"

"Not this time. You'll be one of six men-at-arms, different from the ones I took last time. I'm a fair man, but I will not tolerate incompetence. You'd better start preparing. Go see Sir Michael. He'll provide you with a helmet, gambeson, mail, and boots. I will see you at dawn in two days."

"Thank you, my lord. I will."

David did as Henry ordered. Michael equipped him with everything the baron's other men-at-arms had. He wore them into the castle to the chamber he shared with Bryce, who was resting on his bed. He sprung up when David entered.

"Donald! I almost didn't recognize you. Why are you dressed like a man-at-arms?"

"Baron Henry is going to see Baron Geoffrey, and I'm going with the other men-at-arms."

"That's exciting. I figured he'd take you at some point, but you haven't yet completed your training."

"I wish you were going too."

"Oh," Bryce said. "I didn't know I wasn't. Did the baron tell you that?"

"I'm sorry. He did."

"I'll keep training, and perhaps next time I'll be ready to go."

"I hope so, my friend."

Two mornings later David rose early, dressed in his man-at-arms clothes and mail, took his sword and shield, and said goodbye to Bryce. He ate a light breakfast, being too excited to eat much. The baron and the rest of the men-at-arms already had gathered by the main gate. David was glad Sir Michael was going, as the two of them had become friends. Michael was impressed with David and had expressed it to Henry.

"Good morning, Donald," Henry greeted him. "Are you ready for your first assignment?"

"Yes, my lord."

"Where are your bow and arrows?"

This surprised David. "I thought men-at-arms don't carry them, my lord."

"That's true, but that's because they don't know how to use them. You do. I'll feel safer if you bring them. Hurry. We'll wait for you."

David ran back to his chamber and grabbed his bow, bowstrings, quiver, and arrows. He hurried back to the baron as fast as he could, almost stumbling down the castle stairs.

"I'm ready, my lord."

"Let's go." Henry mounted his horse, and they crossed the drawbridge and began the journey to Northampton.

This time Henry tried to stay close to his escort, even in open country. David enjoyed the march, even as the day wore on and he and the other men tired. Henry let them rest at intervals to refresh themselves with food and water. It was a sunny day, and David was full of confidence during his first experience as a man-at-arms. The other men treated him as an equal, despite his being inexperienced and several years younger than each of them.

It took a while for David to get used to wearing the helmet and mail for hours at a time. At least it was a cool spring day, which increased his comfort. The first night they slept in a stable while the baron took a room at an inn. David did not mind, since he knew he had to learn just how these men lived, and Henry made sure the men were well fed. They continued on for two more days in the same fashion, arriving at Northampton the afternoon of the third day. All the men, including David, were quite tired when they arrived. As usual, Geoffrey was there to greet his friend, and they embraced.

"Henry, welcome. I see you arrived unscathed. Is it true that on your return journey last time that was not the case?"

"Donald, come here." David hurried to Henry's side.

"Geoffrey, allow me to present Donald. He saved my life when I was ambushed by three thieves."

"So, the stories were true," Geoffrey said. "The bodies of the thieves were found in Salcey after you had left, and it was assumed they had attacked your party."

"Not exactly," Henry said. "My men had stopped to rest and, as you know, I have a tendency to get ahead of them. The three scum did ambush me, but Donald here killed two with his bow and wounded the third, who I quickly dispatched. I am forever in his debt."

Geoffrey looked David over. "You're quite young, are you not?"

"I'm sixteen, my lord."

"He's an excellent archer and is becoming very skilled with the sword as well. Come, Geoffrey, I'm tired and thirsty. Enough talk, let's go inside."

Geoffrey laughed. "I'll make sure you are well taken care of. Walter, please take care of Henry's men."

"Hello, Walter," Michael said. "It's good to see you again."

"Walter, this is Donald. He saved the baron's life."

"Welcome, Donald. You're a brave boy."

David nodded in a slight bow. "Sir Walter, I've heard of you. I'm honored to meet you."

David worried that he might be asked where he was from since the small village of Colby Hollow, where he had claimed to grow up, was near Northampton. Luckily, no one did.

"Come, everyone," Walter said. "I'll show you to your quarters and get you some food and drink."

They all followed Walter into the castle to the quarters of the men-at-arms. There were beds of newly replaced straw and benches and a table at which to sit and relax. While they waited for their refreshment, several of Geoffrey's men who were off duty joined them. The conversation for the most part was typical of most men-at-arms—what battles had the York men fought in, talk of women and booty, as well as some more personal questions. One of Geoffrey's men, Mark, looked at David.

"Where are you from, boy? You look familiar."

Michael answered for David. "He's from Coby Hollow, near here."

Mark looked confused. "Coby Hollow? I was born there but ran away as soon as I could. Who are your parents?"

David started to get nervous but answered with the story he had worked on over and over. "My parents died when I was very little. I lived with a family there who took me in." David hoped the questioning would end there.

"What family?" Mark asked gruffly.

"Arthur." David responded with the name of the only person he knew from there.

"Don't know him," Mark said. "But I've been gone a long time." His disposition softened. "Come, boy, have a mug of ale with me."

David felt relieved as the subject changed, and Mark did not inquire any further. David was not sure why Mark thought he looked familiar, as he did not remember ever seeing him before. He was certain he would have recognized him if he had.

He began to feel more comfortable among men such as these, and he could sense they were getting more comfortable with him. He was learning their coarse way of speaking, and while he did not like it, felt he had to speak that way to fit in and not to arouse any suspicions. He also had to hide his literacy, since these men were totally illiterate. If he slipped up, he may have some difficulty explaining how he learned those skills. He was extremely careful not to give any indication of his education.

David's greatest concern, however, was when the men talked about Jews. So far, no one had even the slightest inkling he was Jewish. Though he made sure he did not join into any conversation that mentioned his people, it was extremely hard for him to listen to the cruel comments and the jesting that often started after a few mugs of ale. For them it was a common topic—making fun of Jews. Especially disturbing for David was when they hoped for an opportunity to rape Jewish women or rob and kill Jewish men. They lamented that Baron Geoffrey protected Northampton's Jews. Michael told them Baron Henry did as well, primarily, they believed, because the king commanded them to. David believed none of these men was responsible for the death of his mother, but he always listened for any clue that might lead him to the culprit. He hoped to one day avenge her murder and would not hesitate if he had the chance.

The two barons were getting drunk, as the wine kept coming and they continued drinking. Their conversations ranged from news from London to the results of their latest hunts.

"Tell me, Henry, this boy Donald who saved you. How did he learn to be an archer, and how did he obtain his equipment?"

Henry took another long drink of wine. "This is good wine, Geoffrey. I'm afraid I may drink all of your stock."

Geoffrey laughed, then repeated the question.

"Geoffrey, I know what you're thinking, that he's the one who took the forester's weapons."

"Well, is he?"

"Does it matter?"

"It may. What do you know about him?"

"Not much. Just what I told you already. He is, however, a natural talent with the bow and is showing great promise with the sword as well."

Geoffrey put down his wine and looked at his friend. "Henry, I'm very glad he saved you, but I would like to know what happened to the forester. Remember he was my cousin."

"I remember. Very well. You may send for him if you will keep his secret and let him stay with me."

"Agreed, as long as there was no foul play."

Geoffrey called for Cyrus to fetch David. After a few minutes, David entered the great hall and approached the two barons, bowing. "My lords."

Henry spoke first. "Donald, I want you to tell Geoffrey how you found your bow and arrows."

David could not contain a look of shock and fear. Henry noticed it and calmed him. "Don't worry, Donald. Geoffrey only wants to know what happened. I know you didn't do any harm to anyone except the outlaws."

David took a deep breath. "That's the truth, my lord. I swear it. I was walking in the forest and found the forester dead with no wounds or anything. I had always wanted to be an archer, so I made a quick decision to keep the weapons."

"I see. Why didn't you report this?"

"I was afraid if I did, I would lose the weapons and perhaps be accused of causing his death."

"So, you practiced in the forest in secret until the ambush?"

"Yes, my lord. Please forgive me if I committed any wrongdoing. I meant no harm."

"Very well. Since you saved the life of my dear friend, and I know Ronald's death was not caused by any attack, I forgive you and will honor your secret. Henry is quite fond of you, and I can understand why. I like you too, Donald."

David bowed deeply. "I am grateful, my lord. I only wish to be of service to Baron Henry and do him proud."

"I believe you shall. You may go." David bowed again and left the hall.

"So," Geoffrey began, "now that mystery has been solved. However, I cannot tell the sheriff, who is still trying to discover who took them, since I promised you I won't."

"You may tell him you know who took them, that the matter is closed, and he should not continue looking."

"Yes. I certainly can do that."

"Thank you, my friend. It's important to me. I'm certain Donald had nothing to do with the forester's death. People do die under circumstances that cannot be explained."

Geoffrey thought about Abbot Hubert and the poisons Mordecai had given him but had not been used and smiled. "Yes, they do. Yes, they do."

Chapter Eighteen

West End – May 1268

David walked briskly through Northampton, wearing his helmet, and keeping his head down as much as possible to avoid being recognized. Townspeople were used to seeing men-at-arms at all times, so no one paid attention to him. As he entered West End, almost everyone he passed he knew, although they too minded their own business and did not care about this soldier. Finally, he arrived at his house. The door was unlocked and he slowly opened it. His father, brother, and sister all were startled to see a man-at-arms trying to enter their home. Mordecai started to yell at this stranger, until the soldier removed his helmet.

"David! It's you!" They all ran up and hugged him. Then they looked incredulously at him, dressed in mail, carrying a sword, and wearing a crucifix, since he had forgotten to take it off.

"What's happened to you?" his father asked. "Are you now a Christian?"

"No, Father, I am not a Christian. Let's sit and I will tell you everything, but you must promise never to tell anyone. I could be imprisoned or executed if you do." They promised in unison never to repeat to anyone what he was about to tell them.

The three of them sat spellbound as David shared his story. They knew about the three dead thieves, and Mordecai told David he was not surprised it had been him.

"Father, did you know about the bow and arrows?" David asked.

"I suspected as such, but I did not want to have you followed. Benjamin tried to get details from Avram, but he wouldn't divulge anything except you were fine."

"Avram is a good friend. I'd like to see him."

"David," Rachel began, "you said you have to live as a Christian, but you're not a Christian. I don't know what that means."

David hugged his sister. "It means I am pretending to be a Christian. I'm still a Jew and will always be a Jew."

"But how?" Benjamin asked.

Mordecai looked sternly at his oldest child. "You have eaten forbidden foods, have you not? You have broken the Sabbath, the High Holidays, and most likely many more of our laws as well. Your mother would be so ashamed, as I am."

"Father, I meant no disrespect. I had no choice. When Baron Henry made his offer to me, I had to accept. It was the one chance to possibly become a champion of our people. I couldn't come and tell you. You probably wouldn't have let me go, and how could I explain to Baron Henry I lived in West End? Please, Father, don't be angry with me."

"I still don't understand how you've pretended to be a Christian all this time without anyone becoming suspicious."

"It hasn't been that difficult. I'm very observant and able to learn quickly. I pick up small details and know how to talk to them, especially the men-at-arms. The hardest part was to remember I told them my name was Donald. I thought that sounded Christian."

"So obviously, no one has seen what would give you away immediately."

Benjamin smiled at this, as he understood, but Rachel did not. "Seen what, Father?" she asked. Before Mordecai could answer, Benjamin whispered the answer in her ear, and she giggled.

"No, Father. They don't bathe very often, and when I do, I am very careful to do it alone. I have to be extremely careful."

"How long can you stay, David?"

"Since I told them I came from Coby Hollow, I must return by nightfall tomorrow. Father, can you send Benjamin to bring Avram here?"

"I don't think that would be wise. It's not that I don't trust Avram, but it would look strange for him to ask Avram to come here. With what excuse? I understand how much you would like to see him, but I think it may be too dangerous."

"Very well, Father. Can we eat soon? I miss our meals together."

"Certainly. Come, children. Let's prepare a meal for your brother to welcome him home."

David was still wearing his man-at-arms clothes and mail. After getting help to remove the mail, he went into his old room and found some of his clothes. However, nothing fit him anymore. He was not the same boy who left West End not so long ago.

After a meal of chicken soup, roast chicken with vegetables, and some sweets for dessert, Mordecai sent Benjamin and Rachel to bed so he could talk more to David.

"David. What do you think you can accomplish? Even if you become a great warrior, you are only one man. It would take an army of other Jews like you to defend and protect our people."

David sighed and nodded in agreement. "I know, Father. I am not so naïve to think I can change everything. I just want to show them our people can fight and we must be respected and not ridiculed. I also want to avenge mother's murder, as I've told you."

"David, my David," Mordecai said, sighing. "Perhaps one man can change the world. Abraham did. Moses did. Solomon did. However, you are not anywhere near them. Even if you complete your training and become a knight, you never could reveal your identity. And what if someone recognizes you? Aren't the risks too great?"

"Yes, Father. I know the risks, but I don't care. I want to do this. I'm a good swordsman and an excellent archer. I've earned the respect of Baron Henry and many of his men."

"I imagine you may have made a few enemies as well, am I not correct?"

"None that I know of. Since I saved Baron Henry's life, he warned all his men I was not to be mistreated in any way or he would punish them. The baron wanted to be sure none of the six men who accompanied him from Northampton on that day would harm me for embarrassing them."

"David, you are my oldest child, and you know I love you very much. I cannot stop you from this foolish endeavor of yours. Anyway, I believe you are too deep into it already. You probably would have to leave England if you decided not to return to York."

"I must return, Father. I must. I will complete my training, and someday I will make you proud of me for standing up to the abuse and tyranny our people suffer. Perhaps I can get other Jewish boys and men to join me. Then I can teach them what I've learned, and they can teach others, and so forth."

Mordecai shook his head. "It's a dream, David. A dream. A dream that will never come true. Your motives are commendable, at least when it comes to defending our people, but unrealistic. I will not speak of this again. I will pray you will stay safe and won't be discovered. I also will pray you never forget you are a Jew, and one day you will stop masquerading as a Christian and will practice your Judaism again. That is what your mother, may she rest in peace, and I would wish for."

"I will Father. I promise you. If I could live openly as a Jew now, I would." He paused for a moment. "Father, are you angry with me for all I have done against our teachings and customs? I know I have committed great sins. I am sure the rabbis would forbid me from practicing Judaism. If they can excommunicate someone like the Christians do, I am sure they would."

"David, that's my greatest dilemma about what you have done and are doing. I made it no secret that if you had the opportunity to become a warrior, I would let you. I must admit I said that with the belief it would never, ever happen. I now have learned one always should expect the unexpected. Yes, you have broken some of our most sacred laws. I am sure if they knew, the rabbis and elders would enact herem, our form of excommunication. It shuns one from the community. I certainly hope they never do. I'll pray for you as I always have."

David hugged his father. "Thank you. I want to please you, but I need to follow my destiny, and I believe God has given me this opportunity, so I must pursue it."

David noticed tears in his father's eyes. "Then make us proud, David. Make us proud."

Hedgestone Priory – May 1268

Abbot Hubert walked into the refectory, where Bartholomew sat munching on a small piece of bread and sipping on a cup of water. Hubert had not spoken to him very often and had never asked the old prior for advice on anything. Bartholomew and Father Ambrose had not hidden their dislike of him. It was better for everyone if they avoided each other as much as they could.

"Hello, Bartholomew." Hubert greeted him in an unusually friendly tone.

"Abbot," Bartholomew answered coldly.

"May I join you?"

Bartholomew nodded, and Hubert sat down across from him.

"I see you are well. I'm glad."

Bartholomew did not hide his feelings. "Of course I'm well. I could have remained prior, and I believe the priory would have been better off."

"You're not pleased with the improvements I have made?"

"They are cosmetic. While I admit that on the surface Hedgestone looks better, the monks are fearful of you. They are trying to make your ventures succeed but are worried of your wrath if they fail. They also know that while you have forbidden us to even speak with the Jews, you do so as you wish."

"The monks will do as I say, as will you. It is not for you or anyone to question my motives or me. I do not have to explain myself to anyone except the bishop. Don't forget that."

"Did you wish to speak to me about something?"

"Yes, I do. I would like your assistance. I need to negotiate a second loan with Baruch, and I would like you to attend the meeting to support me."

Bartholomew made no effort to hide his surprise. "My support? What possible help could I be?"

"Do you know Baruch?"

"No, I don't. I met his brother Mordecai, but not him."

"But you do have a strong relationship with the Jews, do you not?"

Bartholomew wondered if Hubert was trying to bait him. "I used to, as you know, but not since you became prior and stopped all interactions with them."

Hubert smirked. "So, you've never had any contact with them since my edict?"

Before Bartholomew could answer, Hubert continued. "No matter. I believe your presence could help me."

"Why should I help you? Since you arrived, you have done everything you could to reverse the good work we were doing. You have consistently intimidated the monks and sabotaged the inroads we were making with the Jews. You forced me from my duties of serving God that gave me deep inspirational comfort. You made me feel like a prisoner in my own priory."

"My dear Bartholomew. Please believe me that was never my intention. You know Bishop Basil gave me an assignment, and I must complete it in my own way from his directions. If you do not want to help for my sake, you should for the bishop's."

"Humph," Bartholomew grunted. "And why should I do that? Basil isn't even my bishop. All our work is supposed to be for God and the Church, not for any individual. I have always practiced that. I'm afraid you and he are more interested in your personal gains."

Bartholomew stood and put his face directly in front of Hubert's. "I may be old, and I may have been relieved of my duties, but I will not compromise what I believe in for you, the bishop, or anyone." He stormed out of the refectory.

Hubert laughed quietly to himself. The old fool, he thought. No wonder he spent so many years here in this hole. Anyway, I don't need him. I don't need anyone, not even Alwyn.

West End – May 1268

David arose well rested, happy to have slept in his own bed for the first time in quite a while. He figured he would have to stay in the house until he returned to Baron Henry later in the day. The baron was willing to let him visit his family, but only for a short while. David wanted to be cautious as well, fearful he could be discovered. He spent the day visiting with his father, Benjamin, and Rachel. They made David tell the same stories about his experiences several times, never seeming to tire of them. As the day wore on and it was late in the afternoon, David dressed in his man-at-arms clothes, mail, and helmet. He hugged all of them several times. "Be healthy and safe," he said. "I hope to see you again soon."

"You do the same," they all said, as he walked into the street. He hurried back to the castle, keeping his head down until he was past West End. He arrived at the castle gate, where the guards greeted him. He made his way to the quarters of Geoffrey's men-at-arms, where Michael and the others sat drinking mugs of ale. "Donald. You've returned. Come, have a mug with us."

"Gladly, my friends." He sat next to Michael while one of the men filled a mug for him.

"How was your visit?" Michael asked.

David did not want to talk too much about it, since they believed he was seeing the fictitious people in Coby Hollow he had told them about.

"It was fine. They are well and were happy to see me."

The conversation then changed to the women in the castle and Northampton the men had seen. While ordered to remain in the castle during the day, Henry permitted them to go to a tavern in town the previous night, with an upstairs brothel they all took advantage of.

"Donald, you should have been with us. There's a redhead who is perfect for you. I hope we can return there before we must leave," Michael said.

"Sorry I missed it," David lied. He had not thought about the possibility of the men going to a brothel. How could he not join the other men if they did return there? He would have to pretend to be sick. There was no other way. Luckily, it was raining fairly hard, so they all stayed in the castle that night.

The next day Baron Henry summoned David to the great hall with his bow and arrows. David entered, bowing to Henry and Baron Geoffrey, noticing an archery target had been set up at the end of the hall.

"So, here again is your savior," Geoffrey said. "He's a fine young lad. He will make a good man-at-arms."

"He wants to be a knight. I think he has the talent to become one," Henry said. "Donald, I want you to show Geoffrey your archery skill."

"Yes, my lord." David took an arrow from his quiver, notched it, took his position, pulled back on the bowstring and shot. The target was about thirty paces away, and the arrow landed dead center.

"Very nice," Geoffrey commented. "Try again from ten more paces back."

David did as the baron instructed. The second arrow did not hit dead center but was still in the center circle. David shot three more arrows, and they all landed in the center circle.

"I'm quite impressed, Henry. Donald, how did you become such a fine archer?"

"The baron's man James taught me."

"Donald," Geoffrey began, "I've thought about what you told me, how you found my cousin Ronald, the forester, dead in Salcey. However, there is one thing that puzzles me."

David became nervous. He thought this matter had been closed. "What is that, my lord?"

"It was reported to me near where his body was discovered were two sets of footprints that appeared to have been made by boys probably about your age. I think you told me you had been alone when you found him and took the weapons."

"That's correct, my lord."

"Do you swear by Our Lord Jesus you're telling the truth?"

"I swear, my lord, in Jesus' name, I was alone. I cannot explain what was reported to you."

"Very well. I trust you would not commit a sacrilege using Our Lord's name. You may go."

"Well, Geoffrey," Henry said, "are you convinced? I hope you'll stop doubting Donald. For me, at least, because the matter should be closed."

"Henry, I believe him, but there were still two distinct sets of footprints, one larger than the other, in a remote place. No one goes there, I understand. Could Donald be protecting someone? I would just like to know the truth is all."

"You have been told the truth. I'm sure of it. Now, let's talk of tomorrow's hunt. I'd love some fresh meat."

Hedgestone Priory – May 1268

Baruch sat across from Abbot Hubert in the same small room where they previously had met. He speculated Hubert was going to press hard for the second loan, and to ask for much more than he had originally said. Hubert initiated the usual small talk, and then got right to the point.

"Baruch, tell me, have I not performed exactly, even better than what we had agreed upon?"

"Yes, you have, surprisingly. To be honest, I thought you wouldn't be able to honor our agreement."

"I should be insulted at that remark, but I understand. I hope I have alleviated all your fears and we may negotiate the next loan."

"I'm listening," Baruch said, his voice low and unemotional.

"After doing a great deal of thought and considering all aspects, I have decided the three-step plan will take too much time, and a two-step plan will be better for both of us."

"Better for both of us? I don't think so. Nothing has changed in my mind."

Hubert began pacing. "I want one thousand pounds as the final loan. I will not ask for any more."

"With no guarantor, I assume?"

"That is correct. I have upheld my part of our agreement in good faith. I expect you to do the same."

Baruch stood. "Apparently, you have a very short memory. I thought I made myself quite clear that without a guarantor, I will not loan you anywhere near that amount. In fact, we're done. I expect you to continue to repay the balance of the fifty pounds of our agreement. Good day, Hubert."

Hubert moved to block Baruch. "Not so fast. I think you will loan me the rest, and at very attractive rates."

"You are mad. Goodbye, Abbot."

"Am I, coin clipper?"

Baruch stared at Hubert. "What did you say?"

"You heard me."

Baruch knew what this could mean. If Hubert was willing to falsely accuse him of coin clipping, he was capable of almost anything.

"I have never clipped a coin in my life, and you know it. How dare you try to use a false accusation to force me to give you what you want."

"I have not accused you of anything, yet. Though it would be easy to do and give the sheriff some, shall we say, evidence to support the claim."

"You're a fool, Hubert. I should report you to the sheriff."

Hubert laughed. "Report me? Who do you think he'll believe—an abbot or a Jew?"

"I know the sheriff, and I believe he's an honest man."

Hubert looked slyly at Baruch. "Perhaps. While he may believe you, I am sure the townspeople will not."

"Now you threaten to stir up the townspeople against me? Goodbye, Hubert. We're done here. I want no further dealings with you. I expect the remainder of the payments under your obligation to be made on time."

Baruch stormed out and left the priory. Alwyn had been standing outside and watched as Baruch hurried out. He could not help but notice the angry look on the moneylender's face. Alwyn found Hubert still in the room.

"What happened, Hubert? Baruch ran out of here looking quite upset."

"Close the door and I will tell you. However, you must swear never to repeat anything to anyone about this. And that includes Bishop Basil."

Alwyn felt he had no choice. "I swear I will never repeat this."

"Very well. But remember, I still hold your secret, and will divulge it if you renege."

Alwyn nodded.

"I realized Baruch was never going to give me a loan as large as I asked for, and large enough to please the bishop. So, I threatened to expose him as a coin clipper if he did not give it to me."

"I cannot believe you did that. Baruch is respected by Baron Geoffrey, the sheriff, and, as I understand it, all who have done business with him. Why should anyone believe you?"

"Alwyn, I am not a fool. I have evidence. Clipped coins Baruch gave me from the loan."

"That's not evidence. Anyone could have clipped them. In fact, you probably did it yourself."

"Perhaps you clipped them for me." Hubert suddenly stopped, realizing he had gone way too far. "Alwyn, I'm sorry. I didn't mean to make you angry or involve you. I must be successful, and I thought I could intimidate Baruch. Instead I made him angry and fearful of me."

"No, he's not fearful. He lost all faith and trust in you. No man wants to be threatened, especially of being wrongfully accused of committing a serious crime."

"You're right. Do you think if I apologize he will forgive me?"

"Hubert, humility is not one of your strong points, I'm afraid."

Hubert laughed. "For once I agree with you. Alwyn. I must find another way."

West End – May 1268

Mordecai had received a message that his presence was required at the castle. One of the men-at-arms had fallen ill, and his condition was worsening. As he walked down Green Street, he saw Avram. "Shalom, Mordecai. Have you heard from David?"

"Shalom, Avram. I hope you and your family are well."

"Mordecai, you didn't answer my question. Have you heard from David?"

"Yes, I have, and he is well."

"I'm glad to hear it. Did he write you? How did you hear from him?"

Mordecai hesitated, as he did not know how to avoid telling him. He motioned for Avram to follow him to an alcove so they could speak more privately.

"Avram, David is here in Northampton."

"Here?" Avram exclaimed.

"Keep your voice down. He came to see us, and wanted to see you, but I was afraid it was too dangerous and risky for him. Can you understand that?"

Mordecai told Avram what he knew about David's life at York, intentionally leaving out the details of his pretending to be a Christian. The fewer who knew about the sins David had committed to hide his identity, the better.

"So, he is here with Baron Henry as a man-at-arms? Will you see him again?"

"No, I'm afraid not. The baron gave him a little time to see what he was told was David's adopted family in Coby Hollow, but he must remain with the other men-at-arms. I believe they will be returning to York soon."

"Thank you for telling me. I promise I won't say anything to anyone."

"It's very important you don't. Just one mistake could cost David his life."

They said goodbye, and Mordecai continued on to the castle. The ill man-at-arms was one of Geoffrey's men, not Henry's. Mordecai previously had treated him and was hoping he could at least get a glimpse of David, but when he arrived at the castle, he learned David had accompanied Henry on his hunt with Geoffrey, along with several men-at-arms. David showed his skill at archery in the hunt, where he killed a boar and two ducks. While he had never hunted before, he did not find it difficult. His archery skill was evident in the ease with which he was able to kill the prey, especially the boar. However, the boar had gored one of Henry's men-at-arms, and he required medical attention. While Mordecai completed his treatment of the first man, two of Geoffrey's guards brought the wounded man into their quarters, accompanied by David. They looked at each other, neither acknowledging the other. As Mordecai treated the wounded man, David stayed back, out of the way. After Mordecai cleaned the wound and closed it, one of the guards asked David to escort the apothecary out of the castle.

"David," Mordecai said in a low voice, "it's very strange to be walking with you here and you dressed like that."

"I'm Donald," he answered. "Please only call me that here."

"Yes, of course. When are you returning to York?"

"Baron Henry has not said. I imagine soon. Can his man travel?"

"No. He should be left behind until he has healed."

They reached the main gate of the castle. In order not to raise the slightest suspicion, David merely thanked the apothecary for his services, turned and walked back to the guards' quarters. How strange that was, he thought. My father treating a wounded man-at-arms and me escorting him.

West End – May 1268

Baruch had come to see his brother. He was very upset about what had happened that day and wanted his brother's counsel. Baruch related what Hubert had said.

Mordecai put his hand on his brother's hand. "I'm worried, Baruch. This abbot is ruthless if he would even threaten you. Coin clipping is a serious offense. Many have been imprisoned and hanged for it, even when innocent."

"I'm aware of that. I may tell the sheriff what he said."

"Can you trust the sheriff?"

"I think so. These days it's hard to know who you can trust. Tell me, have you heard from David?"

"Baruch, in confidence, I tell you he's here in Northampton." Mordecai related everything that had happened.

"I'm not surprised," Baruch said. "I felt all along he was the one who had the weapons, and when he mysteriously went away after the three thieves were killed, it made perfect sense to me. I won't say anything. If you see him again, please tell him I'm proud of him, and I support what he's doing."

"I will. But I don't think I will see him again for a while. He'll be returning to York shortly."

Chapter Nineteen

Northampton – May 1268

"Men, I have some good news," declared Sir Michael. "Baron Geoffrey has ordered a festival be held in three days, and we'll stay to enjoy it. The festival will include contests among the knights and men-at-arms. Donald, Baron Henry wants you to win the archery tournament for him."

The news excited the men. They were enjoying their stay in Northampton and were hoping to get back to the brothel. David, however, did not like this announcement. To shoot in the archery tournament meant there was a good chance he would be recognized, if not by any Jews in attendance, but by Gentiles who might know him. He did not know if there was any way he could get out of it. He would have to try to stay out of sight as much as possible.

"Donald," Michael continued, "Baron Henry wants you to practice as much as you can. Baron Geoffrey wagered his archer will beat you, and Baron Henry hates to lose."

"I'll do my best for the baron."

As preparations were being made for the festival, David practiced for several hours each day. He did not worry about his skill, but about his nervousness of being seen in public. While he would be wearing his helmet and man-at-arms clothes, he could not get it out of his head that before the end of the festival he could be in trouble. The night before the tournament, he was resting in bed when Michael came to see him.

"Donald, are you ready to make us proud? You're the best archer we have, you know."

"Thank you, Michael."

"Come. We are all going back to the Swords Point tavern for ale and some female company."

David thought quickly. "Michael, tonight I had better stay here and rest. If I drink too much or in any way am not well rested, I won't be able to shoot well."

"Perhaps you're right. We'll go back tomorrow night to celebrate your victory."

David did not reply. He laid back on the bed as Michael left.

As news of the baron's order to hold a festival on such short notice spread, there was excitement in Northampton. Most of the Jews did not plan to attend. They tried not to mix with the Christian population, not wanting to suffer the usual humiliations. While these were primarily verbal and often due to too much drinking, violence often would occur.

Avram heard the news and went right to Mordecai's house. "Mordecai, have you heard? Baron Geoffrey is holding a festival with an archery tournament, and Baron Henry's man Donald is to compete against Geoffrey's man. Donald is really David, right?"

"Yes, Avram, I have heard. And, yes, Donald is our David. I'm very worried that someone will recognize him, and he'll be in trouble."

"You will attend, won't you?"

"Yes, I feel we must attend, although we must stay as obscure as possible. We cannot let anyone suspect that David is who he is. Please make sure you do the same."

"I will, Mordecai."

Hedgestone Priory – May 1268

Alwyn had just returned from Northampton with Brother Gabriel. He went right to Hubert's chamber and knocked. Hubert was taking his afternoon nap.

"What is it?" he yelled, irritated at being awakened.

Alwyn entered. "Hubert, I have just returned from Northampton. Baron Geoffrey is holding a festival tomorrow with tournaments and contests."

Hubert had not attended any festivals since he arrived. "A festival on such short notice? Why would Geoffrey do that?"

"Apparently, Baron Henry of York is visiting and has a skilled archer with him. Geoffrey wants everyone to see his own archer defeat him."

"Alwyn, I think we and all the brothers should go. They've been kept in the priory too long, and it will be good for them. Please make the announcement."

The next day turned out to be a beautiful spring one. It was cool in the morning, but warmed nicely as the day wore on, the sun shining in an almost cloudless sky. The festival was held in the meadow just outside the town. Stalls had been set up with vendors selling everything from various foods to pottery and glassware. The crowds were large, as everyone was happy to take a break from their mundane lives. The tournament activities would begin in the afternoon. David reluctantly accompanied the other men-at-arms as they browsed the stalls, always worried he might be recognized. He did see one man he remembered he had fought with a couple of years before, but with David dressed as a man-at-arms, the man merely walked past him without even a glance. David looked around for any Jews he might know but did not see any at all. Maybe they will not attend, he thought, and I won't have anything to worry about.

Mordecai, Benjamin, Rachel, and Avram arrived at the festival, staying away from the crowds as much as they could. For the tournament, Mordecai said they should find places in the rear.

Hubert, Alwyn, and all the monks except Gabriel, who was ill, also arrived. Hubert had instructed the monks to enjoy themselves, but not to do anything to embarrass him or they would be punished. Hubert strolled through the stalls, greeting everyone. Alwyn accompanied him as usual. They occasionally would stop at a stall and buy something to eat. Everyone eagerly waited for the competitions to begin. Hubert and Alwyn then arrived at the tournament field and took seats in the front.

Avram left Mordecai and his family and strolled through the stalls by himself, ignored for the most part, although several times someone gave him a push, saying, "Out of my way, Jew." He made his way to the tournament field and decided to sit near the front. He saw two churchmen sitting in front of him but thought nothing of it.

Benjamin saw Avram sitting up close, and asked Mordecai if he could join him. His father said yes, and Benjamin ran up to Avram, slapping him on the back.

"Avram, can I sit next to you?"

"I suppose so. Where are your father and sister?"

"They're in the back. Father preferred it that way. I wonder if Uncle Baruch is here. I'm sure he'd want to see David."

"Be quiet, Benjamin. We must not say his name."

Hubert, who was sitting in front of the two boys, overheard the mention of Baruch's name, and turned around to see who had said it. He kept silent, trying to hear every word they said.

After a while, the crowd filled the seats and the grassy areas around the field. Baron Geoffrey, Lady Catherine and Baron Henry arrived and took their seats under the canopy in the center of the stand. Geoffrey called for the events to begin. From one end of the field a parade of knights on horseback, men-at-arms carrying swords and shields, and a group of men with bows and arrows circled the field. When David walked past, Benjamin could not contain his excitement. "Look, Avram. There's David."

Avram again tried to quiet him. "Benjamin, I told you be silent. No one is supposed to know who he is."

Hubert heard every word and became very interested in those two, especially Benjamin. What is going on, he wondered? Who is the one he called David, and why would he be on the field? Is David a Jew? If so, how could a Jew be part of the tournament? Hubert realized he might be gaining some very interesting and potentially useful information. He looked at Alwyn, who appeared totally oblivious to it all.

As the parade circled the field, David tried not to look around but found it hard not to. As he marched past Avram and Benjamin, he nodded slightly, acknowledging them. This was not lost on Hubert, who began studying his every move.

The group completed their entry march, and the tournament began. First was the joust. David was enthralled with all of it. Only a few years ago he had been here watching such an event with his father. Now he was on the field, soon to be a part of it.

The first joust was between Sir Paul of Bristol against a visiting Spanish knight, Sir Rodolfo de Madrid. David could not take his eyes off them. They were not using sharp-tipped lances, but blunted ones. As the two knights galloped towards each other, there soon was a clash of lance against shield. Sir Paul's lance shattered, but he remained on his horse. Rodolfo leaned to the side but also managed to stay upright. David marveled at their warhorses. They were huge, and so well trained they obeyed their knights without hesitation.

The match was declared a draw, and the two knights waited for the next pair. This went on for a while, until there were only four knights left—Sir Paul, Sir Rodolfo, Sir Keir de Courteney, and Sir Edward of Nottingham. One knight, Sir Eugene de Augustine, was injured and taken away. When it was over, Baron Geoffrey was not happy the Spaniard Rodolfo had won the day, since it made the English knights look bad. The crowd, however, did not care, and cheered for the victor.

David watched as a group of swordsmen entered the field. Upon the baron's command, they began to fight. The swords were not wooden, and care was taken not to kill or wound. Normally, many knights would take part in the melee. Due to the festival and tournament being announced only days before, the number of knights participating was smaller than usual.

The crowd was getting eager for the main event—the archery tournament. After the melee, luckily with only a few minor wounds, the targets were placed and it was time for the archery contest to begin. Everyone listened intently as the Marshal announced the contestants. However, no one listened more closely than Hubert. As each archer's name was called, he stepped forward. When the one he had heard as being David answered to Donald of Coby Hollow, Hubert's suspicions grew. He planned to watch this Donald very closely.

There were ten archers in all, and five targets. Eliminations occurred as the targets were moved further back and there were more center misses. Eventually only two archers remained—David and Baron Geoffrey's man, Richard de Tal.

"Well, Geoffrey, it looks like it's just between our men," Henry said. "Shall we increase the wager?"

Geoffrey gulped his wine. "What are we up to, fifty pounds? All right, let's make it one hundred "

"Agreed," Henry said. "One hundred it is."

Everyone watched as Richard notched his arrow, aimed, and shot. The target was one hundred paces away. The arrow flew straight and landed in the bottom of the center circle. David then took an arrow, inspected it first to be sure it was true, notched it, aimed, and released. It landed dead center. The crowd cheered. Richard looked over at his opponent. "Nicely done, Donald. You definitely have a talent."

"Thank you, Richard. Your fame as an archer is well known. I am honored to compete against you." Richard had been Geoffrey's archer for several years. A seasoned warrior, he was almost forty years old, and had won many contests for his master. Today, however, he was worried this young man might defeat him.

The target was moved back another ten paces. This time David was to shoot first. While his arrow did not hit the exact center, it did hit the center circle. Richard's second shot also hit near David's. Again, the target was moved back another ten paces. The crowd was silent as Richard pulled back on his bowstring and released. The arrow missed the center circle and landed slightly below it. David took a deep breath as he stepped up to the firing line. He took an arrow, inspected it, and decided to use another instead. He carefully notched it, pulled back the bowstring, aimed, and released. All he heard was the crowd letting out a tremendous roar. The two men who had been moving the target started carrying it. As they got closer, David saw his arrow had landed perfectly in the center. He had won.

"Well done again, my young friend," Richard said, patting David on the back. "You have defeated me, and I must say that doesn't happen very often."

"Many thanks, Richard. I don't know what to say."

Even with the cheering, Hubert could hear the two boys behind him. "He did it, Avram. He did it!" Avram again reminded Benjamin to stifle his excitement, although he was beaming as his best friend, a Jew, had defeated Baron Geoffrey's famed archer.

"Well, Geoffrey," Henry said, "it looks like you owe me one hundred pounds."

Geoffrey was in a foul mood, as his drinking coupled with losing the wager did not make him a happy man. "Henry, what a fine archer you have," Catherine said. "What do you know about him? The Marshal said he's from Coby Hollow. That's near here at the edge of Salcey, is it not?"

Henry was uncomfortable with her questions, as he wanted to keep the secret of David's finding the weapons. He decided to answer her simply.

"He lived with a family there after his parents died. He came with me to York after he saved my life. That's all I know. Let's eat, shall we? I'm famished."

The two barons, Catherine, and the rest of their entourage left the stands and returned to the castle. As the crowd dispersed, Hubert kept a watchful eye on the two boys. He was especially interested when he saw Benjamin approach an older Jew whom he recognized and embrace him. *This Donald is a Jew. But how could a Jew become an archer for Baron Henry? He is wearing a crucifix. Is he pretending to be a Christian? If so, I may be able to use this but I must be sure.*

Benjamin could not control his excitement, though he did keep his voice down. "Father, did you see? My brother won the archery tournament. My brother. We have our own champion!"

"Quiet! We must not let anyone suspect he's from our family. Let's return home, and we can talk about it there." Mordecai, Benjamin, and Rachel left the field, and began to walk back to West End, not noticing the two churchmen walking behind them. Mordecai heard a voice addressing him. "Aren't you Baruch's brother?"

Mordecai stopped and turned around. "Who is asking?"

"Remember me, Mordecai? Abbot Hubert?"

"Of course I remember you. Yes, Baruch is my brother. Why?"

"I've done business with Baruch. Has he ever mentioned me to you?"

"No, he doesn't discuss his business with me. I also have not seen him for a while." Mordecai did not want Hubert to know he was aware of Hubert's threat.

"Mordecai, do you have any children other than these two?" He did not want to answer.

"Abbot, you are the one who removed Prior Bartholomew and commanded the monks not to even speak to Jews. You are breaking your own rules. I don't wish to continue this." Mordecai turned and with Benjamin and Rachel hurried away from the churchmen.

"What was that about?" Alwyn asked.

"Nothing. At least, not yet."

Northampton – May 1268

Baron Geoffrey recovered from his foul mood and ordered a great feast be held in honor of Baron Henry and Donald for his victory. David returned to his quarters, and the men all cheered him with mugs of ale. They spoke of the upcoming feast, and that Donald could have his pick of any of the girls at the castle. "They'll all be willing to spread their legs for the champion," Michael told him. "You'll be fighting them off, so give us your discards." They all laughed and David laughed with them, worried again that he could not be put in such a position.

That night as David entered the great hall, Baron Henry called him over. "My lord. Baron Geoffrey. Lady Catherine," he said, bowing.

"Donald, you made me proud today, as well as one hundred pounds richer." Geoffrey frowned and grunted at Henry's statement. "I want to reward you." Henry handed David a purse. "There are twenty pounds in there. My gift to you for today."

David bowed again. "My lord is too kind. I'm pleased to serve you as best I can."

David returned to his table, where he enjoyed a variety of foods, wine, and ale. He figured if he were drunk he would not have to worry about being put into a situation with any of the castle's maids. One, however, kept serving him, leaning very close, with her ample breasts half-exposed. Michael and the other men kept prompting him to go take her, but he kept holding off until he eventually passed out on the table. Michael and one of the other men carried him back to his quarters and put him to bed. They joked that he again had missed another opportunity for female companionship. They, however, would take advantage of it whenever they could.

Hedgestone Priory – May 1268

Hubert considered what he had learned this day, believing this Donald is not who he pretends to be, but he needed to be sure. He summoned Brother Andrew.

"Andrew, I want you to do something for me. Do you know where Coby Hollow is?"

"Yes. It's a small village at the edge of Salcey. I passed through it once returning from a pilgrimage."

"I want you to go there first thing tomorrow and inquire if there was a boy named Donald who used to live there after his parents had died. Come right back after you have questioned everyone, and report only to me. And tell no one about this."

"Must I go alone through the forest?"

"Very well. Take Brother Dominic with you. Make sure he keeps silent as well."

Alone again, Hubert thought about his plan. *If it is true, and Donald is David, Baruch's nephew, Baruch will give me the loan or I will expose him.*

The next day Hubert watched the two monks leave at first light for Coby Hollow. Hubert knew it would take most of the day until they returned. The hours passed slowly for him until at last he saw them returning. He motioned for Andrew to follow him to his chamber.

"Well, what did you learn?"

"No one ever heard of a Donald, let alone someone who had lived with a family after his parents had died."

"I see. Thank you. You must be tired, so go rest and refresh yourself."

Hubert smiled. *I knew it,* he said to himself. *It was all a lie. Does Baruch know what David is doing? I did not see him at the tournament.*

He may not be aware of this deception and may not believe me. However, if I threaten to go to Baron Henry with this accusation, as his uncle he cannot take the risk. I have him. He must cooperate with me now. He must.

Northampton – May 1268

David awoke with a massive headache, feeling awful. While he was sorry he drank so much, at least he again avoided being betrayed by his circumcision. He saw Michael standing over him.

"Good morning, my friend. Feeling a bit ill today?"

David moaned. "Michael, I feel terrible. My head is pounding."

"You'll be better soon. I brought you some food and water. No ale or wine for you for a while."

"Thank you. When do we return to York?"

"Tomorrow, I believe. Baron Henry is eager to get back."

"I'm not ready to get up. Let me rest some more."

David laid a while, thinking about his success yesterday. He had defeated a famous archer. He was training to hopefully become a knight. His father knew about what he was doing and was as supportive as he could be. So far, everything was going well. However, he reminded himself he must never let his guard down and stay vigilant at all times. So far, no one in Northampton or West End had recognized him. His secret was safe. And he was determined to do whatever was necessary to keep it that way.

West End – May 1268

Baruch was examining his accounts. Only three were late with their payments, and he had given each of them a little more time. They were good, hardworking people, so he did not worry. He heard a knock at his door and rose to answer it, since his housekeeper was ill. He was surprised to see Abbot Hubert standing there.

"Hello, Baruch. I am sorry to come unannounced, but I must speak to you."

"Hubert, I told you I did not want to do business with you after your threat." Baruch began to close the door on him.

"I think you will for your nephew David's sake."

"David? What's he got to do with you?"

"If you let me in, I'll explain."

Reluctantly, Baruch opened the door and Hubert entered.

"May I sit down?" Baruch motioned him to do so and sat across from him.

"What's this about, Hubert?"

"Were you at the tournament the other day?"

"No, I wasn't. I'm not interested in them."

"This time I think you would have definitely been interested. Did you hear anything about what happened?"

"No, I didn't. Please get to the point."

"Well, the archery contest was won by one of Baron Henry's men, a man called Donald who said he was from Coby Hollow."

"What of it?"

"At the tournament, I sat in front of two boys, and one of them was named Benjamin. I overheard him talk about his brother David. When this Donald paraded past him, he said he was his brother."

"So? Who is this Benjamin?"

"I think you know. He's your nephew. How many Benjamins are there in Northampton? Or should I say in West End? And how many have a brother named David? I'm not a fool."

"You must be mistaken. David is a Jew and studying in Germany. He could not be an archer."

"I sent one of my monks to Coby Hollow. There was never a Donald living there as this man said."

"So, he lied. He must have his own reasons."

"And how do we know David is really in Germany? I heard Benjamin not only identify David but ask where his uncle Baruch was. Donald is David, your nephew, a Jew pretending to be a Christian. Now, what do you think Baron Henry would do if I told him that?"

This man Donald must be David, Baruch thought. Mordecai must have kept the truth from me for secrecy. He realized there was no use denying David's new identity. If he did, Hubert would immediately go to the baron or the sheriff, and they would question not only David, but Mordecai and the children as well.

"What do you want, Hubert?"

"I think you know. Give me a one thousand pound loan, and I will not say anything."

"Without a guarantor?"

Hubert laughed. "I have a guarantor. David's secret."

"You're an evil man, Hubert."

"No, I'm not. If I were evil I would expose him, and he and his family would be arrested, and you too, no doubt, and then who knows what may happen. I simply have a need, and now have a way to fulfill it."

Baruch swallowed hard to contain his anger. "Very well. I will have the documents drawn up and the money ready. I will meet you at the archa in three days."

Hubert smiled. "I knew you'd be agreeable." He rose to leave. "One more thing. I'm not the only one who knows of David's masquerade. If anything happens to me, the secret will not be a secret anymore."

"Get out. We are done here." Baruch slammed the door behind him.

Hubert returned to Hedgestone jubilant. Perhaps he should have demanded more from Baruch? No, he can always ask for more. He was proud of himself for the last lie, since he had not shared the secret with Alwyn or anyone else. Baruch did not know that, and he never would.

Baruch was furious at what had happened. He did not care about the money. He was worried about Mordecai and all three children. Hubert was ruthless. Who knows what else he would do in the future? Baruch did not know what he should do. Tell Mordecai? Warn him and David? He would have to think about it. He also thought about Hubert's last statement. Did others at Hedgestone know about David? The more he thought about it, the more he thought Hubert lied about that. If a Christian suspected a Jew of pretending to be a Christian, he would have to report it. Hubert could not trust anyone else with that information. It would be too risky. Hubert must be stopped and he would have to find a way. A way that would protect David and the rest of his family, without anyone finding out.

Chapter Twenty

Northampton – June 1268

Baron Henry ordered his men to be ready to return to York. Along with the others, David gathered his pack, ate a light breakfast, and headed for the courtyard. It was quite early, and most of the people in the castle had not yet arisen. David still was marveling at the whole experience. He was getting more comfortable with his role in Baron Henry's entourage. Winning the archery contest not only increased his standing with the men, but also proved to himself he was born to do this. He must continue to improve his skills, become expert with a sword, and convince Henry he eventually should earn knighthood.

Henry wanted to get an early start. This time he would stay with his men as long as they were in Salcey. He managed to survive the last ambush and did not want to press his luck.

Baron Geoffrey said goodbye to his friend, who again hoped he would return soon. Henry returned the invitation, and Geoffrey promised to visit York in the near future.

Henry mounted his horse and led his escort across the drawbridge. People began to appear on the streets as David marched through Northampton. Suddenly a young girl ran up to David and handed him a small package wrapped in cloth. "This is a gift for winning the archery contest," she said. "Don't open it until you return home."

This startled David and made the other men incredibly curious.

"Thank you," David said. "Who's this from?"

"I don't know," she said. "I was just told to give it to you."

The men-at-arms laughed. "Donald, it's from a wench who wants you to stay and pleasure her. It's probably one of her undergarments. Show us what it is."

David laughed as well. "If it's from a wench, I won't share it with any of you. I can wait until we return to York."

David placed the package in his pack, and they continued on to York, stopping at the same inns they did on the way to Northampton.

When they arrived at York, Henry dismissed the men and gave them some time to relax. David waited until they had all fallen asleep, as they were quite tired from the journey. He took the package and went off to a spot where he knew he would not be disturbed. He carefully untied the thin rope that held the cloth wrapping together. Inside was a small wooden box. He opened it and saw a parchment inside. He carefully unfolded it. All it said was 'Hubert knows.' What does that mean, he asked himself? Who is Hubert, and what does he know? What am I supposed to do with this information? David sat down and thought. Hubert must be someone in Northampton. I do not remember anyone with that name at the baron's castle. I will have to ask around discreetly to find out who exactly this Hubert is. The girl who brought this to me wore a crucifix, so she's not a Jew.

David decided he had better burn the parchment. Whatever meaning it has, it probably would cause trouble if found. He saw a torch burning in a corridor and the parchment burned quickly, leaving no remnants.

When David returned to his quarters, the men were awake and all wanted to know what was in the package. He showed them the empty box, saying it must have been a joke. They all believed him, said some wench was teasing him, and he should go back to Northampton and find her. He said perhaps he would, but the baron probably would not let him. It was all in fun, and soon they forgot about the package altogether.

Hedgestone Priory – June 1268

Baruch apprehensively approached the priory. He had never been in a position such as this, but felt he had no choice. He thought about confirming with Mordecai David was indeed pretending to be this Donald. From what Hubert had said, there was no reason to doubt he was correct. Better his brother did not know about this, and the forced arrangement.

He rang the priory bell, Brother Dominick answered and he escorted Baruch to the same room he and Hubert previously had met in several times before. The plan was for Baruch to deliver the money, and then they would go to the archa to record it as required by law. Unlike before, when he made Baruch wait, this time Hubert was there waiting for him.

"Welcome, Baruch. I've been eagerly awaiting you."

"Did you think I wouldn't come?"

"No, you are too smart for that. I know you'd never jeopardize your nephew's safety."

Baruch had two monks carry several chests of coins into the room, Hubert swearing them to secrecy. "Here. One thousand pounds. Count it if you wish."

"That will not be necessary. I know you wouldn't be foolish enough to cheat me."

"Cheat you? You are the one who is cheating, forcing me to give you this loan with your threat."

"I asked you honorably to do business with me, and you refused. I found a way to get what I wanted. It's not cheating. It's using an advantage. No one will be hurt, unless you betray me, and that would be a huge mistake. You don't seem to me a man who makes huge mistakes."

Baruch looked sternly at Hubert. "You're wrong. I made one believing you were an honorable man, a best example of the Church. Obviously, I was mistaken. One day, you will pay."

"Is that a threat?"

"No, I do not threaten. It's a prediction. One I hope I live to see come true."

"Enough of this. Let's go record the loan at the archa."

"Very well."

West End – July 1268

Benjamin and Avram sat by the river, tossing pebbles like David and Avram used to do. Since David had left West End, the boys had become good friends, even though Benjamin was younger than Avram. Together, they each felt the other's connection to David.

"Avram," Benjamin said, "do you think we could go visit David?"

Avram laughed. "Of course not. York is far away. We could never travel there by ourselves, and even if we could, how could we spend time with him? Everyone would question who we are, why are we there, and most dangerous of all, why do we want to see the archer called Donald."

"I really miss my brother, Avram."

"I know. I miss my best friend as well. But he's doing what he always wanted to do, and if we in any way jeopardize that, we'd be hurting him, and I know we don't want to do that."

Benjamin sighed. "You're right. Maybe he'll visit again soon."

"I hope so, Benjamin."

York – August 1268

David continued with his training and saw improvements each day. Baron Henry noticed the young warrior, who seemed to have a sixth sense with a sword, knowing exactly when his opponent would thrust or make any sudden, unexpected movement. Sir Michael had also kept the baron apprised of Donald's progress. Michael agreed Donald was proving himself, and eventually would make a fine knight.

One day after training, David was collecting the axes and wooden swords when he heard a girl's voice behind him. "Hello, Donald." David turned to see Alycia standing there in a bright blue dress, the wind lightly brushing against her flowing hair.

"Oh, hello."

"Are you not happy to see me? It's been a while."

"No, I mean, yes," he stammered. "But I don't think it's wise for me to speak to you. You are betrothed, and even if you weren't, you're noble and I'm only a lowly man-at-arms in training."

She laughed. "You will be a knight someday. I heard my father talking about it. He said you're one of the finest warriors he's ever seen."

Her statement caught him off-guard. "I hope I meet his expectations," he said. "My lady, where's Sir Edgar? Are you not to be wed soon?"

Alycia frowned. "Sir Edgar is a boor. I have no desire for him. My father wants me to marry who he wants. It's my station. I envy the servant girls who can marry someone they love, not someone they're forced to, and someone they're supposed to learn to love. What an awful concept. I'm sure you have many a maiden wanting you."

In the late afternoon light with the sun at her back, her golden hair radiated even more. He marveled at the smoothness of her skin and the glow in her eyes. She looked lovelier than ever. "I have no time for maidens. I must keep improving my skills and can think of nothing else."

"Do you think I'm beautiful?" she asked.

David hesitated. "My lady, I think you are the most beautiful girl I have ever seen. However, like a magnificent sunset, moonlight reflecting on a lake, or sunlight dancing on a meadow in the early morning, I can observe these things, but cannot keep them. Do you understand?"

Tears appeared in Alycia's eyes. "You use words beautifully. A bit strange for a man-at-arms. One would think you were educated."

"No," he replied. "They just come naturally."

"Goodbye, Donald. I'd better go."

David bowed. "Goodbye, my lady." He watched as she disappeared into the castle. I was very lucky to get here, he thought, and so far, I am proving my ability to stay and prosper. Even thinking about Alycia could get me into the worst trouble. Not only would Baron Henry not be pleased, but Sir Edgar would no doubt run me through before I could defend myself. I am sure Alycia would certainly give me away if she knew who I really am. I must not be tempted by this girl.

Sir Michael had observed them speaking to each other.

"So, you're at it again, I see."

"Sir Michael, I didn't see you there. And no, I am not at it again. She came up to me and started a conversation. I did nothing wrong."

Michael laughed. "Not yet, my young friend. I must protect you from yourself. You need something to forget about Alycia. Or should I say someone?"

David began to get nervous. Again, the prospect of his being discovered would be very real if he had to prove his manhood. The other men-at-arms constantly talked about it. While he did not believe even half their stories, he knew they often frequented the whores in the city, and some had had trysts with a few of the maids in the castle. One in particular seemed to be the favorite of several. Her name was Abigail, and she had been married to one of the men-at-arms killed defending the castle against a bold but futile attack by a group of former French soldiers turned outlaw. Baron Henry felt sorry for her, since she had lost her baby due to illness soon afterwards, so he let her live in the castle as a chambermaid. She had become very promiscuous and was known to pleasure almost any of the men-at-arms at various times. Previously an attractive woman, since her misfortunes her appearance had deteriorated, and she had lost much of her beauty. Nevertheless, the men treated her well despite using her whenever they could. David tried his best to avoid her, as she appeared to be attracted to him.

He had to think quickly. "Sir Michael. I appreciate your concern. The truth, that I did not want the other men to know about, is I am pledged to someone in Coby Hollow, and wish to honor that pledge."

Sir Michael looked at David in disbelief. "I've never heard of such a thing with someone like you. You can't be serious."

"I am, Sir Michael. Even in such a small village as Coby Hollow, one can find one's mate."

"Why didn't you mention her before? Did you visit her when we were in Northampton?"

"I wanted to keep her my secret. I didn't want the men to be jealous of me, and yes, I did see her there."

David did not think he had convinced Sir Michael. "Donald, I've been with many women, most whose names I don't remember. I've never been in love, and never have married. I know I sired a number of children, but I don't know who any of them are. If what you say is true, I envy you. If you've found someone you love and loves you, you are a better man than I, and I wish you well."

Sir Michael's confession startled David. Never had he thought this gruff knight who had been in many battles, killed many men, and even had committed rape in his younger years, would lament his never marrying, and approve of David's story.

"Thank you, Sir Michael. Can we please keep this between us? I still don't want any of the men to know."

"Of course, Donald. Your secret is safe with me."

London – August 1268

Father Alwyn arrived in London after a long interval since his last trip. He had delayed his scheduled trips at Hubert's request. He knew he was treading a fine line between the two churchmen but felt he could control the situation. As he sat waiting for the bishop, Eustace exhibited his usual strange behavior. Alwyn did not trust the old priest and made certain he never said anything in front of him he wanted no one else to know.

"Well, Alwyn," Basil said, "I expected you to be here quite a while ago. I was going to send old Eustace here after you."

"I'm sorry, Your Grace, but I wanted to be able to give you a report with a considerable amount of information, and a report that also would please you."

"And now you will or will not?"

"You will be the judge of that."

"Obviously. Now tell me everything."

"Hubert had considerable trouble obtaining the large loan you requested. After he secured a fifty pound loan and more than met its terms, he attempted to secure additional ones in phases. However, the moneylender refused unless he had a guarantor."

"A guarantor? And did he?"

"No, Your Grace. He knew no one would guarantee the loan for him, and he could never ask you."

"He was correct. I would never do that. I do not need Hubert if I am the guarantor. So, did he obtain another loan?"

"The surprising thing is all of a sudden, the moneylender changed his mind and agreed to a one thousand pound loan without a guarantor."

"Do you know why? Has he ever done that before?"

"I tried to find out why and answer that same question but could not. I can only assume he knows a secret about the moneylender. No other possibility makes sense to me."

Basil was silent for quite a while. "Did anything happen about that time that could be connected to this change of heart?"

"I thought about that as well, Your Grace, but nothing I could think of. There had just been a tournament and archery contest when Baron Henry de Percy of York visited Baron Geoffrey, but nothing else."

"Did anything unusual happen there?"

"Not to my knowledge. One of Henry's men won the archery contest, a young man named Donald. I believe he's a peasant boy who saved the baron's life last year. Henry has been training him to be a man-at-arms and took him to Northampton."

"A peasant boy, you say? How did he save Henry's life?"

"I don't know. Everyone was very secretive about it. Some speculate that when a forester was found dead some time ago and his weapons were missing, this boy found them and taught himself archery. Since it happened, the sheriff has been trying to find whoever took them."

"Was the forester killed?"

"It appears he died of natural causes."

Basil grunted. "I don't see what that has to do with Hubert obtaining the loan. So, where is the money?"

"This is the part you won't like. Hubert didn't tell me about the loan. I learned it from one of the clerks who keeps the archa. To be blunt, he's kept the money for himself."

Basil was furious. "Himself? He knew you were coming to give me a report, did he not?"

"Yes, but he doesn't know I know about the loan. He thinks I will report his unsuccessful efforts."

"I knew he couldn't be trusted. Alwyn, I want you to return to Hedgestone immediately. Find out more about this. Do you know who the moneylender is?"

"Yes. His name is Baruch."

"Do you know anything about him?"

"Not much. He has no immediate family but has a brother who is an apothecary. I believe the brother's wife was killed in the riots a few years ago."

"Do either have any children?"

"I know the brother does."

"Talk to this Baruch, find out everything you can. If you need to talk to the brother, do that as well. I think what you told me may be connected. This moneylender changed his mind awfully quickly. There must be a good reason for it, and I'm certain Hubert's involved."

"Very well, Your Grace. I'll find out what I can."

"Make certain you do it very discreetly. I don't want Hubert to know what you're doing or I know anything about it, understand?"

"Perfectly. You can count on me."

Alwyn left the bishop's palace and began the return trip to Hedgestone. Throughout the journey he could think of nothing else except Basil's orders and various scenarios surrounding the bishop's speculation. He must be right. Why would Baruch all of a sudden give Hubert what he wanted? It made no sense unless he was forced to. Did the coin clipping threat work, or did Hubert discover another way to threaten this Jew?

Upon arriving back at Hedgestone three days later, Alwyn first reported directly to Hubert.

"Well, what did you tell him?" Hubert asked sternly.

"Exactly what you told me, that the moneylenders will not lend large sums without a guarantor, even with all your efforts."

"And how did our friend respond?"

"He wasn't happy, but said I was to thank you for your efforts, and you were to continue to try. He also said he was pleased you continue to keep the brothers away from the Jews."

Hubert nodded. So far, his plan was working. Basil does not know I have the money. I have Baruch whenever I need him, although I must remain cautious. He is a very smart, shrewd man, and I must stay one-step ahead of him at all times. I also do not trust Alwyn. I am certain he is more loyal to Basil than to me, but that is no matter. I can keep him under my control.

Chapter Twenty-One

Northampton – September 1268

Baron Geoffrey thought about this talented young archer named Donald, as well as what to do about Abbot Hubert. Now that he had answered the question about Ronald and the missing weapons, he was quite happy it had turned out that way. Henry was his friend, and if something had happened to him, Geoffrey would have been very distraught. This Donald, however, should have reported finding Ronald and taking the weapons. No doubt, I would have let him keep them anyway. Geoffrey felt he understood why a peasant would think that way, however. Most of the common people were fearful of him, the sheriff, and most of the king's men, and he could not blame them. With only the slightest suspicion, anyone could be arrested, and it was very difficult to prove one's innocence. Geoffrey laughed to himself, thinking that under those circumstances, he probably would have done the same thing Donald did. He would try to find out more about this Donald if he could, to satisfy his own curiosity if nothing else.

Hubert, of course, was another matter. Now that Geoffrey knew the truth about why Hubert excommunicated his brother, he meant to do something about it. Still, he could not decide how, where, or when. The more he thought about it, the more he wanted to learn more about Hubert. Who else hated him? Bartholomew, of course. The Jews? Father Alwyn? The monks? He either had to send someone to spy on him, to inquire discreetly about what was really going on at Hedgestone or get the information from someone inside. But who? Then it dawned on him—Father Ambrose. He hated both Hubert and Alwyn, and no doubt would tell me everything he could. But how can he get word to Ambrose? Almost instantly, he knew. He would send for Ambrose to hear Geoffrey's confession. He never would let Hubert or Alwyn hear it. Then he could question Ambrose and perhaps get him to keep me informed about what is going on at Hedgestone.

"Cyrus, go to Hedgestone Priory and tell Father Ambrose, not Father Alwyn, I want him to hear my confession here at the castle."

"Yes, my lord. Will he or anyone else not think it strange you won't go to the church for your confession?"

"You're right, Cyrus. Tell them I'm ill and cannot travel now. That should be sufficient. And remember, only Father Ambrose is to come. No one else, understand? Take a horse. Tell the stable master I order it."

Cyrus nodded. "Yes, my lord, only Father Ambrose."

Cyrus ran down the stairs to the stables. The stable master gave him a smaller brown mare, saddled it, and Cyrus proceeded out over the drawbridge. He rode as fast as he could through Northampton and West End, where he paid no attention to anyone on the streets. He pulled up at Hedgestone, dismounted, and pulled the bell cord. After a few minutes a monk appeared.

"Yes, lad. What do you want?"

"I come from Baron Geoffrey. He requests Father Ambrose come to the castle immediately to hear his confession."

"Immediately? Is he dying?"

"No," Cyrus responded. "He's not dying, but too ill to travel here."

"Wait here. I'll return shortly."

Cyrus waited for what seemed to be an eternity until finally the door opened.

"I'm Father Ambrose. What's happening that I need to rush to the castle?"

"I'm sorry," Cyrus answered. "I don't know. I'm only obeying the baron."

Ambrose looked at the boy, who appeared nervous that if Ambrose did not come with him, he would be punished. "Very well. I'll go with you."

They both rode on Cyrus' horse, Ambrose seated behind Cyrus. It was not a comfortable journey, but since it was not long, it was tolerable. They reached the castle and Cyrus led Ambrose to the baron, who was sitting in his private chamber. Geoffrey rose to greet him.

"Ah, Father Ambrose, is it? I'm glad you could come. I'm sorry it was on such short notice. I hope I didn't take you away from anything important. Cyrus, you may go."

Cyrus left, and Geoffrey closed the door behind him. "Please sit down, Father. Can I get you anything?"

"No, thank you, my lord. I wish to hear your confession and return to Hedgestone. Tell me, the boy said you were ill. You don't look ill to me."

"Ambrose, may I call you that?" Ambrose nodded. "I confess not only am I not ill, but I wanted you to come here so I could speak to you in private. I regret having to deceive you, but it was necessary. Please, have some wine."

Geoffrey poured two cups from a pitcher on the table in front of them and handed one to Ambrose.

"Very well. To your health, my lord."

"And yours as well," Geoffrey said. "Tell me, Ambrose, what do you think of Abbot Hubert and Father Alwyn?"

Ambrose spit out the wine in his mouth as Geoffrey mentioned both names. "I'm sorry, my lord, for my reaction. I think you now understand."

Geoffrey knew he had made the right decision. "Ambrose, do you know why I hate Hubert and have no love for Alwyn either?"

"I believe Hubert had your brother excommunicated, after which he killed himself?"

"That's correct. I found out why Hubert did it and want to get my revenge. However, I have no way of learning about what is going on at Hedgestone. I cannot formulate any plan without knowing."

Ambrose sipped his wine. "I see. You want me to inform on them for you?"

"Inform is such a harsh word. Shall we say, educate me?"

"Baron, as a priest I don't want anything to do with your request. As a man, though, I will be happy to, as you say, educate you. Actually, your timing is excellent. I have just learned something about Hubert that I believe you will find most useful."

Geoffrey leaned forward. Ambrose, however, remained silent.

"Well," Geoffrey said. "Tell me."

"And what is in it for me if I become your educator?"

"What do you want?"

"Baron, while it may not be directly in your power, should something happen to Hubert, I want to be prior, and I may need help from outside the Church, as well as a donation. Can you give me that?"

"I would be happy to see you prior and make a donation. Anyone other than Hubert or Alwyn."

Ambrose told Geoffrey as much as he could about what had happened at Hedgestone since Hubert arrived. While he was not privy to everything, it was difficult to keep secrets, as the monks always tried to hear what they were not supposed to. Finally, Ambrose divulged the latest and most important piece of information. "Baron, Hubert just obtained a loan of one thousand pounds from Baruch, the Jewish moneylender, with no security or guarantor. The money was supposed to go to Bishop Basil, but Hubert decided to keep it a secret from him and Alwyn, although I know Alwyn found out. Alwyn has been spying on Hubert for the bishop, and no doubt told him the truth during his latest visit to London."

"Is that true? Is Hubert mad? Why on earth would he deceive the bishop?"

"I don't know. Frankly, I'm afraid Hubert will initiate another round of violence against the Jews in order to harm Baruch."

"But that doesn't make sense," Geoffrey said. "Even if something were to happen to Baruch, the loan is registered in the archa. Hubert wouldn't dare to tamper with that. The king would have his head."

"You don't know him. I fear he'd do anything for his plan to succeed."

"One thousand pounds is not a huge fortune. Why risk one's life or position in the Church for that?"

"Again, Baron, I don't know. There's speculation Hubert may know something about Baruch that Baruch does not want anyone to know. Hubert had been trying to obtain a large loan from him, and Baruch refused to loan him more than fifty pounds without a guarantor. All of a sudden, he changed his mind. To answer your question about why he would risk so much for one thousand pounds, I wouldn't be surprised if Hubert either demands another larger loan, or even the money outright if he does indeed hold something over him."

Geoffrey began pacing. "Interesting. I think the speculation actually may be the truth. Father Ambrose, thank you for sharing your information with me. I promise I will hold it in the strictest confidence. If you hear anything else, you will tell me?"

"Of course, my lord. I hope somehow Hubert will be removed, and Alwyn with him. If I can be of any assistance to you in this regard, you can count on me."

Geoffrey laughed. "It seems our friend Hubert has many enemies. Perhaps we can even identify a few more. Goodbye, Ambrose, and thank you again."

Geoffrey again thought if there was any way he could destroy Hubert without killing him. That would be an even better revenge. He poured himself a cup of wine. Soon he fell asleep in his chair, without coming up with a definitive solution.

York – September 1268

Henry recently had ordered David to begin training in horsemanship to further increase his skills. David was thrilled, as this would put him even closer to becoming a knight.

One late afternoon as David was about to put his practice weapons away, he turned and saw Alycia. She looked more radiant than ever. She wore a low-cut dress that exposed the top of her ample breasts. Her skin looked to be as soft as a butterfly's wings. He tried not to stare at her cleavage but found it difficult.

"Donald, you've been avoiding me," she said teasingly.

"Lady Alycia, hello."

She smiled and giggled softly. "I've missed you. It seems if you aren't training, I don't know where to find you."

David felt embarrassed. Why does she need to find me? He was afraid he might say something that would anger her or, even worse, Baron Henry. "I've been quite busy, and I'm also quite tired after each day's training."

"You don't like me."

"I know my place, Alycia, and you are betrothed. I am not permitted to," he paused, "like you."

David did not know Sir Edgar had just arrived. Alycia looked up and saw him walking towards her. David's back was to him, so he could not see the knight approaching. Suddenly Alycia started crying. David, still oblivious to Edgar, was surprised by her tears. He did not think he had said anything to upset her. Then he heard a brusque male voice behind him.

"What's going on here?" Edgar shouted.

David turned to see Edgar with his sword drawn.

"Edgar, my love, Donald said you are not worthy of me and will never make me happy, and it upset me."

David stared at Alycia, shocked she would lie like that. Should he deny it, thereby accusing Alycia of lying? Edgar never gave him a chance to respond. David was still holding a steel practice sword with a blunted edge. Edgar thrust his sword at David's stomach without saying a word. David blocked the blow, and the two of them began fighting. Alycia realized what she had started. "Stop this. Edgar, you'll kill him."

"He insulted me."

"No, Edgar. I made a mistake. He didn't say that. I made it up. Please don't hurt him."

Edgar ignored Alycia's wishes. They continued to fight, Edgar launching heavy blows, being much stronger than David. But David was quicker, able to hold his own, avoiding blows when he could, and blocking others. David saw out of the corner of his eye Alycia had run off. A small crowd had gathered to watch the knight fight the boy in training who was not even a squire. David was beginning to tire, not only from defending himself, but it had been a long day of training. Then he heard Baron Henry's voice. "Stop this at once, I command both of you!" David realized Alycia had run to fetch her father. He lowered his sword, but Edgar thrust one more time and the point of his sword slid into David's left thigh. He dropped his sword and fell to the ground, holding the wound that was bleeding profusely. Alycia screamed.

"Edgar!" Baron Henry exclaimed. "What have you done? I ordered you to halt. Donald did, and you attacked him anyway."

Edgar showed no remorse. "He insulted me and made Alycia cry. I was only defending my honor as well as hers."

"You fool. Donald didn't say anything like that. Alycia told me she made it up and told you too. You also knew Donald is under my protection, and you didn't question either of them. Go to your quarters. I'll deal with you later."

Edgar grunted, turned, and left, muttering under his breath.

Henry called for servants to carry David to an empty chamber, where they placed him on the bed. Oliver had tied a cloth around the wound as a tourniquet, but the wound was deep and required medical attention. Bryce had not witnessed the initial confrontation between David and Edgar but was in the small crowd that had been watching them and accompanied David to the chamber.

"Bryce, run and fetch Nehemiah, the Jewish physician. I believe only he can treat Donald. I don't want any of those idiot monks to even look at him," Henry ordered.

Bryce nodded and ran out of the room. It took about an hour until Nehemiah arrived. Meanwhile, David was getting weaker, drifting in and out of consciousness.

"My lord," Nehemiah said, bowing as usual. "Bryce told me what happened. Let me see the wound."

"You must make sure he's completely healed. This lad saved my life, and he is special to me. Do everything you can for him. If you need anything, just ask," Henry said.

Nehemiah looked at David, who was barely conscious. "What's your name?" Nehemiah asked. David had lost a lot of blood and was very weak. Nehemiah put his ear to David's mouth and thought he heard the name David. Bryce then answered for him. "His name is Donald."

Nehemiah opened his bag and removed a knife. He began to cut David's breeches and undergarments away to get better access to the wound. In doing so, he was able to see part of David's genitals. He suppressed his surprise at what he saw, and quickly covered them up. "Everyone must leave. I will take care of this better alone."

"Are you sure?" Henry asked.

"Yes. There is much less risk of infection if I am alone."

Henry nodded, ordered the room cleared, and the door closed.

Using the hot water Henry had brought in before Nehemiah arrived, Nehemiah cleansed the wound, prepared some herbs he placed around it, and carefully sewed it closed. It was deep, and if not properly treated, gangrene would set in and David would lose his leg. Nehemiah sat with him for a while, checking for a fever that would indicate an infection. He was happy to see there appeared to be none. Nehemiah heard the door creak open and saw Baron Henry. "How is he, Nehemiah?"

"My lord, I have done what I can for him. However, he is not out of danger. I will stay with him until he is."

"Very well. Let me know if you need anything at all." The door closed and they were alone again.

Nehemiah looked hard and long at his patient. He wore a crucifix but was circumcised. Is he a convert? While that was the most likely explanation, he would wait until this boy could speak to him before jumping to any conclusions. Several hours passed, and finally David began to wake up. He saw Nehemiah, who he quickly identified as being Jewish. Without thinking, he said, "Shalom. I am David ben Mordecai. Who are you?"

"I am Nehemiah. A physician. I treated you."

David began to realize he had broken his masquerade and tried to correct his mistake. "I am Donald, a squire in training."

Nehemiah leaned over to get closer. "No, you are not. You first told me your name was David, and I know you are circumcised. You are a Jew."

David realized he could not continue to lie to this man.

"You haven't reported me?"

"No, why should I? Tell me, why are you pretending to be a Christian, which you are doing, am I correct?"

David nodded. He was still weak but felt he could speak clearly. He quickly told Nehemiah his story.

"So you are the one who saved Henry's life. Henry is a good man, although if he found out the truth about you, I don't think he would take kindly to it."

"You will keep my secret?"

"Not only will I keep it, I will help you with whatever I can. We Jews do need a champion. If I were younger, I would join you in your mission. David, I will come several times to check on you, but not too often as to raise suspicion. In the meantime, I will get you new breeches and undergarments, since we have to make sure your condition, shall we say, never gives you away."

"Thank you, Nehemiah."

"I only pray you know what you're doing."

"As do I."

David was resting when Nehemiah opened the door and saw Alycia. "How is he, Nehemiah?"

"He's resting, and actually doing quite well considering the depth of the wound."

"I'm glad. I will never forgive Edgar for what he did. I will not marry him, even if my father insists on it. May I see him?"

"Yes, but only for a few minutes."

Nehemiah waited outside as Alycia entered. David was awake and opened his eyes when he saw her.

"Lady Alycia."

"Are you all right, Donald? I'm so sorry about what happened."

"The physician says I should fully recover. But I don't understand why you lied to Edgar."

Alycia lowered her eyes. "I can't forgive myself. Can you forgive me?"

"Perhaps, if you tell me why you did it."

"I wanted you to defeat him so he would be humiliated."

"Me, defeat a knight? I'm only in training. He's a knight who has fought many battles. How could I defeat him? All you did was make him angry, and he could have killed me. Does he know the truth?"

She nodded. "I told him again, and my father spoke to him. Edgar said he didn't believe either of us, that my father was only covering for me. My father is very angry with me."

"What do you think will happen?" David asked.

"I hope my father will see Edgar for the savage he is, but I'm sure he'll still insist the marriage take place, and probably soothe Edgar with a larger dowry. That's something I'll have to deal with. Now I'm worried I made you his enemy. Even so, I hope you can forgive me."

David saw remorse in her eyes. "Of course I forgive you. We all make mistakes."

"I knew I would find you here, Alycia," Baron Henry said. "Have you apologized to Donald for your stupidity?"

"Yes, Father, I have. And Donald has forgiven me."

"Well, he's a better man than I. If I were him, I would insist on punishing you severely."

"Father, forcing me to marry Sir Edgar will punish me for the rest of my life."

"Alycia, you will not be marrying him."

Her eyes lit up, and David tried to lift his head to better hear the baron. "What did you say?"

"While I don't approve of what you did, I didn't know Edgar had such a short temper and would also violate the rules of chivalry as quickly as he did. Your mother and I discussed it, and we're worried he might harm you for some small, insignificant comment or transgression. We'll find you a better husband that will still provide benefits to us."

"Oh, Father. Thank you. That's the best news. But isn't Donald in danger now?"

Henry put his arm around his daughter. "I don't think so. I told Edgar again Donald is under my protection, and if he harmed him again in any way he would pay for it. Edgar is smart enough to understand that and gave me his pledge."

Alycia hugged her father. "Father. I would never be happy being married to Edgar." She looked at David as she said that, but he pretended not to notice.

"Donald," Henry said, "I want you to be fully recovered before you return to your training. I want you to regain all your strength and be sure your leg never will affect your fighting ability. A wound that does not heal properly can change one's life."

"Yes, my lord. I promise I will not do anything to hurt my recovery."

Nehemiah, standing outside the door, heard everything. "I believe I'm done here for today. I'll return tomorrow to see how our patient is doing." They all thanked him, and he left.

"Come, Alycia, let Donald rest," Henry said.

David laid back on the bed, thinking about everything that happened. I fought a knight, and while I did not defeat him, he did not defeat me. He cheated and attacked me after I had lowered my sword and the baron ordered him to stop. Should I ever see him again, I must be wary, for I do not believe he will honor his pledge, especially if he ever finds out who I really am. For that matter, if anyone finds out who I really am.

Chapter Twenty-Two

York – December 1268

Henry noticed David's walking was getting better. He was not limping and seemed able to put all his weight on both legs.

"Donald," Henry called out one morning. "I see you're healed. Are you truly ready to train again?"

"Absolutely, my lord. I'm afraid Bryce is well ahead of me now."

Henry laughed. "Bryce is coming along, but he will never be the warrior you'll be. Don't tell him that, although I think he knows it himself. You may resume training tomorrow. I'll inform James and Oliver."

"I won't tell Bryce, my lord. Thank you."

"Donald, promise me if you feel any pain or weakness you will stop and report it to me. I don't want to take any chances with you."

"I promise, Baron Henry."

David sat on a bench as he watched Henry return to the castle. He closed his eyes, thinking of his father, brother, sister and Avram, wondering what they were doing right now. How I miss them, he thought. Somehow, I have to see them. He then heard the sound of light footsteps.

"Daydreaming about me?"

"Alycia. I didn't see you coming."

"My father told me you're completely healed and will start training again tomorrow. That's good news."

"Yes. I'm eager to return. I hope I haven't lost much of my skills."

"I doubt it. My father thinks you'll become a knight faster than you think. He even wants to tell the king about you. Perhaps he'll soon ask him to knight you."

Her statement took David aback. "Tell the king? About me? But I'm nowhere near being ready to be knighted. I'm just learning horsemanship and have never jousted or even fought in a battle."

"You will. My father has great hopes for you." Alycia sighed. "He also wants to ask the king for help in finding me a suitable husband."

"Has there been any word about Sir Edgar?"

"Edgar's father sent a message to my father asking him to reconsider."

"Did he respond?"

"He wrote back he would not, and he hoped Edgar soon would find a bride better suited for him."

David, as usual, found it hard not to stare at her. She wore a bright yellow dress under her woolen cloak that was partially open despite the cold, and a matching yellow bonnet. Her eyes were always radiant, and he could see she was beginning to shiver as the wind picked up. "My lady, you should go sit by the fire. You're freezing."

"I'm fine. Donald, I need to ask you something."

David became nervous. He always worried he would let his emotions get the better of him, and it could destroy him. "Yes?"

"Do you remember what you said to me before the incident? That you are not permitted to like me?"

"I do."

"I'm giving you permission to like me."

"Alycia, that's very kind of you, but I believe the kind of like you are referring to, you can't merely give to me. Perhaps if I were a knight and held lands. However, I am not and do not, and have no reason to believe I will anytime soon."

"You know my father is extremely fond of you."

"Yes, and I'm grateful for that."

Alycia lowered her head, and then raised it. David saw tears streaming down her cheeks. "I love you, Donald. I think I've loved you since I first saw you at the banquet. I know you were looking at me, and I am sure Sir Michael and all the men-at-arms told you to stay away and forget about me."

David knew his shock was evident. Not only was his inexperience with girls obvious, but he did not know how to respond. While he felt a strong desire for her, he knew the reality of the situation.

"Alycia, I am honored by your admission. But I am too young and inexperienced to know what love is. I imagine you are as well. I don't understand why people are attracted to one another. I do understand that no matter what, you are the baron's daughter, and we can never be anything other than friends. I pray the man who gets your hand in marriage appreciates who he's getting and treats you with the love and respect you so richly deserve."

Alycia's tears continued.

"Donald, even though I know you're right, I can't help my feelings. I believe I do love you. I also resent these rules that prevent two people from finding happiness because of their birth or station. I'd change them if I could." Alycia suddenly stopped crying and briefly laughed. "I am not permitted to marry you any more than I am a Jew."

"That is true, Alycia. Very true."

West End – December 1268

All preparations for the marriage of Mordecai to Hannah were completed. The ceremony would take place in the West End synagogue, with a celebration party to follow. Rabbi Ezra, Hannah's brother, would be conducting the wedding ceremony.

Since they met a few months before at Passover, Hannah had decided to stay in Northampton so she and Mordecai could spend more time together. She was very good to Benjamin and Rachel, both who encouraged their father to ask her to marry him. After thinking it over and discussing it with Baruch, he did, and she immediately accepted.

Mordecai noticed Baruch had become somewhat withdrawn the last few months. When questioned, Baruch always would respond nothing was wrong, and only that he had a few things on his mind. Mordecai did not believe him, and repeatedly told him he was available to help him.

The day of the wedding, Mordecai sat dressed in his finest clothes, thinking about his late wife, Sarah, and his son, David. He thought Sarah would approve of Hannah and would have liked her as a friend. Heavy on his heart was that he wished David could be there. Benjamin had stopped asking to go visit him at York, understanding the danger that would have created for them all.

It was time to leave for the Shul. As the three of them made their way through the dusty street, Mordecai wondered about the future. He felt he was making the right decision but regretted the circumstances that led to it. Rabbi Ezra was already there.

"Shalom, Mordecai. Are you ready?"

"Shalom, Rabbi. Yes, I am. Where is Hannah?"

"She's in my study, waiting for you."

Members of both families and most of the small Jewish community attended the ceremony. The synagogue was their central focus, and it was customary for everyone to share the happy times as well as the sad. They all managed to squeeze into the small sanctuary. After Mordecai and Hannah both signed their marriage contract, called the ketubah, it was signed by two witnesses—Baruch and Rabbi Ezra. They then walked together to the chuppah, the marriage canopy, supported by four men holding poles.

Hannah wore a simple, light-colored dress, her face covered by a thin veil she then lifted. The couple stood under the chuppah as Rabbi Ezra chanted the blessings. She then circled Mordecai seven times. Mordecai recited the traditional marriage vow—behold, you are consecrated to me with this ring according to the laws of Moses and Israel. He placed the ring on her finger, and Rabbi Ezra read the ketubah to the assembly. After several additional blessings, a glass was placed on the floor and Mordecai stepped on it, breaking it into dozens of pieces. Everyone cheered mazel tov, and the couple lightly kissed.

The party afterwards consisted of a number of foods the guests had brought—roast chicken, challah bread, various vegetables, some raw and some cooked, and numerous sweets. There was wine as well, and some of the men definitely drank far too much. As was the custom, the men and women not only sat separately, but danced separately as well. The couple also was given the honor of the chirala, where they each sat on a chair held high by several strong men while the three musicians played and everyone sang.

As the celebration wound down and the guests began to return to their homes, Mordecai sat next to Hannah. "Are you happy, Mordecai?"

"Yes, Hannah. I am happy. I'm sure it has been difficult for both of us, losing our loved ones, but I welcome you to our home and family, and promise to give you the best life I can."

Hannah smiled and took Mordecai's hand as Baruch sat next to his new sister-in-law. He was holding a cup of wine, and apparently had been drinking quite a bit himself. "L'chaim to the bride and groom," he said, lifting his cup, and finishing it with one long gulp.

"Mordecai," Baruch began, "I need to talk to you." He was slightly slurring his words.

"Now? This is hardly the time, my brother."

Baruch got up, sat next to his brother, and spoke at a level a little louder than a whisper. "Abbot Hubert knows about David. He forced me to loan him one thousand pounds or he threatened to expose him."

Mordecai was stunned. "How long have you known this?"

The wine continued to affect Baruch. "For a few months. I fear Hubert will continue to use this against me."

Hannah looked over at her new husband and brother-in-law. She could not hear what Baruch was saying but could hear Mordecai.

"How did he find out?" Mordecai asked.

"I don't know," Baruch lied, not wanting Benjamin to feel guilty about giving away David's secret.

Hannah noticed Mordecai's expression of joy quickly transformed into what looked like extreme worry. "What's the matter, my husband? What did Baruch say to you?"

Baruch understood her, even in his inebriated state. "Tell her Mordecai. She should know," he said, slurring his words even more.

"Hannah, please take Rachel home. I need to get Baruch to his. I will tell you everything later. Benjamin, come help me with your uncle."

Mordecai and Benjamin got Baruch to his feet and managed to support him as he stumbled with each step toward his house. Mordecai helped him to his bed, and he fell asleep almost immediately.

"I'm afraid he'll wake up with a pounding headache," Mordecai told Baruch's housekeeper. "Let me know if he needs something for it. I have a mixture that should reduce the pain."

Mordecai and Benjamin arrived home. Hannah had put Rachel to bed and was waiting for them. "Benjamin, please go right to bed. I need to speak to Hannah."

"Good night, Father," Benjamin said, kissing him. He then kissed Hannah good night as well.

Alone, the newlyweds sat next to one another. "I am pleased Benjamin kissed you. I hope in time they both will call you mother."

Hannah smiled. "Rachel did tonight. Now, tell me what you were going to."

"Are you sure? I don't want to frighten you, since sometimes it's better not to know certain things."

She took his hand. "Mordecai, I love you and the children, and want to share our joys and sorrows. Do not forget what we both have experienced, and what eventually brought us together. I want to be your partner and will always be by your side."

Mordecai leaned over and kissed her. "I am very lucky I found you."

He proceeded to tell her about David, concluding with what Baruch told him. She listened intently to every word, asking a few questions to clarify anything she may not have understood completely.

"Mordecai, there is much here to contemplate. It is late. The children are asleep. Let's complete our wedding day as newly married couples do. We'll discuss this further tomorrow."

Mordecai smiled and kissed her again. Without saying another word, they quietly entered their bedroom and closed the door. They did not go to sleep for quite a while.

Hedgestone Priory – December 1268

Abbot Hubert was taking his daily inspection walk around the priory. A light snow had fallen the previous night, and he liked to gently kick the soft flakes aside with his fine leather boots. It had been about three months since he received the money from Baruch, and he had not had any contact with the Jew since. With Christmas and the New Year approaching, it was time for the next step in his plan. How wonderful it is, he thought, when one knows something the other person does not want anyone else to know. It is the easiest way to get what one wants.

He also thought about Alwyn and was very proud he had been able to keep the thousand pound loan a secret from him so he could not tell Bishop Basil about it. He also had managed to keep Father Ambrose from becoming closer to him, even though Ambrose seemed to be trying over the past several weeks. At first, Hubert was suspicious of Ambrose's motives, but then he assumed he was just trying to enhance his position at Hedgestone. After all, he had not caused Hubert any problems for quite a while, and actually had been very cooperative.

Bartholomew had kept to himself, attending prayers regularly, while spending most of his time in the scriptorium. He enjoyed copying books and had a definite talent for doing so. He said leaving books behind after his death would be his legacy, and he hoped future generations would benefit from his labors. Hubert was quite happy Bartholomew had resigned himself to this.

As Hubert continued his walk around the grounds, he decided he would go to Baruch and demand money without it being a loan. Yes, it was beneath his station as an abbot, but Baruch was a Jew. Hubert felt there was nothing wrong with what he was doing. I am a man of God, he said to himself to justify his ambitions. I have heard of other churchmen who have done far worse things.

Hubert informed Alwyn he was going to Northampton and left the priory on horseback. He rode slowly, contemplating what might happen when he presented his latest demand to Baruch. A cold, early-winter wind blew, and he was quite chilled when he arrived.

"What are you doing here?" Baruch asked gruffly.

"Now Baruch, is that how one friend greets another?"

"You know you're not my friend." Baruch started to close the door in his face. Hubert quickly slid his leg partially inside, preventing the door from closing.

"I think you should let me in. What will the West Enders think if they see the Prior of Hedgestone standing at your door?"

While most probably would assume the abbot was there for a loan, everyone knew Baruch rarely did business at his home. "Come in but make it quick. I don't want you here."

Baruch almost slammed the door as Hubert entered and sat in one of Baruch's very comfortable chairs. Baruch remained standing. "Are you not going to offer me some wine?" Hubert asked.

"No, I'm not. What do you want?"

Hubert's attitude changed, and he looked sternly at Baruch. "It's time for us to discuss a payment."

"Payment? Your first payment is not due for three more months as we agreed."

"I know. The payment is from you to me."

Baruch immediately knew what Hubert was implying. "I see. You want to take money from me without me loaning it to you. You are mad, as I told you before."

"Let's say it's a donation, shall we?"

"Get out. I won't give you a penny. I should never have loaned you the thousand pounds in the first place."

Hubert stayed calm. "Baruch, I'm not a greedy man. This will be the only time I ask you to do this."

"Perhaps you didn't hear me. I said I won't give you a penny. Now honor the loan agreement registered at the archa, and don't return here again."

"Have you heard from your nephew? I wonder how he's doing. I wonder if anyone suspects he's a Jew. Perhaps I should make a journey to York?"

Baruch grabbed Hubert's robe and pulled him to his feet. A look of terror came across Hubert's face as he saw the anger in Baruch's eyes. Yet the words Baruch wanted to say never came. After a few moments, he released Hubert and pushed him back into the chair.

"How much do you want?"

"Two thousand pounds."

"Two thousand? You have lost your mind. I have only to inform the king of what you are doing, taking money that would be his upon my death, and extorting it for yourself."

"Now Baruch, I said it would be a one-time donation. You will not tell the king, or David will be exposed, and I will expose him. And remember, if anything happens to me…"

There would not be any reasoning with this man. Baruch needed time to think. "I will consider your donation request and let you know my answer in a week. Now, get out!"

Baruch again grabbed Hubert by his robe, pulled him up, and shoved him out the door, slamming it behind him. Several townspeople witnessed the event and scurried away when Hubert ordered them to. He quickly rode off, muttering under his breath. He did not notice there was another witness, who did not scurry away.

Chapter Twenty-Three

West End – January 1269

Baruch sat by the fire on a bitterly cold day, a light snow falling. Christmas and New Year's had come and gone. The week Baruch had told Hubert he would get back to him had passed more than three weeks ago, and surprisingly Hubert had not tried to contact him since his recent visit. Baruch knew this grace period would not last much longer. Hubert was an ambitious man, and Baruch believed when it came to dealing with Jews, he had no scruples at all. I cannot give him the two thousand pounds, he thought. He only will keep asking for more, and he will end up taking everything I have. I cannot put David at risk either. There must be something that can be done. Just then there was a knock at the door. Baruch slowly opened it. Mordecai stood before him.

"Shalom, my brother."

Baruch showed his obvious relief. "Shalom. I was afraid it was Hubert."

"I'm worried about you. We haven't seen you for quite a while."

"I'm sorry. I've had a lot on my mind. How are Hannah and the children?"

"They are fine. It's you we're worried about. Tell me what's wrong."

Somewhat reluctantly, Baruch told Mordecai about Hubert's demand, and he had not yet responded to him.

"He must be stopped," Mordecai said. "I agree he will not honor his pledge that this is a one-time demand. He'll do it over and over."

"What can we do? Have him killed?"

"No, we cannot. For one, I don't know how we could complete the task without suffering for it. We must discredit him somehow."

"Discredit him? How? As long as he's alive he'll threaten to expose David."

"There are potions that will make a man appear to be insane and can also affect one's memory. Perhaps if we can administer one to him, no one will ever believe anything he says, and he will have forgotten about David."

Baruch raised his eyebrows. "Could that work? How could we do it? He probably would be leery of eating or drinking anything I give him."

"I believe I may know a way. Do you know who Prior Bartholomew is?"

"You mean the old prior who Hubert replaced?"

"Exactly. He hates him. I don't think he would be part of a plot to murder him, but I am certain he would help to discredit him."

"Can you make such a potion?"

"I never have before, but I believe I can. In the meantime, we need to get word to Bartholomew."

"Leave that to me."

"What will you do now? I don't know how much time we'll need."

"I'll try to stall him. Perhaps I can give him a small amount just to placate him, say two hundred pounds, promising the rest later. That should buy us some time."

"Very well. I'll try to get what I need as soon as I can."

If this works, Baruch thought, it might solve our problem. If not, I do not know what I will do.

York – February 1269

David continued his training despite the cold temperatures and snowy conditions. His horsemanship was steadily improving, even though the snow made the animal more difficult to maneuver. Sir Michael offered to help train him, and his knowledge and experience proved invaluable. David again showed he was a quick learner. He mastered the quintain after only two weeks and was getting better at holding a lance while charging. He started with a light training lance and was working his way up to the heavier jousting weapons.

Bryce continued to train with him but grew frustrated at not being able to match David's skills. While still a student himself, David was able to tutor Bryce. Baron Henry, Sir Michael, James, and Oliver all commented he was an excellent teacher. Bryce appreciated David's help, recognizing that his own skills were improving under his tutelage.

David's greatest improvement involved his skills with the blade. He was defeating not only the other trainees and Oliver, but also Sir Michael on a regular basis.

"Donald, come here," Michael commanded after a rather long training session.

"Yes, Sir Michael?"

"Baron Henry has ordered me to take a group of men to find and eliminate some bandits who've been robbing travelers on the road to Sheffield. Would you like to join me?"

"Yes, of course. Thank you."

"We'll all be on horseback, and it won't be easy. These are desperate men, and they will stop at nothing."

"I understand."

"Good. Bring your bow. It may be useful."

The next morning Sir Michael, David, and ten men-at-arms, all riding palfreys, assembled ready to leave. Two of them were dressed as merchants to serve as bait to draw out the thieves. David saw Baron Henry and Alycia approaching.

"Men," Henry said, "find these brigands and bring them to justice. I wish you all Godspeed." Henry then walked up to David.

"Are you ready, my boy?"

"Yes, my lord. I'm ready."

"Good. Be careful. Michael, look out for our young friend."

"I will, Baron Henry."

Alycia walked up to David as her father started to return to the castle. "I wish you a safe and speedy return, Donald."

"Thank you, my lady."

Sir Michael led them out of the castle. David turned to see Alycia was still looking at him. He quickly looked forward, and soon they were out of sight.

West End – February 1269

Mordecai looked through his list of herbs, trying to figure out the best way to help his brother. There were several substances that could produce the desired effect if they could be administered properly. He decided to try a combination of henbane and mandrake. He had a little of each, so he checked his code parchment and found them. He carefully poured small amounts of each onto a small plank, being extra careful not to touch them. He ground them together and placed the residue into another small jar, labeling it with the Hebrew letter "hey" for Hubert. I believe this should do it, he thought. Now to have it administered.

The South York Road – February 1269

Sir Michael sent the two men-at-arms dressed as merchants ahead of the group, instructing them to keep their eyes and ears open. They had swords hidden under their cloaks. Michael, David, and the rest stayed back, just out of sight. They walked their horses slowly for more than two hours, when they approached a section with snow-covered bushes on either side that extended for several hundred feet. It was an ideal spot for an ambush, even in winter. The two front men noticed how quiet it had become and suspected their quarry was hidden in the brush. Even though a cold wind blew, David's excitement kept him warm. Sir Michael suspected something might happen soon and told his men to slow down and keep quiet.

Suddenly, six men jumped from behind the bushes, three on each side, and surrounded the two apparent merchants. Both men yelled for Sir Michael and drew their swords. Sir Michael heard them. "There they are! Get them!"

The bandits saw ten men now galloping towards them and retreated into the bushes.

"Sir Michael, three are hiding on each side," one of the front men reported.

"Donald, take five men and search the left side. The rest of you come with me and search the right."

The group separated and began searching. With the tracks in the snow, it did not take long for each group to find their quarry. David readied his bow as they searched. Suddenly three men jumped out, each pulling a man-at-arms off his horse. David notched an arrow and shot one in the chest before he could attack the man on the ground. As he notched his second arrow, one of the bandits ran a man-at-arms through with his sword before another man-at-arms dismounted and with a slashing stroke cut off his head. The third man started to run, but David's shot landed in his back.

"Nice work, Donald," one of the men-at-arms said. "Too bad about Kendrick," he added, looking at his dead companion.

"We need to see if Sir Michael needs help," David said. "Follow me."

David led the four men to the other side of the bushes. The remaining bandits had tried to flee without attacking and were easily chased down and slain.

"Sir Michael, I see you didn't need our help."

Michael noticed David was leading only four men. "What happened?" he asked.

David described how they were attacked, how Kendrick was killed, and the three were dispatched.

"I knew your skill with the bow would be useful."

They retrieved their comrade's body and returned to the castle. As they approached, David saw Alycia looking out from one of the crenels. He was too far away to see the huge smile on her face when she saw he was all right. They reached the stables, where Sir Michael ordered the horses to be taken care of, Kendrick's body to be taken to the priest, and David to accompany him to Baron Henry. They found him in the great hall, and Alycia was with him.

"My lord," Sir Michael said as he bowed. "We were successful. The bandits have been permanently removed."

"Any losses?"

Michael told the baron what happened, highlighting David taking care of two of the bandits himself.

"Nicely done. Make sure Kendrick has a proper burial. I believe he was married with children. See they're taken care of, and order extra ale for the men. Michael, you may go. Donald, please stay. How was your first real action?"

"It happened so quickly I had no time to think about it."

"I understand. That's how it is sometimes. You did well. I am also impressed you were given leadership responsibilities and again proved yourself. That is good. Many men do not know how to lead. I believe you were born to."

"Thank you, my lord. I'm grateful for your kind words."

"Father, I think you should reward Donald for his bravery and his leadership."

"And what do you propose?"

"In the spring I'll be making my journey to London. Let Donald lead my escort."

Baron Henry thought for a moment. "The road to London can be dangerous. Donald, do you think you'll be up to the task?"

"Yes, my lord," he answered. "I would be honored to lead Lady Alycia to London. I'm sure I will prove myself worthy."

"Very well. If you are far enough along in your training, and I give my final approval, you may lead her escort."

David could not help but notice the huge smile on Alycia's face. He bowed and left.

"Alycia, I know you're attracted to Donald. He's a fine, young man, and you know I am quite fond of him. I almost think of him as a son. Remember, though, you can never marry him."

She gave him the pouty look that usually worked to get her way. "But Father, are you not going to London soon yourself to tell the king about Donald? I am sure when he hears about his great deeds, the king will have him knighted, and then if he wants me, I can marry him."

"My dear Alycia. You are so much like your mother. So headstrong. Yes, I will tell the king about Donald, but knighthood is not easily awarded. I'm hopeful it won't be too long before he will be knighted, and perhaps given lands as well. But that takes time. Sit, my child."

Alycia sat across from her father and Lady Elizabeth joined them. "Ah, my dear, I'm glad you're here. I was about to tell Alycia about my upcoming meeting with the king."

"I don't think I'm going to like what you're going to say, Father."

"Alycia, your mother and I decided I must ask the king to help find you a suitable husband. Your journey to London in the spring will require you to stay there for a while."

Alycia looked stunned. "Why? This isn't what I want. You know that. You want me to be at court?"

"We've been in touch with Lord Essex," her mother said. "He's spoken to the king about you, and he has agreed to assist us. The king is very grateful for your father's loyalty during the Baron's War."

Alycia stood, furious. "I don't care. I won't let anyone choose a husband for me. Please don't send me to London under those conditions."

"The matter is closed. You will travel to London in the spring and present yourself to his majesty," Henry said. "I'm leaving next week to finalize the arrangements."

"Is Donald going too?"

"No, he must stay here and continue his training." He looked disapprovingly at his daughter, who had not hidden her reaction to this news. "Perhaps I should not have agreed to let Donald lead your escort."

"You promised, Father. If I cannot have him, at least I can enjoy his company before my imprisonment."

"You will soon forget him. There are plenty of noble young men available in London. I am sure a suitable one will be found for you."

Alycia ran out of the room in tears. She hurried to her chamber, slammed the door, and fell onto her bed. Donald will be mine, she thought. I'll ask the king myself to grant my request. I know how to get what I want.

Northampton – February 1269

Sheriff John de Oxenden sat with his wife as they sipped wine.

"John, are you sure of what you saw?"

"Of course I'm sure. He threw him out of his house. Why would he do that? I've never seen or heard of such a thing before. He's an abbot, for heaven's sake."

"I don't know, John. Why don't you ask them?"

"I can't ask Hubert, but I could ask Baruch."

"Then go do so. I'm tired of listening to you think."

The next day, the sheriff went to Baruch's house and his housekeeper answered. "Hello, Sheriff. If you've come to see my master, he's not here. He left for York two days ago."

"York? For what reason?"

"I don't know exactly. Some business, he said."

"I see. Tell me, do you know why he booted Abbot Hubert out a few weeks ago?"

The woman looked afraid. "I do, but my master made me swear not to tell anyone."

John patted her on her back. She was the same one he saw before, about fifty years old, with white hair. "I'm the sheriff, appointed by the king. You can tell me anything. His majesty would insist."

She thought for a moment. "I guess it's all right. I would never disobey his majesty."

She then told him everything she had heard that day. John listened carefully to every word.

"Thank you. You've done a great service for the king. Remember, don't tell your master I was here."

"Oh, no, my lord Sheriff. I would never do that. I hope you don't tell anyone either."

So, he thought, our friend the abbot is trying to extort money from Baruch. But why? Does he know something about the Jew that Baruch does not want everyone to know?

York – February 1269

Baruch was not afraid to travel alone. He usually went to York once each year to meet with other moneylenders. They had developed a strong bond, based not only on business, but on friendship as well. While he typically made the journey in the summer, he decided his being gone for a while would help stall Hubert. As his horse made its way through the road covered by only a few inches of snow, he kept trying to think of a way to thwart the abbot. His journey took four days, and even stopping at inns along the way he encountered no trouble. The weather helped to keep the troublemakers away, he figured.

When he arrived at York, he immediately went to the house of Aaron, the chief moneylender.

"Baruch. Shalom. What brings you to York in the winter? Come warm yourself by the fire."

"Shalom, Aaron. Thank you, I will."

Aaron lived in a large house and had two servants working for him. Baruch sat in front of the roaring fire, while one of the servants brought him a glass of warm wine.

"So," Aaron said, "how are things in Northampton?"

Baruch took a sip. It was slightly sweet, with a tangy flavor. Its warmth started to remove the chill from his body.

"I have a problem, Aaron, and I was hoping to get your advice and counsel."

Aaron appeared surprised. "I have never known you to ask for advice and counsel. Usually you are the one being asked for them."

Baruch laughed. "Not this time. Tell me, has anyone ever tried to extort money from you?"

"Is that what's happening to you?"

Baruch looked around the large parlor. While he did not see anyone, he still was highly suspicious. "If I tell you, it must be kept secret and in the strictest confidence. Is it safe to speak here?"

Aaron shook his head. "Come with me." The two men went into a small room on the second floor, and Aaron closed the door.

"Now, tell me everything."

Baruch related the situation to Aaron, omitting nothing. Aaron was shocked at what he heard. "David is here? In York, pretending to be a Christian? I have heard of this young man called Donald after he won the archery contest. Are you going to try to see him?"

"As much as I want to, I fear I cannot. It's too dangerous. Why would a Jew from Northampton want to look for a Christian who is supposed to be training to be a knight?"

"You are right. At the very least, many would be asking questions, and could lead to his exposure. I see your dilemma. Once you give in to this Hubert, he will not stop until you're ruined or he exposes David or both. Do you think your brother can prepare something that will discredit him?"

"I don't know. My brother is a wise apothecary, but his knowledge of something so unique may be lacking."

"May I suggest something? We have a very knowledgeable physician, Nehemiah, whom I trust. I would like to summon him and obtain his counsel on this. It may help to solve your problem."

"Are you sure you can trust him? The more who know about this, the greater the chance of discovery."

"Do not worry. I assure you he can be trusted."

"Very well. You may summon him."

Aaron called one of his servants to bring Nehemiah back with him. Aaron and Baruch chatted until the physician arrived about one hour later.

"Nehemiah, thank you for coming. I want you to meet a friend of mine, Baruch from Northampton."

Baruch grasped the older man's hand. Nehemiah wore a blue robe with Hebrew words embroidered in white on it. "Shalom."

"Shalom, Baruch. Aaron, how can I help you?"

"Please listen to Baruch's story, and promise to keep it just between us."

"Of course, if that is what you desire."

Baruch repeated the story. He noticed Nehemiah's eyebrows rise when he mentioned David the first time. Nehemiah did not acknowledge anything until Baruch had finished speaking.

"Baruch, I've met David."

"What?" Baruch exclaimed. "When?"

"I treated his wound a few months ago. When I had to cut away his undergarments, it was apparent to me he was a Jew."

"Did anyone else see that?" Baruch asked. He then realized if anyone had, David would have been exposed by now.

"No. I immediately made everyone leave. I was able to speak to him, and he told me who he was. I promised to keep his secret."

"Is he well?"

"Yes, he's completely healed." Nehemiah related how David received his wound and all that had happened during his treatment.

"Baruch, do you want me to get word to him?"

"Could you? He must know about Hubert."

"I will try. I don't have a legitimate excuse to see him, but I'll find a way."

"What about the potion?" Aaron asked.

"One must be very careful when trying to make someone appear to be in such a state of mind. I must admit I have never attempted anything like this. I will consult my resources and get back to you."

"Thank you, Nehemiah. I appreciate your help. Perhaps we can find a solution to this and protect David." They all nodded, understanding it would be difficult, if not impossible.

"How long will you be in York?" Nehemiah asked.

"I don't know. I'm staying to help David by avoiding Hubert. It may be quite some time."

"He can stay with me as long as he likes," Aaron said. "We must be careful. Hubert may have spies about, looking for a reward if you're discovered here."

"That is true," Baruch said. "I'll be careful."

York – February 1269

Baron Henry strutted onto the training field where David, Bryce, and the others were training.

"Donald, I'm leaving for London, where I will tell the king about you. I want you to look out for Alycia while I'm gone. Make sure she's kept safe and stays here. I don't trust Sir Edgar. I still believe he may try something to get his revenge. Keep training and improving your skills. Sir Michael will be here with you. I'm taking six men with me."

"Please be careful, my lord. I won't be around to save you."

They both laughed as the baron patted David on the back.

"Goodbye. I'll be back before Alycia leaves for London."

"God speed, my lord."

David watched as the baron and his escort, all on horseback and carrying crossbows, rode away. As he turned around, Alycia stood before him.

"Donald, I understand you're to keep me safe. I think that means you should never leave my side."

"I'm sorry, my lady, but it does not mean that. I must continue my training, and you must stay inside the castle walls. That's what your father ordered."

"Donald, this is our opportunity. We can spend time together."

As much as David wanted to agree, he knew he could not. "I'm sorry, but you know we can't. Now, please let me train."

Alycia watched him walk back to the training area. Rather than cry, she started developing a plan.

Chapter Twenty-Four

Hedgestone Priory – March 1269

Abbot Hubert paced the floor of his chamber. *Where is Baruch? He has been gone for more than two months. I should have considered this. After all, he has no immediate family. I believe his brother does not know where he is. A clever tactic, I must say. But he cannot escape me forever. He has too much at stake here, and he knows that eventually I will find him. He does not have any other family I know of. Did he go to London? Could he have reported me to Basil? No, then I would expose his nephew.*

"Alwyn," he called. "Come here."

Father Alwyn, always required to be ready to serve Hubert, obeyed. "Yes, Hubert."

"I want you to do something for me. Baruch was supposed to complete another loan for me, but I have not heard from him. I suspect he may have left Northampton to avoid me. I want you to try to find out where he may be."

Hubert's order annoyed Alwyn. "Hubert, that's below me. You should send Brother Dominic."

"No, I only want you to go."

Alwyn showed his displeasure. "Hubert, how can I find out where he has gone? I doubt his brother or even his housekeeper will tell me. I cannot travel around England searching for him."

"No, and I don't want you to. Go speak to the other moneylenders in Northampton. Perhaps they may provide some insight. Jews are a close-knit group. They always know what each other is doing."

"Very well. I will. But that's all."

Alwyn left the priory, unhappy with Hubert's assignment. *I am just his lackey*, he thought. *He treats me with disrespect, and I am tired of it.*

Alwyn walked to West End, where he asked some men on the street where the moneylenders lived. One man told him he only knew of three, Baruch, Simon, and Ezra. He first went to Simon's house, who told him he had no idea where Baruch could have gone. They were not friends, but occasionally would speak at gatherings. Alwyn also had no luck at Ezra's. There are more moneylenders here, I know it, he said to himself. He then stopped another man, who said he was a moneylender as well.

"Do you need a loan, Father?" the man said.

"No. I need some information. I am trying to find out where Baruch might have gone. I have to get a message to him."

The man looked Alwyn over, wondering if he should help him. "What's the message?"

"I'm sorry, but it's only for Baruch. Do you know where he might be?"

"I don't, but he sometimes travels to York to meet with Aaron the moneylender."

"York. Thank you. That's very helpful."

Alwyn returned to Hedgestone, where Hubert eagerly waited.

"York, you say? You served there. Do you know this Aaron?"

"I know of him," Alwyn replied. "He's very successful. I believe Baron Henry borrows from him."

"Of course! He went to York to warn David. It's so obvious I should have deduced that right away."

Alwyn assumed what was coming next. "I suppose you want me to go to York?"

"No, I don't. I believe he'll return soon, and I'll receive my new loan at that time. You may go."

Hubert sat down and poured himself a cup of wine. *It is of no matter. Even if he warns David that I know, nothing has changed.*

London – March 1269

Baron Henry bowed deeply to King Henry III and kissed the ring on his outstretched hand. Approaching seventy, the king was quite gray, and moved much more slowly than Baron Henry remembered. It had been quite a while since the two had met.

"Welcome Henry," the king said. "It is good to see you."

"Thank you, Your Majesty. It is good to see you as well."

"I never have forgotten your loyalty and support during the traitorous Baron's War. What can I do for you?"

"I have but two requests. The first concerns my daughter, Alycia. She was betrothed to Sir Edgar, but he proved himself unworthy. I would like for her to become a lady-in-waiting, and perhaps find a suitor here in London, as Lord Essex advised you."

King Henry smiled. "Of course, my friend. I would be happy to honor that request. There are many suitable young nobles here. And your second request?"

Baron Henry related the story of how Donald had saved his life and proved himself by eliminating the bandits. The king listened intently.

"So, it seems like you have found a true champion."

"Yes, Your Majesty. I'm sure I have. He and I only wish to serve you."

King Henry nodded. "So, what do you want?"

"I would like him knighted. I realize he's young, but I feel he deserves it. He is also a born leader, and by becoming a knight he will be able to serve the realm in a greater capacity."

"There is more to your admiration for this Donald, is there not?"

"Yes, Your Majesty," Baron Henry replied. "I actually like to consider him to be the son I never had."

The king stood and walked over to the baron. "I will think about your request. Knighthood for this young man may be appropriate, although I am concerned he may not yet be ready. Come back in three days, and I will give you my answer."

The baron bowed. "Thank you, Your Majesty. I appreciate your consideration."

Baron Henry felt a bit disappointed. He had hoped his request would be immediately granted, although he knew such a request was not only unusual, it went against the normal route required for knighthood. Donald had not even been a squire. Still, Henry firmly believed an exception in this case was justified.

He spent the next two days walking around London, visiting with a few old friends and enjoying the atmosphere of the city. He visited the armory to see if any new weapons had been developed, and spoke with the armorer about improvements he could make to his own arsenal. Finally, it was time to return to the king.

King Henry was in a surprisingly barren room in the White Tower. There was an older table, eight chairs, and a few tapestries on the walls. The wood floor was quite scratched.

"Ah, Henry de Percy," the king said as he saw the baron enter and bow.

"Your Majesty."

"Did you enjoy your few days in London?"

"Yes, Sire. I saw some old friends and spent some time with your armorer."

"Very good." The king paused. "I have thought seriously about your request. I am sure this Donald holds a special place in your heart. However, even though he has performed some great deeds, including saving the life of my loyal baron, I feel he must continue his training and gain more experience in battle. If in the next year he has done this, come back to me with him. Perhaps then I will grant your request. Knighthood cannot be granted so quickly."

Obviously disappointed, Henry bowed. "Very well, Your Majesty. I will obey and am confident Donald will meet with your approval."

The baron gathered his men, who were quartered with the castle guards, and left for York. On the journey, he pondered how he could help Donald. He stopped at Northampton to see Baron Geoffrey, but he had gone to France and would not return for quite a while.

York – April 1269

Alycia's plan was ready. She would disguise herself as a castle servant and walk out of the main gate when no one was paying attention. She would hide in the Forest of Galtres outside of York until Donald came looking for her. He then would have to stay with her to ensure she stayed inside the castle, and this way she would have him all to herself. While she feared the forest and its dangers, she did not think it would be too long until Donald found her. She was not planning to make it hard for him to find her. He always checked on her every morning before his training session. She would leave as soon as the castle began stirring. It was common for servants to fetch fresh water in the early light, so after putting on her disguise, she found a bucket and headed towards the main gate. Keeping her hood pulled as far over her lowered head as she could, she left the castle grounds without anyone saying a word to her. When she was out of sight of the walls, she dropped the bucket and headed for the forest. It took her two hours to reach it. Even in the morning light, it still was somewhat frightening. Every sound was magnified a hundred times. Every rustle of the just starting to bud branches scared her. She walked into the forest for about an hour and found a hiding place. She spotted a small cave a little off the forest road and thought it would be perfect to wait for her rescue. Having ignored the dangers of the forest, even though she knew better, she was not prepared for what happened next.

David awoke, performed his usual morning preparation rituals, ate a quick breakfast, and went to check on Alycia. His normal routine was to go to her chamber, where her servant Helen would be sitting outside her door. He found Helen there, asleep and shook her awake.

"Helen, you were sleeping. Is Alycia all right?"

"I'm sorry, Donald. I'll check on her."

She slowly opened the door, and they both saw the room was empty.

"She's not here. She must have gone out while you were sleeping," David said, obviously quite perturbed. "We must find her."

The two of them began searching the castle, asking everyone they met if they had seen her. No one had. David decided to go back to Alycia's room to see if perhaps she had left a clue as to where she might be. He pulled up the covers of her bed and found a small piece of parchment. On it was drawn a few trees.

That stupid girl, David thought. He quickly gathered his sword, bow, and arrows, and headed to the stable. He saddled a horse and rode out of the castle towards the forest road. Sir Michael saw him and called out to him to stop, but David did not hear him.

He rode hard until he reached the edge of the forest. He slowed to keep his ears open, as he knew danger often was alerted by carefully listening to sounds, or the lack of them. He continued until he heard a faint cry for help. The cries got louder, and he soon realized it was definitely Alycia's voice he heard, along with the grunts of what sounded to be a wild boar. He dismounted, tied his horse, and proceeded carefully towards the sounds. He saw Alycia, using a tree for protection, as a huge boar kept her from escaping.

"Donald! Help me!"

"Quiet," David whispered. He did not want the beast to turn on him. The boar was a large male with long tusks. David slowly took his bow, notched an arrow, and aimed. He knew a wounded boar would be even more dangerous. As he released the arrow, the boar turned to face him. The arrow found its mark into the boar's brain, and it dropped dead. David slowly approached the animal, drew his sword, and to be safe, thrust the blade into it. It was not necessary.

"What have you done? Your father left you in my care for safekeeping. He told you not to leave the castle. You could have been killed."

Alycia hugged him. "I'm sorry. I was so scared. You saved me. My father will reward you again."

David did not hide his anger at her as he pushed her away. "He will not reward me. He will punish me for not watching you more carefully. He may punish you as well."

She looked at him, hoping to soften Donald with her gaze. "We don't have to tell him. It can be our secret."

"Absolutely not. I will not hide this from him. If he punishes me, I'll accept it."

Alycia knew it was futile to try to change his mind. "Very well. Let me tell him, since it was all my fault."

David did not trust her to keep her word, but he reluctantly agreed.

"Come, let's return to the castle. I'll send servants to fetch the boar."

Alycia rode behind David, trying to chat with him during the ride back, but David told her he was not in the mood. Here sat behind him a noble's daughter he knew he could never have. She held him tightly around his waist. Sometimes he thought her hands were intentionally moving down to where they should not, even though he wished he could experience that with her. Again, his frustration with the separation between his people and hers he did not understand. We are all humans. What if we have different beliefs? What if we come from different backgrounds? What if we have different customs? Why is one better than another? David mulled this over as they rode.

"Donald, I'm thirsty. Can we stop at the creek up ahead?"

David guided the horse to the edge of a small creek, dismounted, and helped Alycia down. On their knees, they both scooped up some of the cool, fresh water. When they stood, without warning she placed her lips against his. His passion got the better of him, and he met her sweet tongue with his own. She pressed herself against him, hoping to feel his excitement. Then reality set in, and he quickly pushed her away.

"Alycia. Please don't."

"Why? You wanted me to. I know you did. I love you. I want to be with you."

"Alycia. I'm very flattered and honored you think you love me. But you know very well nothing can change who we are. Your father would never accept me as your husband. I am nothing. You are a baron's daughter."

Tears began to stream down her cheeks. He wanted to wipe them away, but hesitated. "Come. Let's go. It's chilly, and we need to return to the castle."

Reluctantly, she let him lift her back onto the horse. "Donald. Even though what you say is true, I will never stop loving you, and will try everything I can to make you my husband."

David turned around. "Alycia, please remove those thoughts from your head. I will never be able to marry you. Never."

Yes, you will, Donald my love, Alycia thought. Yes, you will.

York – April 1269

Upon his return from London, Baron Henry de Percy sent a servant to find David and Alycia. After her escapade, Alycia was more than a little apprehensive about telling her father what she had done. They both arrived at the same time.

"Donald, are we still going to tell my father what I did?"

"Of course. He must know. I won't hide anything from him."

Alycia nodded as they both entered the room.

"Ah, there you both are. Did things go well while I was away? After you tell me, I'll tell you about my discussions with the king."

David started to speak, but Alycia interrupted. "I ran away, Father, and Donald found me and killed a boar that had cornered me. It was all my fault. Donald took good care of me."

The baron nodded as he listened. Before he could answer his daughter, David spoke, bowing his head. "My lord, you entrusted me with Alycia's care, and even though she did leave the castle without my knowledge or permission, I must in good faith still take responsibility for her actions. You may punish me as you see fit."

"Donald, my daughter certainly has a mind of her own. I assume she ran away because she wanted you to find her and then, not trusting her, you would have to be by her side until my return."

"Father, that's exactly correct. Upon our return, Donald assigned two men-at-arms to guard me so he could continue training. Please don't punish him."

Henry laughed. "Donald, you continue to amaze me. Tell me about the boar."

David related the entire episode, how he found Alycia's note, and then, after hearing her cries in the forest, slew the boar.

"Donald, I spoke to the king about you. While I couldn't convince him to grant you knighthood at this time, he said if you have proven yourself in battle during the next year, he might knight you then. Based on what I heard today and know about you already, you may not have to wait even that long. Alycia, the king agreed you should go to London to be a lady-in-waiting. I was planning to send you later in the spring. Since you disobeyed me and almost got yourself killed, I want you to leave by the end of this week. I should change my mind about letting Donald lead your escort, but I won't, since I trust him more than I do you."

Alycia was upset by her father sending her away so soon, but with Donald still leading her escort, she smiled. "Very well, Father. I'll need a few days to prepare."

"You have four. Donald, I want you to take eight men with you, and Sir Michael. I will instruct him you are in command, and he will be your advisor. I want you to present Alycia to the king so he can meet you. You may stay in London for a few days. If you wish, you may also stop in Northampton if Baron Geoffrey has returned from France. You may also visit your old village again."

"Thank you, my lord. I won't let you down."

"I know you won't. Alycia, you may go. Donald, please stay a moment."

"Donald, again I'm grateful to you for a great deed you have done. Not only did you save me, but now you've saved my daughter. She did a very foolish thing, hiding in the forest. She knew the dangers, and she certainly could have been killed. Your skills and courage again have been proven to me. If I could, I would knight you right now. However, I must obey the king."

"I understand, my lord. Thank you again for your belief in me."

David returned to his quarters and laid down to rest. Baron Henry was not only entrusting the safety of his daughter to him but was allowing him to present her to King Henry. He smiled as he thought about it. A Jew from West End was going to go before the King of England as a warrior, not a moneylender or anything else. As he continued to think about it, he looked up to see Sir Michael standing over him.

"So, my new warrior not only saves the baron's daughter, but now gets to go before King Henry. I'm proud of you."

"Sir Michael, I'm glad you'll be going with me. The baron has given me a great responsibility, and I don't know if I'm experienced enough."

Michael patted David on the shoulder. "You are. You know how to lead men, and your fighting skills have improved. With me along, all will go well."

"Thank you. I hope so."

They discussed which men-at-arms should go, what they should bring, and other logistical considerations. Alycia would ride in a carriage with storage in the rear for her personal items. David requested to Sir Michael Bryce be allowed to go. Michael agreed, since Bryce's skills had improved, and the experience would be good for him. David told Michael he wanted to tell Bryce himself.

After they had finished their planning, David went to find Bryce. He found him resting in the castle courtyard. As always, Bryce was happy to see his friend.

"Donald. Where have you been?"

"Baron Henry summoned me. He wants me to lead Lady Alycia's trip to London in a few days. Sir Michael is going as well, and we were making our plans. Tell me, can you get away from here for a few weeks?"

Bryce could not contain his excitement. "You mean you want me to go along?"

David nodded. Bryce hugged his friend. "Thank you. I was going to ask you if I could go."

"You'd better go tell your parents."

York – April 1269

Nehemiah had tried to see David three times without success. He felt he would arouse suspicion if he came to the castle too often without being summoned. Since meeting Baruch, no one there required his services, so he did not have a legitimate reason for being there. Twice was when David had left the castle, once because of the bandits and the other when Alycia ran away. The other time David had gone to confession. Nehemiah had met with Aaron and Baruch several times, and they decided he had to try again. He entered the castle grounds, where he happened to see Baron Henry supervising a training session. The baron recognized him immediately.

"Nehemiah. What brings you here? Were you summoned?"

Nehemiah bowed slightly. "No, my lord. It has been some time since I was here, and I wanted to make sure my former patients had healed correctly."

"I believe they are fine."

"Even Donald? He did have a deep wound. I don't see him training."

"He's not here. He's taking my daughter to London to the king. She's to be a lady-in-waiting. Donald is leading her escort along with Sir Michael. You need not worry. He is as strong as ever."

Nehemiah tried to hide his disappointment. "I'm glad he healed completely. Please call on me should the situation arise."

He left the castle and went straight to Aaron's house.

"I'm sorry, Baruch, but I missed him. He's on his way to London."

Baruch's face showed his concern. "If he stops in or near Northampton, he may see Hubert. He is unaware Hubert knows his secret, which could be a problem. Now there is nothing we can do about it. He's in God's hands."

Chapter Twenty-Five

The Road to Northampton – April 1269

The rain picked up, and the wind blew harder. The road, already muddy from the melting snow and earlier rains, was growing more difficult to traverse. Riding in the covered carriage driven by Bryce, Alycia poked her head out the window.

"Donald, can we stop somewhere? I don't like this weather, and I'm cold and hungry."

David turned to Sir Michael. They both were leading Alycia's escort. "What do you think, Michael?"

Michael wiped the rain from his eyes. "Hedgestone Priory is up ahead. Perhaps we can find shelter there."

David turned towards Alycia. "We'll stop at the priory until the storm is over."

"Thank you, Donald. Will they let a woman in?"

David could not answer that question. He knew little of priories and monks. "I hope so. If not, we'll stop at the castle."

The rain fell even harder as they reached the priory. David pulled the bell rope and banged on the door. After a few minutes, a monk appeared, opening the small viewing window.

"What do you want?" he asked.

"My men and I are taking Lady Alycia to the king. May we please have shelter from the rain?"

The monk shook his head. "Abbot Hubert is not here. We cannot allow a woman to enter the priory without his permission."

David heard the name Hubert and tried not to wince. "Did you say Hubert?"

"Yes, Abbot Hubert."

Sir Michael was standing next to David. "Let us in, you dog."

The insult did not sway the monk. "Go away. We can't let you in."

The monk tried to close the viewing door, but Michael jammed his sword in it. "Get your master. I must speak to him."

David saw the monk turn and run back into the priory. "Sir Michael, let's seek shelter at the castle. It's not far. It seems we're not wanted here."

"These monks lead an easy life. There's no reason why they shouldn't help us."

After a few minutes, another man ran out of a building and to the door, his cloak protecting him from the rain.

"I'm Father Alwyn. Who are you?"

David decided not to give his name, suspecting this Alwyn might know his identity as well. Michael answered before David had a chance. "I'm Sir Michael. We come from Baron Henry of York. We're escorting his daughter to be presented to the king. We ask only for shelter from the rain."

David listened to those words with mixed emotions. Since he suspected that Abbot Hubert of Hedgestone Priory is the Hubert he was warned about, he did not want to stay there.

Alwyn looked closely at the young warrior standing in the pouring rain, water dripping from his helmet and cloak. He thought he looked familiar but could not place him. "I'm sorry, Sir Michael, but the abbot has given strict orders—no women or Jews are permitted entry for any reason. I cannot disobey the abbot."

Michael was about to curse Alwyn, but David stopped him. "Michael, let's go to the castle. It will be a better place anyway to stop."

Michael spat at Alwyn as he closed the viewing window, just missing him.

"I'm sure you're right, Donald. I just hate these lazy monks who always seem to ask for help but never want to give it."

Alycia again leaned out of the carriage. "Aren't we staying here?"

"No, my lady. They will not permit a woman to stay here. We'll seek shelter with Baron Geoffrey." She grunted and pouted her unhappiness with the situation. "Very well. Let's get there quickly."

They mounted their horses and proceeded towards the castle. The rain had let up slightly, but the road was becoming almost impassable. David thought about what Alwyn had said—no women or Jews were allowed in. He could not have been referring to him, could he? No, he must have been speaking in general. He could not know who he really is.

As the castle came into sight, everyone in the entourage felt better. Soon they arrived at the gate, and one of the guards recognized David.

"Donald, isn't it? The lad who won the archery contest? That was fine shooting."

"Thank you. We're taking Lady Alycia, Baron Henry's daughter, to the king and seek shelter."

"Of course. I'll tell Lady Catherine you're here. Baron Geoffrey is in France."

The group crossed the drawbridge and proceeded into the courtyard. By then the rain had stopped, although the cold wind continued to chill everyone.

"Donald! Donald!"

David looked up to see Cyrus running towards him.

"Donald! Is Bryce with you?"

"Hello, Cyrus. Yes. Bryce, come here."

Bryce ran up to Cyrus, and they embraced.

"Bryce, go spend time with your friend. We'll call for you later."

David then saw Lady Catherine and Sir Walter. He helped Alycia out of the carriage, and she stepped onto the muddy courtyard. David bowed.

"Lady Catherine. Sir Walter. I am Donald, leading Baron Henry's daughter to the king."

"I remember you," Lady Catherine said. "Come in, all of you, and warm yourself by our fires. Walter, please take care of the men-at-arms."

"My lady, Walter," Michael said, bowing to Catherine as well.

"Michael. Nice to see you. Come, and bring your men. We have warm quarters for all of you, with hot food and ale," Sir Walter said.

The men gave a slight cheer as they followed Walter and Michael into the castle.

"Donald, you and Alycia, come with me. Cyrus, prepare chambers for our guests."

David smiled. *A chamber for me?* The two of them followed Catherine as Cyrus ran on ahead with Bryce following him. "So, Alycia, how are your father and mother?"

"They are well, Lady Catherine."

"I understand you were to be wed to Sir Edgar."

"Yes, but he's a brute, and thanks to Donald for saving me and getting wounded in the process, I will never marry him."

Catherine noticed Alycia could not keep her eyes off Donald. "Alycia, this is your chamber. Donald, continue down the corridor, go up the stairs, and you will find Cyrus at yours."

"Thank you, my lady."

Catherine and Alycia entered Alycia's room. There was a large bed covered with a canopy, and a table with a washbasin and a mirror. A fire recently started began to heat the room.

"Alycia, come sit down. May I ask you a question?" Alycia nodded.

"Am I correct you have feelings for Donald?"

"Are they that noticeable?"

"A woman senses these things. You know I don't have any children. Geoffrey and I have tried without success. While I have not had the experience of raising a daughter, you may speak freely to me. I imagine that might be difficult for you to do with your own mother."

Tears appeared in Alycia's eyes. "You're very wise. I tried to talk to my mother about Donald, but from her and my father I get the same answer. He's not a knight, not nobility, and I cannot marry below my station. Now I'm on my way to London, where my father asked the king to help find me a husband, and I'm to be a lady-in-waiting."

Catherine put her arm around Alycia. "I understand completely. You know, before Geoffrey was awarded his title, we were just commoners as well."

"I had forgotten that. Are you trying to say that perhaps I will have a chance with Donald?"

"Do you love him?"

"I do, Lady Catherine. I do."

"Does he love you?"

Alycia hesitated. "I think so, but every time I try to talk to him about us he says the same thing—that he's not allowed to, and it can never be. I think he says that not to hurt my father. He treats Donald like the son he never had, but I don't treat him like a brother."

"I see," Catherine said. "I can only give you this advice. Donald, from what I understand, is a fine warrior who probably will be a knight. If you want him, I suggest you bide your time until he obtains his rank and title. There is no other way. Even if you would renounce your birthright, he will never disgrace your father. You must be patient. However, at court your heart may take a different course, and you may find that Donald is not your true love."

"Is that possible, Lady Catherine? How do you ever know if any man is the right one?"

"Alycia, you are so young and beautiful. These are both blessings and curses. They can complicate a woman's reasoning about a man. I don't know how to answer your questions. They say when you meet him, you know. I'm not so sure. It is true the older we get, the wiser we become. I hope you never lose your beauty like I have."

Alycia looked at Catherine with disbelief. "You have not lost your beauty, my lady. I think you are very beautiful."

"You are very kind, Alycia. Age does change one, physically and mentally. You will find that things that seemed to be so important when you were younger are not so as you get older."

Alycia laughed. "My mother told me the same things. Somehow, they're more believable when you say them. I will take your advice and try to be patient. I will wait for Donald to be knighted and will not pursue another. I know what I want, and I will try everything to get it."

Catherine kissed Alycia on the cheek. "I hope you do get what you want. And if I can help you do that, I most certainly will."

"Thank you, Lady Catherine."

London – April 1269

Bishop Basil was fuming. "You failed me, Hubert. Failed me terribly. I told you to get me the largest loan from the Jews you could. Instead, you tell me all you got were fifty pounds. Are you telling me the truth?"

Hubert tried to stay still but could not. He was sweating profusely, even though the fireplace was cold, and there was a distinct chill in the room.

"Your Grace, I was working with the best moneylender in Northampton. He's very difficult to deal with. We even gave him detailed plans to increase our revenue, but he rejected all of them."

"Why didn't you use someone else?"

"There is no one else. Baruch is the only one in Northampton who has the resources. Besides, they all speak to each other."

Basil stood and glared at Hubert. "You're a liar. I know about the one thousand pounds."

Hubert was stunned. "Your Grace, let me explain."

Basil sat. "Very well. Explain."

"I admit I obtained a thousand pound loan from Baruch. I kept it a secret from Alwyn, but it was properly recorded in the archa. I was holding the funds until I could obtain more before delivering them all to you. I don't trust Alwyn. I was afraid he would steal the money for himself."

Basil seemed unconvinced. "Nonsense. Why would he do that?"

"Alwyn and I are cousins, as you know. He grew up very poor, and his parents are quite ill. I believe he would have used the money for them. Also, I have to report he has been communicating with the Jews against your and my orders."

Again, Basil looked unconvinced. "I do not believe you. Alwyn has been under my orders, and I seriously doubt he would go against them."

Hubert was not prepared for the bishop's ranting. That traitor Alwyn, he thought. He found out about the thousand pounds and told Basil.

"Your Grace," Hubert said humbly, "I'm sure we can settle our differences to your satisfaction."

"How?"

"Baruch has gone to York, but I'm sure he will return soon. I promise you I will obtain more from him and turn all of it over to you."

Basil looked sternly at Hubert. "Very well. I'll give you three months. I've heard the king will be issuing a new edict soon with more restrictions against the Jews, but I don't know what they are. If moneylending is halted, you will not be able to please me."

Hubert was not aware of any new restrictions and became worried that, depending on what the king had in mind, everything could change. He would have to work fast.

"I will please you, Your Grace."

Hubert left the bishop, and as he walked down the street, he did not stifle his anger at Alwyn as well as Baruch. I cannot trust anyone, he whispered to himself. I still have Baruch because of what I know about his nephew, and that alone will be the difference. Baruch cannot avoid me forever, and he will not sacrifice David for money. I will sacrifice him if I do not get my way. Three months. Not a long time, but it will have to do.

Northampton – April 1269

The rain started again, and with no end in sight, David and Sir Michael decided to stay at the castle until the skies cleared. The spring was already one of the wettest anyone could remember. David enjoyed sleeping in his chamber and had the best night's sleep he had had since he slept in his own bed at home. He wondered if he could get away for a while to see his family, but decided it was too risky.

The weather made it too difficult to train, so David spent much of the day with Michael and the men-at-arms playing dice. As evening approached, the rain slowed, and Walter took Michael and David into Northampton to a tavern he frequented, the Swords Point. They ate mutton, drank ale, and talked of battles and fighting skills. When the subject of women came up, which was quite frequently, David did his best to ignore it as best as he could. As he looked around the tavern, he noticed two shabbily dressed men sitting near them. They were drinking heavily, and talking loud enough that David could hear.

"Remember when we attacked the Jews with de Montfort?" one of the men said.

"Aye, it was five years ago, but I remember it well. We killed a number of them. Some fled to the castle, but we had our fun."

David tried to hear more of their conversation, but with other men talking, it was difficult. After a while, Walter and Michael said they were tired, and were going back to the castle. David told them he wanted to stay a bit and would return soon. After a few minutes, he approached the two men.

"Evening, gentlemen. May I buy you a round of ale?"

The two men looked at each other, and then at David. "That you may, my friend. Join us."

David sat and called the barmaid, who brought a pitcher.

"What's your name?" one of the men asked.

David decided not to give his assumed name. "Robert. Who are you?"

"I'm Ralph," the first man said, "and this is Tom."

"I overheard you talking about the attacks on the Jews. Can you tell me more? I was too young to have participated."

"You missed a good time. Simon de Montfort ordered us to ransack their homes, taking whatever we wanted, killing as many as we could find," Tom said.

Ralph smiled. "It was so easy. Nobody fought back. They had no weapons, no training. They're all cowards."

"Not all," Tom said. "Remember that one woman? She fought me with a knife and cut me before I hit her hard and killed her. This is the scar it left." The man pointed to a long scar on his right cheek.

They kept drinking, and David kept the ale coming. "A woman, you say. Do you know who she was?"

Ralph answered David's question, slurring his words a bit, as the ale was taking effect on both of them. "She was the apothecary's wife, I believe. No one else was in the house. We never knew what happened to her husband and any children."

David ordered one more pitcher, and the two men gulped it down.

"It's getting late," Tom said, obviously drunk. "I'd better get on home."

"Me ... too," Ralph said slowly, and they both got up and staggered to the door.

"Thanks for the ale," Ralph said.

"My pleasure," David said. "Let me help you men home. In your condition, the streets can be dangerous."

"You're a good man, Robert," Tom said.

David led them out of the tavern and down the street into an alley.

"Where are we going?" Ralph said, trying to keep his eyes open.

"I know a shortcut. Trust me," David said.

He led them down the alley where it ended at what appeared to be an abandoned building. He then pushed both of them down to the ground and drew his sword. The two drunken, startled men became frightened.

"What are you doing?" Tom said.

"Keep quiet, both of you. Such brave men. Killing innocent Jews. Killing innocent women."

"Innocent Jews?" Ralph said. "Why should you care about Jews or a Jewish woman?"

David knelt and put his face in front of both of them. "Before you die, know that my name is David. I am a Jew, and the woman you killed was named Sarah. She was my mother."

Both immediately looked shocked and terrified. Even in their condition, they knew what was coming. David took their purses, threw them away so it would appear robbers had killed them, and wiped the blood from his sword. "You are avenged, my dear mother."

When David returned to the castle, Sir Michael was standing in the courtyard.

"It's about time you came back. I was getting worried about you."

David smiled. "No need, Michael. I took a walk around town for a bit since the weather had improved."

"Yes, it has. We should leave in the morning."

"Fine with me. I'm getting tired of being here with no action and not much to do."

Chapter Twenty-Six

London – May 1269

David gazed in awe at the king. Henry stood over six feet tall with a full beard, his long, gray hair falling under his crown and onto his shoulders. He had an imposing look and was known for his piety. However, David knew this king was no friend to his people. He built the Domus Conversorum to house Jews who had converted to Christianity and had imprisoned and heavily fined many leaders of the Jewish community. What would he think if he knew Donald's true identity?

Alycia and David were led into a room with two high-backed chairs. The king sat in one, but the other, for Queen Eleanor, was empty. The room was cold and dark, with few windows, and many of the candles had burned down and not been replaced with new ones. The wooden floor was old, and the entire room was musty. There also was a table with ten chairs around it. A faded tapestry hung on one wall.

Alycia wore a new dress with embroidered flowers made by her mother's seamstress. It was a subtle yellow David thought complemented her hair. He could not help noticing it was low-cut and exposed more of Alycia's bosom than he thought was proper.

Henry motioned for them to approach. After bowing, the king signaled for both to rise.

"You are Baron Henry de Percy's daughter?"

"Yes, Sire. Alycia."

The king looked at David. "And you?"

"I am Donald of Coby Hollow."

"Ah, yes. I remember. You are the lad who saved Baron Henry's life, and I believe defeated Baron Geoffrey's champion archer."

"Yes, Sire. Baron Henry has been very generous to me."

The king looked at Alycia. "Your father asked me to help you find a husband." Alycia frowned. "You are not happy with his request?"

Alycia looked up, her gleaming blue eyes at maximum sweetness. "Your Majesty, my parents mean well, but they don't know my heart. I wish to find my own true love." She glanced at David.

Henry laughed. "Such innocence. You are a baron's daughter and cannot marry just anyone. Can you imagine what would happen if we allowed those of rank to do that? I would never permit it. I do admire your courage, though, to express your desire. Alycia, I promised your father to make you a lady-in-waiting and introduce you to potential suitors. Your father was a loyal supporter of me during the Baron's War, and I've never forgotten it. I expect you to honor his wishes."

Again, Alycia could not hide her disappointment. "Sire, I will try."

"I am sure you shall. Now go with Rose. She will inform you of your duties."

Alycia bowed and left with the servant girl, looking back at David, as he did to her as well. Henry then turned to David.

"You are the one Baron Henry wanted me to grant knighthood."

"I am honored the baron would be so bold as to ask your permission, Sire."

"Do you think you deserve to be knighted?"

"That is not for me to judge, Your Majesty. I am proud of my accomplishments, and I only wish to serve you and Baron Henry to the best of my ability. Yes, I wish to be a knight, but only when I have earned the right."

Henry stared at this young warrior for what to David felt like an hour. "I am impressed with you, Donald. Most men would not be so humble and would request immediate knighthood." The king looked to his left and, to David's surprise, said, "Edward, please come here."

David had not noticed the figure sitting in a darkened corner.

"Edward, this is Donald, a young warrior who saved Baron Henry de Percy's life. Perhaps you should take him on crusade with you?"

Shocked he would be introduced to the future King of England, David bowed to Prince Edward. He was extremely tall, like his father, with long, black, curly hair. He wore a magnificent black tunic, with polished leather boots. "Your Grace. I am honored."

Edward looked David over without any enthusiasm. "If he wishes it. It's of no importance to me, Father."

David definitely did not want to go on crusade. He knew traveling crusaders often would put entire towns of Jews to the sword. He also wanted to stay in England to be able to defend his people when the time came.

"Sire, Prince Edward, I thank you for your consideration, but I must return to Baron Henry to complete my training. I hope you'll understand."

The king nodded. "Very well. Edward is not leaving until next year. Perhaps you will be ready then. You may go. Give Baron Henry my best."

Relieved, David bowed to the king and the prince, and quickly left. A Jewish crusader. How ironic that would be. No, I could not. Too many of my people have been massacred by crusaders. I cannot be a part of that and do not know how as one man I could stop it. He returned to the barracks, where Sir Michael was waiting for him.

"Is it Sir Donald now?" he said with a hearty laugh. "Did the king make you his new champion?"

"Very funny, Michael. I did meet him and Prince Edward. When will we return to York?"

"Are you in such a hurry? Baron Henry said we could stay in London for a few days."

David did not like that idea. Even though he had never been to London, he was eager to get back to York. He did not know why, but believed the longer he was away, the more dangerous it would be for him.

West End – May 1269

The elders had called for a meeting after evening prayers. Feeling honored to be included, Mordecai waited for the meeting to start. Rabbi Ezra silenced everyone.

"Gentlemen. I called you here because we have been informed the king continues to issue more edicts against us. These new ones forbid us to own land, and do not allow our families their due inheritances.

Some of you are landowners, and you must now sell your holdings for a mere pittance, taking a severe loss. For most of us, not being able to provide for our families after we are gone is by far more serious."

Rabbi Tanchum, Moshe ben Jacob, and Joshua ben Isaac all nodded. "I think we should consider leaving England," said Rabbi Tanchum.

"Leave England?" Ezra said. "To where? When our fathers and forefathers settled here, they did not know the language, and experienced many difficulties with the local population as well. Most of us do not speak French. We must stay here and make the best of it."

Mordecai decided to speak up, even though he knew he was considered more of a guest than a member of the council.

"Gentlemen. We have all been through this before. Frankly, are we not all tired of it?"

"Of course," Rabbi Tanchum said, "but what can we do? We must obey the king."

"Must we? Why don't we try to resist? To at least talk to him? To do something other than just take what is put upon us?"

"I agree, Mordecai, but it is unrealistic. We have no legal rights. We are the king's possessions, to do with us as he pleases," Moshe said.

"I know, and that makes me mad. Why do we put up with being treated like that?"

Rabbi Ezra stood. "Mordecai, while I understand your frustrations, we have no choice. We must not antagonize the king."

"No choice? Why not? We are men just as they are. Just because we have a different religion does not make us lesser men."

Everyone except Rabbi Ezra expressed his agreement.

"Mordecai, in the eyes of the Church, we are infidels. We are in a Christian country where we aren't considered English. The populace considers us infidels. What options do we have? We don't have our own country. Mordecai, you're starting to sound like your son used to. By the way, where is your son? Have you heard from David?"

"I pray he's well. He left to find his fortune. He did not want to live the way we are forced to." A murmur rang through the group.

"Find his fortune? A Jew can't do that. There are severe restrictions. If he's discovered, it will only bring harm to us," Joshua said.

"Bring harm to you, is that your concern? You are all weak. You are like sheep who cannot think for yourselves. I am ashamed to be one of you."

Rabbi Ezra became incensed. "Mordecai, you are naïve, and you are not one of us. Henry instituted the Statute of Jewry against us seventeen years go. We could never get him to change his mind. I asked you to join us with the hope your insight might be helpful, but I now regret doing so. Your son was a troublemaker, and you are one as well."

The anger rising in Mordecai could not be masked. "Very well. I will happily leave you. I don't want to be associated with your decisions and lack of courage. You are fools. Nothing will change for our people unless we try to change it. Shalom."

Mordecai stormed out, mumbling to himself his displeasure with these old men. *No wonder our people are treated the way we are. David was right. I am sorry I did not tell him so. I pray I will have the opportunity to do so.*

Northampton – May 1269

John de Oxenden had finished questioning everyone he could find who was supposed to have been at the tavern the night Ralph and Tom were killed. Most declared they had not seen or heard anything. The barmaid, however, remembered quite well the handsome young man-at-arms who had been talking to both men after his friends left. While she had never seen him before and did not know his name, she did say he had been with Sir Walter, whom she knew from his frequent patronage.

John thanked her and immediately went to the castle to talk to Sir Walter. He was disappointed to learn he had left with an entourage guarding Lady Alycia to London and would not be back for quite a while. He had a feeling the young man-at-arms could be the one he was looking for and wondered who he might be.

London – May 1269

Alycia stared out the window of the small chamber she was assigned. It contained a bed, a table and chair, and a wardrobe for her clothes. Rose had given her some basic instructions on how a lady-in-waiting should act.

Ladies-in-waiting were generally girls of noble birth who were more companions to a queen than her attendants were. Rose helped Alycia dress into a new gown, light blue with floral decorations, for her first meeting with Queen Eleanor.

"Rose," Alycia said, "why don't you go in my place? I don't want to be a lady-in-waiting."

Rose looked at her incredulously. "My lady, I am but a poor servant girl, trying to earn my keep for my family. You are a baron's daughter."

"To me it's a curse. Tell me, have you ever been in love?"

Rose looked at this attractive young lady. Rose herself was not unattractive. She was twenty-one, about five foot three, with a nice figure, brown hair, and smooth skin. She looked embarrassed at the question.

"Actually, I'm in love right now. He's one of the men-at-arms. We hope to be married soon."

"I'm happy for you. I can't marry whom I want because of my birth. I would trade places with you, but then I would deny you your happiness."

"Thank you, my lady. Is it Donald?"

"Yes, he saved my father's life, and mine as well."

"I hope you'll find your happiness soon. You should know I heard the queen talk about your coming, and of some of the suitors she wanted to meet you."

Alycia scowled. "I don't want to meet any of them. I want to make my own happiness."

"I understand. I'm sorry, but it seems as long as you are here, your destiny will be decided for you."

Alycia nodded, a small tear forming under her left eye.

Queen Eleanor was forty-six years old and quite lovely, with dark brown hair and what Alycia thought were sensual eyes. Educated and a poet, she and Henry had four other children besides Edward—Margaret, Beatrice, Edmund, and Katherine, who died at the age of three in 1257. Alycia heard Eleanor still grieved for her. Rose led her into the queen's drawing room, where she sat with three other ladies-in-waiting. Alycia approached her and bowed.

"Your Majesty," Rose said, "this is Lady Alycia, Baron Henry de Percy's daughter."

"Thank you, Rose. You may go. Rise, my child, I want to look at you," Eleanor commanded.

Alycia stood and faced her. "You are more beautiful than I was told. I should have no problem finding you a husband."

"Your Majesty, you are very kind. May I make a request?"

"Certainly. What is it?"

"I don't want to seem ungrateful, but may I return home?"

Eleanor looked surprised. "Return home? Why?"

"I don't feel right here. I don't think life at court is for me, and I want to choose my own husband."

Eleanor laughed. "My dear girl, you do not understand how our world works. We live in a man's world, and we of the nobility must do as we are told. You have only just arrived. I am sure after you are here awhile, you will get used to life here, and when you are married, you will be glad your father sent you to us. My husband is very grateful for your father's loyalty, and we will honor his wishes."

Alycia decided not to challenge the queen. "Yes, Your Majesty."

"I wish to rest now. You all may go."

Alycia and the other ladies-in-waiting, to whom Eleanor did not introduce Alycia, all left together. Outside the queen's chamber, one of them stopped her. She was slightly overweight, with reddish hair.

"Alycia, I am Olivia, the daughter of Baron Gilbert of Cornwall. I've been here for almost a year. My father sent me here for the same reasons yours did, and I wanted to tell you I feel the same as you do."

"The queen has not found you a husband yet?"

Olivia blushed, embarrassed at the question. "I am not beautiful as you or the other ladies-in-waiting. She introduced me to several suitors, but none has been interested, and frankly, none has interested me. To be honest, I'm in love with someone from home, but he's not noble, and so my father refused his permission to marry me."

"I'm in the same position. The man I want to marry is not noble, although I believe he will be knighted soon, and when he obtains lands and title, then I hope to marry him. But if I'm married off to someone else, my dreams will be shattered. Tell me, Olivia, have you ever thought about leaving here?"

Olivia nodded, tears in her eyes. "Many times, but I don't know how I could travel home. And even if I could, my father would merely bring me back. They probably would chain me up so I couldn't do it again."

"Perhaps your lover could come and get you, and the two of you could run away together?"

Olivia shook her head. "My father already thought of that and threatened to throw him in the dungeon forever if he tried. My father believed I'd be married soon after I arrived here. I'm still hopeful somehow he and I can be together."

"My poor girl," Alycia said, embracing Olivia. "I've learned we must try to make our own happiness. I don't want anyone to make it for me."

"Are you thinking of leaving? Don't worry. I would never betray you. I wish I had the courage to leave. You don't have to answer. I wish you luck if you do."

"You are a warm, loving person, and I truly hope you do find your happiness. I'm glad we met, and if I can help you in any way, I will."

"Thank you."

Alycia returned to her chamber and summoned Rose to help her get out of the gown and into more comfortable clothes.

"My lady, did Queen Eleanor tell you about the ball?" Rose asked.

"No. What ball?"

"I heard other servants talking, that the king and queen are planning to hold a ball next week to introduce you to eligible suitors. Everyone believes you will be betrothed in no time."

A sense of panic arose in Alycia. I cannot stay here, she thought. Somehow, I must leave immediately.

Hedgestone Priory – May 1269

Hubert summoned Alwyn as soon as he returned from London. The entire way back, he thought of how or even if he should confront his traitorous cousin. Alwyn was expecting the worst, assuming Basil revealed what Alwyn had told him. He decided to let Hubert make the first move. To his surprise, the abbot was extremely friendly.

"Hello, Alwyn, it's good to see you and be back. Anything happen while I was away?"

"Hubert," Alwyn replied, "welcome back. No, nothing happened. I've been checking, but Baruch has still not returned."

"Most unfortunate," Hubert said. "I need to talk to him. Basil gave me three months to fulfill his orders. I need to get him back. I am going to prepare a letter, and I want you to go to York and deliver it to him."

"Letter? What letter?"

"I am going to write him that his brother and his family have been arrested and taken to the castle dungeon. If I know Baruch, he will run back here to try to help them."

"Yes, I'm sure he will. When do you want me to leave?"

"Tomorrow at first light. You remember where you will most likely find him?"

"At the home of Aaron, the moneylender."

"Good. Go on horseback, take one of the monks with you, and return as soon as you have delivered it."

Alwyn nodded and left, fuming again he had to be Hubert's errand boy. He will pay me back for his treatment of me, he said to himself.

Chapter Twenty-Seven

London – June 1269

David, Sir Michael, Sir Walter, Bryce, and the rest of the men were ready to leave. It was early morning, and the sun had not yet risen. The courtyard was still quite dark, so no one saw the petite, dark-clad figure sneak into the back of the carriage, raise the cover, and hide underneath it.

David wanted to get back to York as soon as he could. His goodbye to Alycia the night before had been brief, but painful for him. She begged him to take her with him, but he told her he could not. The king expects you here, and you cannot go against your father, he repeated. He wished her luck and happiness. He also told her he hoped whomever she married appreciated the wonderful woman he was getting. Her tears at their parting tugged at his heart, and he reminded himself again even if he is knighted he could never marry her without giving up his Judaism, which he would never do. He did not know where this masquerade would end, but he knew he could only marry a Jewish girl. There was no other way. He thought about how she had tried to kiss him, and how he reluctantly managed to push her away. Her image was in his mind and would always stay with him.

They left the castle grounds with Bryce driving the carriage, and headed through London's narrow, dirty streets until they were out of the city. David looked back, again thinking about Alycia. What have you done to me, he asked himself.

After several hours they stopped to rest and eat at a small inn, leaving the carriage briefly unattended while they all went inside. Bryce was to get his food and then guard the carriage. No one saw the stowaway get out from her hiding place and run into the brush to relieve herself. She quickly returned, hungry and thirsty, but willing to wait until it would be too late to turn back.

After a while, everyone else returned. Bryce again was the driver, and they continued north. As darkness approached, David and Michael decided they should seek shelter for the night at an inn near

St. Albans. The men-at-arms took care of their horses and those of David, Michael, and Walter. Bryce was assigned to feed the carriage horses and guard the carriage itself. David had Bryce's meal brought out to him, while everyone else had supper inside. The weather was fair, and Bryce enjoyed his roast chicken while sitting on the driver's bench. As he ate, he thought he heard stirring in the back of the carriage. Placing his plate down, he jumped onto the ground and walked to the carriage's back. He slowly moved away the cloth.

"Bryce, please don't say anything. Help me."

"Lady Alycia. What are you doing here?"

"I just couldn't stay in London any longer. I want to go home."

Bryce was never comfortable in Alycia's presence. He also was attracted to the baron's daughter and did not know what he should do.

"Could you get me something to eat? I'm famished," she asked him in a voice that was low but very sweet.

"I must report this to Donald."

"No. You can't. He'll just return me to London. Please keep my secret," she whispered.

Both of them failed to notice Sir Michael and Sir Walter had stepped out of the inn and heard Bryce speaking. Bryce quickly covered Alycia before either of them could see what he was doing.

"You must report what to Donald, Bryce?" Michael asked. He was holding a mug of ale he handed to the boy. "Here, I thought you might be thirsty."

"Thank you, Sir Michael. I think one of the wheels is loose, and Donald should know about it."

Michael checked all four wheels and pronounced them fine.

"I think you're too tired, my friend," Sir Walter said. "Go inside and get some sleep. I'll get one of the men to watch the carriage."

"Thank you, but I'm all right. I can stay on watch for a little longer. I'm still hungry, though."

Walter went back inside the inn and brought out another plate of chicken, along with a large slice of bread. "Here. If you can wait a while, we'll get some sleep and get relief for you later."

The two knights disappeared inside the inn. Bryce uncovered the cloth, and handed the plate to Alycia. "Here, my lady."

"Thank you, Bryce. I promise I will never tell anyone you knew I was hiding here."

Alycia ate quickly, and Bryce took the plate from her. The night passed without incident, as Bryce was relieved and slept in the room with the rest of the men-at-arms. David, Michael, and Walter shared another room. After a light breakfast, they resumed their journey. Bryce tried not to turn around too much as he guided the carriage but found it difficult due to who he knew was in the back. Alycia did her best to be still, but it was becoming more difficult with each passing hour. She was getting quite stiff from being forced to stay in one position in the very uncomfortable back of the carriage. The several times they stopped to rest, she wanted to jump out from her hiding place. She feared if she did it too close to London, they would just turn around and take her right back.

At one of the rest stops, Bryce parked the carriage so the rear was hidden by some bushes. This enabled Alycia to quickly get out, relieve herself, and hurry back. Again, no one saw or heard her.

There was one more night stop to make before they would reach Northampton. Not finding an inn, they stopped at a farmhouse, where they paid the farmer for a meal and a place to sleep in the barn. Donald felt it was not necessary for anyone to stand guard there. Bryce again was able to sneak some of his food to Alycia, and again in the middle of the night she snuck out since no one was watching. She suspected she probably would not be able to keep her secret much longer, and she was right.

David was up early the next morning, heading outside to freshen up at the well before anyone else was up. He poured a bucket of water over his head and decided to use a part of the cloth covering the back of the carriage as a towel. He pulled a section of it up and was stunned at what he saw.

"Alycia, what in God's name are you doing here? Are you mad?"

She looked up at him with those striking eyes. "Donald, don't be angry with me."

"Get out! Of course, I'm angry with you. Do you have any idea what you've done? No doubt, the king has sent out men looking for you, and I'll be held responsible. And what will your father say?"

Even though she had been hiding in the carriage for almost three days, David could not help noticing how pretty she still looked. As he kept looking at her, he started to wonder what Sir Michael and Sir Walter would say. He did not have to wait long to find out..

"By Lucifer, what's going on?" Sir Michael said. "Donald, what have you done?"

"I just found her here. I swear I knew nothing about this."

"This is all my doing," Alycia said. "I hid in the back of the carriage. Donald just found me."

"It's been almost three days," Walter said. "You must not have eaten anything. Bryce, get Alycia something to eat."

While Bryce knew that was not true, he went into the farmhouse to get her something.

"I'm sorry if I caused any of you a problem, but I had to leave London, I just had to."

"This is terrible," Michael said. "I cannot imagine any good can come of it."

"What do you suggest?" David asked.

"I think we should turn around and take her right back to London," Sir Walter said.

"No! I won't go. If you take me back, I'll run away again," Alycia yelled.

"Donald, you're our leader. It should be your decision as to what we should do," Michael said.

David walked away, thinking about what should be done.

"This is what I order. Two of the men-at-arms will return to London and inform the king what Alycia did, and that she is safe. The rest of us will stop at Northampton and confer with Baron Geoffrey, who should have returned from France. We may send for Baron Henry instead of bringing her back to York, asking for his counsel."

Walter and Michael looked at each other and nodded.

"Very wise," Michael said. "If we return her to London, she probably will just do it again. Her father must be informed and decide what to do. I agree. What do you think, Walter?"

"I also agree. It makes sense and is the best way to handle this."

David looked at Alycia. "You heard my decision. Will you promise not to run away, or do I need to tie you up?"

"Tie me up? All right, I promise I won't run away, as long as you guard me."

Michael and Walter smiled at each other. "Very well," David said. "You will stay with me until we get to Northampton."

David selected two of the men to return to London with the message. Then the rest of them left the farmhouse and continued on to Northampton.

York – June 1269

Alwyn and Brother Andrew arrived at York late in the afternoon. Alwyn knew where the Jewish Quarter was and asked someone where Aaron the moneylender lived. He was directed to a large, two-story stone house with a stable in the rear. He found it and a young girl answered.

"Is Aaron at home?" Alwyn asked.

"My grandfather is with someone. Who's calling?"

"Tell him I have a message for Baruch."

The girl closed the door. A few minutes later, an older man appeared.

"I am Aaron. Who are you?"

"I am Father Alwyn from Hedgestone Priory in Northampton. I was told Baruch of Northampton was staying here, and I have a message for him."

"I'm sorry, but I know no Baruch. You must be mistaken." Aaron started to close the door, but Alwyn held out his arm with the parchment and stopped him.

"I am not mistaken. I know Baruch, and I know he's here. This is an important message about his brother and his brother's children he must be given."

Alwyn saw Baruch at the door. "Father Alwyn. What about my brother and his family?"

Alwyn handed Baruch the parchment. He opened it and read it.

"Is this true, or did Hubert put you up to this?"

Alwyn hesitated. "I was told it is true."

"If so, why are you delivering the news to me and not one of my people?"

Hubert had devised a cover story in case Baruch was skeptical. "Rabbi Ezra came to Prior Bartholomew for help, but he's too old, so Abbot Hubert offered to help. Since I'm from York, I said I would go."

"Do you know why they were all arrested?"

"I'm sorry, but I don't."

"What do you think, Baruch?" Aaron asked.

"I'm not sure. Hubert is cunning, and this may be his way of getting me back to Northampton. If Mordecai and his family are in trouble, I must be there to help them. I can't take the risk this is true and I'm not there to help."

Baruch turned to Alwyn. "Tell Hubert that if he is responsible for lying to me, he will regret it. And you will too if I find out you were an accomplice."

"I'll tell him," Alwyn said, as he quickly placed another parchment, this one quite small, in Baruch's hand, hiding it from Andrew.

As they left, Andrew looked at Alwyn. "Is it true, Father Alwyn?"

"Who knows what the truth is anymore, Andrew? Who knows?"

Northampton – June 1269

Alycia embraced Lady Catherine with tears in her eyes.

"Am I a bad person? I know I disobeyed my father, but I couldn't help it."

Catherine lightly stroked Alycia's hair to help soothe her.

"My dear child, I believe you are too young to be placed in such a position. Our society requires us to be directed by men. We are not free to follow our hearts. Nobility can be a blessing and a curse at the same time."

Alycia rubbed her eyes. "Lady Catherine, what am I to do?"

"Frankly, I don't know. My husband should be returning any day now. Donald wants his counsel about this matter. I suspect Geoffrey will send for your father, who will be quite angry with you for leaving the king without a by-your-leave."

Alycia regained her composure.

"I don't care. I will do what I want, not what anyone else wants. It's time to change these archaic customs."

Catherine smiled at this vivacious, strong-willed girl.

"You may be right, Alycia. It may be time to change. Though it will not be easy and will not take place overnight."

Baron Geoffrey did return three days later. He met with David, Michael, and Walter in the great hall.

"Well, she certainly has caused a problem. You were right to bring her here. I will send for Baron Henry. I believe he must deal with her directly, and it would be better here than in York."

"Thank you, Baron Geoffrey," David said. "I must admit I don't have any experience in these matters. My wish is to serve Baron Henry, and I don't want to fail him."

Geoffrey gave David a reassuring look.

"Trust me, Donald, Henry knows his daughter well. I doubt if he'll be surprised to hear what she's done, and I'm sure he will not blame you."

"I hope you are correct. He trusted me to lead her escort to London, which I did. I never expected this to happen."

"And you couldn't have. Honestly, I would not have as well."

Northampton – July 1269

Alycia sat in her chamber, contemplating what seemed to be a bleak future. She knew her father would take her back to London himself, and then arrange it with the king to ensure she could not run away again. Would she be imprisoned? Guarded at all times? What will her life be? No, she said to herself. I will never live like that. Never. I would rather die. If I cannot have Donald, I will never be happy. Why cannot anyone other than Lady Catherine understand what I am feeling? I should be grateful for the life I was given but I would trade it in an instant if I could have Donald. She decided she had to try one more time. She went down to the courtyard, where she found David sharpening his sword. He smiled when he saw her. She had bathed, was wearing a bright green dress Catherine had given her and had scented her body with one of Catherine's perfumes.

"Hello, Donald."

"Alycia. You look much improved from the trip here."

Alycia blushed. "I never wanted you to see me like that, but I had no choice." Then she paused for a moment. "Donald, I need to talk to you about something serious."

"All right. Let us move away from anyone who may be listening."

They walked to a hidden alcove in a corner of the courtyard. There was a bench there, as it was a place for reflection. He was certain his feelings for her would be so apparent that trying to hide them would prove futile. He guessed what she wanted to talk to him about, knowing that he again could only answer her one way, but admitting to himself it was getting harder and harder to refuse her advances. He worried he might break down at any time. What man in his right mind could refuse such a woman? Her beauty was undeniable, and the more time he spent with her, he learned she seemed not to be what most perceived women like her to be like. She had a down-to-earth quality that made it even harder to push her away. Reality set in again, though. I am a Jew and will always be one. Then a seemingly impossible thought came over him—does she love me enough to renounce her religion and convert? No, it would be heresy, and no doubt Father Zacharias would have her sent to the stake. It cannot be. Then, David had another thought. I always was told I could never be a warrior, and look, I am closer than ever. Has God placed me in this position to change Alycia? Could this help to reconcile my people and hers? No, he concluded. That was too much to hope for.

"Donald. You don't take me seriously, do you?"

"Alycia, how many times must we talk about this? A baron's daughter cannot marry whomever she wants. A baron's daughter cannot marry me, and no matter what my desires are, I can never marry a baron's daughter."

Alycia tried to maintain her composure. "Donald, don't you believe that true love is more important than anything else? I believe that."

David raised his voice slightly. "What I believe doesn't matter. What matters is what your father and the king believe and dictate."

Alycia took David's right hand. "Donald, I love you enough to renounce my birthright and spend my life with you. That's the only thing that matters to me."

Even though David had heard her express her love before, this was the first time she had taken it this far. This, and her manner and inflections, affected him deeper this time. His voice warbled, and he became nervous.

"Alycia, Alycia. You cannot renounce your birthright. Why do you persist and make it so difficult for me?"

"Because I know we love each other. I know that no matter what you say, your feelings override them. You want me, you love me, and if we leave before my father gets here, we can run away and be together."

As their eyes locked, he could not resist. Their lips met, the passion between them greater than even he could understand. He held her tightly as their tongues almost became one. David could feel his excitement growing quickly. Alycia reached down and felt the result of her advances. David came to his senses and pushed her away.

"No, stop. Please. I can't do this to your father."

"My father? You would deny yourself my love and my body because of my father? He doesn't have to know. It can be our secret."

David began to get angry. "No. I will not dishonor him."

"You want me, I know you do. Now is your chance."

David walked a few steps away and turned around.

"Of course, I want you. I want you more than you could know. But my honor and future as a knight is at stake, and I can't jeopardize that."

"Even for me?"

"Alycia. Please don't make this harder than it is. Go back to London. Get married and raise your sons and daughters and forget about me."

Alycia looked at David, and she suddenly sensed there was something he was not telling her.

"Donald, you're hiding something from me, aren't you?"

Taken by surprise, he became defensive. "I don't know what you mean."

"Yes, you do. You keep using my father as your excuse, but I think there's more to it."

"No, Alycia, there isn't. You know becoming a knight must be my first priority, and I can't let anything or anyone get in my way. Unfortunately, that means you as well. Don't wait for me, as I have no idea how long it will take, or even if it will happen."

"No, Donald. My father will make sure you are knighted. The king himself may do so himself in a year. I can wait. I will wait. We will be together. You cannot deny me."

Alycia turned and started to run back to her chamber, almost crashing into Sir Michael, who noticed she was upset and holding back tears.

"Lady Alycia. Are you all right? Have you been talking to Donald again?"

She nodded.

"Alycia, I'm sorry, but I must tell you something. Donald is pledged to a girl in Coby Hollow where he is from."

Alycia's face betrayed her shock.

"What? How do you know this?"

"Donald told me in confidence. He always had an excuse not to go with us to the brothels, so he told me the reason why. I would never want to see you hurt, but you needed to know that."

The devastated look on her face frightened the seasoned warrior. "But he just told me he wanted me. Why didn't he tell me that when I admitted my feelings for him again and again? Why? Why?"

She did not wait for Sir Michael to answer. She sped back to her chamber, locked the door, and collapsed on the bed, sobbing uncontrollably.

"My life is over," she whispered to herself. "I don't want to live anymore."

Chapter Twenty-Eight

Hedgestone Priory – July 1269

"So, Alwyn, what did Baruch say when he read the parchment?"

"He asked me if it was true, or if it was your way of getting him to return."

Hubert laughed. "He is smart, that Jew, but not smart enough. When will he arrive in Northampton?"

"I imagine any day now. He told me to tell you if he discovered this was a lie of your doing, you and I would regret it."

Hubert laughed again. "Oh, he threatened me, did he?" Alwyn frowned when Hubert said me and not us.

"There's nothing he can do to me. Nothing at all. Alwyn, I want you to send one of the brothers to watch for his return, let me know immediately when he's back, and make sure he's discreet."

This time I will demand even more, Hubert thought, and he will give it to me.

Northampton – July 1269

John de Oxenden hurried to the castle. His wife had overheard in the marketplace Sir Walter had returned to Northampton with Lady Alycia, who had run away from London. The sheriff wanted to question Walter and the young warrior who he had been told was with him the night Ralph and Tom were found dead.

The guards at the castle gate knew the sheriff, and waved him in. He went searching for Walter, who was resting in the barracks.

"Walter, I need to talk to you," John said sternly.

Walter sat up. "What about?"

"Do you know what happened the night before you left for London?"

"No, I don't."

"Two men who had been at the Swords Point were murdered, apparently right after they left. I was told by a barmaid they left with a young man-at-arms who had been sitting with you. Who is he?"

"Do you think he killed them?"

"I don't know, but right now he's the prime suspect."

"John, this man saved Baron Henry de Percy's life and his daughter's as well. He's under Baron Henry's protection. You'd better be certain before accusing him. Who were the men?"

"They were nobodies, former followers of de Montfort, I understand."

"Perhaps they had done something to deserve it or were set upon by robbers. It does happen, you know."

The sheriff grew irritated with Walter's apparent lack of cooperation and nonchalance.

"Walter, as sheriff it's my responsibility to try to find the killer. Now, who is this man?"

"His name is Donald, and he's here in Northampton waiting for the arrival of Baron Henry. Come with me, and I'll take you to him."

John followed Walter out of the barracks, and found David sitting alone with a mug of ale. He looked up to see Walter with another man.

"Donald, this is John de Oxenden, Sheriff of Northampton. He wants to talk to you."

"Sheriff, what can I do for you?"

"I understand you were at the Swords Point tavern a few weeks ago with Sir Walter here."

"Yes, with him and Sir Michael."

"Did you leave with them?"

David knew what the sheriff was trying to get out of him and assumed someone, probably a barmaid, told the sheriff he was present. "No, I stayed and drank some more with two men who were talking about their experiences. I was interested to hear what they had to say. We left together, but I went back to the barracks since we were leaving for London the next day. Why do you want to know?"

John looked suspiciously at David. "They were murdered near there that night."

David's eyebrows elevated, his mouth agape. "I had no idea. I suppose you think I killed them?"

"Did you?" the sheriff asked.

David felt slightly nervous but managed to keep calm. "Sheriff, why in Our Lady's name would I kill them? Baron Henry had entrusted me with the safety of his daughter. I'm trying to become a knight. Do you think I would kill two men I had just met for no reason, possibly ruining everything I am working toward?'

"No, I don't suppose you would, unless you had a reason."

"Did you find their purses on them?"

"No."

"Then they must have been ambushed by robbers. They were quite drunk, so they would have been easy prey."

"John, I can vouch for Donald. If he said he didn't kill them, then I'm sure he didn't."

The sheriff turned to David again. "Do you, as a good Christian, swear on Our Lord Jesus' name you did not kill those men?"

David stood and faced John. "As a good Christian, I swear on Jesus' name I did not."

"Satisfied?" Walter asked John.

"I suppose so. I'm sorry to have bothered you."

"No bother, Sheriff. You're only doing your job. I hope you find the one or ones who did it."

"Thank you. I intend to."

West End – July 1269

Upon arriving at West End, Baruch immediately went to Mordecai's house and banged on the door. Rachel answered.

"Uncle Baruch. Is everything all right?"

"Rachel, you aren't arrested. Where's everyone else?"

"Arrested? No one has been arrested. Father is out, and Benjamin is at cheder."

"I knew it," Baruch said. "That swine Hubert tricked me into returning. Well, it won't work. I won't give him a penny, no matter what he threatens."

"Hubert?" Rachel asked. "I don't know what you're talking about."

Baruch hugged his niece. "I'm sorry, Rachel. I hope I didn't upset you. I was told the family had been arrested, but apparently it was someone's idea of a bad joke. All is well. Tell your father I'll see him later."

Baruch went home. He noticed his housekeeper had maintained it well in his absence. There must be a way to thwart Hubert's plan, he thought. There must be. He pulled out the second parchment Alwyn had slipped into his hand and reread it. And suddenly it came to him. The question was would Alwyn help him? Baruch would risk he would.

Northampton – July 1269

Alycia knew her father would arrive at any time. She spent a few days sulking after Sir Michael had told her Donald was pledged to someone in Coby Hollow. She avoided everyone, staying primarily in her chamber. Even when Lady Catherine came to check on her, she lied and said she was fine. David had not tried to see her, thinking it was better to leave her alone before she no doubt would return to London with Baron Henry.

Her mind began to wander, and she started to fantasize about a life with whom she referred to as her Donald. This caused her confidence to grow, and she decided she still would not give up. After all, why would an up-and-coming knight choose a peasant girl over her? Donald loves me, he wants me, and it is only a matter of time before he and I are betrothed, she convinced herself. She would try to talk to her father again, and perhaps under the circumstances he might change his mind about sending her back to London. If not, she had to be prepared to do something else, although she did not know what that would be.

West End – July 1269

Rabbi Ezra was dumbfounded at what he had just heard.

"Baruch, tell me again."

"I want to distribute my wealth to the poorest families in West End, as well as to the synagogue."

Ezra took a moment to take in what Baruch told him. "Tell me why."

Baruch shook his head. "Rabbi, it's better you don't know why. Let's just say that since I have no immediate family, and under the edict all my wealth will go to the king upon my death, I wish to be remembered as a great philanthropist."

"I see. We will leave it at that. How do you wish to proceed?"

Baruch sat with his hands held together. "I will bring you an accounting that includes everything, including all outstanding loans. With one exception, they will all be forgiven."

"Are there Jewish and Christian debtors?"

"Yes, there are both. Most are for smaller amounts, although I am sure those families will be better off if they don't have to pay any more back."

"Baruch, whatever your reason for doing this, I want to thank you. Your kind gesture will bring relief to a number of people. I assume you will take care of your brother on your own?"

"I haven't told him yet, but yes, I will set aside some for him and his family."

Ezra's expression quickly changed. "Baruch, is it legal for you to do this? Are not the loans registered in the archa, and will not the king require the payments go to him?"

"I'll have documents drawn up that show all payments have been received. I do not believe there will be any problems."

"Baruch, I only hope you will not regret your incredible act of charity."

"I'm sure I won't."

Northampton – August 1269

"Alycia, I cannot believe what you've done! You have shamed me."

"Father, I meant no disrespect, I swear. I just couldn't stay there another day."

"You were hardly there. Only a few days."

"They were enough. Please, Father, please don't send me back. If you do, I'll run away again."

Baron Henry de Percy paced around his daughter's chamber. "I told your mother this might happen, but she said you would honor our wishes."

Alycia looked innocently at her father. "Father, I thought I would. Please believe me. I just couldn't."

"Is it Donald? Is he why you left?"

Tears began to flow down her cheeks. "I'm sorry, Father, but I love him so much. I must be his wife. I can't stop thinking about him. Please help me to be happy for the rest of my life."

Henry adored his daughter, even though she had a mind of her own, and always exhibited a somewhat rebellious nature. Henry himself held this Donald in his highest admiration, even though he was not nobly born, and did not know much else about him. Henry had not cared, since Donald had saved his life and Alycia's as well, and he never thought Alycia truly would be interested in someone out of their rank.

Donald also had demonstrated a high degree of character. He was quite different from the other men-at-arms, squires, and most of the men the baron had known, and Henry did not understand how that could be. A peasant boy raised in a tiny village after his parents had died? He was unique. In his heart, Henry believed Donald would make a fine husband for Alycia, regardless of his birth. Could he help his daughter to get her wish?

"Alycia, are you absolutely certain Donald wants to marry you?"

Alycia was taken aback by the question. Even though Donald had told her it was impossible, and Michael had told her about him being committed to another girl, there was only one answer she could give her father.

"I am certain, Father."

"Very well. No doubt I will suffer for this, but I want you to be happy."

Alycia could not believe it. "Did I hear you correctly? You will help me to marry Donald?"

"There is only one way—if he is knighted. But you must wait until that happens. Can you do that?"

"Yes. Yes. Of course, I can. But I will not go back to London."

"That I cannot promise, but I won't make you return right away. I'll first seek Geoffrey's counsel. If the king was offended by your leaving, you will have to return and beg his forgiveness. We can't have his majesty angry with us. Don't you realize that may hurt our chances to have Donald knighted sooner than later?"

The joy on Alycia's face vanished. "I never thought of that. I pray I haven't made a terrible mistake."

Henry tried to soothe her. "Let's not jump to conclusions. We don't know if the king really cares. He does have more important matters to worry about, and Donald had nothing to do with your leaving."

"I hope you're right." Alycia hugged her father and kissed him on both cheeks. "Thank you, Father. I was beginning to think my life was over, and now you have given me new hope."

"Alycia, I don't want you to tell Donald about our conversation."

"But, why not? He will be so happy to hear the news, and perhaps try to earn his knighthood sooner."

"You must not tell him because we don't want to get his hopes up. We have much to do for you to get your wish."

"Very well," she reluctantly said. "I won't tell him."

Hedgestone Priory – August 1269

Hubert knew he was running out of time. The three months Bishop Basil gave him were over. Basil will not care Baruch escaped to York to avoid him. Now that Baruch was back, it was time to confront him before Basil either sent for him or possibly showed up at Hedgestone. Just as Hubert prepared to go to Baruch's house, Alwyn appeared.

"Hubert, Baruch is here to see you."

"What?" Hubert exclaimed. "He's here?"

"Yes, he just arrived."

"Excellent. I will meet with him in the scriptorium."

Hubert was overcome with joy. Baruch must have come to his senses and realized he cannot avoid me. Hubert waited for several minutes, and then hurried to meet the Jew.

Baruch and Alwyn were both in the scriptorium when Hubert arrived.

"Baruch, I'm glad you've returned. You should have told me you were leaving."

"Why? I don't answer to you."

"No, but you don't want to anger me." Hubert looked at Alwyn. "You may go, Alwyn."

"No," Baruch said. "Alwyn will stay."

Hubert nearly exploded. "Who are you to rescind my order?"

"Sit down, Hubert," Baruch ordered. "Listen to me."

Alwyn smiled. "You had better do as he says, Hubert."

Hubert sat down, wondering what was going on.

Baruch stood and pointed at the abbot. "You are finished trying to control and threaten me. I have liquidated all my assets, and you can get nothing more from me."

Hubert's jaw dropped. "You can't do that. Besides, I will expose your nephew if you fail to do as I demand."

Baruch shook his head. "No, you will not expose him."

"Why not?"

"Because if you do, Alwyn will testify he caught you and me together. I don't think the bishop would approve of that."

Hubert looked at Alwyn. "You know what I will do to you if you betray me."

"Brother Thomas is dead. I learned that when I was in York delivering your parchment. You have no witnesses."

Hubert stood, fuming. "You would lie for this Jew? And you, Baruch, would risk being ostracized by your people, or even worse?"

"This Jew has more morality and integrity than you ever had," Alwyn said. "I don't share your feelings against the Jews. If I can help to destroy you, I will happily do so, and am willing to take any risk."

Hubert sat down. Baruch must have paid Alwyn off, he thought.

"Well, Hubert?" Baruch asked. "Are you finished with your scheme?"

Hubert glared at Baruch. "I am not finished with you. You will not get away with lying about me. No one will believe either of you."

Baruch laughed. "Is that a risk you are willing to take? The bishop will no doubt deal harshly with an abbot who he believes acts in that way, especially with a Jew, don't you agree? The Church cannot have known sodomizers leading its flock, now can it?"

Hubert was fuming. It is not over, he thought.

Northampton – August 1269

Baron Geoffrey listened carefully to everything Baron Henry told him. While the king had been very grateful to both of them for their previous service during the Baron's War, Geoffrey did not know how King Henry might react in this situation.

"Henry, my friend," Geoffrey said, "I think you let the love for your daughter color your judgment. Donald may never be knighted. The king certainly may want her back as a lady-in-waiting, only because she ran away without permission. She may never get what she wants."

"I know, Geoffrey. I'm going back to London to explain to the king what happened. My hope is he'll understand the motivations of a young girl."

"When are you leaving?"

"First thing tomorrow. May I leave Alycia here with you? I also would appreciate it if Donald and Sir Michael can remain here as well. I'll take the other men-at-arms with those I brought for more protection."

"Of course. They may stay as long as you would like them to. I will make sure Donald resumes his training with Michael and Walter."

"Thank you. I am in your debt."

"Not at all. I'm glad to help."

West End – August 1269

Mordecai stared at his brother, shocked at what he had just heard.

"Tell me again, Baruch. I don't think I heard you correctly the first time."

"I am cancelling almost all outstanding loans and giving away all of my money. Well, almost all of it. Some I have well hidden. I will give some to the synagogue, some to the poor, and I have some for you, Hannah, and the children. By the way, have you heard anything from David?"

Mordecai was still trying to absorb the news.

"No, I haven't. But why? Why?"

"To thwart Hubert, of course. If I don't have any money, he cannot demand any from me. It's the only way. Hubert will take everything if I don't stand up to him, and he'll expose David anyway. I'm sure of it. His lie to me about you and the children being arrested proves it. He will stop at nothing."

"Yes," Mordecai said, "but then he will expose David."

Baruch shook his head. "No, my brother, he won't. I've taken care of that."

"I don't understand."

"You don't have to. The less you know, the better."

"Will you be leaving Northampton then?"

"No, not right away. I must be sure Hubert doesn't try anything." Baruch and Alwyn had discussed the possibility Hubert might even try to kill Alwyn.

"Good. Still, I'm afraid that no matter what you think you are doing is under the law, the sheriff will think differently. You may be arrested."

Baruch shook his head. "I don't think the abbot will allow that. He would not want my reason for divesting my assets to be divulged."

"I hope you know what you're doing."

"Trust me. I believe I do."

Hedgestone Priory – August 1269

Abbot Hubert paced in the scriptorium. He decided he was not surprised at Alwyn's betrayal. *He was always scheming against me*, he thought. *He most likely even approached Bishop Basil with the idea of spying on me. I should never have trusted him, never. God only knows what he told the bishop.*

Hubert sat down and poured himself a glass of wine. He took a long drink, savoring its flavor as he began to formulate his plan. He took a parchment and quill and began to write. When he finished, he rolled it up, melted the sealing wax to seal it, and stamped his seal into the soft wax.

He leaned back in his chair. *No, Baruch and Alwyn, you cannot thwart me. I am smarter and much cleverer than both of you. The only way to stop me is to kill me, and neither of you has the stomach to do that.*

Hubert left the scriptorium and found Brother Dominic. He pulled him off to one side and whispered to him.

"Dominic. Take this parchment and wait seven days. If you do not hear from me, I want you to go to York and personally deliver it to Father Zachariah, and only him. You must not tell anyone about this, especially Father Alwyn, understand?"

"Yes, Abbot. I understand."

"Good. You will be well-rewarded for doing this for me. Now, hide it and go about your business."

Hubert felt incredibly pleased with himself. *There, Baruch, I am not the only one who can expose David as a lying Jew. You cannot outsmart me.* Now, I must find a way to stop the bishop. I suspect either he will come to see me himself or will send that lackey Eustace to fetch me. However, I may never be able to satisfy Basil. Perhaps I should speak to Baron Geoffrey. Maybe I can convince him it was Basil who ordered his brother excommunicated and not me, and I was only sheltering the bishop. If he believes that and he takes out his revenge on Basil, I will be in the clear with him. Geoffrey also hates Alwyn. Perhaps I can also convince him Alwyn was involved as well.

The more Hubert thought about that idea, the more he liked it, although he realized it was extremely bold and risky. After all, it was certainly plausible. *The land my brother wanted is next to Church land, so we were only following the bishop's orders. Geoffrey will believe it. He must.*

Chapter Twenty-Nine

Northampton – September 1269

David felt extremely uneasy about remaining in Northampton. The more he thought about the sheriff, the more worried he became. *Can he link me to Tom and Ralph somehow? While I do not think so, he is very inquisitive. I believe he still is looking for the one who took the forester's weapons. What if he learns of my story about Coby Hollow? It wouldn't be hard for him to discover my lie. I can only hope Baron Henry returns soon.*

Alycia spent most of her days watching David train. Sir Michael and Sir Walter continued to work with him. They both were pleased with David's progress. His skills with the sword and shield had increased tremendously, and he regularly defeated both of them. His jousting also had improved, and both knights found it quite difficult to best him.

"Donald," Sir Michael said after another long day of training, "you are the best student of the art of fighting I have ever seen. I am proud of your accomplishments. I'll report to Baron Henry your initial training has been completed."

"Thank you, Sir Michael. I've been blessed with excellent teachers, especially you and Sir Walter."

Alycia was standing nearby and heard every word. Smiling, she ran up to David.

"Donald, I'm so proud of you! Perhaps now you'll be knighted very, very soon!"

Sir Michael laughed as David looked at her. A slight breeze blew her hair in front of her eyes, but he still could see and feel their radiance. She wore one of her low-cut dresses, which always brought excitement to him, and stares from the other men. Alycia knew it, and hoped they made David feel jealous. *Every day she seems to get lovelier,* he thought. *My dearest God. She can only mean trouble for me. She would never keep my secret. She would feel betrayed just like everyone else. No one had ever heard of a Christian marrying a Jew. Who would even* marry us if we kept our own religions? The rabbis would never accept me, even if I refused to convert. Why can't all men and women be free to choose their own destiny and their loved ones? These clerics quote scripture and say it is God's will. How do they know what is God's will? Why aren't they challenged on these seemingly arbitrary ideas and restrictions? I don't understand it at all.

"Donald? Are you there?" Alycia asked.

David realized he had been in a daze, and she brought him out of it.

"Yes, Alycia. I'm sorry. I guess my mind was off somewhere else."

"I hope you were thinking about me," she said almost whispering.

David brushed the windblown strands of her hair away from her eyes.

"Alycia, Alycia. How could any man not think of you?"

"You know I don't think about any man except you."

David tried not to react to her, but he knew he could not resist. Kissing her in front of Sir Michael, what he really wanted to do, was impossible.

"I don't know what to say. I never know what to say when you speak to me like that."

Alycia took David's right hand. "Just say you love me."

"Alycia, I'm more afraid of even thinking of loving you than I am of being in battle. I've told you before. I am nothing. You are the baron's daughter. Please stop teasing me."

"Donald, you are mistaken. I am not teasing you. You are not nothing. You will be a knight, and as soon as that happens, my father has agreed we can be wed."

"No, that's not possible. You can't be correct."

She held his hand even tighter. "It's true, my love. My father and I discussed it before he left for London."

"Will he be asking the king again to grant me knighthood?"

"I don't know. He first has to explain why I ran away. I'm praying when the king, and hopefully the queen, hears his explanation, he'll be generous and offer it."

David made her release his hand, and he began pacing. This has gone too far, he thought. What if Baron Henry succeeds with her wishes? Never in my wildest dreams did I ever believe this may be a possibility, and now it actually may be. I cannot hide my being Jewish forever, especially on our wedding night.

"Let's wait and see what your father says when he returns."

"Yes," she said with a huge grin. "Until he returns."

Northampton – September 1269

John de Oxenden fixated on the murders and the answers this Donald gave him. No, there is no proof he had anything to do with the murders, but there is no proof he did not, only his word and Sir Walter vouching for him. Who is this man, anyway? I need to learn more about him.

John returned to the castle to speak to David again. As he approached the gate, he saw the same guards.

"Good day, Dirk, Stephen."

"Good day, Sheriff," they replied.

"Any excitement today?"

Both laughed. "Nothing," Stephen answered, "except me trying to keep Dirk from falling asleep."

"Do you know if the man called Donald is in the castle?"

"Donald? Oh yes, you mean the man from Coby Hollow who won the archery contest last year."

The sheriff looked confused. "Coby Hollow? Archery contest?"

"Aye," Dirk said. "Remember when Baron Henry's man defeated Richard de Tal, Baron Geoffrey's archer last year? I heard he was from Coby Hollow."

"Coby Hollow. There's nothing there but a few huts and some serfs. I've been there. How could that dung heap produce a champion archer?"

Dirk shook his head. "I don't know."

"And you are certain this Donald is the same person?"

"Aye, Sheriff. I was present at the tournament, and now he's returned with Lady Alycia, Baron Henry's daughter."

"Thank you, my friends." He handed a few pennies to Dirk. "Here, buy yourself some ale with these. But don't tell anyone what you just told me."

"Keep buying us ale and we won't speak another word to anyone ever," Stephen said, laughing.

John returned home. All of a sudden, he thought he had figured it out. This Donald must be the one who found the weapons since Coby Hollow is on the Salcey road. He must have taught himself archery, and somehow became the baron's champion. I cannot prove it, but it must be true. Yet I still cannot tie him to the murders of Tom and Ralph. I need to know more about him. Tomorrow I will go to Coby Hollow and make inquiries. Someone there will be able to tell me about him.

Alycia decided to take a walk around the castle grounds before it got too dark. She was beginning to be a familiar face, and most of the servants and castle guards knew who she was. As she strolled, she approached the castle gate. Dirk and Stephen were still on duty.

"Good evening, my lady," Dirk said.

"Good evening. It's a fine evening, is it not?"

"Yes, my lady," Stephen said.

"Tell me, earlier I saw the sheriff speaking to you, but he didn't enter the castle. Did he want something?"

Dirk appeared nervous and did not answer.

"I asked you a question. Don't you respond to a baron's daughter?"

"We're sorry, my lady," Stephen said, "but the sheriff made us promise not to say anything and gave us pennies to keep quiet."

"I see. Well, I will give you twice as much to tell me what he wanted." Alycia thought if the sheriff was inquiring about her for the king, she had to know about it.

"I'm sorry, my lady, but we'll be in trouble with the sheriff if we tell," Dirk said.

Alycia became angry. "I'll have you flogged if you don't tell me, and you won't get paid. Now, what will it be?"

The two guards quickly changed their minds.

"Very well. He was asking about Donald."

"Donald? Why would he be interested in him?"

"We don't know. He asked about him, and we simply mentioned he was the champion of the archery contest last year. Suddenly he became much more interested."

"In what way more interested?"

"I'm not certain. I believe it was because he's from Coby Hollow."

"Anything else?"

"No, that's all."

"I'll send a servant with the pennies for each of you. I won't tell anyone you told me, and you had better not tell anyone, do you understand?"

"Yes, we understand, and no, my lady," they said in unison. "We won't."

Alycia walked back towards the castle, becoming slightly panicked. Why would the sheriff be interested in Donald? Did he commit a crime? He could not have. I must find out to protect him.

Baron Geoffrey could not believe Abbot Hubert had come to speak to him. *What in God's name could that cur want to talk to me about? He knows I hate him and would kill him if I could.* Geoffrey initially planned to have Hubert sent away. Then his curiosity got the better of him, and he decided to hear what the man had to say.

Geoffrey had Hubert brought into the great hall. He bowed, to Geoffrey's surprise.

"Baron Geoffrey. Thank you for seeing me. I hope you are well, and I hope after you hear what I have to say we may put aside our differences."

Geoffrey grunted. "You can cut out the courtesies, Hubert. What do you want?"

"May I sit down?"

Geoffrey motioned for him to sit in front of him.

"Baron, I must tell you the truth about what happened with your brother's excommunication."

"I know the truth. You were responsible."

"Not exactly."

"What do you mean?"

Hubert put his hands together. "Bishop Basil ordered me to falsely accuse him."

Geoffrey looked incredulously at the abbot. "That makes no sense. Basil had nothing to do with it."

"Baron, your brother's land is next to Church land, is it not?"

"You know it is."

"The bishop ordered me to get your brother to sell the land, but when he refused, Basil told me to falsely accuse him of heresy. Alwyn also was involved."

"I don't believe you. You wanted that land for your brother. Besides, Basil is in London, is he not? And I remember when you forced me to give you shelter a few years ago, you told me you had been summoned by Bishop Basil but didn't know him, and Alwyn didn't either. I'm not a fool. Now, get out of here before I put you in irons."

Hubert had forgotten what he had told Geoffrey. Without bowing or saying anything he hurried out of the castle. I made a huge mistake, he said to himself. I need another way to stop Basil, but I do not know what.

Alycia ordered a servant to bring Cyrus to her. After a few minutes, he appeared.

"My lady," he said, bowing. "You summoned me?"

"Come here, Cyrus. I need your help."

"My help?" he asked, quite surprised.

"Do you know where Coby Hollow is?"

"Yes. It's a small village at the other side of Salcey."

"Would you go there for me at first light tomorrow?"

"I first must ask Baron Geoffrey's permission."

Alycia had not considered that. Geoffrey would want to know why, and he could not know. She had to try something else.

"Never mind. Can you have a horse ready for me so I can go? And you must not tell anyone."

"By yourself, my lady? It's too dangerous. The baron and Donald will be furious when they discover what you have done."

"You're right. Forget I even talked to you."

"I've forgotten already."

Alycia sat on her bed, wondering if there was anything she could do. I'm at a loss, she said to herself as tears began to stream down her cheeks. If the sheriff arrests Donald, if he truly is guilty of something, he may never be knighted and I will never be his wife. I must know what he is up to.

Coby Hollow – September 1269

It was a beautiful morning when John de Oxenden arrived at Coby Hollow on horseback. As he looked around at the few huts that made up this so-called village, he realized it looked the same as it had several years earlier when he had been there while traveling through Salcey. The only thing new, he noticed, was a small chapel.

The men were working in the fields, and he saw three women doing a variety of chores.

"You there, come here," he shouted.

One older woman, with stringy gray hair and wearing a torn, filthy old dress, answered.

"Who are you to order us around?"

"I am John de Oxenden, Sheriff of Northampton. How dare you speak to me like that."

The old woman spat on the ground. "I'll speak to you any way I want."

"Answer my questions, and I will give you each a silver penny."

At this, the three approached the sheriff, who did not dismount. "Well, what do you want to know?" the old woman asked.

"I was told there used to be someone here named Donald."

Again, she spat. "Another asking about a Donald. We don't know anything about him."

"Someone else asked about him?"

"Some time ago a monk came here asking the same question," one of the other women said.

"What you are saying is there never was a Donald living here?"

"Give us our pennies first before we say anything else," the old woman demanded.

John opened his purse and threw three silver pennies onto the dirt. "There, now tell me the truth."

Each of the women picked up a penny. "There hasn't been a Donald here since I was born," the old woman said.

John nodded, turned his horse around, and started back to Northampton.

Well, he said to himself, this Donald is a liar. Also, if a monk was inquiring about him, then Hubert must have something to do with it. But why would Hubert be interested in this Donald? This Donald must be hiding a deep secret. Somehow, I must discover what it is, and when I do, no doubt it will answer a number of questions I have been asking these last few years. I am sure of it.

Northampton – September 1269

Sitting in the castle courtyard, David saw Alycia approaching. Her hair was tied back, and she was wearing a bright blue dress that complemented her eyes.

"Alycia, you wanted to talk to me?"

"Donald, yes, I must tell you something."

"Well, what is it?"

She told him of her conversation with the two guards.

"The sheriff was asking about me and where I came from?"

"Yes. Why would he be interested in you? Did you do something wrong?"

David was not surprised to hear of the sheriff's continued questioning about him. He now was certain the sheriff would go to Coby Hollow and no doubt find out he had been lying. He realized he could not leave until Baron Henry returned. He tried to decide what course of action to take, but Alycia kept pestering him with questions.

"Donald. Why is the sheriff so interested in you? Tell me. I must know."

"The sheriff thinks I killed two men before we left for London."

"Did you?"

"I told him I didn't."

"But why his interest in Coby Hollow? What could he learn there?"

"Alycia, what I'm going to tell you, you must never tell anyone, promise?"

"Of course, my love. I would never betray you."

"Remember how I saved your father's life?" Alycia nodded.

"One day while walking in Salcey, I found a forester who had died. There were no wounds or blood or anything to suggest how he died. I took his weapons and secretly taught myself archery. That's how I was able to save your father. The sheriff never found out who took the forester's weapons and has not stopped trying."

This confused Alycia. "But you didn't kill the forester. Why can't the truth now be told?"

David shook his head. "No, I did not kill the forester, but I was afraid I would be accused of doing so, and it could be said I stole the weapons."

"That was a long time ago. You've proven yourself. My father will protect you and not allow this sheriff to arrest you. I'm sure of it."

"It's not that simple. You see, I'm not from Coby Hollow."

"You're not? Then you don't have another girl there."

"No, I don't. I had to make up that story because I didn't want to go to the brothels with the men-at-arms."

A huge smile erupted on Alycia's face as she hugged David tightly. "Oh, Donald, that's the best news. When Sir Michael told me about another girl, I was devastated. So where are you from?"

"It's not important. I hope it doesn't matter to you."

"No, I don't care where you're from. I don't care if you did take the weapons, or even if you did kill those men. No doubt they deserved it. I only know I love you." She paused. "Donald, does my father know about this?"

"Yes. Your father and Baron Geoffrey know I took the weapons and did not kill the forester. They do not know I am not from Coby Hollow."

"Good. I'm glad they know. And I swear by Our Lady I will never tell anyone what you told me. You know you can trust me."

"I hope so, Alycia. I truly do."

Chapter Thirty

Northampton – October 1269

Hubert could not stop pacing. I will not be thwarted he kept saying to himself. I will call Baruch and Alwyn's bluff. Baruch will not risk the ramifications of his lies, and Alwyn never will throw away his future opportunities by cooperating with and defending a Jew. I first will go to Baruch and tell him I will inform Geoffrey Donald is a Jew. That should change his mind.

Hubert called for Brother Andrew to accompany him. They rode into West End to Baruch's house. "Open up, it's Abbot Hubert."

Baruch answered the door himself. "I have nothing to say to you, Hubert," he said, starting to close the door in the abbot's face.

"Not so fast, Baruch. I think you'd better listen to me."

Baruch let Hubert enter while Andrew waited outside.

"What do you want?"

"I'm giving you one more chance. Give me the two thousand pounds, or I'll tell Baron Geoffrey who this Donald really is."

"I told you I don't have any more money. All my funds have been liquidated."

"I don't believe you. If that's how you wish to proceed, I will go right now to Baron Geoffrey and expose David. I understand he's here in Northampton, waiting for Baron Henry to return. I can expose the lying Jew to his face."

Baruch grabbed Hubert by the front of his robe. "You are a wicked man, Hubert. I wish I had the courage to kill you here and now. But you will be defeated. Bishop Basil will punish you for me." Baruch let go of the abbot. "Now get the hell out of here!" he shouted, as he pushed Hubert out the door.

"Come with me, Andrew. I'll show you how to deal with Jews."

Hubert and Andrew mounted their horses and rode to the castle. At the gate, Hubert demanded to see Baron Geoffrey.

"Your Grace, I'm sorry, but Baron Geoffrey left strict orders not to admit you ever again," said one of the guards.

Hubert was not swayed. "Oh, he did, did he? Tell him I have information about a lying traitor who is now in his castle. Go, tell him."

The abbot intimidated the guard. "Yes, Your Grace, I guess that changes things." He ran to find the baron.

Hubert waited impatiently until the guard returned with Sir Walter.

"You are Abbot Hubert?" Walter asked.

"Yes. Take me to Baron Geoffrey."

"Follow me, Abbot, and only you."

Hubert told Andrew to wait at the gate, and he followed Walter into Geoffrey's great hall.

"What the hell are you doing back here, Hubert, with a story of a lying traitor? You had better not be playing tricks, or I swear by St. Cuthbert, this time I will slap you in irons."

"Baron Geoffrey, I swear to you I will speak the truth. It's about Baron Henry's man Donald."

Hubert then noticed there was another man in the hall.

"Well, Baron Henry has just returned from London, so I imagine he'll be most interested to hear what you came to say." Turning to Henry, Geoffrey said, "He's a snake, Henry, and a liar. I wouldn't believe anything he says."

Henry nodded. "What about Donald?" he asked Hubert.

Hubert bowed. "Baron Henry, I regret to inform you your man Donald is a Jew."

Geoffrey and Henry looked at each other and burst out laughing.

"You're mad, Abbot," Henry said. "How dare you accuse the man who saved my life, and my daughter's, of being a Jew?"

"It's true. He is David, the son of Mordecai the apothecary here in Northampton, and the nephew of Baruch, the moneylender."

"How do you know this?" Geoffrey demanded.

"I overheard two Jewish boys talking at the archery tournament last year. They clearly identified Donald as David, the brother of one of the boys."

"This is absurd," Henry said. "Donald is a warrior, he was baptized, and attends church. He's not a Jew."

"He also says he's from Coby Hollow. I sent a monk there, and no one ever heard of any Donald."

Henry grunted. "That means nothing. I'm sure he can explain that. It doesn't mean he's a Jew."

Hubert smiled. "There's one simple way to find out."

"How dare you come here with false accusations? I don't know your motives, but I reject your lies."

"My Lord Baron, perhaps if you were to bring Donald, I mean David, here, the truth can be quickly determined," Hubert said.

"Cyrus," Geoffrey ordered. "Bring Donald here at once, but don't tell him why he's being summoned."

Cyrus found him in the garden with Alycia.

"Donald, Baron Geoffrey requests your presence at once in the great hall. Lady Alycia, your father has just returned as well."

"I wonder what this can be about," Alycia said. "Perhaps father has some good news?"

The two of them followed Cyrus into the main hall. Donald approached the barons and bowed.

"My lord, you sent for me?"

"Yes. This is Abbot Hubert of Hedgestone Priory. He has made a serious allegation against you."

So, this is the Hubert of the message, David thought. I must be very cautious, since I have not prepared myself to be discovered like this, and I am not aware of what this abbot may know or not know.

"I'm sorry, but I don't know you, Abbot."

Hubert grunted. "No, but I know your uncle Baruch. You're a Jew."

David hid his shock. If he can tie me to my uncle, my family may be in danger.

"You're wrong, Abbot," Alycia said. "He's not a Jew. He's my lover, and I can attest to that."

The hall became silent. David stared at Alycia, completely surprised by her defending him.

"Alycia. Is that true? Have you given yourself to him?" Henry asked.

"Father, please don't be angry. It's not Donald's fault."

Hubert also was stunned by her confession. "My lords, she's trying to protect him. I swear to you he's a Jew. Check for yourself."

Henry became incensed. "How dare you challenge my daughter?

Geoffrey told me what a liar and immoral person you are. Get out of here now before I run you through."

"It's true! I swear it on Jesus' name."

Geoffrey called for his guards. "Throw this scum into the street and instruct every man-at-arms if he tries to enter the castle again, they have my permission to kill him."

Hubert screamed as the guards dragged him out of the castle. Andrew could not help laughing under his breath as they pushed Hubert onto the dirt.

"Donald, come here." Geoffrey said.

"Do you have any idea why Hubert would make such an accusation?"

"No, my lords. I never met him before. We stopped at Hedgestone on a stormy night when we were taking Lady Alycia to London, but he wasn't there and they wouldn't let us in because of her."

"Donald, you've been almost like a son to me," Henry said. "Tell me the truth. Are you a Jew?"

David knew there was only one answer he could offer. "I swear on Our Lady I am a Christian." He then crossed himself.

Henry nodded. "What about you not being from Coby Hollow?"

"I never meant to deceive anyone. I've lived in several places and simply decided to tell everyone I was from there. I didn't want to be seen as an outsider in this shire."

"That's good enough for me." Henry turned to Alycia. "Come with me. We need to talk."

Alycia looked at David as she left the hall with her father. David still could not get over what Alycia had done. She had told everyone she was no longer a virgin. Even though David had not slept with her, why would she so quickly defend him, and in such a way? Could she have believed Hubert and did it to save him? Why would she save a Jew? If so, she truly must love me, and perhaps this was her way for us to be lovers. As he tried to figure out her motives, Sir Michael patted him on the back.

"Donald, Baron Henry asked me to look after you. He told me what just happened. How absurd. Jews are not warriors and are forbidden to have weapons. The abbot is an idiot. The thought that you're a Jew." Michael laughed.

"Sir Michael, I have no idea why the abbot did that. I don't even know him."

"Geoffrey has instructed Walter to find out. Walter will be talking to the sheriff as well, but Baron Geoffrey has ordered him not to talk to Hubert, since we can't trust anything he says, and we can't let anyone, even a churchman, falsely accuse our fighting men, especially one that should be knighted soon."

David nodded. "He must be mad. It's the only explanation I can think of."

Henry struggled with what to say to his daughter.

"Alycia, how could you say that in front of everyone? Have you no shame?"

"I'm sorry, Father. I needed to stop that awful abbot from hurting Donald."

"Donald easily could have proven his Christianity himself. You didn't even give him a chance."

Alycia looked at her father. "I couldn't help it. I love him and will do anything for him."

"I believe you do love him. I won't ask you any details of your tryst. I also won't punish Donald, although I am disappointed in him."

Alycia was relieved her father did not question her again about her confession. She could not tell him the truth. While she was certain Donald was a Christian, she did not want to plant even the slightest seed of doubt in his mind. "Come now, Father, mother told me about the two of you before you were married."

"Oh, she did? While I don't condone what you did, I can understand it."

"You never told me what happened in London."

"No, with what happened, I didn't. The king understood why you left, and while he said I should punish you for not asking permission, you don't have to return. But Donald cannot yet be knighted. He needs to prove himself on the battlefield, or by performing a great deed for the king. Then, hopefully, he can be knighted and you can be wed."

Alycia expressed her joy at not having to return to London, but her disappointment at still having to wait. "Thank you, Father. I guess that's the best I could hope for right now."

Later that day, Alycia sought out David. She found him sitting at a table in the barracks, sipping a mug of ale.

"Alycia. You shouldn't be here in the barracks. Let's find a place to talk."

They proceeded to the alcove where they could have some privacy.

"So, are you happy with me?" she asked.

"Why did you tell everyone in the hall we are lovers?"

"Donald, I believe you are keeping some secret from me, but I don't believe you're a Jew. This was the only way I could think of to silence that evil man, and it worked. Besides, it's only a matter of time before we are lovers."

"Your father will have me flogged or worse for what you said."

"No, Donald, he told me he will not punish you."

"I'm glad. Still, I must apologize to him."

"No, you don't have to. He was young once himself, and I know he and my mother didn't wait either."

David caressed her left cheek. "I don't mean to keep anything from you, but I'm afraid that for the time being at least, I must. I hope you won't hold that against me."

"I love you, Donald, with all my heart. I know when you're ready, you will tell me everything."

They kissed, David feeling the push of her breasts against his tunic, and his passion swelling as their tongues met. Then reality returned. *What will she say when she does learn the truth?* he wondered. *What am I going to do? What will the barons do to me?*

Hedgestone Priory – October 1269

Hubert was livid. Not only was he made to look like a fool, the barons did not even try to verify what he said was true. They also did not summon Baruch or his brother, and they did not say they would question them or his family. He would have to redeem himself by proving Donald is indeed David, a Jew. He would let Father Zachariah in York do it for him. Baron Henry would listen to Zachariah, and since this David was training at York, perhaps it made more sense for him to be exposed there. He called for Brother Dominic, who appeared with Alwyn, Ambrose, and Bartholomew.

"What are all of you doing here? I only summoned Dominic. The rest of you I have no use for, as you are all against me."

Dominic stepped forward, holding the parchment Hubert had given him. Hubert noticed it had been opened, and therefore read.

"Hubert," Bartholomew said. "We are all against you. Brother Dominic brought us the parchment, and we read it. We never believed you would stoop so low, accusing Baron Henry's man of being a Jew to stir up resentment against the Jews because your plans were thwarted."

Hubert was astonished. "No, that's not true. Baron Henry's man is a Jew, Baruch's nephew. Alwyn, you know that. Tell them!"

Alwyn shook his head. "I know nothing of the sort."

"You lie. You were here with Baruch, his uncle, and both of you threatened me."

Alwyn addressed the others in the room. "See, he is mad. He continuously makes up stories. Abbot, I am afraid you need a long rest. We must inform the bishop of your condition."

Hubert lunged at Alwyn and began choking him. "I'll kill you, Alwyn!" he screamed. The others quickly pulled him off and tackled him to the ground.

"Get some rope and tie him up until he calms down," Bartholomew said.

Dominic and Ambrose held Hubert down while Alwyn tied him up. They gagged him as well since he did not stop yelling.

"What do we do now?" Ambrose asked.

"We get word to Bishop Basil of Hubert's madness. Until then, we will lock him in the cellar," Bartholomew said.

Northampton – October 1269

John de Oxenden left the castle after speaking with Sir Walter. So, Hubert accused this Donald of being a Jew. Baruch's nephew. Walter confirmed what I discovered that Donald is not from Coby Hollow, while Lady Alycia defended him. Walter told me his explanation for lying about where he was from, but is that the real reason? All this is very strange. The sheriff was convinced these events, including the missing weapons and the murders of Tom and Ralph, were all connected. But what ties them together? Is it this Donald? John first went to Baruch's house to question him.

"Sheriff. Please do come in," Baruch said.

"I'm sorry to barge in on you, but I must. I have some questions to ask you."

"Certainly. May I offer you some wine?"

"No, thank you. Tell me. Do you not have a nephew David?"

Baruch knew what was coming next. He and Mordecai had prepared a story in the event of something like this happening.

"Yes, I do. He used to live in Northampton, but he left quite some time ago to study in Germany. We have not heard from him since."

The sheriff believed he could gauge a man's honesty by his eyes. "I see."

"Why do you ask?"

"Abbot Hubert told Baron Geoffrey and Baron Henry that one of Henry's men who calls himself Donald is really your nephew David."

Baruch laughed. "Abbot Hubert, I am afraid, is going mad. First of all, how could a Jew become a man-at-arms? Secondly, Hubert has continued to try to borrow large sums from me, but without the proper collateral, I refused him. He may have made up this story to try to get back at me. Things have not been going well for him, I believe. I understand he has run the priory poorly, and the monks are all against him. This must have affected him."

"Do you remember a few years ago there was a forester found dead in the forest, and his weapons were missing?"

"Of course. I believe you were investigating it."

"Did your nephew go to Germany, as you say, about the time that happened?"

"Sheriff, I assure you he is not the one you are looking for. My nephew was not a good student, and my brother sent him to Germany hoping the yeshiva there would turn him around."

"Yeshiva? What's that?"

"It's one of our houses of learning, especially for older children. Come now, you don't seriously believe he or any Jew could be the culprit, do you?"

"I suppose you're right. It's just so maddening to me. The missing weapons, the two men murdered."

"Two men murdered?" Baruch asked.

"Did you not know two of de Montfort's old soldiers were murdered one night? This Donald had been drinking with them just before, but he denied any part of it."

"No, I did not know about this. I had been away in York for a while. I hope you find out who did it."

"Thank you, Baruch. I intend to."

The sheriff left. David must have found out these men had something to do with his mother's death and killed them, Baruch thought. It makes sense. John de Oxenden is a smart sheriff. If he can tie any of these things together, David will be exposed, and Hubert proved correct. That would be a disaster. I must prevent that from happening.

Baruch hurried to his brother's house.

"Baruch. Is something wrong?" Mordecai asked as his brother entered.

"Hannah, Mordecai, I must speak to you. Send Benjamin and Rachel upstairs."

Rachel began to obey, while Benjamin resisted. "Why can't I stay? I'm not a child."

"Please, Benjamin," Baruch said. Benjamin then agreed and followed his sister, staying out of sight while trying to listen.

Baruch told them everything that happened with Hubert and the sheriff. Hannah took her husband's hand as she saw the worry on his face.

"What can we do, Baruch? David is here, but we cannot get to him. That only would raise suspicion. How can we silence Hubert and stop the sheriff from finding out everything? Even though some believe Hubert mad, if he is proven right, his credibility will be restored."

"I believe we can take care of Hubert. Bishop Basil ordered him to obtain a large sum from the Jews. While I had to loan him one thousand pounds, I refused his demand for two thousand more and told him I had liquidated my assets. Father Alwyn told me when the bishop finds out Hubert has failed, he will send him away. Hopefully, that will solve that problem."

"We need to get word to the bishop."

"I will speak to Father Alwyn. He is also against Hubert and will certainly help."

"Very well. But what about the sheriff?"

"I have no answer for that. We can only hope and pray he does not find out anything and gives up."

"I suppose you're right."

Northampton – October 1269

Baron Geoffrey stared at the two small clay jars of poison Mordecai had provided.

"Geoffrey," Baron Henry, said, "I think Hubert's humiliation is a better punishment than his demise. It seems he has gone mad. Bishop Basil will no doubt relieve him of his duties."

"Yes, that does appear so. Although I was truly hoping to kill him for what he did to my brother."

"Where did you get these poisons?"

"From Mordecai, the apothecary who Hubert said is this David's father."

"Geoffrey, this entire situation is quite curious."

"How so?"

"Just think about it. It started with the missing weapons, did it not? Then my life is saved by this boy Donald, who said he was from a nearby village, and now it's clear he is not from there."

"What are you saying? That Donald may not be who he says he is?"

"What if Hubert is right?"

"Henry, your daughter's confession. Doesn't that satisfy you?"

"Alycia loves Donald, of that I am sure. But I am not convinced they are lovers."

"Why?"

"Because Donald is too honorable. He seems so different from our other men. I have no doubt Alycia has tried to lure him, and she has not been with anyone else. Even though she said what she did, I don't think she has ever seen his cock, and that surely would give him away."

Geoffrey listened to his friend. "Henry, your daughter is extremely attractive. You know the men all stare at her, and we can only imagine what they are thinking. Donald is a handsome, virile young man. I think it would be difficult, if not impossible, for him to resist her advances."

"Perhaps you're right. Besides, it's all so improbable. A Jew becoming a man-at-arms. I've observed them at York, and they are quite different from us. Donald does not act like them at all."

"Henry, I don't need these poisons anymore. Will you take them?"

"I doubt if I would have a use for them, but one never knows."

Geoffrey handed him the jars. "Just be careful. I would not want them to kill the wrong persons."

"I will be. Geoffrey, I need to return to York. If you don't mind, we'll leave tomorrow."

"Of course," Geoffrey replied. "We'll help you prepare."

Chapter Thirty-One

The Road to York – November 1269

As October became November, David felt the winds biting into him even more. He drove the carriage sitting next to Alycia, charged with her protection. Henry rode at the head as usual, while his men followed closely under the watchful eye of Sir Michael behind them. They traveled through Salcey Forest without any trouble, meeting only a few merchants on their way to Northampton. David noticed one of them was a Jew, who some of the men-at-arms made fun of. David said nothing, seething inside as he heard the insults.

They stayed at a small inn the first night, the baron and Alycia getting their own rooms, while David, Michael, and the men-at-arms shared two small rooms. After a light breakfast, they continued their journey. A cold, light rain fell, making the trip quite uncomfortable. Alycia tightened a thick, woolen cloak around her. She and David glanced at each other at various times but did not speak.

As they approached a section of the road later that afternoon, Henry became suspicious. He turned around and rode back to the rest of the group. "Keep a sharp eye out, men. I fear some evil may be about."

Suddenly ten men jumped out from behind rows of bushes and surrounded them. They carried swords and crossbows, although no one attacked. Then David saw him, and Henry did as well.

"Tell your men to drop their weapons!"

"Edgar. How dare you!" Henry yelled.

"Tell them, or they're dead."

Henry looked back at Michael and his men. "Do as he says."

They obeyed, and dropped their swords, shields, and crossbows. Edgar's men gathered the weapons and put them in the back of the carriage.

"And you as well, Baron." Henry unsheathed his sword and dropped it. It was placed with the others.

Edgar bowed slightly. "Hello, Baron Henry. Lady Alycia. I see you still have that young arse with you." David stared at Edgar.

"What do you want?" Henry demanded.

"I want my betrothed."

Alycia started to stand, but David put his hand on her shoulder and held her down.

"She's not your betrothed," Henry said. "I'm sorry she ever was."

"That was your doing, not mine. Alycia was given to me, and I want her back."

Henry looked at Edgar's men. They looked like an unkempt lot, and he was sure his men could take them if given the opportunity.

"Tie everyone together except the baron and that young arse," Edgar ordered, and his men obeyed.

"Baron, and you, get down," Edgar demanded, pointing to David.

"Donald, I'm frightened," Alycia whispered to David.

"Don't worry. It will be all right."

Henry dismounted, and David jumped onto the ground. They both stood in front of Edgar. Edgar did not notice David's sword had been lying at his feet in the carriage, covered to protect it from the weather.

"So, Edgar, I see you've become an outlaw," Henry said.

Edgar scowled at the baron. "No, I'm not an outlaw. I only want what's mine."

"I will never be yours. You'd better let us go or the king shall hear of this."

Edgar laughed. "Be quiet, my love. I'll deal with you later."

"Sir Edgar, I have no quarrel with you," David asserted. "You recall I never said anything against you. Alycia had made it up. I also have forgiven you for the wound you gave me."

Edgar grunted. "You mean nothing to me. I should kill you and be done with it."

"Edgar," Henry said, "think of what you're doing. I will never give Alycia to you. I was fearful for her safety and happiness because of what you did before, and now even more so. I demand you let us go. If you do it now, I'll forget this ever happened, and say nothing."

David saw the anger in Edgar. It was obvious this knight had a dangerous temper, and one wrong move could set him off.

"I don't believe you. I'm taking Alycia." He turned to three of his men. "Tie the baron and the boy together by that tree." The men did as he ordered. Then Edgar turned to Alycia.

"So, my love, you aren't happy to see me? You look more beautiful than ever."

Alycia turned away from him. It appeared he had been away for some time. His clothes were dirty, and it was clear that he had not washed for a while.

"Get away from me," she screamed. "I hate you!"

"This wench needs some discipline, Edgar," one of his men said, laughing.

Edgar was not amused. "Take their horses. We'll leave them here to hopefully freeze to death."

"Edgar, it's almost dark. No one travels these roads at night, so you're just leaving us here in this miserable weather?" Henry said.

Edgar laughed. "Warm yourself with the boy."

"I won't go with you," Alycia said, and she tried to jump off the carriage. Edgar's man grabbed her arm and pulled her back.

"Do that again and I'll have to tie you up," Edgar yelled.

Alycia then realized David's sword was covered by a blanket, and decided if she were not tied, perhaps she would have a chance to use it. Hopefully, Edgar's man would not notice it.

"Very well, Edgar. I won't do it again."

"Good. Let's go, men."

Henry and David watched as Edgar and his men and the carriage with Alycia soon were gone in the darkness. Henry and David struggled to free themselves from their bonds, but they could only slightly loosen them.

"Donald," Henry said. "Can you reach into my pouch?"

"Yes, I think so. Why?"

"I have a small dagger inside it. The sheath broke, and I put it there in the meantime. Edgar must have thought the pouch too small to hold a weapon and didn't check it."

David struggled to pull on the ropes to get a little more slack. He maneuvered enough to reach the pouch, but he could not open it.

"Baron, can you move to the left a bit?"

Henry did, and that enabled David to carefully open the pouch and grab the small dagger.

"I have it."

"See if you can cut the rope."

It was difficult, but David's dexterity helped him to slowly cut it strand by strand. The rope was poorly made, and it did not take David long to get through it. He and Henry removed their bonds, and then freed Michael, the men-at-arms, and Bryce.

"Baron, what do we do now?" one of the men-at arms asked.

"We'll follow their tracks until we catch up to them. They can't travel very fast."

"But we have no weapons."

"They won't be expecting us, so we'll surprise them. Our weapons are in the carriage, and we may be able to take some of theirs. Come men, we have a score to settle."

Farmhouse off the Road to York – November 1269

"Are you comfortable, Alycia?" Edgar asked.

She scowled at him. "I will never be comfortable around you."

Edgar knew of an abandoned farmhouse just off the road and had directed his men there for the night. He planned to leave at first light back to his father's castle. He did not know how his father would react to what he had done, but he was going to find a priest to marry him and Alycia before arriving there, so it would be too late to do anything about it.

"You'd better get some sleep. We have a long journey tomorrow."

The farmhouse only had two rooms. Edgar put Alycia alone in the back one that had a very small window, too small to crawl out of. It had been used as a storeroom. Edgar posted a man outside at the door, and he and the rest of his men slept blocking the storeroom door, so Alycia could not get out.

Edgar had an old bed in the farmhouse moved into the storeroom for her, but it was in horrible condition, and she refused to lie on it. She stayed awake, thinking how she could escape her captors. As the hours passed, all she heard was the snoring coming from behind the storeroom door. She was afraid to try to open it, not wanting to risk waking Edgar or any of his men. Then she heard a light knock on the window. She got up to investigate and smiled at what she saw.

It had not been difficult to find Edgar and his men, even in the relative darkness. There was enough moonlight to follow the carriage tracks, and they saw where it had left the road. There it was, in front of the old farmhouse. While Henry, Michael, and the men-at-arms stayed hidden, David quietly crept up to it, noticing the sentry had not fallen asleep. David slowly made his way to the back. He carefully looked into the window. With a little moonlight at his back, he was able to see Alycia pacing inside. He lightly tapped on the window and saw her turn to see him. With a huge smile, she quietly opened it.

"Alycia," David whispered as low as he could, "are you all right?"

"Yes," she whispered back.

"Are they all inside?"

"I believe so. Except for the one guarding the door."

"Are our weapons still in the carriage?"

"No. They brought them inside. Except for your sword, which is still hidden."

"Close the window and stay quiet. I'll be back."

She blew him a kiss and did as he said.

David returned and reported what he had learned.

"What do you think we should do?" Henry asked.

"We should rush them while they sleep," Sir Michael said. "We can surprise and easily overtake them."

Henry shook his head. "That's too risky. The guard may sound the alarm, and they can quickly get their weapons before we can find ours."

"My lord. I have an idea. It's bold, but should work," David said.

"Go ahead."

"You still have the two poison containers Geoffrey gave you?"

"Yes, they're in my pouch."

"I can get them to Alycia. She can offer to make porridge for Edgar and his men for breakfast. They probably are quite hungry. Our carriage has the provisions. If she can put the poison in their food, we can at least weaken them, if not kill a few of them. Then we can attack."

Henry nodded. "Donald, it's a risky plan, but it may work. Here, take my pouch. Tell Alycia to put some of the poison in their bowls, but don't cook it, as it will weaken it. Warn her to be very careful. They must not see what she's doing."

"I will."

David carefully crept back to the farmhouse and tapped on the window. Alycia was waiting for his return.

"Donald," she whispered, "are you going to attack?"

"No. We don't have any weapons. Here. Take these two jars of poison and be careful with them. When they're awake, offer to cook porridge for them. Everything you need is in the carriage. Somehow, before you serve them, you have to put a little poison in each bowl. If you can, put a little more into Edgar's. After they're affected, we'll attack. Can you do that?"

"Yes, I think so."

"Be careful."

"I will," she said, slowly closing the window. She hid the jars in a pocket inside her cloak.

David crept back to Henry and told him the plan had been conveyed. Now they had to wait.

As dawn approached, Edgar arose and checked on Alycia. He found her lying down on the old bed, wrapped in her cloak. She had dozed off after David's second visit.

"Good morning, my lady," Edgar said. "I trust you slept well?"

Alycia sat up. "It's hard to sleep well under these conditions. Anyway, I'm starving. We didn't eat last night, you will recall. There are provisions in the carriage. I can prepare groats for all of us."

Edgar nodded. "That's a good idea. We're all hungry. Go ahead. We'll get a fire started in the old hearth. I'll have one of my men fetch water."

"The groats, a caldron, and bowls are in the carriage."

"We'll get them."

Edgar woke up his men, and had the items brought into the farmhouse. Some men gathered firewood while another brought water from the well. After the fire was lit, one of the men placed the pot over the fire and filled it with water. When it was boiling, Alycia poured in the groats, stirring occasionally. They all ignored her as she spread out the bowls. There were not enough for all of Edgar's men. She also worried about diluting the poison so it would be ineffective, since she had never done anything like this before.

After it had boiled for several minutes, she took the ladle and tasted it. She thought it was vile but did not spit it out. With her back to Edgar and his men, she carefully took out the poison jars. In one bowl, she poured a little more, and then ladled some of the runny substance into it. This would be for Edgar. She prepared the remaining bowls the same way, being extra cautious. Her cloak worked well to keep any prying eyes away.

She picked up the bowl for Edgar and handed it to him.

"Here, my lord. I hope you like my cooking."

Edgar took the bowl and laughed. "I will expect much better than this slop." Alycia watched as he quickly downed the contents. She served the other five bowls, and those men downed them quickly as well. She then refilled them without any poison, handing them to the other men, including the one who had been guarding outside.

After a few minutes, Alycia saw Edgar begin to exhibit the effects of the poison. He complained of dizziness, pressed his hands against his stomach, and fell to the floor. The other men who had eaten in the first round also began to feel the effects, and soon all were on the floor, moaning.

"What have you done?" Edgar said, barely able to speak.

The four men who had not had the poisoned bowls were confused and did not know what to do. Suddenly, the door burst open and Baron Henry, Sir Michael, David, and the men-at-arms all jumped on Edgar and his men. David was holding his sword he had retrieved from the carriage after disarming the sentry, and the other men grabbed whatever weapons they could find. Edgar's men surrendered without a fight, most too sick from the poison to resist.

Edgar looked up at Alycia. "You poisoned me, you witch," he spurted out, retching as he spoke.

"Yes. Die, you bastard."

Edgar's body began shaking, and his eyes became glassy. In a few minutes, he was dead. The other men who had eaten the poison were ill, but probably would survive. Apparently, the poisons were too diluted to kill them. Henry had them all tied up. Alycia ran to her father and embraced him.

"Father. You saved me."

"It was Donald, my dear. It was his idea."

Alycia tightly embraced David. "Again, you have saved me. You're not only brave, but also clever. It was a very good plan."

Sir Michael then called out. "My lord, you must see this."

Henry and David went outside, where Michael stood at the carriage. "Look, Henry."

They saw a small chest, and when Michael opened it, they saw it was filled with silver coins. The chest had the crest of King Henry carved into its lid.

"My God," Henry cried. "The king's tax money. Edgar must have killed the tax collector and stolen it." Henry turned to David. "Donald, when the king hears of what you have done, I'm sure you finally will be knighted."

David could not believe what he had heard. "My lord, I thank you for that, but I still haven't fought in a tournament or a battle."

"Knighthood may be won in different ways and saving the king's taxes I would wager is one of them."

Alycia took David's hand and squeezed it. "My love, now I'm sure we we'll be wed sooner than later."

David tried not to show any expression of panic. *If what Baron Henry says is true, I may be knighted sooner than I thought. However, I will not be given any lands. I do not believe I could marry Alycia without an income. Just being a knight would not be enough. I must stall her as long as I can.*

"We must return to Northampton with the tax money and turn it over to Geoffrey," Baron Henry said. "The king is known to visit Northampton, and Geoffrey will ensure he gets it."

They placed Edgar's body in the back of the carriage and prepared to take his remaining men back as prisoners.

"You cannot take me," one protested.

"Why? Who are you?" Henry asked.

"I am Jonathan, Sir Edgar's brother. When my father hears of this, he'll have you all punished."

Henry laughed. "You were part of this group that abducted my daughter and stole the king's tax money, serious crimes, and you think just because you say you are Earl Tristan's son you should be treated differently? King Henry will no doubt have your head, and I hope I'm there to witness it. You will stay tied with the rest of these scum and await Baron Geoffrey and the king's pleasure."

Jonathan spat at Henry but missed. "We shall see."

Northampton – November 1269

Geoffrey ran his hand through the coins in the king's chest.

"Edgar did this?"

"Yes," Henry answered. "We found it in the back of our carriage."

"We should inform his father. Do you think he'll believe what his son has done?"

Henry shrugged. "I don't know. Earl Tristan knows his son has a temper. That's why we broke off his betrothal to Alycia. He may not believe his son abducted my daughter and stole tax money from the Crown. He also may want an inquiry into his death. And Jonathan may lie about what happened."

"I've sent for the sheriff to report the entire incident. With the tax money as evidence, and plenty of witnesses, I don't expect any problems. The sheriff will question Edgar's men, and he's quite skilled at learning the truth. It was Donald who came up with the plan to use the poison I gave you?"

"Yes, it was."

"I believe he's proven himself several times already. The king will most certainly grant him knighthood now," Geoffrey said.

"Yes, I believe he will, and sometime afterwards he'll be my son-in-law."

John de Oxenden left the castle after hearing about the entire encounter Baron Henry had with Sir Edgar. Edgar's men were locked in Geoffrey's dungeon. Jonathan was kept separate, since Henry worried Jonathan may order his men to lie.

John thought the explanation very plausible. He again wondered why this Donald was involved, but he could not argue with success. Edgar might have gotten away with abducting Alycia, but his theft of the tax money was a serious crime, punishable by death, so he got what he deserved.

The sheriff returned home and told his wife what he had learned.

"I think you should forget about your suspicions of this Donald. When the king learns what he has done, he will no doubt be rewarded handsomely."

"I believe you are correct. Imagine. Hubert accused him of being a Jew! No Jew could ever be that brave and accomplish those feats. It's not possible."

"No," his wife agreed, "it's not possible."

After being summoned by Baron Geoffrey, Mordecai hurried to the castle. I wonder what he could want, he thought. He had hoped not to prepare more poisons. The guards let him in, and he was led to the great hall, where Geoffrey and Henry were there, and to his surprise, David.

"Ah, Mordecai," Geoffrey said. "Welcome. Let me introduce you to Baron Henry de Percy of York."

"My lord," Mordecai said, bowing.

"And this young warrior is Donald."

"I met him the last time I was here, my lord." Mordecai nodded to his son.

"I called you here to tell you your poisons were put to good use."

Geoffrey then related the story to Mordecai.

"So, you unknowingly helped to stop an abduction and the theft of Crown taxes. You should be proud."

"My lord, I am glad for the outcome, but I am a healer, and do not wish any of my work to be used for harmful purposes."

"Hah," Henry said. "See, Jews have no stomach for anything except prayer and study. And to think Donald was accused of being one."

"My lord?" Mordecai said.

"Mordecai, Abbot Hubert accused Donald of being a Jew and your son."

Mordecai looked at David. "My son is in Germany, studying. This man may resemble him, but he's a Christian, so he cannot be my David."

"So that's it," Geoffrey said. "Donald resembles your David. Hubert must have misunderstood what those boys were saying, or they were confused at the archery tournament."

David smiled at his father. "May I escort this Jew out of the castle?"

"Certainly," Geoffrey said. "Go, Mordecai. I will send for you if I need you."

David walked next to his father, waiting until they were alone to speak to him.

"Father, it's so good to see you. Is everyone well?"

"Yes, but we've been worried since we haven't had any word from you."

"You can see I've been busy."

"Do you really think you can continue like this? Eventually they'll discover who you are."

"Yes, they might, but I'm becoming the warrior I always dreamed of, and rest assured, I will always help our people. Father, I have avenged our mother's death."

"What? Those two men the sheriff was asking about?"

"Yes. Tom and Ralph. They were the men of de Montfort who killed her. They went to their end knowing it was a Jew and her son who was killing them."

Mordecai shook his head. "I am glad they have been punished, but not that it was you who performed the deed."

"I only have killed to protect, or for that act of revenge."

They were soon at the gate. "Be on your way home," David said. "The baron will send for you if he needs you." David made sure the guards heard him.

Mordecai left the castle without looking back. *David, my David. You are becoming a warrior. But how can one man help our people? We need an army. A Jewish army. And that we do not have. If only there were more like you …*

Hedgestone Priory – November 1269

Alwyn sat in the cellar with Hubert. Ambrose and Brother Dominic stood at the top of the cellar stairs to make sure Hubert did not try to escape his confinement.

"Alwyn, when are you going to come to your senses and let me out?" Hubert asked.

"We expect the bishop to arrive any day, and he will decide what to do with you."

"It is you and the rest of those rebellious monks here who will be punished. Your plan will never work."

"You're wrong. This man Donald you falsely accused of being a Jew rescued Baron Henry's daughter from a Sir Edgar, who it turns out stole Crown tax money. The king will probably come to Northampton and reward him. Perhaps he'll even knight him."

"That's impossible. You know as well as I do Donald is David, Mordecai's son, and Baruch's nephew. You admitted it."

"Did I? You can't prove that. Prior Bartholomew learned Mordecai met this Donald and told Baron Geoffrey he resembles his son. Apparently, what you overheard was incorrect this whole time. Mordecai's son has been in Germany studying for several years."

"Lies. All lies. I'm sure of it. Just to protect another lying Jew. If any of this were true, why did Baruch all but admit it?"

"I'm not here to argue with you. Your accusations have been proven false, and that, along with all of your other misdeeds, will be punished when Basil gets here."

Hubert stood. "You're a fool, Alwyn. You and everyone else here at Hedgestone. I know I'm right, and so do you. If I can't convince the bishop now, then so be it. My time will come. This David or Donald or whoever he is cannot live his lie forever. His circumcision will give him away."

"Hubert," Alwyn said, "you've deceived the bishop, and we have proof. He will not believe anything you say. Your credibility has completely vanished. He should defrock you and you should be banished from England."

Hubert shrugged. "Perhaps. Do not underestimate me, Alwyn. It will be a huge mistake to do so."

"The mistake was yours, Hubert," Alwyn said, as he walked up the cellar stairs, leaving Hubert alone again, and locked the door.

"Alwyn," Ambrose said, "one thing Hubert said does bother me."

"What is it?"

"What he said about Baruch. The moneylender did admit this Donald is David, his nephew."

"Not really, Ambrose. Baruch was not at the archery tournament, so he did not see this Donald there. He was only going with what Hubert told him. If this Donald does resemble David, then that would explain the confusion."

"Perhaps you're right."

Chapter Thirty-Two

Hedgestone Priory – December 1269

Bishop Basil arrived at Hedgestone accompanied by Eustace. After refreshing himself from his journey, Basil met with Alwyn, Ambrose, and Bartholomew. Alwyn related all he knew about Hubert demanding the money from Baruch, and his accusation regarding this Donald.

"So, Father Alwyn, it appears my suspicions about Hubert have been proven correct."

"Yes, Your Grace. We believe Hubert planned all along to betray you. He failed because I discovered his plans, and when his accusation of this Donald being a Jew and the moneylender's nephew was proven false, he went berserk. Baron Geoffrey gave his men leave to kill him if he tried to enter the castle again. We feel he's gone mad and must be relieved of his duties."

"I agree. From everything you have told me, we cannot let him serve any more. Where is he?"

"We have locked him in the cellar for his own protection."

"Take me to him."

"Very well, Your Grace, but he continuously spouts lies, and may get violent."

Ambrose led Basil to the cellar. "Leave us. He will not harm me."

Basil carefully went down the stairs. The cellar was lit by several candles and had a musty odor. Hubert stood when he saw the bishop.

"Bishop Basil. I am glad you're here." Hubert knelt and kissed the bishop's ring.

"I'm very disappointed in you Hubert. Alwyn has told me everything."

"He told you lies."

"Did he? You received funds from this Baruch, the moneylender, and kept them for yourself. Then you tried to extort more money from him, and when he refused, you falsely accused a Christian boy of being his Jewish nephew."

"Your Grace. Let me explain. I told you I was never going to withhold funds from you. I swear I was only trying to obtain as much as I could. When I discovered the truth about this David, I only used it to try to fulfill my obligation to you."

"And you still insist this Donald is a Jew?"

"Most definitely. He is David, nephew to Baruch, the moneylender, and son of Mordecai, the apothecary. I'm not mad."

"Hubert, I understand Baron Henry's daughter admitted they were lovers and she could verify his being a Christian. You don't believe her?"

Hubert shook his head. "She's a child who thinks she is in love with him. She would say anything to help him."

"But not if she knew he's a Jew. It doesn't make any sense."

"And there's another thing. Alwyn knows as well. He and Baruch were going to bear false witness against me if I revealed his secret. I know I'm right."

Basil glared at Hubert. "That's preposterous! Why would Alwyn conspire with a Jew? Hubert, I want you to turn all the funds you received from this Jew Baruch over to me. Then you will accompany me to London, where I plan to have you sent to a priory in Wales, not as prior, but as a brother."

Hubert became livid. "No, Your Grace! You cannot do that to me. I've served you well, and exposed a Jew masquerading as a Christian, a serious offense."

"You have done nothing of the sort. You refuse to admit your sins and show no remorse for what you have done."

"I've done nothing wrong."

Basil pointed a finger at Hubert. "You will do exactly as I say, or I will excommunicate you. Which I may do anyway."

The bishop began climbing the stairs.

"Do not leave me here, cousin."

Basil grunted. "You will stay here until I'm ready to leave."

Hubert stared at the closing door, stunned. Alwyn was at the top of the stairs when the bishop returned.

"I believe you are correct, Alwyn. Hubert must have gone mad. He still insists he was not going to keep any of the money, and this Donald is definitely a Jew. He also accused you and this Baruch of conspiring against him with some false tale."

"What additional proof do you need? Why would I cooperate with a Jew? What are you going to do with him, Your Grace?"

"I will take him to London with me, and then he will be sent to Wales as a brother, not an abbot or prior. He is also to turn all the money he borrowed over to me."

"Do you think he will cooperate?"

Basil nodded. "He has no choice. I will excommunicate him if he doesn't, and perhaps hold him for trial if necessary."

Alwyn smiled. "I will be happy to testify against him."

"I'm sure you would, Alwyn."

Northampton Castle – December 1269

"Henry," Geoffrey said, "I've sent a messenger to King Henry to tell him what happened. I hope you'll stay here until we receive a response."

"I would be more than happy to stay. The king occasionally comes here, doesn't he?"

"Yes. I keep a separate chamber for him no one else can use."

Suddenly Cyrus appeared. "My lord, Prior Bartholomew is here to see you."

"I wonder what he wants," Geoffrey said to Henry, who then turned to Cyrus. "Well, bring him in."

"My lords," Bartholomew greeted them, bowing.

"What brings you here, Bartholomew?"

"My lord, I thought you should know about Abbot Hubert. Bishop Basil is here, and Hubert is being dismissed."

"What?" Geoffrey exclaimed, getting up from his chair. "Is this true?"

"Yes, my lord. The bishop caught him stealing Church funds, and he is being declared mad for his insistence this Donald is a Jew. The bishop is taking him back to London with him, and then sending him to Wales as a mere brother. He is disgraced."

Geoffrey's excitement nearly poured out of him. "Excellent. This is the best punishment for him. Let's all drink a toast to this wonderful news. Cyrus, bring wine and glasses."

"Who will be the new prior? Will you return?"

"I do not know. Father Alwyn has been spying on Hubert for Basil, so perhaps he will be, or Father Ambrose. I am too old, and don't want the job anymore."

Cyrus arrived with the wine and glasses, poured them to the top, and handed them out.

"Here's to revenge. It is so sweet." The three drank, and even Bartholomew did not hide his joy.

"When will the bishop leave?"

"Soon, I think. He's eager to return to London."

"I'll offer him an escort," Geoffrey said. "Bartholomew, tell the bishop my men are ready to accompany him."

"A good idea. Hubert may escape if armed men are not there to guard him."

"My thoughts exactly."

A huge smile illuminated Alycia. "Donald, my love, this is what we've been waiting for. I know this time you'll be knighted, and perhaps given a manor with lands and serfs." She turned to her father. "Soon Donald will ask you for my hand in marriage."

Henry nodded and smiled, while David remained expressionless. "Alycia, please do not speak like that. I told you, I have much to accomplish before I can even consider marriage."

She gave him that look he always had trouble resisting. "We shall see, my love. I told you, I always get what I want."

David knew he was in trouble. *Is it possible the king will confer knighthood on me here in Northampton? If so, I wish my father could be there. As much as I desire knighthood, my plans could be thwarted by this Christian girl who does not know she is in love with a Jew. And if she finds out, who knows what will happen?*

London – December 1269

King Henry received the messenger from Baron Geoffrey and read his letter. He handed it to his son. "Well, Edward, it looks like a traitor has been eliminated. We cannot tolerate those who steal tax money. And Earl Tristan's sons Edgar and Jonathan. I doubt if the earl had anything to do with it. This is very disturbing."

"Quite. This Donald who Geoffrey writes about, is he not the same boy who was here with Alycia, Baron Henry de Percy's daughter?"

"I believe he is. He's the one who saved Henry's life, and who he asked me to make a knight, but I said I wouldn't until he had proven himself in battle."

"I wasn't impressed with him when he was here, but perhaps I misjudged him."

"Edward, I think I'll travel to Northampton after the New Year and honor this Donald."

"With knighthood?"

"Why not reward him for what he has done? He has earned it, and perhaps it will be an inspiration to others." Henry turned to the messenger. "Tell Baron Geoffrey I hope to come to Northampton in early January to collect the tax money, and I plan to knight this Donald. I will send word to my exact coming."

The messenger bowed. "Yes, Sire, I'll tell him."

"Edward," the king said, "I also will use this trip to announce further edicts against the Jews. They are becoming less useful to me."

Hedgestone Priory – December 1269

Bishop Basil finished his preparations to return to London. As promised, Baron Geoffrey provided four men-at-arms to accompany him, even though Hubert agreed not to try to escape. He decided to do so would further prove to Basil he was guilty and could not be trusted, on top of his credibility now being in question. Somehow, Hubert had to convince the bishop he had not been planning to keep the money he received from Baruch, as well as his certainty about David.

Basil installed Father Alwyn as interim prior, ordering Father Ambrose and Bartholomew to assist him. This pleased the brothers, as they had grown to like and respect Alwyn for standing up to Hubert. Alwyn and Ambrose had become good friends and agreed to work together. They even planned to resume contact with the Jews after Basil left.

The entire complement of monks gathered in the courtyard to say goodbye to Hubert, though it was obvious they were happy to see him go. All except Andrew, who did not entirely believe Hubert was mad. Andrew's skepticism primarily came from his belief Hubert was correct about this Donald, even though he had no proof. While he did not know what he could do about it, unlike the other brothers, Andrew would not accept the explanations given, and decided he would continue to try to prove Hubert correct.

Northampton – December 1269

With Christmas approaching, Baron Henry de Percy wanted to return to York to be with his wife. He decided to wait, however, until Geoffrey's messenger to the king had returned.

A few days later, Geoffrey's messenger did return. After hearing the message, Geoffrey summoned Baron Henry, David, and Alycia. When they arrived at the great hall, Lady Catherine was there as well.

"Welcome. I have excellent news, and I wanted to tell you all together."

The four of them looked at each other, curious what this announcement could be.

"I sent a messenger to the king with a letter detailing how Henry and Donald saved what amounts to more than twenty thousand silver marks. He responded he is most grateful for his loyal subject's deeds and honesty and will be coming to Northampton to personally show his gratitude and collect the money."

David and Alycia looked at each other. "King Henry is coming here?" Alycia asked. "When?"

"He hopes in early January, and he will notify us. I also suspect our young warrior here may be well rewarded," Geoffrey said.

"That's wonderful news. Are there any details?" Alycia said.

"No. That's all the king said, other than he will send word as to when he's coming. Donald and Alycia, you may go." Geoffrey waited until they left before continuing.

"Henry, my friend, the king is coming to Northampton to make Donald a knight of the realm. My messenger reported it, but I did not want to divulge it."

"That is good news, but shouldn't we tell Donald?"

"It's up to you, but I think not. Let him be surprised. It will also keep your daughter off his back. I imagine if she knew, he wouldn't be able to keep her away from him."

Henry laughed. "I believe you're right. It means I must leave for York tomorrow. You will send word as soon as you know when Henry is coming?"

"Of course. As soon as I know, I'll send a messenger to you."

"Thank you, my good friend. I just hope I can keep the secret myself."

Northampton – January 1270

Jonathon sat chained to the wall in the cold, dank cell. It was on the other side of a thick wall, isolated from the main dungeon where the rest of his men were held. Geoffrey is smart, Jonathan thought. Even though they were guilty of everything Henry accused them of, he should have tried to convince him they had rescued the tax money from the actual thieves who had stolen it and were on their way to return it when they encountered Alycia, Henry, and his men. Edgar's passion for Alycia, he would argue, resulted in his taking advantage of the situation. While Jonathan loved his brother, he was jealous Edgar was a knight and he was not. Edgar was more than ten years older than Jonathan, and with two other brothers in front of him, Jonathan would never inherit his father's castle, lands, and title.

He heard footsteps approaching and saw Baron Geoffrey standing at the cell door.

"Enjoying my hospitality, Jonathan?" Geoffrey asked.

"The food could be better, and there are no women," Jonathan said.

"Sorry. This is all you get, unless I send you an old hag for your pleasure. I thought you should know, the king will be here this month, and I've notified your father."

Jonathan grunted. "Why? To watch my execution?"

"You will get what you deserve. Are you ready to tell us about killing the king's tax man and stealing the taxes?"

Jonathan spat on the floor. "I know nothing about that. I met up with Edgar just before he ambushed Henry. He never told me about it. I had nothing to do with any of it."

"The other men told us a different story. They said it was your idea to steal the taxes."

Jonathan laughed. "And you believe them? Lying to save themselves, I imagine."

"No matter. You will all hang, unless the king wants you drawn and quartered."

"I am an earl's son. I have rights."

Now Geoffrey laughed. "Traitors have no rights, except to be executed."

At this, Jonathan tried to rush the cell door to get to Geoffrey, but the chain around his ankle stopped him. "You won't get away with this. I'll be freed because I'm innocent."

Geoffrey laughed as he turned and left. "The only freedom you will know is from life."

While waiting for the king, David continued to practice his fighting skills. Even in the cold weather, Alycia would wear a warm cloak and watch him. The cold did not seem to bother him. While she was no expert, she could tell his swordsmanship had improved greatly. Sir Michael's training provided him with an extremely skilled warrior. David also had improved his horsemanship and jousting, and he was comfortable with the axe and mace and chain. Baron Henry had ordered him to continue to practice his archery to maintain his skills. David also began training on the crossbow, although he preferred the bow.

As much as he tried to avoid Alycia, he found it difficult. She spent some time with Lady Catherine, where most of their conversations were how to prepare for a wedding. Though not trying to replace Lady Eleanor, Catherine began to treat Alycia like the daughter she never had.

One afternoon as they sat by the fire, Catherine decided to ask Alycia something that had remained in the back of her mind.

"Alycia, we have become quite close these past few weeks. I'm glad about that."

Alycia nodded and smiled. "I am too. It's definitely easier to talk to you than my own mother."

"May I ask you a personal question?"

"Of course."

"You defended Donald when Hubert insisted he is a Jew, but you were not being truthful you two were lovers, am I correct?"

Alycia blushed. "No, we are not lovers, yet. How did you know?"

"I didn't know, but I suspected. Tell me, are you sure Hubert is wrong? What if he's right?"

Alycia's expression changed to one of near-terror. "What are you saying? Do you believe Hubert?"

Catherine took Alycia's hand. "No, my child. I'm not saying that. I was just wondering what you would do if in fact Donald is not who he says he is."

Tears began to flow down Alycia's cheeks. "Lady Catherine, I would be devastated. But how could that be possible? Donald has proven himself. How could a Jew do what he has done?"

"Have you ever met a Jew?"

"I've seen them in York. A Jewish physician cured my father a few years ago and treated Donald when Edgar wounded him, and I briefly spoke with him. I've been told all my life they are quite different from us since they never accepted Christ. My Donald has accepted Christ. He attends church. He wears a cross. No Jew would ever do that."

Catherine nodded. "I'm sure you are correct. They are so different from us Christians. They could never pose as one of us, especially a warrior. I'm sorry to have brought this up."

"I will not let Hubert's lies affect me anymore. Donald will be mine. It's only a matter of time, and hopefully not too much longer."

Baron Geoffrey was surprised when he heard Earl Tristan had arrived, since the king had not yet informed Geoffrey when he was coming. The earl brought a small entourage consisting of six men-at-arms.

"My lord," Geoffrey greeted him, bowing. "I was not expecting you so soon."

"I could not wait. First, let me thank you for bringing my son's body to me for burial. Your man, Sir Walter, told me what happened. My son was a hothead, and he made mistakes. He never got over Henry's refusal to honor his betrothal to his daughter. I am afraid he got what he deserved. I understand you're holding my youngest son, Jonathan."

"He was captured with the rest of Edgar's men along with the tax money. The king will decide his fate, and of the others."

"Geoffrey, he's only a boy. He idolized Edgar, and unfortunately was influenced by him. Is there any way you can find it in your heart to release him?"

"I'm sorry, my lord, but we already have informed the king of his crimes, and we await his pleasure. He may be young, but he must take responsibility for his actions. Abducting Baron Henry's daughter and stealing tax money are both serious offenses, as you well know."

"I understand. But know I will ask the king for mercy. Perhaps his punishment could be to serve the king. If not, he could prove his innocence by trial by combat."

"Jonathan is not a knight. He's not eligible for such a request."

"No, but Edgar was, and since he cannot defend him, Jonathan should be allowed to."

"I doubt if King Henry will agree."

"He may not, but I will try. May I see my son?"

"Certainly. I'll take you to him."

They went down two levels to a dark corridor with steps that led to the dungeon. Jonathan was kept in the lowest level. The only light was a torch just outside the cell. Jonathan rose when he saw the earl.

"Father! You've come to rescue me!"

The earl looked at his son. His clothes were filthy and torn, and he had lost weight, even from the relatively short time of his captivity.

"Jonathan. Are you all right?"

"As best as can be expected. When can I get out of here?"

"I'm afraid it's not so simple. You're accused of serious crimes."

"I had nothing to do with the tax money or the abduction. I met up with Edgar afterwards, and I never touched the baron's daughter. It was all Edgar."

"Perhaps. But you were caught with him. I'll ask the king to pardon you, or reduce your punishment, but I'm not optimistic he'll grant it."

"You must try, Father. I swear I had nothing to do with any of this. Edgar kept me at the old farmhouse when he went to ambush Baron Henry and abduct Alycia. I even tried to stop him. And I didn't even know about the tax money until Sir Michael found it. I swear it."

"Very well. I'll plead with the king and do the best I can."

The earl and Geoffrey returned to the great hall. "What do you think, Geoffrey?"

"It is hard to say, Tristan. How old is Jonathan?"

"Almost eighteen."

"King Henry may feel he's old enough to know better. Is he telling the truth?"

"Jonathan is a spirited boy, but he has never lied to me. I do believe him. The question is, will the king?"

Chapter Thirty-Three

Northampton – February 1270

King Henry finally made good his promise to come to Northampton, sending word a fortnight before his arrival. Baron Geoffrey sent a messenger to Baron Henry as soon as the king's letter arrived.

Geoffrey and Lady Catherine made certain all arrangements were completed. The king's special chamber was cleaned and prepared, as well as one for Queen Eleanor, who was accompanying her husband. Fresh meats were delivered to the baron's kitchen, and the bakers busily prepared breads, cakes, and pies. Geoffrey wanted to ensure the king's visit would be a memorable one. Theresa, his cook, was hard at work preparing everything.

Baron Henry arrived several days before the king with Bryce and his usual contingent of six men-at-arms.

"Henry! At last the time has come."

"Yes, my friend, I left as soon as I received your message. Luckily, the weather has not been too bad. The snows were light, and we had no problems."

"This is all who you came with?"

"No. I brought my priest, Father Zachariah. He is staying at Hedgestone with Prior Alwyn."

Upon hearing of the baron's arrival, David and Alycia ran down to greet him.

"Father! Father!" she cried. "At last you've returned. They embraced as he kissed her cheek.

"You're looking well. I suspect Donald has been watching over you."

"Hello, Baron Henry," David said, bowing.

"Donald. Have you been continuing your training here?"

"Yes, my lord."

"And he's gotten even better," said Sir Michael, who just joined them.

"I'm most glad to hear it, but not surprised. Come, Alycia, I want to hear what you've been doing."

"How is Mother? Why isn't she here?"

"Your mother, I'm sorry to say, became ill with a fever the day Geoffrey's messenger arrived. Nehemiah treated her but advised against her traveling in winter. She'll be fine."

David watched as the two of them walked into the castle. Then he saw Bryce, and the two friends embraced. "My friend, it's good to see you."

"It's good to see you, too. Donald, everyone in York has been talking about you and Alycia."

David raised his eyebrows. "Why?"

"Why? You must be jesting. After you're knighted, you most certainly will marry her. The men-at-arms are so jealous, I swear they'd kill you if they thought they could have her. No one ever believed you of all people could ever win her."

"Not so fast, Bryce. First of all, we don't know if I'll be knighted, and if so, I may not be granted lands. I'm still quite young. Besides, we aren't ready for marriage."

Bryce laughed. "You still don't understand women, or at least Alycia, do you? Baron Henry made it clear you are who she wants, and when you become a knight, he'll approve of it if the king grants you lands and permits the marriage."

David turned away so Bryce could not see the worry on his face.

"Donald. Are you all right? You seem troubled."

David turned back to Bryce. "Yes. I'm fine. Come, you must be hungry and thirsty."

Hedgestone Priory – February 1270

Prior Alwyn and Father Zachariah sat in Hubert's old room, eating bread, cheese, and drinking wine. Alwyn related what happened with

Hubert, telling him only what he wanted the priest to know, leaving out anything that might make him suspicious. However, he felt he had to tell him about Hubert's accusing Donald of being a Jew, since he would find out anyway.

"So, Alwyn, what you have told me is very interesting. I've never heard of an abbot going mad. It is most unusual."

"I've been with him for several years, and there is no doubt in my mind of his condition."

"Very well. If you say so. But don't you think it strange he would risk so much to falsely accuse this Donald of being a Jew?"

"Not for a madman. You said you know Donald."

Zachariah nodded, tearing off a piece of bread. "Yes, I met him when he first came to York. He had no crucifix, so I had Baron Henry get him one. He also had never been to confession, so I heard his first one. I didn't think it strange at the time, but now, I'm not so sure. What if Hubert is right?"

"Come now, Zachariah. Donald was just a peasant boy with nothing. There are many like him."

"I suppose. I've observed him regularly at church, and Baron Henry is quite fond of him. Still, he has qualities unlike any other boy I know of."

"Does that make him a Jew?"

"No. It's true I've seen him eat their forbidden foods without hesitation, and he has an exceptional fighting ability. I've watched him train, and must admit he's become quite skilled, and has proven his bravery and cunning several times already."

"There. No Jew would ever be able to do that. And no Jew would eat pork. It would be a major sin and abomination."

"Perhaps. Or perhaps not. There are exceptions, you know, and maybe this Donald is one of them. I think I'll watch him more closely than I have been. If he is pretending to be a Christian, he'll slip up, and then I'll expose him. But after what you told me, I must be sure. I will not end up like Hubert."

West End – February 1270

There was a knock at the door, and Mordecai answered it.

"Cyrus, is it not?"

"Yes, Mordecai. Baron Geoffrey sent me with a message for you."

"Well, what is it?"

"King Henry will be arriving any day to honor one of Baron Henry's men, and Baron Geoffrey would like you to attend the ceremony. I'll be back to tell you exactly when as soon as he knows."

"He wants me to attend? Why?"

"I don't know. I was only told to tell you this so you could prepare."

"Very well. Please tell the baron thank you, and I will await further instructions."

Cyrus left, and Hannah came out from a back room. "What is it?" she asked.

"Baron Geoffrey invited me to attend a ceremony when King Henry is here."

"Just you?"

"Yes. I wonder why. I've done nothing to warrant such an invitation."

"Mordecai, we all have heard the stories that one of Baron Henry's men saved the king's tax money and the baron's daughter from an abduction. Could it be they know he's your son David?"

"No, that cannot be. Cyrus said the king was going to honor one of Baron Henry's men. It must be David from what we have heard. But if they knew who he really is, they would never withhold it from the king."

"You are right, my husband. Your invitation must be related somehow. Wait! We heard the outlaws were poisoned. Maybe it was the poison you prepared?"

"You may be right, my dear. That would be the only connection, the poison. And if that is true, I may have helped my own son to get his wish."

Northampton – February 1270

King Henry arrived with the usual fanfare one would expect for a king. His seneschal had arrived the day before and was quite pleased with all the arrangements Geoffrey had made.

Geoffrey, Lady Catherine, Earl Tristan, Baron Henry, Alycia, and David, who was there at Geoffrey's insistence, waited at the castle gate as the king's entourage approached. Geoffrey ordered trumpets blown as the king drew near and was pleased with how good they sounded. King Henry rode a magnificent white warhorse, followed by an exquisite carriage containing Queen Eleanor and two of her servants. Several knights and a number of men-at-arms followed. The king wore a blue velvet cape over a cloak made from what appeared to be the finest furs. He dismounted in front of Geoffrey.

"Welcome, Your Majesty," Geoffrey said, kneeling. Lady Catherine and the rest knelt as well.

"Thank you, Baron Geoffrey. Lady Catherine. You may all rise. It is good to see you again. I've been away from Northampton too long."

"All is ready for you, Sire. May we escort you and the queen to your chambers?"

"Yes. We are tired and cold from our journey."

The king then recognized David. "Donald, my boy. Come here."

David approached the king and bowed.

"So, you are the one who saved my tax money?"

"I assisted, Your Majesty. I was one of many."

"It was Donald's plan that rescued Baron Henry's daughter from Edgar," Geoffrey said, "and it was after that when the stolen tax money was discovered. Without Donald's plan, we may never have found it."

"I see. I owe you a reward for saving my tax money and eliminating a traitor."

"I only wish to serve you and Baron Henry, Sire."

"How old are you, Donald?"

"Seventeen, Sire. I will be eighteen in May."

"So young and so brave. I wish we had more like you. I'll be here for a few days and will announce your reward while I'm here."

Alycia heard the king, and her face showed obvious disappointment. "Father," she whispered. "I hoped he was going to knight Donald. He must so we can be wed."

Baron Henry's eyes told Alycia she should be quiet. Both barons also were surprised, based on what Geoffrey's messenger had reported.

Queen Eleanor alighted from the carriage, and after the traditional greetings given to royalty, retired into the castle with Lady Catherine. Alycia stayed outside with her father.

"Father, you must speak to the king."

"Be patient, my dear. We don't know the king won't knight Donald."

"He said he would announce his reward while he's here. What does that mean?"

"We'll have to wait to find out."

Baron Henry noticed Earl Tristan had accompanied Geoffrey with the king into the castle, and the earl was whispering something in the king's ear.

That night everyone attended a huge banquet in honor of his Majesty. While there were toasts to Sir Michael and Donald, thanking them for what they had done, nothing was mentioned about any reward. Alycia grew more nervous the king had changed his mind. As much as David wanted to be a knight, he was also apprehensive. He felt at times he had dug himself into a hole from which he could not emerge.

The next afternoon an announcement was made that the king had commanded everyone to the great hall. Cyrus informed Alycia, who hurried down, wondering what this was all about. When she arrived, she saw the Queen, Baron Geoffrey, Lady Catherine, her father, Earl Tristan, Donald, Sir Michael, Father Zachariah, and to her shock, Jonathan, the earl's son. There were the knights who arrived with the king, as well as his seneschal. She also noticed several men who she believed were Jews. Two of Geoffrey's finest chairs had been set up as thrones for the king and queen. Geoffrey told the king everyone was in attendance, and the king addressed his audience.

"I have asked you all here because I want to honor and reward bravery and loyalty, as well as to show mercy and compassion. I also will be making an announcement."

A murmur scattered throughout the room, everyone wondering what the king would say. Mordecai was present, arriving separately from the elders, who were ordered to attend. After his admonishment, there had not been any reconciliation. However, the castle guards made him stand with the elders, separating the Jews from the Christians. They all acknowledged each other's presence but did not speak.

Mordecai looked around and could just barely make out David near the front, dressed in a fine tunic. He could not see it had Baron Henry's coat-of-arms embroidered on the chest. Mordecai worried one of the elders would recognize his son and possibly expose him. So far, David's back had been turned to them, and since they were at the rear of the great hall, they could not see him with everyone standing in front of them.

"First, I want to thank Baron Geoffrey for his hospitality," the king continued. "You have continued to prove your loyalty, and while we expect it, we appreciate it, as traitors may appear at any time." The king motioned for Jonathan to approach and he knelt before him.

"This is Jonathan, son of Earl Tristan of Northumberland. His brother, Sir Edgar, became an outlaw who stole Crown taxes, killed my tax collector, and abducted Baron Henry de Percy's daughter. Jonathan was brought here for trial and execution for his part in these crimes. However, I have heard his testimony and the plea of his father. I believe he joined his brother after Edgar had stolen the tax money, was not present during the abduction, and caused no harm. Therefore, I am pardoning him with the stipulation he must return to York with Baron Henry for one year, where his behavior will be watched closely. If he performs any misdeed, he is to be put in chains and sent to me for punishment."

Alycia immediately turned to her father. "Why does he have to come to York? I don't want anything to do with him or his family. Did you know about this?"

Henry shook his head. "I did not."

"Secondly, my messengers will be riding throughout the realm to announce further tallages against the Jews. By Easter, each town with an archa must pay ten thousand marks to the Crown."

Everyone turned towards the Jews, who murmured amongst themselves. David turned around and could just barely make out his father standing in the back. He also saw the elders and became nervous he might be recognized, but there was nothing he could do about it now.

"Donald, please come here," the king instructed.

David's heart raced as he approached the king, who stood. "Your Majesty."

"This young man is the pride of England. He is only seventeen, and yet he saved Baron Henry, his daughter Alycia, and Crown tax money. He very cunningly used poison Baron Geoffrey had given Baron Henry to defeat our enemies. Donald, please accept this reward of fifty pounds."

Baron Henry and Alycia stared at each other. Henry was surprised no mention of knighthood was made, and Alycia only wanted one reward. "No!" she cried. "He should be knighted!"

Before he could stop her, Alycia ran up to the king. "Your Majesty, please. Donald deserves more. He should be knighted."

Baron Henry quickly followed her. "Your Majesty, I apologize for my daughter's behavior."

King Henry waved him away and smiled, looking at Alycia. "So, you not only ran away from us in London, now you question your king?"

"I'm sorry, Sire. Donald and I cannot be wed unless he is a knight."

"Oh, I see," Henry said, turning to Queen Eleanor. "What do you think, my dear?"

"Come here, my child." Alycia obeyed.

"Do you love him that much?" She nodded. Then the queen looked at David.

"Donald, do you love Alycia?"

David was not prepared to answer this question in public. He realized he had never actually expressed that to Alycia, even though he felt it. He could not say no. It would devastate Alycia and cause a scene. But what would his father think if he admitted his love like this? "Your Majesty, who could not be in love with Alycia?"

Even though David did not answer the question directly, it seemed to satisfy everyone, including Alycia, her smile as big as he had ever seen it.

"Baron Henry," the king said. "If Donald is knighted, will you approve of their marriage?"

"Sire, Donald is one of the finest men I have ever met, despite his youth. While he holds no title or lands, I would bless their marriage once he is a knight."

The king sat. He leaned over to the queen and whispered something to her, which she acknowledged with a nod.

"Jonathan, come here." Jonathan came forward and stood next to David.

"Have either of you jousted before? Jonathan?"

"Only in training, Sire."

"Donald?"

"The same with me, Sire."

"Very well. This is what we have decided. You two will joust against each other. Jonathan, if you win, I will relieve you of my order to go to York. Donald, if you win, you will be knighted. I will give you both two days to train before the match. Geoffrey, do you have armor for our young opponents?"

"Yes, Your Majesty. I'm sure we can equip both of them."

The crowd murmured, most people pleased with the king's declaration. Jonathan immediately said he agreed with the king and welcomed this chance, as did Earl Tristan. David said, "As you wish, Sire." Alycia was about to protest again, but her father stopped her. The king then dismissed everyone.

"Alycia. The king has decreed. You cannot question him. Anyway, I'm sure Donald will win."

"What if he doesn't? He's earned his knighthood. He shouldn't have to prove himself again."

"I'm sorry. The king feels differently, and we must follow his command. Donald."

"Yes, Baron Henry."

"I've watched Sir Michael train you in the joust. We'll get the armor Geoffrey has so you can practice while wearing it. I don't know anything about Jonathan's skills, but I'm sure you can defeat him. Sir Michael will help you train. You must also observe Jonathan. Watch what he does. If his brother trained him, he may try to cheat, and if it isn't noticed he may get away with it."

"I will, my lord."

"Donald," Alycia said, taking his hand. "I know you'll win. For us."

"Yes, Alycia. For us," David said without thinking.

As everyone filed out of the hall, David saw Mordecai had not left with the elders. His father signaled to follow him outside, but David noticed Father Zachariah was nearby and he had to ignore him.

"Donald," Zachariah called. David turned around.

"Father Zachariah. Will you bless me before the joust?"

"Of course, and I will pray for your victory. I am sure you will as well."

"I certainly will, Father. You can rest assured."

David and Jonathan spent the next two days training at the lists just outside the city. Baron Geoffrey and Baron Henry both watched them practice with great interest. Alycia said she could not, and stayed in the castle with Catherine, or spent considerable time in the chapel praying.

Geoffrey had supplied older, experienced jousting horses that had been retired from active service for over a year. Training lances, made of soft wood and equipped with a blunt tip, would be used in the competition. David did not believe Jonathan exhibited any more skills than he had. His horsemanship and technique with lance and shield were average, according to Sir Michael. A quintain and practice targets were set up, and each boy took turns. Jonathan trained with his father, and it appeared to everyone watching that Jonathan's skills were far below David's.

They both wore the borrowed armor Geoffrey provided. Jonathan's was a little too large in the body, but his helmet fit perfectly. David's body fit well, but his helmet was a little too large. Sir Michael stuffed some cloth into it, but David would have to be careful so his sight did not become impaired.

The third day arrived, and everyone was excited to see them compete against each other. There was speculation that Jonathan must hate Donald for being responsible for his brother's death, no matter what Edgar had done. Hate could be an asset or a liability, depending how one handled it. David festered no animosity towards Jonathan. He did notice him staring at Alycia, but he was not the only one, so it did not concern him.

The joust was to take place at noon. After a light breakfast, David spent the morning resting. Sir Michael stayed with him, discussing tactics. This would be David's first competitive joust.

"Donald, are you nervous?"

"A bit. I'll be fine."

"You've proven yourself in training and in the field. You have the skill and courage of a knight. All you are lacking is the title, and I'm sure that will be earned shortly."

"Thank you. I'll do my best."

As noon approached, everyone gathered at the lists. The contest was announced throughout Northampton, and a large crowd had gathered. Vendors took the opportunity to sell various baked goods. Several taverns had brought wagons with barrels of ale and wine to sell, and business appeared to be brisk.

Each boy had a tent in which to prepare. Sir Michael helped David put on his armor, and Baron Henry stopped by. "Remember, Donald. Lean forward and hold the lance close to your body to center the weight and stabilize it. Strike your opponent off-center and deflect his lance."

"I will, Baron Henry."

"I hope the helmet will not impede you."

"It will have to do."

"Donald, Alycia sends her love. She's too nervous to tell you herself." Henry handed David a small scarf. "This is hers. She wants you to carry it for good luck."

"Please thank her for me," he said, as he pushed it into his breastplate.

"I will. Good luck, my boy. Make us proud with a quick victory."

Baron Henry left to sit with Alycia. Sir Michael accompanied David to his horse and would serve as his squire. Jonathan was at the other end of the list, with his father serving as his squire. David surveyed the crowd, trying to see if his father was there, but he did not see any Jews.

On the main grandstand he saw King Henry and Queen Eleanor, both wearing heavy cloaks in the cold February air. Barons Geoffrey and Henry sat nearby, along with Alycia and Lady Catherine.

David mounted his horse and adjusted the reins. Then he and Jonathan rode up to the king and queen without their helmets and lances. King Henry stood.

"Good people of Northampton. We are here to witness a joust between Jonathan of Northumberland and Donald of York. Are you both ready?"

"Yes, Sire," David said. Jonathan nodded, saying nothing.

"You both know the rules. The Marshal will give the signal, and then you will joust. May God be with you both."

The two rode to their respective ends, put on their helmets, and were handed their lances. Under his breath, David recited "Shma Yisroael Adonai Elohainu Adonai Echad," one of the most important Hebrew prayers. He then crossed himself, knowing if he did not it would look suspicious. He saw Jonathan do the same.

David positioned his lance, his too-large helmet still a problem even with the cloth inside. He adjusted his head so he could see properly and watched as the Marshal dropped the starting flag. David kicked his spurs into the sides of his horse. Jonathan did the same, and the two soon were about to clash. What seemed like a long time only took a few seconds. David aimed off-center as he was taught and saw Jonathan's lance coming right at him. David's lance hit perfectly, breaking as it was supposed to, but it did not knock Jonathan off. Jonathan's hit high on David's shield, but did not break. David absorbed the impact, causing him to lean dangerously to his right and he was unable to stay on his horse. Sir Michael rushed out to help him get up. Suspicions grew that something was amiss. The Marshal ran up to Jonathan and took his lance. He examined it and took it to the king.

"Sire, this is not a practice lance. Jonathan cheated and broke the rules. He should be disqualified and Donald declared the winner."

"No!" Jonathan yelled. "I defeated him. This is the lance I was given. I did nothing wrong."

King Henry examined the lance. "The Marshal is correct. This is not a practice lance. But Jonathan may have used the wrong lance by mistake. I declare there be another round. Marshal, make sure the proper lance is used this time."

"Donald, are you all right?" Sir Michael asked.

"I'm fine. A cheater. I'm not surprised."

"Can you go another round?"

"Of course. And this time I'll win."

Jonathan continued to argue he had won, to no avail. His father told him to concentrate on the next joust. He handed the Marshal a lance, who examined it and declared it legal. Then the two boys finished their preparations and waited for the signal. The Marshal returned to the center of the list, everyone watching Jonathan to be sure he did not try to switch lances.

The signal was given and again the two charged each other. The crowd was silent as the two got closer and closer. David again hit Jonathan's shield perfectly off-center, the lance shattered, and Jonathan lost his balance and fell. It happened so fast Jonathan's lance glanced off David's shield and this time broke into several pieces. The crowd cheered at David's victory. Alycia hugged her father, who kissed his daughter on her head. "He did it, Father. I knew he would. Now he will be knighted and we will be wed!"

David removed his helmet and rode a victory lap around the list. He did not notice the lone Jew at the top of the stands applauding. Mordecai smiled as David rode past him. *My son,* he said to himself. *I believe you have done it. May God protect you, for you will need His protection more than ever.*

David stopped in front of the king. Alycia had stood, almost overcome with joy. "Donald!" she yelled. "You did it, my love. You did it!"

David nodded to her, dismounted, and knelt in front of the king.

"Your Majesty, I hope I have pleased you."

"Donald, or should I say the soon-to-be Sir Donald of York? You have earned your title. Spend tonight in prayer as is accustomed, and tomorrow I shall perform the ceremony."

The king then called Jonathan over.

"Jonathan, you have shamed your father and your house, as well as your king and everyone here. I believe you tried to cheat but were caught. I gave you a chance to redeem yourself honorably, and you failed. You will go to York with Baron Henry. You will obey the soon-to-be Sir Donald, and perhaps he can make an honorable man out of you. Remember my decree."

Jonathan hung his head. "Yes, Sire. I remember and will obey Donald."

"Sir Donald. Do not forget that."

Jonathan looked at David. "No, I will never forget that."

Chapter Thirty-Four

Northampton – February 1270

After bathing, David dressed in the white vesture for purity, a red robe for nobility, and black hose and boots that symbolized death. The time seemed to pass too slowly as he spent the night in the chapel, his sword and shield placed on the altar. Father Zachariah stayed with him for a while but was soon falling asleep and decided to leave him alone. David still remembered most of his Hebrew prayers after years of repeating them, though it had been almost three since he had left West End. As he whispered the words, he looked at the large crucifix mounted on the altar. Synagogues do not have any such sculptures, as there is a commandment against graven images. That was always something he could not understand about the Christians. While they could believe Jesus was the Son of God if they wanted to, how could they have images of him? David was glad he did not have to learn Latin. Participation in church mostly consisted of listening and repeating amen.

Eventually he fell asleep on the floor but woke up at first light. Father Zachariah came to escort him to Mass, where the sermon included the duties of a knight. While he listened, he thought about Alycia, and how he was going to respond to her persistence they wed. Did she love him enough she would not care he is a Jew? Would she keep his secret if he did marry her? Would she only keep it if he converted? He had no idea how she would react. He knew one day his being Jewish would come out, and even thought about how and when he would disclose it. David wanted as many Christians as possible to know a Jew not only could be a warrior, but a knight capable of defeating them. He wanted his people to earn the respect he felt they deserved. Christians admired strength, and for more than one thousand years, the Jews were denied the opportunity to exhibit the courage and fighting ability he knew they would have if they had the chance. In his mind, what he was doing was a first step to changing the status quo.

King Henry wanted to return to London as soon as possible, so he commanded the knighting ceremony be held in the morning. David entered the great hall and was greeted by the two barons, Lady Catherine, Sir Michael, Sir Walter, Bryce, Cyrus, Baron Henry's men-at-arms and Alycia. Father Zachariah, Earl Tristan, and Jonathan stood silently off to the side. Queen Eleanor was not in attendance. "Donald, come here."

David approached King Henry and knelt on the knighting stool that had been set in front of the king. "Sire, I am here to serve you."

Baron Henry, acting as David's sponsor, handed the king David's sword and shield, which had been blessed by Father Zachariah. Baron Geoffrey acted as David's second sponsor, and presented him to the king to begin the ceremony as David took his vows.

"My Lord King and noble barons," he began, "I swear my undying allegiance to you. I will never traffic with traitors, never give evil counsel to a lady, always treating her with respect and defending her against all. I will observe all fasts and abstinences, hear Mass, and make offerings in church."

The king rose, took the sword and shield, and with the flat of the sword tapped him on his right shoulder. "I dub thee sir knight, Sir Donald of York. Do you swear to honor our code of chivalry, defending the realm against all enemies and infidels, in the name of Jesus Christ Our Lord and Savior?"

David tried not to react to the reference to infidels. He bowed his head. "I do swear, Sire." The accolade had been performed. He crossed himself and stood. Barons Henry and Geoffrey then put spurs on his boots and girded his sword, completing the ceremony. Alycia wrapped her arms around him and kissed his right cheek.

"I am so proud of you, my love." Her father pulled her away. "There will be time for that later, Alycia." Reluctantly, she released David and stepped back.

"Sir Donald," the king said. "You will return to York with Baron Henry and serve under him. At such time in the future when you have further earned it, we will consider awarding you lands and a manor. You are still very young. There will be time for this, and perhaps then we can consider your marriage to Alycia."

"Yes, Sire. I will do my best to earn those as soon as I can."

"My lords, it's time for me and the queen to return to London. Baron Geoffrey, I thank you for your hospitality. I wish you well."

Geoffrey commanded cheers for the king, and everyone shouted, "Long live King Henry," three times. Henry nodded and left the hall as the assembly all bowed. Baron Geoffrey followed him to be sure all his final arrangements had been made.

Alycia took David's hand. He thought she had never looked more beautiful. Her golden hair glowed against the sunlight that shone through a small window. She smiled as her eyes spoke to him without words. Her pride was bursting.

"Alycia," he said softly, "you have been by my side supporting and encouraging me. I am grateful."

"Donald," she replied, "our future is now apparent. Even though I was hoping we could be wed soon, now you are a knight I know you will earn your lands and manor sooner than you think."

The king's words brought David relief. *I still have some time*, he thought.

Baron Henry approached them. "I think it's time we returned to York. We've taken advantage of Geoffrey's hospitality far too long. I will order a celebration in honor of Donald's knighthood when we return. Alycia, go pack your things. We'll leave tomorrow. I'll inform Geoffrey and Sir Michael."

David decided he would sneak out of the castle to see his family one more time. He would have to be very discreet, for he could not risk anyone following him.

David returned to his chamber to get his helmet, sword, and cloak. With the cold weather, he could more easily hide from anyone he might meet. He left the castle, walking quickly away. Since Coby Hollow was in the same direction as West End and many still believed he came from there, he felt more confident he would not arouse suspicion if anyone at the castle watched him leave.

As he entered West End, he realized how much he had missed it. Only a few people were out as a light snow had begun to fall. He reached his old house and knocked on the door. No one answered. *Strange*, he thought. *Where could everybody be?* He knocked again, and still no answer. He was uncomfortable standing there, but he could not return to the castle so soon. He decided to see if Avram was home but had the same result. Then he looked towards the synagogue and saw people filing out onto the street. The children were in costume. He realized it was Purim, and his family must be at the synagogue. He strolled back and forth for a few minutes, aware he stood out. Then, out of the corner of his eye, he saw a group of six young men who had been standing off to the side. His instincts told him they were planning to make trouble for Jews returning home. He kept watching them as he saw his father, a woman he did not recognize, his brother, sister, uncle, and Avram walking towards his home, with the six waiting to jump them.

David drew his sword and began to walk towards them. He saw the men block the path of his family.

"Hey, Jews," one of them said, "Where are you going? And what's with the costume? It's not All Hallows Eve." Rachel was dressed as Queen Esther.

"Get out of our way," Baruch said.

"Well, a tough-talking Jew," their apparent leader said. "I think we should teach them a lesson."

Rachel began to cry. "Father, I'm frightened."

Baruch stood in front of the leader and repeated. "I said get out of our way."

Two of the others grabbed Baruch and held him. "Hit him, Hugh. Teach him a lesson," one of them said. Hugh was about punch Baruch in his stomach when he stopped.

"I wouldn't do that if I were you," a voice from behind said. He turned to see David standing in front of him.

"What business is this of yours, Sir Knight? And since when do knights defend Jews?"

"Since now. You need to make a decision. Hit him and die or get out of here now."

While this was happening so fast, his family recognized David, but did not say a word.

Hugh signaled to release Baruch.

"That's better. You boys are really brave, attacking those who cannot defend themselves. If I ever see any of you bothering Jews or anyone again I won't be so kind. Now, leave." David raised his sword and slapped it against Hugh's behind as they all ran away, cursing under their breath.

"David, David, is it really you?" Benjamin said.

"Let's get out of here. I don't want to attract attention." They all hurried back to Mordecai's house, where they showered David with hugs and kisses. Avram stared at his friend, unable to speak.

"David, first I want you to meet your stepmother, Hannah," Mordecai said.

David had seen the ring on her finger and guessed who she was. He embraced her. "Welcome to the family." Hannah smiled, and kissed him on his cheek.

"Is it true?" they all asked.

"Yes, it's true. I am a knight."

Baruch put his hand on David's shoulder. "David, my nephew, do you realize the danger you're in? You're playing a very dangerous game. A Jew knighted and swearing loyalty to the Church? God forbid you're discovered. They'll burn you at the stake after torturing you."

"Everyone, please don't worry. Every step I take I'm closer to helping our people. You saw an example of it today. Who knows what may have happened if I wasn't there?"

"I want to be a knight, David," Benjamin said. "Will you teach me?"

"This is madness," Mordecai said. "You can't continue this masquerade. It's inevitable you'll be discovered. Abbot Hubert almost exposed you, and now your brother wants to be a knight. Is that what you want?"

"What I want is to show the Christians we can defend ourselves, and to earn their respect. Now let me tell you my latest adventures."

They all gathered around and he told them how his plan rescued the baron's daughter, saved the king's tax money and led to him being knighted. Avram, Benjamin, and Rachel sat spellbound, hanging on to every word he said.

"David, you're a hero!" Rachel exclaimed.

"My sweet Rachel. I only hope I can help to make life better for our people. I know it's a daunting task."

Baruch stood. "I want you all to know I will be leaving England."

This surprised David. "Leaving? Why? Where will you go?"

"I must leave. I helped to destroy Abbot Hubert, and even though Alwyn has promised to keep our secret, I cannot fully trust him. I illegally gave up most of my money, and if I'm discovered, I'll be imprisoned and tortured. I won't tell you where I'm going, in case you're questioned."

"But that means we may never see you again, Uncle." Benjamin said.

"Most probably. I'm afraid it can't be helped. I've been able to protect you, David, but if I'm arrested, or if any of you are, your secret may be in jeopardy."

"When will you leave?"

"Tomorrow. The longer I stay, the more dangerous it is."

Mordecai embraced his brother. "You are a good man, Baruch. I'm sorry I ever thought ill of you for your moneylending success. You've used it for the good of our people. I hope you find peace and happiness in a new land."

Baruch then embraced David. "David, you've made us all proud. God has given you a unique opportunity, and you have so far been successful. But I caution you to be more careful than ever. You must have made some enemies, and I'm certain they won't hesitate to destroy you if they could." Baruch went into a back room and came out with several purses.

"I want each of you to have some of the money I kept. Avram, you've remained a loyal friend to David, and I want you to have some too."

Baruch gave each one a purse. "I don't know what to say, my brother," Mordecai said as they all thanked him.

"No need to say anything. I must go now."

"What about your house?" Hannah asked.

"I'm giving it to Emma, my housekeeper. I'm sure the king will have the sheriff confiscate it if I give it to you. I've instructed Emma after I leave you're to take all my Jewish items."

"I see," Mordecai said. "We'll take good care of them."

"Goodbye. I love you all, and I do hope we'll see each other again." Each one embraced Baruch. "David, again I say, be extra careful."

"I will, Uncle."

Hedgestone Priory – February 1270

Prior Alwyn sat in the refectory with Bartholomew and Father Ambrose.

"Have things improved already since Hubert's been gone?"

"Absolutely," Ambrose said. "There is no more fear in the brothers. They do their duties willingly, unafraid that Hubert will spy on them to try to discover them doing something he didn't like."

"Good. I want there to be an openness at Hedgestone. Does either of you have any concerns?"

"I have one," Bartholomew said. "Beware of Brother Andrew. I fear he thinks Hubert was not mistaken about Donald and may try to prove him right."

"Yes. I should never have taken him to York with me, as I believe he became suspicious then. We must protect the secret, or we'll be in serious trouble."

They all nodded. "I am sure many would think what we have done is a sacrilege," Alwyn said. "I do not. This David cannot change the world. He is one man doing something I believe has never been done before, and no doubt will never be done again. He cannot possibly continue to pretend who he is forever, and when he is exposed we, of course, will plead ignorance if questioned. After all, there is no proof we knew, only speculation because of Hubert's ranting. We managed to get rid of him, and to me, it was worth it."

With that, they all drank a toast to the future of Hedgestone without Hubert.

West End – February 1270

After the family ate a wonderful meal of roast lamb Hannah cooked, Mordecai took David aside.

"David, am I right that after tomorrow we may not see you for quite a while?"

"I'm afraid so. Now that I'm a knight, my duties will change, and either I must stay longer at York or may be called away."

"I see. There is one thing that worries me the most. The baron's daughter, I believe Alycia is her name."

"Yes, Father."

"She says she's in love with you. Are you in love with her?"

"I've tried not to, but I am. She's not only beautiful, but she has a sweetness about her I cannot resist. She's always there for me, and her persistence makes it harder."

"David, you cannot marry her. Never, while remaining a Jew. You said you would never convert."

"And I won't convert. I'll always keep that promise, for you and Mother, may she rest in peace. Don't you understand how important it is for me to keep my true faith through all of this? Don't you understand the torment I feel every day? I want so much to tell everyone Sir Donald is Sir David, a Jew! I want to dispel everything wrong the Christians say about us, but I can't. At least, not yet."

"I am worried you'll marry her and hope she won't betray you. But how could she not? When she finds out who you really are she will feel deeply betrayed, and her faith forbids such a union. As does yours."

"So, you do not believe love is stronger than faith?"

Mordecai shook his head. "Not when it comes to love between a Christian and a Jew. It is forbidden in both worlds and would be severely punished."

"What if Alycia were to convert?"

"You are mad if you think even for a moment she would do that."

"Why? If she truly loves me, the differences in our faiths won't matter, and I will insist I must honor my pledge."

Mordecai had tears in his eyes. "David, I'm afraid we will lose you. If not in battle, then in your discovery, or Alycia's temptation will be too great and you will become a Christian. You cannot have it both ways. Perhaps someday two people can marry for love without the shackles of religious and royal decrees that rule men's lives. But that is not today."

"Father. I understand what you are saying, and perhaps part of what I'm doing is to try to break those shackles."

"No, my son. Those shackles cannot be broken by you or anyone else. Only God can break them, and if he does, it will be at a time of His choosing."

"Then let me be God's hand."

Northampton – February 1270

David returned to the castle in time to attend a great going away feast Geoffrey had ordered prepared. Strangely, no one asked where he had been. David assumed they had been too busy preparing for tomorrow's journey.

At the feast, Henry and Geoffrey honored the new knight, and with Alycia at his side, David was the envy of all the men. As happy as this moment was for him, he could not get the words of his uncle and his father out of his head. While he had heard them many times, now he had reached this previously impossible goal, and a feeling of fear crept down his spine. Would my family be in jeopardy if I were found out? Could they be questioned and even tortured?

Alycia continuously looked over at him, the warmth in her smile further accentuating her beauty. He met each smile with one of his own. He could not help thinking, is this a dream? No, this is reality. You made your dream come true, and now you must follow through with it. There is no going back.

"Donald," she said, "are you happy?"

"Becoming a knight comes with great responsibilities. Yes, I'm happy for what I have achieved, and now I must continue to serve the king and your father. There are many who are oppressed because they may have different beliefs or values, and they should be defended as well. I believe in what Our Lord Jesus said, to treat others as we ourselves want to be treated. I hope my newfound title will help me to do that."

Alycia looked confused. "All I know is I want to treat you with all my love and devotion. Nothing else matters to me. Can you understand that?"

"Yes, Alycia, but even though we are just two people, we cannot close our eyes to what's happening in the realm. We must work towards helping all good people, no matter who they are."

"Donald, you're speaking strangely. As long as we're together, I don't care what you do." She paused. "Donald, maybe now you'll tell me the secret you couldn't before?"

"I will when the time is right, and this is not that time."

"Very well. I will wait, but not forever. A husband and wife should not have secrets from each other," she said.

"True. But we are not even betrothed."

"No," she said. "Not yet."

Epilogue

York – March 1270

David sat by the fire late at night in his own chamber, earned after being knighted by the king, thinking how far he had come in three short years. He had achieved something he never believed was obtainable. He sipped a mug of ale, thinking about his family in Northampton. He was glad they knew about his accomplishment but regretted he still must maintain his secret among everyone else. Then his mind turned to Alycia. After the knighting ceremony, they had spent a little time talking, and he was more at ease with her. Perhaps his title made him more confident. Then a light knock on his door brought him out of his head. It was Alycia, wrapped in a cloak.

"Alycia. It's late. You should be in bed."

She smiled at him. "I intend to be."

She entered his chamber, closed the door behind her and set the bolt lock. Before David could utter a word, she turned to him and dropped the cloak.

David stared at her in a daze. This was the first time he had seen a naked woman. Before him was the baron's daughter who had been pursuing him for such a long time. He knew he could not resist her forever, nor did he want to. She pulled him to her and they kissed, as both their passions rose to the point of no return. He forgot the danger such a union could bring. He forgot he was not Sir Donald, but a product of another religion, another culture. They continued kissing as they made their way to David's bed. She laid down as he quickly tore off his clothes and joined her. She must not touch me, he thought.

Alycia's mind wandered as he caressed her and awkwardly kissed her soft, smooth skin. She could feel his excitement swell against her thigh as she readied herself and he positioned himself to enter her. With his first thrust, she felt the break. The pleasure. "Donald, I love you," she moaned.

"Alycia, my sweet Alycia." They both lost track of time. He could not hold back any longer. His burst filled her as they kissed, their tongues becoming almost one. Then it was over. They kissed again while both were almost out of breath. Before saying a word, and without thinking, he rolled over. The dim light from the fireplace was just bright enough for her to see it. But he did not see the shock on her face.

Author's Note

My lifelong interest in the Middle Ages led me to learn about Jewish life during those difficult times. It amazes me how, despite the restrictions and persecutions, our people managed to survive while they could not fight back. This inspired the premise for *The Fate of the Arrow*.

My intent was to give readers a basic understanding of Jewish life in England in the mid-thirteenth century through David and his family. While incorporating some historical aspects, I took the liberty of including some things that occurred at a different time. For example, pews were added to churches in the fourteenth century, but I included them as part of the improvements made by Hubert. I also wanted to show that there were tolerant Christians who maintained good relations with the Jews.

It is my hope that readers have gained some understanding of the extreme hardships Jews faced during the medieval period in England in particular, and that they will learn more on their own. If we could all understand each other better, perhaps we could make a dent in the prejudice and hate that have no place in the world.

The story will continue in the sequel *The Point of the Arrow*.

Glossary

Archa ~ special box to contain agreements of loans made by Jews

Challah ~ braided bread made with eggs

Cheder ~ school

Denier ~ French unit of currency

Minyan ~ ten men required for a prayer service

Purim ~ Jewish festival to celebrate the survival of the Jews from the Persians

Shabbos ~ Sabbath

Shacharit ~ morning prayer service

Shul ~ synagogue

About the Author

SHEL PAIS has been interested in the Middle Ages since he was a boy. He never missed watching Roger Moore in *Ivanhoe* and Richard Greene in *The Adventures of Robin Hood* TV series. Errol Flynn's *The Adventures of Robin Hood* and Robert Taylor's *Ivanhoe* are still the definitive classics he enjoys. As part of his medieval interests, he has made a hobby of Robin Hood, collecting more than 80 fiction and nonfiction books, and numerous movies and television series. He "owns" a square foot of Sherwood Forest to help preserve what little remains. Born, raised, and living in the Chicago area, he is a diehard Cubs fan.

Website
Shelpais.com

Twitter
@SHP49

Instagram
@shelpais

Made in the USA
Middletown, DE
09 February 2019